SHADOW SCHOLAR

LESSONS IN THE DARK

DOMINIC DORSEY

Written by Dominic Dorsey
Published by UrbanFellowship Strategic Capital LLC
Belleville, IL
Contact: ufstrategiccapital@gmail.com

This is a work of fiction. Names, characters, places, and incidents are products of the author's imagination or are used fictitiously. Any resemblance to actual persons, living or dead, events, or locales is entirely coincidental.

First Edition
Printed in the United States of America

Library of Congress Control Number: 2025919570

ISBNs
eBook: 979-8-9931197-0-0
Paperback: 979-8-9931197-1-7
Hardcover: 979-8-9931197-2-4
Audiobook (forthcoming): 979-8-9931197-3-1

To my kids:
You are the reason I build.
You are the reason I finish.
This legacy is stamped with your name.

To the ones who threw shade—
You lit the fire. I'll keep it burning.

TABLE OF CONTENTS

Prologue: Just Another Memory 1

Act I: Before the Fall 5

Chapter 1: The Outer City Life...............................7

Chapter 2: The Edge of Two Worlds 16

Chapter 3: The Invitation 32

Chapter 4: "Inner City" Dreams and "Outer City" Shadows.........39

Chapter 5: The Double Life Begins 59

Chapter 6: Shadow's Summer 71

Chapter 7: Between Two Worlds 93

Chapter 8: Elijah's Morning Realization................102

Chapter 9: Emotional Fallout...............................118

Chapter 10: A Way Out 133

Act II: Names Like Ghost....................................145

Chapter 11: Into the Crossfire..............................147

Interlude I: No Loose Ends 163

Chapter 12: Shattered Peace................................167

Chapter 13: A House Divided 176

Chapter 14: Blood Ties and Blind Spots 188

Chapter 15: Neutral Grounds 199

Chapter 16: Quiet Bleeds 211

Chapter 17: Fuel to the Fire 220

Act III: The Cuts That Don't Heal............................**235**

Chapter 18: Ping...237

Chapter 19: Where the Lies Lived..............................253

Chapter 20: The Check-In......................................260

Chapter 21: Cracks in the Glass...............................272

Chapter 22: The Ones Who See Through You......................281

Chapter 23: The House We Buried...............................287

Chapter 24: Ashes Don't Bury Themselves.......................295

Chapter 25: Brotherhood in the Balance........................302

Chapter 26: Doc's Reveal......................................308

Act IV: The Reckoning **317**

Chapter 27: House of Cards....................................319

Chapter 28: Love on the Line..................................326

Interlude II: The Devil's Hand.......................**331**

Interlude III: Neutral Ground **335**

Chapter 29: The Breaking Point 339

Chapter 30: No More Names.....................................344

Epilogue: Shadows Never Leave.........................**367**

About The Author **373**

Acknowledgements **375**

JUST ANOTHER MEMORY

The smell of lemon oil and cigar smoke meant he was home.

Elijah sat on the studio couch, legs swinging, back straight like his mama taught him. The faint buzz of the speakers hummed in his ears, mixing with the distant clink of glasses and the low murmur of voices from the control room. The scent of lemon oil clung to the cracked vinyl cushions, blending with the sharp tang of sweat and dust baked into the foam. Warm overhead lights poured down like a spotlight, making the room feel more like a stage than a workspace. He tried to sit still, but his toes tapped on instinct, mimicking the beat pulsing through the floorboards. He couldn't have been more than nine, still in his school uniform, backpack half-zipped with math homework poking out the top.

Across the room, Jules stood behind the mixing board, nodding to the beat. His fingers moved across the knobs with effortless precision, adjusting faders like he was carving sound from stone. The bass rumbled low, shaking the walls in rhythm with the slow tap of his foot. His shoulders rolled to the groove, rhythm rooted in his bones. A fresh gold chain hung heavy around his neck, catching the dim light. His voice, gravel wrapped in velvet, poured through the speakers.

"Real ones don't fold, even when the paper do..."

Elijah didn't understand all the words yet, but he felt their gravity. He watched the way the room responded, how even the air seemed to pause when his father spoke. It was like magic. Power. Presence. Command.

Jules slid off the headphones. "Yo, Lij. You feel that?"

Elijah blinked. "Feel what?"

"The pockets." Jules tapped his chest where the bass had landed. "That's where the truth lives. Not in the lyrics. Not in the rhymes. In the pockets."

Jules crossed the room and knelt in front of him. "Don't ever let anybody write your verses for you. Life or music. You write your own. You feel me?"

Elijah nodded, small and serious. A hush seemed to fall over the studio, the hum of the speakers the only thing left alive. His chest tightened, and he didn't know why. Maybe it was pride, maybe it was fear. But something told him this moment would follow him for a long time. It felt like both comfort and pressure, like being handed a torch still lit from generations before.

"Good. 'Cause one day, this whole thing: the studio, the label, the streets watching your every move? That's gon' be yours." Jules pressed a hand to Elijah's chest. "Keep that clean, and you'll never lose yourself. Dirty it up..." He paused, voice lowering to a near whisper. "Then you're just another memory."

Years later, the studio would burn. The streets would forget Jules Knight's name. His legacy, once spoken of with reverence, would crumble to whispers and smoke. And Elijah: the good son, the star athlete, the golden child, would disappear into a shadow he never saw coming.

But in that moment, he wasn't a myth in the making or a kid born to inherit an empire. He was just a boy, tucked in the heartbeat of his father's world, clinging to the belief that if Jules's hands could hold the world together, maybe, just maybe, they could hold him together too.

BEFORE THE FALL

CHAPTER 1

THE OUTER CITY LIFE

The mansion stood tall in the distance, glowing in the soft light of the late afternoon. A light breeze rustled the ivy climbing up the stone walls, and the chirping of birds echoed through the still air. From the outside, the house looked like a dream-big, beautiful, and full of success. Elijah Knight's home had perfectly trimmed gardens and expensive details that reflected his family's wealth. But to Elijah, it didn't feel like home. It felt like a trap. A golden one-but a trap all the same.

He stood at the large window in his bedroom, looking out over the neatly trimmed lawn. A layer of fog hovered in the distance, making everything seem far away and unclear-just like how he felt. The "Outer City," as his parents proudly called it, was their dream come true. Clean streets, peaceful neighborhoods, and none of the chaos found beyond its borders. But as Elijah stared out, he couldn't shake the feeling that he was missing something important. Something real.

Not that he hated his life. On the surface, he had everything anyone could ask for. Perfect grades, a future full of possibilities, a shot at an Ivy League school, and a strong athletic career. But deep down, he felt empty.

He glanced down at his desk, where an old subway ticket was stuck beneath his charger. That's when the memory came rushing back.

* * *

I remember how dusty the subway windows were and how Ty's music blasted through his earbuds, like it was the soundtrack to our little adventure. We weren't supposed to leave the Outer City, especially without an adult. My parents would've been furious. Honestly, I didn't even want to go at first. I was nervous about breaking the rules, about getting caught. E said he definitely wasn't going. Said he wasn't about to get grounded over some park trip. But Ty talked me into it. He said we weren't doing anything crazy, just checking out a different part of town.

When we got off the train at Bellridge in the Inlands, it felt like we'd stepped into a different world. The buildings were packed tighter, older but full of personality. The neighborhood had a heartbeat. People chilling on porches, walking dogs, barbecuing, kids racing each other on bikes.

We found a public park with a basketball court a couple blocks from the corner store. It wasn't anything fancy like the gyms I was used to. The paint was faded, the net was ripped, and the ball looked like it had been through a hundred games. But we didn't care. We played like scouts were watching. No parents. No pressure. Just us, talking trash, dripping sweat, and pushing each other harder. I remember one kid in a gray hoodie who wouldn't stop running his mouth until I hit a stepback jumper right in his face. Ty laughed so hard he nearly dropped his phone.

For once, I wasn't Elijah Knight: the straight-A student, the future Princeton guy, the polished athlete with the perfect plan. I was just a kid playing ball with his best friend. And for the first time in a long time, it felt real.

* * *

The memory faded like a song cut off mid-beat. Elijah blinked, staring at his reflection in the glass. Trapped in the perfect house, the perfect life, the perfect lie.

This life wasn't really his. It was the one his parents had carefully planned. Elijah had become the person they wanted, but not the person he wanted to be.

"Elijah," his mother, Vivienne "Vivi" Knight, called out, snapping him back to reality. "Dinner's in fifteen minutes. Don't make me call you again."

Her voice was sharp and in control, just like she always was. Everything about Vivi was polished and intentional. Each morning, she left his schedule on the counter next to his smoothie, color-coded and highlighted. Even her hugs felt like check-ins rather than affection. She had fought hard to earn her place in a world that didn't welcome women like her. And she did it with power and grace. But Elijah wasn't sure he wanted to live in the world she had built. There was no room to mess up, no space to breathe. Everything had to be perfect. And he was tired of it.

His reflection looked flawless: athletic, well-dressed, confident. But it was just an image. His deep brown eyes told a different story. In the glass, he didn't see a real person; he saw a mannequin in a store window, perfectly styled but hollow inside. The tie he wore felt more like a leash, and the smile he used in school pictures felt fake.

He turned away from the window just as his phone buzzed. Tyrell "Ty" Foster: his best friend. Ty was the only one who really understood him, even if he didn't know everything Elijah was dealing with. Steady, loyal, and always there. Elijah quickly typed:

You busy?

Ty: *Nah, just chilling. What's up?*

Elijah: *We gotta talk.*

The message sat heavy on the screen. Ty always knew when something was off. But Elijah didn't know how to explain the gnawing emptiness inside him. It wasn't just stress. It was something deeper. Something that made him question whether all the things his parents gave him: the house, the cars, the reputation, meant anything if he didn't feel whole.

The door creaked open, and Elijah turned to see his mother watching him. She always had that look, like she was reading a report card written on his face.

"Elijah," she said, her tone softer now. "You've been quiet lately. Is everything okay?"

He forced a smile. "I'm fine, Mom. Just school stuff."

She walked further into the room, her heels tapping softly against the hardwood. Her gaze never left him. "You've always been a top student. I know you can handle anything. But I can tell something's bothering you."

She wasn't wrong. Elijah had always been the good kid. But what was the point if none of it felt like his?

"I'm just tired," he said.

Vivi's face softened, just slightly. She wasn't the type to coddle, but there was a flicker of concern behind her eyes. "You know I want what's best for you. You're going to do great things. Your future is set. I already spoke with Princeton alumni, they'll take you. You've earned this."

Just hearing "Princeton" made Elijah's stomach churn. It was the plan. Their plan. But the road ahead felt flat, predictable. Like a script someone else wrote.

Later, at dinner, his father, Julian "Jules" Knight, sat silently at the head of the table. He didn't speak much these days, but when he did, people listened. Jules had lived two lives. One in the streets, the other in the spotlight. From drug dealer to famous music producer, his rise was legendary. But now, he seemed distant, as if trapped in his own success. Suits replaced swagger, and meetings replaced music.

"Elijah," Jules finally said, his deep voice breaking the quiet. "How was graduation practice today?"

"Fine," Elijah replied.

"You've seemed off lately," Jules said, narrowing his eyes. "What's going on?"

Elijah straightened in his seat. His father didn't need many words to make an impact. Still, Elijah couldn't tell if the concern was real: genuine care or just worry that he'd mess up the image they worked so hard to build.

"I'm fine," he repeated, too quickly.

The table fell silent again. No one pushed. It was like even his parents were afraid to crack the perfect picture they'd painted.

As dinner dragged on, Elijah stared at his plate. He thought about vanishing. Just hopping on a train and getting lost in the pulse of the city. Would they even notice? Or just be angry that he'd broken the routine?

His eyes drifted back to the window. Beyond it, the world called to him. A world that moved with rhythm, with heart. A world that wasn't boxed in by expectations.

His fingers twitched. His chest tightened. He didn't know if he wanted to escape. Or if he just needed to feel something.

* * *

As the night wore on, Elijah retreated to his room, his mind spinning. He picked up his phone and typed out another message to Ty.

The room felt heavy and quiet. Elijah sat on the edge of his bed, staring at the screen, his fingers frozen. He hadn't typed much yet, but the weight of everything he wanted to say pressed down on him. As he typed, his heartbeat quickened. Thoughts of his parents filled his mind. The strict expectations they held. The image of perfection they insisted on. It all felt like a barrier, keeping him from the life he quietly craved but had never dared to explore.

He hit send.

I need to get out of here. All this... prep school, family dinners with small talk, and pretending to smile. It's not it anymore.

Ty replied almost instantly.

Meet us at the spot in ten...

A second later, another message buzzed through.

Ty: *We got you.*

Elijah didn't think twice. He jumped up, grabbed his jacket and keys, and headed for the door. The night air would be better than the tight, polished silence of his house. The spot wasn't far away, just the basketball court by the park where he, Ty, and E used to meet up when life felt easier. He could still remember the echo of the ball hitting the concrete and the fresh-cut grass in the heat of summer. Those sounds and smells used to mean freedom before he had to be perfect all the time. That place still held a piece of who he really was.

His parents didn't know about these late-night runs. Once, his mom almost caught him sneaking back in through the side door. He'd stopped cold when he heard her footsteps, heart pounding, and only moved again after the kitchen light went off. Even though that memory stuck with him, he kept going out. Part of it was the thrill. But mostly, he just needed space: air that wasn't filtered through someone else's plan for his life. They never asked questions. Maybe they didn't want to know. But for Elijah, it wasn't about hiding. It was about finding a space that belonged to him.

He needed to breathe, to test the limits, to figure out who he really was.

* * *

When Elijah got there, the streetlights cast long shadows on the cracked pavement of the court. Ty and E were already there, casually shooting hoops. Their figures moved under the dull orange glow of the lights. The air was crisp, each breath sharp and clean. A faint smell of pine and maybe even someone grilling nearby hung in the background. Ty looked up and gave a small nod as Elijah walked closer. E leaned against the fence with a smirk.

"What's up, man?" E asked, his tone easy and joking. Ethan "E" Bishop was always the chill one, the guy who could keep things relaxed even when things got tense. His neat look didn't show the quiet fire inside, but Elijah knew that both E and Ty could always see past his mask.

"Same old stuff," Elijah muttered. He shoved his keys into his pocket and leaned on the fence next to them.

"I don't know what it is, man," Elijah said, his voice tight. He wasn't sure if he was talking to them or just thinking out loud. "I'm tired of pretending everything's okay. Tired of... this." He waved at the park, like it represented everything in his life.

Ty looked confused. "What are you saying?"

Elijah rubbed his face and stared out into the night. A strange chill ran down his back. What if he couldn't change? What if he was stuck like this forever? He didn't have one clear reason for feeling like this. It wasn't just his parents or their high hopes. It was something deeper. A feeling that something important was missing.

"I don't know," Elijah said. "It's like I'm stuck living this perfect life, but it doesn't feel real. I look in the mirror and don't even know who I'm looking at."

E's face changed. "You've been living the dream, man. But dreams aren't everything. What do you actually want? What are you searching for?"

Elijah wanted to answer, but nothing came out. He wasn't sure what his plan was. He just knew the one laid out for him wasn't it.

Ty leaned in. "We get it. But if you really want something different, you gotta go see it. Remember when we talked about that? About the city?"

Elijah nodded. They had talked about it, how the Inner City was this mysterious place, close but far, full of stories and energy they'd never really experienced. He hadn't gone yet, not because he didn't want to, but because deep down he was scared. He hadn't admitted it before, not even to himself.

E had never wanted to go. He said it was too dangerous, said he didn't need to see it to know it wasn't for him. But Elijah had always wondered what it was really like. And now, more than ever, he felt that pull.

"I'll go," Elijah said quietly. Right then, he made up his mind. As soon as he said it, his chest tightened, not from fear but from excitement. Maybe even hope. Maybe this would help him figure things out. "Let's check out the city. Let's see it for ourselves."

* * *

I was eleven, my chest buzzing with nervous energy, like bees trapped in a jar. I sat cross-legged on the gym floor of the Inner City rec center, the same place my dad once went to high school back when it still had proper funding and the walls weren't cracked and peeling. The air smelled of waxed floors and greasy pizza from boxes stacked high on the back tables.

Jules stood tall at the podium, dressed in a sharp suit, his gold watch flashing under the dim lights with every movement. He spoke with power and confidence, his voice cutting through the background noise like it had weight. It was a community event: free backpacks, free pizza, and a message of hope packed into every handout.

People from the neighborhood showed up not just for the giveaways, but for him. Because once, he had been one of them. Drug dealers, guys from the block, single moms, even elders in wheelchairs filled the crowd. I remember watching, caught between admiration and jealousy. These were people who had seen the worst of life, yet they looked at Jules like he had made it out unscarred, proof that escaping the streets wasn't just a dream but something real.

"You don't escape where you come from," Jules said, his voice echoing through the gym. "You evolve it. You rewrite the story."

The room erupted in applause. I clapped too, my palms stinging from how hard I smacked them together. But I didn't care. I wanted to believe every word.

* * *

"You good?" Ty asked.

Elijah blinked, coming back to the basketball court.

E looked surprised. Ty, though, just nodded like he'd been waiting for Elijah to say that.

"Alright," Ty said. "We'll hit the East Side tomorrow. Time to stop being scared of the real world."

Elijah stood there for a second. The wind brushed against his skin, and he felt oddly calm. He knew this wasn't just a random night out. It was something bigger. A step toward a truth he'd been missing.

"Yeah," Elijah said. "Tomorrow."

CHAPTER 2
THE EDGE OF TWO WORLDS

The last day at school felt different. Fridays were usually loud and full of energy, but this one carried a weight, like everyone could sense something was about to shift. The halls buzzed with noise: students shouting across lockers, sneakers squeaking on tile, music blaring from someone's phone. But for Elijah, the usual end-of-week hype wasn't what had him restless. It was the night ahead. The trip to the Inner City wasn't just an idea anymore. It was happening.

As he moved through the crowd, nodding at classmates and flashing his usual easy grin, his mind was already elsewhere. The contrast played in his head like a movie. The Outer City was polished and safe: tree-lined streets, luxury cars, manicured lawns, people who smiled a little too much. It looked like a postcard, but it felt hollow. The Inner City was cracked pavement, graffiti-stained walls, smoke in the air, music that rattled your bones. It was messy. It was real.

By second period, Elijah had already mapped out the night. He spotted E at their lockers, eyes glued to his phone, posture sagging like he was trying to dodge reality.

"You good, man?" Elijah asked, clapping a hand on his shoulder.

E looked up, brow furrowed. "I've been thinking about tonight. Are we really doing this?"

Elijah chuckled, keeping it light. "Come on, E. We've talked about this. You're not backing out now, are you?"

E shifted awkwardly. "I've heard stories. People get caught slipping out there, especially guys like us. I don't know if I'm built for this."

"Relax," Elijah said with a grin. He wasn't entirely sure himself, but somebody had to be the rock. "We're just hitting the mall, grabbing some gear, maybe scoping the scene. Nothing wild."

Ty showed up just in time to catch the tail end. Backpack slung over one shoulder, he smirked. "E, don't tell me you're scared. We haven't even left yet."

"I'm not scared," E shot back. "I just don't want to end up on the news."

Ty laughed. "Man, you already sound like a headline: *Outer City Teen Found Out of Place in the Inner City.* You'll be fine."

Elijah leaned against the lockers and eyed E's outfit: polo shirt, khakis, loafers. "You're sticking out more than anybody. You look like you're dressed for a family brunch."

E glanced down, defensive. "What's wrong with this?"

"You look like you're headed to a yacht club," Ty said. "We're trying to blend in, not host a fundraiser."

E crossed his arms. "Why do we even have to act like we're something we're not?"

Elijah's smile slipped. His tone sharpened. "It's not about pretending. It's about knowing when to adapt."

Ty nodded. "And anyway, we're not out there alone. Elijah's got connections. His dad runs the city. We'll be good."

At the mention of his dad, Elijah's jaw clenched. Something in his chest tightened: resentment, maybe. But he let it slide. "Exactly. Trust me, E. We've got this."

* * *

17

The final bell hadn't even rung before Elijah was already miles away in his mind. He sat in math class, barely registering the formulas on the whiteboard. His pen scratched half-finished doodles in the margins of his notes while his thoughts drifted to the night ahead: how he'd walk, what he'd wear, what he'd say. In history, when the teacher called his name, he blinked, clueless. His head was already across town, somewhere past the Outer City, playing out a new version of himself he hadn't fully met yet. The hum of anticipation buzzed under his skin like static, charging every second that ticked toward the final bell.

By the time school let out, he was no longer just Elijah, the honor-roll kid with polished shoes and a reputation to protect. Something had shifted. The kind of shift that made your hands itch and your pulse quicken. He didn't know what he was becoming, only that he was ready.

Outside, the sun hit the chrome trim of his Mercedes, blinding for a second. Elijah adjusted his rearview mirror and caught his reflection: pressed uniform shirt, a crisp fade, the glint of a school honor pin on his collar. He looked like he was from the Outer City. Rich lawns. Private security. Ivy League prep. But he didn't feel like any of those things. Not today.

In the passenger seat, Ty scrolled through his phone with his left hand, his right fingers tapping rhythmically against the door. In the backseat, E sat quietly, headphones in, gazing out the window at the blur of passing storefronts.

E wasn't sold on this plan. He'd made that clear. But Elijah had talked him into it. They'd start small: new clothes, new energy, testing the waters. One night in the Inner City. No promises, just to see where they fit.

The silence in the car hummed, thick and expectant.

Elijah drove with one hand on the wheel, the other tapping his thigh. Outside the window, the landscape transformed. The Outer City fell away in slow motion. Pristine hedges wilted into overgrown weeds, wide sidewalks gave way to cracked concrete, and the scent of fresh-cut grass was replaced by exhaust fumes and old grease.

Billboards shifted too. First the glossy smiles of private school kids. Then liquor stores, bail bonds, and smoke shops. A man with a limp dragged a broken shopping cart down the shoulder, his expression blank. Sirens whined somewhere in the distance, echoing against brick walls laced with graffiti.

E pulled out one earbud. "You sure about this?"

Elijah didn't answer right away. His jaw clenched, his eyes on the road.

"I'm not going to live my whole life behind gates," he said. "I want to know what's out there."

Ty nodded slowly, like he'd heard it before but wasn't totally buying it.

"Don't forget where you come from," Ty said, voice low.

Elijah shot him a look. "You think I will?"

Ty shrugged, returning his gaze to the road ahead. "Nah. But sometimes it feels like you're trying to."

The words hit Elijah harder than he expected. They pierced through the surface, tapping an insecurity he didn't often admit, not even to himself. Was he running from something or toward something? He stared straight ahead, watching the lane lines blur. In the reflection of the windshield, he didn't see Elijah. Not the old him, not yet the new one. Something in between.

He parked the car outside Crossline Plaza, a shopping center perched at the crossroads of three distinct worlds. On one side, the Outer City gleamed with estates, private schools, and quiet order. On the other, the Inner City waited: gritty and defiant, where survival spoke louder than status. Sandwiched in between was the Inlands, defined by worn-out ambition, working-class hustle, and the pressure of choosing sides. This mall was more than a shopping center. It was the edge, the collision point where all three realities brushed shoulders.

The boys walked through the mall entrance together. Their footsteps echoed off the polished tiles, drawing glances from well-dressed shoppers who quickly looked away. Elijah felt the weight of every stare, every whispered judgment.

Storefronts gleamed: jewelry behind glass, mannequins in designer suits, salespeople too busy to make eye contact. Elijah felt it. They didn't belong here, not entirely.

They weren't here for that life. Not prepwear. Not polos. Their destination was clear: a streetwear boutique tucked between luxury brands.

The glass doors opened with a soft chime. Inside, bold colors exploded from the walls: oversized hoodies, graphic tees, sneakers with thick soles and louder statements. Elijah scanned the shelves, fingers grazing a black shirt with white block lettering across the chest. It felt like something raw.

Something that didn't have to ask for permission or try to fit in.

And for the first time all day, Elijah didn't feel out of place.

* * *

The line at the register wasn't long, but the moment stretched. Elijah stepped up with a hoodie, Gucci shirt and distressed jeans in hand, his pulse steady but his thoughts buzzing beneath the surface. The low thump of music from the store's hidden speakers pulsed behind him, the bass weaving around the quiet tension in his chest.

"This it?" Elijah asked Ty, lifting the shirt slightly.

Ty nodded, a grin spreading across his face. "Yeah, now you're starting to look the part."

E stayed quiet, flipping through a rack half-heartedly, clearly still not sold on the whole idea. His fingers brushed past a pair of cargo pants, then dropped to his sides. "Whatever, man," he muttered, barely audible.

They had been in the boutique for almost an hour, long enough to draw side-eyes from some shoppers and lingering glances from store employees, who couldn't quite decide if the boys were there to shop or loiter. The store smelled like fresh fabric and synthetic vanilla, the air sharp with ambition. Everything about the place, from the sleek lighting to the aggressive playlist, was designed to sell more than clothes. It sold identity, attitude, belonging.

At the register, the cashier, a woman in her mid-thirties with a sharp gaze and practiced poise, looked the boys up and down. Her eyes paused on Elijah's pressed polo, then dropped to his gleaming watch like something didn't quite add up.

"You sure this is what you want?" she asked, scanning the tags with a skeptical brow. "Not really your style."

A younger woman organizing the wall display nearby shot a smirk their way. "Not his usual look, but he makes it work," she said casually. But the way she watched Elijah said more, like she was trying to decode him. Was he legit, or just pretending?

Elijah chuckled, brushing off the comment with a shrug. "Trying something new."

The cashier raised an eyebrow, holding his gaze a second longer than necessary. Then she nodded and bagged the items with no further questions. In her silence was something unreadable: part judgment, part understanding.

As the receipt printed and the final beep of the scanner echoed across the counter, Elijah's eyes flicked toward a slim mirror tucked near the sunglasses display. He barely recognized the face looking back, still baby-faced, neatly lined up like any Outer City kid, but with something different in his eyes. A flicker. A quiet defiance.

The hoodie under his arm wasn't just cotton. It felt like a choice. A first step into something bigger. A subtle declaration of change. Even if no one else noticed the shift, Elijah did, and that was enough to make him stand a little taller as he turned from the mirror.

E leaned against the counter, arms folded. "You really think that hoodie makes you someone else?"

Elijah turned, his lips twitching into a half-smile. "No. But it makes me feel like I could be."

Ty opened the glass door, holding it for them as they stepped back into the mall's fading evening buzz. The air smelled of cinnamon pretzels. But it all felt different now. Like they were carrying something new with them, something less polished, more real.

As they passed a jewelry store, Elijah glanced back at the shop behind them. Its neon sign flickered faintly, fighting to stay lit, trying to hold steady against the gloss.

He didn't know what came next. But for the first time in a long while, he wanted to find out.

* * *

The sun dipped low on the horizon as Elijah, Ty, and E stepped out of the mall, their shopping bags dangling from tired hands. They hadn't changed into their new outfits yet, but something in the air, something in them, had already shifted. Elijah felt it first, like a new version of himself rising beneath the surface.

Ty was practically vibrating, grinning as he glanced down at his purchases like he'd won the lottery. "Yo, wait till people see us," he muttered to himself, head bobbing to a beat only he could hear. E was quieter, lagging a few steps behind. His arms were crossed, his gaze low. He hadn't said much since they left the store, and Elijah couldn't tell if it was hesitation or discomfort weighing on him. The glow from the mall's glass front cast long shadows behind them, mirroring the mixed emotions they carried.

The atmosphere outside was a stark contrast to the mall's polished insides. The scent of sizzling street food mingled with exhaust fumes, replacing the crisp aroma of air conditioning and overpriced cologne. The concrete felt warmer, rougher beneath their sneakers, and the sky was streaked with burnt orange and deep violet as the world shifted into night. The contrast between the Outer City and what lay ahead: the Inner City with the Inlands hovering nearby. It was subtle, but Elijah felt it like a shiver down his spine. Everything about it felt different. Edgier. Louder. More alive.

Elijah reached into his bag and ran his fingers along the edge of his hoodie. Even unworn, it felt heavy. He wasn't just holding clothes, he was holding change, risk, a question mark over who he wanted to become. His parents' expectations had always pointed him in a straight line. This... this was a detour, a curve in the road he hadn't planned for. And somehow, that made it feel more real.

Ty stopped in his tracks, eyes locked on something taped to a nearby lamppost. He yanked down the flyer, the paper limp from sun and weather. Its corners were curled, the colors faded, but the bold print was still legible.

"Yo! Look at this," he said, holding it up.

DOC BLACKWELL — LIVE TONIGHT

Special Appearance by Artists from BY KNIGHT RECORDS

AFTERPARTY at CLUB VERTIGO

Elijah's heart skipped a beat. At the bottom of the flyer, the logo of By Knight Records stared back at him, his dad's label, his dad's empire.

"That's my dad's company," he said under his breath, more to himself than to Ty or E. The sight stirred something deeper than surprise. It brought back studio nights as a kid, falling asleep on the couch to the rhythm of drum loops, the heavy silence between him and his father when words fell short, the trophies that lined the shelves but never made the house feel like home.

Ty's eyes lit up. "Bro, this isn't just some random concert. This is your in. Think about it. We roll in there, name drop, mention the label. People notice that."

E looked uneasy. "We're already pushing it."

Ty waved him off. "This is once-in-a-lifetime shit." He nudged Elijah. "Come on, man. You've been talking about switching it up. This is it. VIP treatment, maybe even meet Doc himself."

Elijah stared at the flyer. He could almost hear the bass now, pulsing in his chest, calling him. This wasn't just a concert. It was a step into the life he'd been eyeing from a distance, one filled with clout, danger, music, and the kind of freedom that burned hot and fast. Fame. Independence. Rebellion. He didn't know if he belonged there, but he wanted to find out.

He looked at Ty, then E, then back at the flyer.

"Let's do it," he said.

And just like that, the night had a destination.

* * *

By the time they arrived at the venue, the Inner City had come alive. The streets were packed with people, most of them dressed in flashy outfits that glittered under the streetlights. Elijah noticed the difference immediately. There was a rawness here, an authenticity and hunger that didn't exist in the polished world he came from. It wasn't just the noise or the fashion; it was the energy, the people, the way they carried themselves like every night could be their last big shot. A part of him felt drawn to it, like this chaos was calling out to a side of him he hadn't fully met yet. His chest tightened, part nerves, part thrill, part recognition of something he didn't want to admit he craved.

The concert venue wasn't a sleek, modern stadium like he was used to. It was gritty, tucked between crumbling brick buildings covered in graffiti and old posters. The scent of sweat, smoke, and fried food lingered in the air. Nearby speakers thumped with bass-heavy music that blended with the sounds of laughter, shouting, and engines revving down the block. The pavement was sticky beneath their shoes, and the faint hum of anticipation crackled like static. A rat darted across the sidewalk, unnoticed by the crowd. The line to get inside wrapped around the block, buzzing with tension and excitement.

"This is wild," Ty said, practically bouncing on his toes.

E shoved his hands into his pockets, clearly uncomfortable. "I'm telling you, this is a bad idea."

Elijah glanced at the bouncer stationed at the front entrance. He recognized the logo on the man's jacket, security hired through his dad's company. The sight brought a tangle of emotions: a flicker of pride, a touch of resentment, and the ghost of conversations where his father promised to keep him away from places like this. Yet here he was, using that same name to gain access. It felt both empowering and ironic. The connection gave him a jolt of confidence.

"We'll be fine," Elijah said. "Stick with me."

They maneuvered their way to the entrance, where the bouncer stopped them with a stern look.

"Names?"

Elijah stepped forward. "Elijah Knight. My dad's the CEO of By Knight Records. Doc Blackwell is signed to our label."

The bouncer raised an eyebrow, then nodded. "Wait here."

A moment later, another man emerged from the venue. He looked Elijah up and down, his gaze lingering on the hoodie and sneakers.

"Let them in," the man said, waving them through.

Ty grinned as they walked past the line. "Told you it'd work."

Inside, the venue pulsed with energy. The air was thick with smoke and sweat, tinged with the acrid bite of cheap cologne, strong perfumes, and the faint smell of weed. Laser lights sliced through the haze, painting streaks of green and blue across the crowd. The bass pounded like a second heartbeat, rattling ribs and vibrating through the soles of their shoes. Elijah felt it all: the rhythm in his chest, the sticky floor underfoot, the shouted lyrics bouncing off the walls. The crowd swayed in unison, hands in the air, lost in the music, their voices rising in a ragged chorus that echoed through the concrete bones of the building.

Doc Blackwell stood center stage, commanding the room with his presence. His lyrics cut through the noise, telling stories of struggle, survival, and triumph.

One line hit Elijah especially hard: "Had to crawl through the dark just to stand in the light." As the words dropped, Doc's eyes locked onto Elijah's for a split second, just long enough to make Elijah's chest seize like he'd been caught.

The words echoed in his mind, sharper than the bass rattling through his chest. It reminded him of long nights alone in his room, staring at the ceiling, wondering if he'd ever be more than his last name, more than the son of a man who built his legacy on shady deals, blood, drug money, and calculated power. That look from Doc wasn't just a coincidence. It felt intentional. Like Doc saw something in him, or was daring him to see it for himself.

It wasn't just about pain or darkness. It was about the grind to become something more. Elijah swallowed hard, the line hitting like a truth he hadn't been ready to admit, as if someone had peeled back the layers of his pride and privilege and called out what lay beneath.

He couldn't take his eyes off Doc. The way he moved, owned the stage, made the crowd chant his name like he was royalty. And yet, he started with nothing. That could be me, Elijah thought.

As the concert continued, Ty and E got lost in the crowd, dancing and shouting along with the music. But Elijah stayed rooted in place, his mind racing.

This was the life he wanted: the rush of being seen, the thrill of breaking rules, the kind of respect that couldn't be inherited but had to be earned in blood, sweat, and tears. It wasn't just about music or status; it was about liberation, about rewriting his story in a place where nobody cared about last names. Elijah craved the kind of power that came from surviving this world on his own terms, not one handed to him by legacy. For once, he wanted to step into a room and feel like he belonged there, not because of who his parents were, but because of who he was becoming. And in this moment, surrounded by flashing lights and echoing beats, that possibility felt real.

The concert ended with a roar of applause, but Ty wasn't ready to call it a night.

"Afterparty at Vertigo," he reminded them, holding up the flyer. "We're going."

E shook his head. "I don't know, man. We barely got into the concert. A club? That's a whole different level."

Elijah glanced at the flyer again. The By Knight Records logo stared back at him like a challenge, bold and unapologetic. His stomach tightened. He thought of the late nights he'd spent watching artists like Doc on TV, dreaming of that kind of power, that kind of freedom. The logo wasn't just a symbol of his father's empire; it was a key to something else entirely. This wasn't just about a party. It was a test. And he wasn't sure if he was ready or already too far in to turn back.

"We'll figure it out," he said.

* * *

The bass hit them before the door even opened, deep, pulsing, relentless, like a heartbeat you could feel in your throat. The air outside the club carried fried food from a nearby cart, cigarette smoke, and something else: anticipation or danger. Neon lights flickered over the entrance, casting the crowd in waves of purple and gold. The line stretched down the block, but Ty was already moving toward the bouncer.

"Let me handle this," he said.

Ty slipped a folded bill into the bouncer's hand. The man glanced at it, then nodded toward the door.

"Go ahead."

* * *

Inside, Club Vertigo was a different world entirely. The bass hit harder, the lights flashed faster, and the energy crackled like static in the air. A wall of heat and sound slammed into them. Elijah felt it immediately, the rush of being somewhere he wasn't supposed to be. It reminded him of sneaking into his father's private studio sessions as a kid: heart pounding, waiting to get caught, craving that rush of rebellion. But this was different. This wasn't about curiosity. It was about becoming someone new.

Ty led them through the crowd toward the VIP section. They weaved past dancing bodies, laughter, and the smell of sweat, cologne, and alcohol. Elijah caught flashes of gold chains, limited-edition sneakers, luxury purses, and the gleam of expensive watches. A DJ spun tracks overhead, mixing trap beats with club anthems, each drop shaking the floor beneath their feet.

This wasn't just a club. This was a kingdom.

"This is it," Ty said, pointing toward a roped-off section.

Doc Blackwell sat in the center like a king on his throne. He wore a black leather jacket that shimmered in the strobe lights, diamond studs in his ears catching every flash. A thick chain hung heavy around his neck, and his presence radiated command. He laughed with his entourage, holding a sleek bottle of champagne in one hand and gesturing animatedly with the other. Everything about him said power. Untouchable. Magnetic. Larger than life.

Elijah couldn't look away. His throat tightened.

"We should go over," Ty said.

Elijah hesitated. Was it really that simple? He only knew him from his dad's stories. Could you just walk into someone else's world and make it your own?

Before they could take a step, a sudden commotion flared near the entrance. Two men were arguing, their voices sharp enough to slice through the music.

"You need to back off," one of them said, low and dangerous.

The other didn't move. Shoulders squared, jaw tight. Tension buzzed through the air like static.

Then.

He reached into his waistband. A glint of metal.

Elijah froze. His breath caught. Time stuttered. The lights slowed, flashing in sluggish intervals. The music felt distant, like it was coming from underwater. For a second, all he could hear was the thud of his own heartbeat.

"Gun!" someone screamed.

That one word shattered the room.

The music cut out instantly. Screams erupted as panic tore through the crowd. Tables flipped. Drinks flew. People shoved and pushed toward any exit they could find.

Elijah jolted into motion. He grabbed E's arm. "Come on!"

Ty was already moving.

They pushed through the crush of bodies, hearts racing, dodging stumbling feet and flying limbs. A girl tripped behind them, her high heels skittering across the floor. Someone shoved Elijah hard, nearly sending him into a speaker.

Then they were outside.

* * *

The cool night air slapped his face. Sirens screamed somewhere close. They staggered to the brick wall across the street, lungs burning, gasping for breath.

Ty let out a shaky laugh, rubbing his hands together.

Elijah didn't laugh.

His mind kept playing it back, over and over: the flash of metal, the suspended silence before the scream. His hands trembled. He pressed his palms to the wall to steady himself.

He had come looking for the thrill. The danger. A taste of something forbidden.

He got it.

But standing under the flickering streetlights, he realized this wasn't just some wild story to tell later. It was the beginning of something. A path he wasn't ready to walk, but one he'd stepped onto anyway.

And now, maybe, he couldn't leave.

The fear he felt wasn't about the gun. Not really. It was about how alive he'd felt. The way it surged through him, raw and electric, and how much he wanted more.

The first taste. The first mistake.

The first step into something darker.

And there was no turning back, not just from the club or the chaos, but from the version of himself he was starting to chase. He had crossed a line tonight. One between innocence and experience, between who he was and who he was becoming.

And he wasn't just a visitor anymore.

CHAPTER 3

THE INVITATION

The sun warmed the Outer City streets on this Sunday morning, casting everything in a soft, golden light. Elijah leaned back on the stone bench in front of the Westmoor Plaza fountain, soaking in the calm. The heat on his skin felt good, like the world was giving them a nod for surviving the night before. Beside him, Ty stretched with a big grin, while E sat upright and tense, clearly not as relaxed.

The plaza buzzed with weekend energy. Kids laughed as they ran past, families browsed small shops, and couples lingered over coffee outside cozy cafés. A saxophonist played smooth notes that drifted through the air. On the surface, everything was peaceful. But Elijah and his friends carried a leftover spark from the night before.

Elijah rested his arm along the back of the bench and smirked. "Man, that club was something else. Tell me that wasn't the livest night we've ever had."

Ty laughed and gave him a slap on the shoulder. "For real! That DJ went off, and those girls? I can't stop thinking about the one in the red dress. She was bad."

E gave a small nod, but Elijah noticed he didn't look convinced. His eyes kept darting around, and he was messing with the edge of his shirt. Elijah could tell something was bothering him.

"Y'all really don't think about the what-ifs?" E said, breaking their laughter. "Like, what if we got caught? What if our parents found out?"

Elijah waved him off. "Come on, E. We didn't do anything that crazy. We went to a club, had fun, and left. Nobody got hurt."

"Yeah," Ty added, smirking. "It ain't like we robbed a store or anything."

E shook his head. "I don't know, man. My mom would go off if she knew where I was. And if your folks found out, Elijah?" He gave Elijah a serious look. "You know your dad would lose it."

Elijah's smile slipped for just a second. His dad's voice, full of pressure and rules, crept into his mind, but he pushed it away. "Look, they did stuff like this too. My dad even rapped about it. And anyway, we were careful."

"Careful?" E raised his eyebrows. "We bribed a bouncer to sneak in. That's not careful."

Elijah chuckled. "Man, you're overthinking it. Nobody's gonna find out unless you tell them."

Ty leaned forward, grinning. "Don't tell me you're scared now, E. What, you scared to go back?"

E sat up straighter. "I'm not scared. I just think we should be smarter about it."

"Being smart means knowing when to take a chance," Ty said quickly. "And last night? That was the move."

"Exactly," Elijah agreed. "Come on, E. It felt good, didn't it? No rules. No expectations. Just us doing our thing."

E sighed and rubbed his face. Elijah watched him closely. He knew E had fun, but he also knew E thought differently. His family had worked hard to leave the Inner City, and E didn't want to mess that up. That kind of pressure wasn't something Elijah carried the same way, even if he understood it.

"Look," Elijah said more gently, "we're not trying to push you. But next time, we do it the right way. No bribing or talking our way in. We get in legit."

* * *

Later that evening, Elijah came home and walked into his room to find his mom sitting on his bed, holding the hoodie he'd worn the night before. His shoulders tightened, and he froze for a second, heart skipping a beat before thudding against his chest. For a moment, he considered backing out, pretending he forgot something. But it was too late.

"Hey, Mom. What's up?" he asked, aiming for casual, though his voice carried a slight edge of nervousness.

She held up the hoodie, her expression calm but sharp. "Where were you last night, Elijah? And where did this come from? It's not something you usually wear."

Elijah's brain scrambled for a response. "Oh, that? I was at Ty's place. I spilled something on my shirt, and he let me borrow it. Said it was his older brother's. You know how wild their family is." The words tumbled out fast and smooth, like he'd rehearsed them. He shrugged, offering his best innocent smile. "Didn't think it mattered."

His mom didn't reply right away. She just looked at him, her eyes narrowing slightly. That look always got to him, like she could see straight through him. The silence between them stretched, heavy and expectant.

"Alright," she said finally, her voice calm but firm. "Just be careful, Elijah. You've got a lot going for you. Don't let one bad decision mess that up."

Elijah nodded, swallowing hard as guilt pressed against his throat. He barely managed to meet her eyes. "I will. I promise."

She stood, crossed the room, and gently brushed his cheek before kissing his forehead. The gesture was familiar, comforting, but it made the guilt sharper. Her love felt undeserved in that moment.

Once she left, the silence in the room deepened. Elijah let out a long breath he hadn't realized he was holding and sat on the edge of the bed, staring at the hoodie in his hands.

It still smelled faintly of smoke, cologne, and the club. He ran his fingers over the fabric, remembering the lights, the noise, the danger. He'd gotten away with it. For now. But her lingering look and steady voice told him she knew something was off.

He leaned back, eyes fixed on the ceiling. "Gotta be more careful," he muttered. He knew he'd dodged a bullet. But even he understood: luck didn't last forever.

* * *

As night settled in, Elijah's phone buzzed. An unfamiliar number lit the room like a flashlight cutting through the dark.

Doc Blackwell: *Heard you were at the club. Saw you during the show, figured it was you. Don't worry. Your secret's safe with me. Let's talk.*

Elijah froze, his eyes locked on the message. His heart pounded, fingers tingling as adrenaline surged through his veins. A drop of cold sweat slid down his back. Just seeing the name Doc Blackwell on his screen jolted him. How did Doc get his number? And why did he want to talk?

His thumb hovered over the screen. Part of him wanted to reply, but another part held back. Doc wasn't just a local celebrity; he was the name in the Inner City: powerful, respected, feared. People spoke his name in half-whispers, stories of loyalty, betrayal, and danger. And now, Doc was texting him, like there was already a bond between them.

Another buzz.

Your dad talks about you all the time. Says you're the future. Maybe it's time we met.

Elijah's breath caught. His stomach tightened as a storm of emotions churned: nerves, thrill, fear, and a strange rush of pride. Being noticed by Doc felt like getting handed a lit match with gasoline at your feet. It was powerful, but it could all go wrong fast.

He thought of his dad's stories, how he and Doc used to run together before everything changed. His dad went legit, built a business, raised a family. Doc didn't. He stayed in the streets and built an empire. And now that man wanted to meet him.

Elijah leaned against the wall and slid down to the floor, the phone still glowing in his hand. After a moment, he opened the group chat with Ty and E and typed quickly.

Doc just hit me up. Wants us back at the club tomorrow. VIP.

Ty replied almost instantly:

Let's gooo! Told you we're moving up! This is crazy!

Elijah could almost hear Ty's voice, amped up, hyped like he was already picking out his outfit.

E, as usual, took his time. When his message finally came, it was short.

I guess. Just don't get us in too deep.

Elijah read it twice. E had always been the cautious one, the one who saw the edge before they stepped off it. His warning echoed louder than Ty's excitement. Elijah felt it too. This wasn't just a party invite; it was something bigger.

He stood up and tossed his phone onto the bed, then began pacing. His thoughts raced. Getting invited by Doc Blackwell didn't just happen. It was a door opening. But once you stepped through, you couldn't go back.

He ran his hand across his head and took a slow breath. If he was going to walk into that club tomorrow, he had to be ready: look sharp, act like he belonged. Whatever waited in that VIP section, one thing was clear: this was the beginning of something new.

And Elijah knew, deep down, that nothing would ever be the same again.

* * *

The next afternoon, the trio walked into the trendy clothing store at Crossline Plaza. Elijah pushed the door open with easy swagger, the overhead chime echoing as cool air swept across their faces. The scent of new fabric, cologne, and fresh leather sneakers hung in the air.

They split up almost immediately. Ty darted toward a rack of varsity jackets, pulling down a royal blue one with bold white stripes. He threw it on in front of a mirror and grinned.

"What you think? Too flashy?"

Elijah smirked. "If you gotta ask, it's probably perfect."

E moved slower, drifting toward the back wall lined with fitted caps, graphic tees, and designer hoodies. His eyes kept snagging on the price tags, hesitation written all over his face. Elijah noticed but kept quiet, tucking it away for later.

Elijah found a clean set: black jeans and a red shirt with bold embroidery. In the fitting room, he changed and studied his reflection. A quick adjustment of his chain, a tug at the shirt. He nodded. It worked.

When they regrouped at the register, Elijah stepped up first. He slid his card across the counter. The clerk, a young woman with a nose ring and a slick ponytail, glanced up and smirked.

"Back again, huh?" she said, scanning his items. "Didn't think you boys were the type to hang out on that side of town." Her eyes flicked toward his watch, quick but sharp.

Elijah leaned casually on the counter. "What can I say? We like to keep people guessing."

She chuckled as she folded the clothes into matte black bags. "Well, just try to stay out of trouble."

He winked as he picked them up. "No promises."

* * *

Outside, they stepped into the early evening buzz, the air heavy with exhaust and the scent of street food drifting from carts along the curb. Car horns blared in the distance, weaving through the chatter of shoppers spilling out of nearby stores. Across the street, the shopping center pulsed with energy, the crowd shifting like a restless tide.

Elijah remembered his dad calling this place a rundown strip mall once. Now it felt charged, like more than sales were being made here. Something tugged at him, familiar but just out of reach. Still, his mind was elsewhere, wrapped in the thrill of Doc's message and what tomorrow might bring.

E glanced over, brows knit tight. "It's weird, right? Doc texting you like this? How'd he even get your number?"

Elijah shrugged it off. "It's Doc Blackwell."

E didn't look convinced. He studied Elijah, as if searching for something unspoken. "Just... be careful. That's not someone you ignore your gut around."

Elijah's phone buzzed again. He pulled it out.

Doc Blackwell: *Club Vertigo. Tomorrow. Don't disappoint me.*

His grip tightened around the phone, a tremor of nerves before the rush of excitement hit. Club Vertigo wasn't just a nightclub. It was the heartbeat of the Inner City, where names were built and reputations destroyed. And Doc was holding the door open.

He slid the phone back into his pocket and turned to the others. "You ready for this?"

Ty's grin stretched wide. "Born ready."

E hesitated, then gave a quiet nod. "Yeah. Let's do it."

As they moved down the street, the sky shifted from gold to indigo. City lights blinked alive one by one, stretching shadows across the pavement. Elijah didn't look back. Ahead lay Club Vertigo. Whatever waited there would change everything.

CHAPTER 4

"INNER CITY" DREAMS AND "OUTER CITY" SHADOWS

The sun crept through the tall windows of the Knight mansion, casting long golden beams across the marble floors. Outside, the serene sounds of the Outer City filtered through a cracked window: birds chirping in harmony, the soft hum of luxury cars gliding down the street, and the distant, cheerful chatter of neighbors on their morning walks. Smooth jazz floated from a neighbor's outdoor speaker, a mellow soundtrack to the picture-perfect neighborhood.

Yet beneath the tranquil surface, something felt off. Elijah had grown up surrounded by this curated beauty, but it always struck him as fake. The lawns looked like they'd been trimmed with a ruler, and the neighbors' smiles never quite reached their eyes. To Elijah, it was like living in a snow globe: glossy, still, and too perfect to trust. The Outer City was clean, safe, and controlled. But it lacked something real. It lacked struggle. It lacked soul.

The smell of breakfast: pancakes, eggs, and sizzling bacon drifted up the grand staircase, snapping Elijah out of his thoughts. His eyes fluttered open, a grin spreading across his face. *Today's the day,* he thought, his heart thudding in his chest.

He swung his legs over the edge of the bed and rubbed the sleep from his eyes. One question lingered in his mind: Why did Doc want me to come on a Sunday? Sundays in the Outer City were for family and rest. Did the Inner City have its own kind of Sunday rhythm? Only one way to find out.

A sudden realization hit him. "Shit!" he blurted out, louder than intended.

From down the hall, his mother's voice echoed, "What did you say, Elijah?"

"Nothing, Mom!" he called back. "I'll be down in a minute!"

He snatched his phone and quickly typed a message to Doc:

Hey, I forgot to ask if two of my friends can come along with me.

He hit send and stared at the screen, waiting for a reply that didn't come right away.

A knock came at the door. "Elijah! Breakfast is ready!"

"Coming, Mom!"

He rushed to get dressed, yanking a shirt over his head and jogging down the grand staircase. The moment he entered the dining room, he froze. His father, Jules Knight, sat at the head of the table, wearing his usual pressed button-down, but his expression was anything but calm. Anger and disappointment clouded his face.

Elijah's excitement dimmed. Sunday breakfast was supposed to be sacred. In the Knight household, it was a rare chance to sit as a family and pretend they were just like any other household. But something was different this morning. The air felt heavy. The smiles were gone.

"Good morning, Mom. Good morning, Dad," Elijah greeted, trying to sound normal.

Jules barely looked up. "Vivi, what's gotten into your son? Why's he so happy this early?"

Vivi, standing at the stove, glanced over her shoulder with a knowing smirk. "I don't know. Why don't you ask him?"

Jules fixed his eyes on Elijah. "Boy, what's got you so excited?"

Elijah paused, his smile fading. Before he could answer, his mother stepped in.

40

"Someone told your father they think they saw you in the Inner City," Vivi said, placing a plate of pancakes on the table. "Of course, he believed them."

Elijah's stomach dropped. "What? That's not true!"

Jules crossed his arms, clearly unconvinced. "You've been acting funny lately. And that sweater? You didn't think your mom would mention it?"

Vivi turned toward Jules, her expression sharp. "You of all people should know better. You grew up in the Inner City. It chews people up. It doesn't care about potential or dreams. And I know my son. He's smarter than that."

"He's got a 4.0 GPA, he's a captain on both varsity teams, and he's got Ivy League schools chasing him," Vivi said, her voice rising. "Our boy is too good to be hanging with drug dealers and gangbangers who don't value life." She pointed at Jules. "And let's not forget, your record label helps keep those clubs alive!"

The room went silent.

Vivi grabbed her purse, slid on her heels, and headed to the door. Her keys jingled in her hand as her pace quickened. Neither Jules nor Elijah spoke. They just watched.

"You two figure this out," she said. "If you're so worried, take him there yourself. Let him see how good he has it here."

She left without another word. Jules watched her go, then smirked.

"Even when she's mad, she's the most beautiful woman alive," he said, eyes following her. "I hate to watch her go—but damn, I love to watch her leave."

He let out a low chuckle. "I'd drink her bath water."

Elijah winced. "Dad, seriously. I'm eating."

Jules laughed. "I'm just saying. Look, I love you, son. I want what's best for you. So I'll let this go—for now. But if I catch you in the Inner

City again, or even hear you've been there?" He shook his head. "That's your ass."

Elijah shifted. "Do you think Mom really meant what she said about the Inner City? If she feels that way, why'd she marry you?"

Jules leaned back in his chair, smiling faintly. "Because I changed. I wasn't gonna lose her. She made me better. When I met her, everything changed. She gave me a reason to grow up."

Elijah listened quietly.

"You need someone like that one day," Jules added. "Someone who makes you better just by being around. That's real love."

Elijah nodded slowly. "You really love Mom."

Jules grinned. "Love's too small a word. What I feel for her? It's everything."

Just then, Elijah's phone buzzed. He grabbed it quickly. Doc's reply had come in:

Of course you can bring your friends. I'll let security know.

Another buzz:

I got you, lil homie. You're like family. And remember, no snitching. See you tonight.

Elijah smiled.

Jules narrowed his eyes. "Why you cheesin' so hard? You got a girl? Getting some ass?"

"No, Dad. It was E. He asked if I'm staying over."

"You like boys?"

"No! I like girls."

"Well, you ain't acting like it. You kinda lame," Jules teased.

Elijah rolled his eyes. "Sometimes I forget you're not my age."

Jules smirked. "When I was your age—"

His phone rang. He checked it. "Doc. Got a session with him today." He stood up. "Remember—no Inner City. I still got people out there."

"Yeah, Dad."

As soon as Jules left the kitchen, Elijah grabbed his phone again. He checked the hallway, then called E and Ty on a three-way call. His fingers trembled slightly, his pulse pounding. This wasn't just another day.

This was the start of something different. And he couldn't turn back now.

* * *

"Ay, we still on for tonight? Doc said we good," Elijah said. He glanced at the clock, heart thumping a little harder, already picturing what the night might hold: music, neon lights, the heat of something dangerous in the air.

Ty's voice crackled through the line. "Wait, you just asked? What if he said naw?"

"Well, he didn't," Elijah snapped. "Matter of fact, fight me, Ty."

Ty chuckled. "Damn. Who messed your day up?"

Elijah sighed, rubbing his forehead. "It's been a long morning."

Ty snickered. "Yeah? You sound stressed. You sure you ain't just mad because you realized you like boys?"

Elijah rolled his eyes, trying not to smile. "Man, what's with everyone saying that today?"

Without missing a beat, both Ty and E chimed in unison, "'Cause you're gay."

Their synchronized laughter echoed through the call, a burst of familiarity and warmth. Elijah cracked a small grin. His shoulders relaxed, the tension in his chest loosening just a bit. They always knew how to break the seriousness, how to anchor him when he was spiraling. It was moments like this that reminded him why he kept them close.

"Whatever," Elijah muttered, shaking his head. "Just make sure you two get your stories straight before tonight. I almost got caught."

E's laughter faded. "Wait—what? How? And how are you still alive? I was sure your parents would kill you if they even suspected something like that."

Elijah rubbed his temples, pacing tight circles. "My dad got word from somebody saying I was spotted at that club in the Inner City."

Ty groaned. "Damn. You know that man got eyes everywhere."

"I know! That's why I was sweating bullets at breakfast," Elijah said. "I thought he was about to flip the whole damn table when I sat down."

"So, what happened?" E asked, voice more serious now.

"My mom defended me," Elijah said, exhaling slowly. The memory still felt unreal. For a second, he'd felt shielded, like she truly believed the lie he wore every day. "She basically told my dad there's no way I'd be caught dead in the Inner City. Said I was too smart for that."

Ty chuckled. "She lied her ass off?"

"Bro, facts," Elijah said, laughing.

Ty added, "Yeah, who the hell thinks you're smart?"

"But you didn't confess, right?" E asked, his voice laced with unease.

Elijah scoffed. "Hell no. I kept my mouth shut. My mom got all worked up though. She went on this whole rant about how dangerous the Inner City is."

E's voice lowered. "She's not wrong, you know."

Elijah and Ty responded in perfect sync, "Shut up, NERD!"

Ty quickly shifted the energy. "Yeah, yeah, we all know it's dangerous, E. But tonight's different. We ain't trying to get involved in anything crazy. Unlike you, E, me and my boy going to the NBA."

Elijah nodded, more to himself than to them. "Exactly. We're just going to observe. I told Doc we'd be there, and he's expecting us."

"Speaking of Doc..." E said slowly.

Elijah's stomach tightened. That name always set something off in him now.

Just then, Jules's voice thundered from the hallway. "Elijah! You better not be on that damn phone all morning! Find something productive to do until you leave!"

Elijah's heart jumped. "Shit, I gotta go. My dad's coming back."

He scrambled to shove his phone in his pocket. Footsteps echoed in the hallway, heavy and unrelenting. Each one sent a jolt of urgency through his chest.

* * *

Jules appeared, his presence immediate and commanding. Though his pace was brisk, he moved with the practiced ease of someone used to being in control. He looked like he had a full plate, but his expression stayed calm, his tone even.

"Elijah, I gotta head out. Almost forgot I have a session with Doc today. You remember Doc, right? One of my guys from back in the day. He used to rap, and I was the one producing his music. Honestly, he's the reason I even picked up a mic. We became this unstoppable duo. No one could touch us. We made it out of the Inner City and never looked back."

Elijah smiled to himself, but the feeling behind it wasn't admiration. It was irony. Jules didn't know the full story. Doc hadn't left the streets like he claimed. Elijah had seen it up close. The knowledge weighed on him like a stone, but he kept it tucked away.

"Yeah," Elijah said casually. "I remember him."

Jules adjusted his jacket and gave his son a once-over. "What's with the grin?"

"Nothing," Elijah said, shrugging. "Just thinking it's wild that you and Doc still keep in touch after all this time."

Jules let out a chuckle. "Yeah, loyalty runs deep. You don't find that often anymore."

Elijah thought back to Doc's last text: *No snitching.* That word, *loyalty,* landed differently now.

"Right," Elijah said, keeping his voice level. "Loyalty."

Jules nodded and moved toward the door. "Alright, I'm gone. You're staying at E's tonight?"

"Yeah. Me and Ty are catching a ride to school with him in the morning."

Jules pointed a finger at him, his tone sharpening. "Be safe."

Elijah gave a quick nod, but something in his dad's eyes made his throat tighten. It was like Jules was searching for something just beneath the surface. For a second, Elijah wondered if his dad already knew more than he let on.

"And remember what I said: if I ever catch you in the Inner City, that's your ass. Just because I don't roll through there anymore doesn't mean I don't still got ears to the streets."

Elijah forced a swallow. "Got it."

Jules smirked, flashing a grin that teetered between playful and warning. "That's your ass."

Elijah let out a nervous laugh. "Yeah, that's my butt."

Jules shook his head as he opened the front door. "I bet you'd like that, huh? Go on, enjoy your little slumber party."

"Dad…" Elijah groaned, rubbing his face. The joke stung, but more than anything, it reminded him of what he was hiding.

Jules's voice floated back from the door. "Just don't be late for graduation tomorrow. That'll be your ass too."

* * *

Later that day

Elijah burst out of his room, his heart pounding with excitement. The warm evening air hit his face, thick with the scent of freshly cut grass and sunbaked pavement. A wide grin spread across his face as he slung his backpack over one shoulder and bounded down the steps. Adrenaline surged through him, not just from where he was going but from what he was hiding. He didn't hear the approaching footsteps until a familiar voice called out.

"Elijah?"

He froze mid-step and spun around, masking his nerves with a cheerful smile.

"Mom?" he said casually. His eyes flicked to his backpack, the zipper halfway down and the sleeve of a black hoodie poking out. He stuffed it back in and zipped it shut, trying not to look rushed.

Vivi Knight crossed her arms, her eyes narrowing with suspicion. "What's got you so excited?"

Elijah scrambled for a believable lie. "Oh, uh… E just got a new game. We're gonna check it out tonight."

Vivi studied his jittery posture and the glint of mischief in his eyes. He wasn't usually this jumpy.

"Hmm. Alright," she said, her voice laced with hesitation. "Just don't stay up too late. You've got graduation in the morning."

"I won't, Mom," Elijah replied quickly, already backing toward the driveway. "Love you. Bye!"

He jogged to the car, his grin stretching even wider. Behind him, Vivi stood still on the sidewalk, watching as the car pulled away. Her instincts prickled. Something felt off.

She pulled out her phone and dialed Jules.

"Yo," Jules answered, his voice muffled by a heavy bass beat in the background.

"You at the studio?" Vivi asked.

"Yeah. Doc's laying something down right now. Why, what's up?"

"It's Elijah," she said, pacing the sidewalk. "He was acting off. Like he couldn't wait to get out the house. Said he's going to E's, but I don't know. It didn't feel right."

Jules chuckled lightly. "Maybe he's got a girl. Or maybe..." He lowered his voice to a teasing whisper. "Maybe he's gay."

"Jules," Vivi warned, her tone sharp. "I'm serious. Something's different about him."

"Relax, babe," Jules said. "He's a teenager. They all act weird sometimes. It'll pass."

In the background, Doc's voice rang out loud and clear: "I brought the bottles and the bitchesssss!"

Vivi's jaw clenched. "You're partying?"

"It's business, babe," Jules said quickly. "Doc's crew is here. We're just vibing."

"Uh-huh," Vivi muttered, clearly unimpressed. "Well, I'm heading to bed. Don't wake me when you get in."

"I won't. Love you."

"Love you too," she replied. But just before she hung up, Doc's voice shouted again.

"Tell your wife I said hi!"

Click. The call ended.

A second later, Vivi's phone buzzed. A message from Jules lit up the screen:

Don't worry, babe. You're the only one for me.

Vivi sighed, shaking her head. "Men," she muttered, then turned and walked back inside.

* * *

The ride into the Inner City felt like entering a completely different world, one Elijah had only imagined through rap lyrics and music videos. As they crossed the invisible line separating the clean order of the Outer City from the gritty pulse of the Inner City, everything shifted. The buildings looked older, battered, standing like crooked teeth under a sky that seemed darker somehow. Streets narrowed, sidewalks cracked beneath their tires, and graffiti covered nearly every surface: mailboxes, brick walls, metal fences, urgent messages left behind by ghosts of the block.

The air felt heavier, laced with the smell of exhaust, faint weed, and fried food drifting from distant vendors. Elijah kept his hands on the wheel, eyes fixed ahead, but he felt every thump of his heartbeat like a bass drum inside his chest. It wasn't just fear; it was the thrill of stepping into something unknown. He'd seen these corners in music videos, heard them referenced in songs, but being here in person made everything feel real.

"Yo, this place is wild," Ty said from the back seat, eyes wide as he leaned toward the window.

Elijah gave a small nod, his grip tightening on the steering wheel. His palms were damp with sweat, but he tried to keep his face unreadable.

E glanced at him from the passenger seat. "Y'all sure about this? It's not too late to turn back."

Elijah didn't hesitate. "We're not turning back. We're doing this."

The car slowed to a stop in front of the nightclub, a squat brick building pulsing with sound and light. Neon signs blinked erratically above the door, splashing the sidewalk in pinks and greens. Outside, a crowd gathered, smoking and laughing, their body language sharp with the confidence. The music thumped through the walls, loud enough to make the car vibrate.

Elijah turned off the engine and sat still for a second, staring at the entrance. "Alright, guys. Let's go."

They stepped out of the car, fixing their clothes, trying to look calm, confident. Ty adjusted his shirt. E wiped his palms on his jeans. Elijah led the way, his legs stiff with nerves. At the door, the bouncer stood like a statue: arms folded, face unreadable, eyes scanning them with a gaze that seemed to miss nothing.

As they got closer, Elijah forced himself to keep walking. He braced for questions, an ID check, anything.

But the bouncer just gave a slow nod. "Doc's expecting you. Go on in."

No resistance. No delay. Just like that, they were in.

Elijah kept his face still, though his heart hammered inside. This was only the beginning. There was no turning back. He was crossing into a world that played by different rules.

* * *

The club wasn't packed, but it buzzed with energy. Deep bass throbbed through the floor, making it feel like the whole building had a heartbeat. Red and violet lights flashed across the walls, bouncing off chrome railings and glossy floors. Elijah's eyes darted around, trying to soak it all in: the women swaying to the rhythm, the men lounging near the bar, and the VIP section roped off like a hidden world at the back.

"Yo, this place is lit. Even on a Sunday!" Ty shouted over the music, peering at the dancers.

They weaved through the crowd toward the VIP section, where Doc sat like royalty on a plush couch. His body was relaxed, but his presence demanded attention. One arm stretched across the backrest while the other held a glass of something dark. A wide grin sat beneath sharp, observant eyes that never stopped moving. Around him lounged an entourage of women and hard-faced men. The women shimmered with gold jewelry and flawless makeup; the men stood stiff in black, like statues with folded arms and cold glares. Doc's posture said it all. He ran this place.

"Elijah!" Doc called out, rising with open arms. "Glad you could make it!"

Elijah forced a grin, masking the nervous energy bubbling inside. "Yeah, it ain't nothing. We were gonna turn up tonight anyway."

Doc clapped him on the back, the impact solid. "Man, I haven't seen you since you were a baby. Your dad won't stop bragging about you."

Curiosity sparked in Elijah's chest. "Why doesn't he bring you around anymore?"

Doc's smile faded slightly. "Your dad wanted to keep his family safe. Out here, people hurt your loved ones just to hurt you. It's a dog-eat-dog world. Only the strong survive." He leaned in. "And me and your dad? We were some of the strongest."

As Doc spoke, Elijah's gaze drifted to the bar. A girl stood there, her dress glittering beneath the pulsing lights. Golden-brown skin glowed like sunlit honey, hips swaying as if she was the beat. Her shoulders were relaxed, her eyes confident, her presence magnetic. His breath caught. For a moment the club noise dulled, time slowing around her. Then she smiled, and the whole room lit.

Doc caught him staring and chuckled. "You like that? That's Jade."

Elijah didn't think. The words just slipped out. "Man... I'd drink her bath water."

Doc doubled over laughing. "Boy, what the hell is wrong with you?"

Elijah winced. "My dad said that... about my mom."

Doc howled louder. "Sounds like Jules." He wiped a tear from his eye. "You want me to introduce you?"

Elijah's stomach twisted. "You know her?"

"Of course. Her folks are good people. Known them for years."

Doc leaned over and whispered to one of his men, who nodded and vanished into the crowd. Elijah watched, unsure whether to be impressed or nervous about how quickly Doc made things happen. It felt like watching a crime boss in a movie.

Then Doc turned back to him. "If you're gonna be out here, you need a name. Elijah sounds like the Outer City. You need something darker."

He paused, then snapped his fingers. "Shadow. Shadow Knight."

Elijah tried it out. "Shadow Knight."

Doc nodded, pleased. "Yeah. Welcome to the Inner City, Shadow."

Moments later, Doc's man came back with Jade in tow. The lights caught her dark hair, her eyes sharp, scanning the room.

"Jade!" Doc greeted her with a warm grin. "How's your mom?"

"She's good," she said, flashing a charming smile. "Why'd you call me over?"

Doc gestured to Elijah. "Wanted you to meet my nephew. Shadow."

She turned to Elijah. "Hey, Shadow. Nice to meet you."

Elijah froze. "H-hi... I gotta go to the bathroom!" And he disappeared into the crowd.

* * *

Cold water hit his face, shocking him back into his body. *Shadow.* Doc's smirk. Jade's voice. The mirror threw his baby face back at him, wide-eyed and unscarred. But behind the glass, in the shadows of his gaze, something else had already taken root.

A switch had been flipped.

This wasn't just a nickname. It was a key to another world.

A new identity. A new rush. And somewhere deep down, a whisper of doubt.

He took a breath, squared his shoulders, and headed back.

Ty spotted him first. "Mr. Casanova! You handled that girl with finesse."

"Shut up, Ty," Elijah muttered, sliding onto the couch. He smirked. "Doc gave me a nickname. When we're out here, call me Shadow."

"Shadow?" Ty wrinkled his nose. "That's a superhero name or something."

"You got something better?"

Ty shrugged. "Nah. Just sayin'."

Elijah—no, Shadow—leaned back into the couch, the bass rumbling through his chest. The name clung to him. Elijah Knight was from the Outer City. But Shadow? Shadow belonged here.

* * *

E glanced at his phone, his eyes widening as the last beat from the club faded into the background. "Damn, it's getting late. We gotta get home before our parents notice."

Ty groaned, stretching lazily. "Relax, E. We're good."

"Nah," Shadow said, checking his phone too. "E's right. I can't be late to graduation tomorrow."

Ty sighed. "Fine, fine. Let's go."

They grabbed their hoodies and headed out, weaving through the thinning crowd. Outside, the night air was cool and still, the music from the club replaced by the soft hum of distant traffic and the occasional flicker of a passing headlight.

Shadow froze. A chill prickled the back of his neck, that unshakable feeling of eyes locked on him from somewhere in the dark.

"See you around, Shadow," a woman's voice called softly from behind.

He turned quickly, heart skipping. Jade? The voice sounded familiar, but he couldn't be sure.

Before he could scan the crowd, two men stepped out across the street. Dressed head to toe in black.

They moved fast, slicing through the shadows like predators.

One pulled a gun from his waistband.

"Yo! Give me all your money before I bust a cap in your ass."

They froze.

Shadow's heart slammed against his ribs. The gun gleamed under the streetlight. This wasn't a video game or a rap lyric. This was real.

E's hands shook as he reached into his pockets, fumbling for his wallet.

"Put your hands where I can see 'em!" the second man barked. "Before I put you on a t-shirt!"

E yelped, throwing his hands up. A dark stain spread across his jeans.

"Oh shit..." Ty muttered, stepping in front of E. "Hey, man. Chill. How we supposed to give you money with our hands up?"

The first robber stepped closer and jammed the gun into Ty's face. "You got a smart mouth, huh? You wanna die tonight?"

The second one laughed coldly. "Put him on a t-shirt!"

The first guy leaned in, voice low and dangerous. "Keep talking slick and they'll be photoshopping you in the clouds. Talkin' 'bout rest in peace."

Shadow forced himself to speak. "Look, man. We don't want trouble. We'll give you what we got."

The gun shifted toward him.

"Good," the guy sneered. "Now hurry the fu—"

Ty lunged.

"No!" Shadow shouted as Ty grabbed the guy's wrist, trying to wrestle the gun away.

POW!

The shot cracked through the night like thunder.

Everything froze. Shadow's ears rang. The robbers stood stunned for a beat, then took off, vanishing into the shadows.

E sobbed, trembling, tears streaking his cheeks. Ty stood frozen, chest rising and falling in sharp bursts.

Shadow blinked. His arm burned. He looked down. His hoodie was torn, a small hole smoldering at the edge of the fabric.

He touched the spot. Blood.

It grazed me, he realized. It should've been worse. I should've been dead.

Ty rushed to his side. "You good? Did you get hit? We need to get you to a hospital?"

Shadow shook his head, still dazed. "Nah… I'm good. Just grazed me. It was close, though."

Sirens pierced the air, growing louder.

Ty's eyes darted. "Cops. We gotta bounce."

Shadow scanned the street. His stomach dropped.

A man lay on the sidewalk, crumpled, unmoving. A pool of blood spread beneath him.

"Oh my God," Shadow whispered. "The bullet must've missed me… and hit him."

E whimpered, locked in place.

Ty yanked his arm. "We gotta go! The cops are coming! I'm too pretty for jail! You know what they'd do to someone like me in there?"

"Come on!" Shadow yelled, snapping E out of his trance.

They ran, feet pounding the pavement, lungs burning, hearts racing. Behind them, the night filled with sirens and shadows.

* * *

The car sped through the dark streets, silence hanging heavy in the air like a thick fog. No one spoke. The usual buzz of Ty's jokes or E's random facts was absent. Only the soft hum of the engine and the occasional bump in the road filled the space between them. Even the city itself felt like it was holding its breath.

Shadow kept his eyes locked on the road, his knuckles white as he gripped the steering wheel. Each passing streetlight lit up his face just long enough to show the tension carved deep into his expression. He hadn't realized how hard he was clenching his jaw until a dull ache started pulsing down his neck and into his shoulders. His heart still hadn't calmed.

After several minutes of tense silence, he finally spoke, his voice low. "We almost died back there, huh?"

Ty glanced over, a nervous grin forming. "Yeah. Low-key... it was kinda exciting." He gave a small laugh. "Besides the almost dying part."

Shadow shook his head, a short, breathy laugh escaping. "You're crazy, man. For real."

"Nah, think about it," Ty said, reclining a bit in his seat, still riding the wave of adrenaline. "That rush? That was wild. Like something outta Grand Theft Auto. We survived, bro. That's what matters. We made it out."

They continued driving, the lights of the Outer City growing brighter in the distance. Familiar streets started coming into view, but they looked strange now. Too polished. Too untouched. It felt like they didn't belong there anymore. They were bringing the night's chaos with them.

Ty suddenly scrunched up his nose and waved a hand in front of his face. "Yo, roll the windows down. It smells like straight-up pee in here."

E groaned from the back, tugging his hoodie over his face. "Shut up, Ty. That ain't even funny."

But the comment cracked through the tension. Laughter spilled out between them, awkward at first, then louder. For a brief moment, it felt like they were just three regular teens again, like nothing had changed. It was a moment of borrowed peace, like the world had hit pause.

Shadow allowed himself a smile. Not because he was okay, but because pretending was easier than unpacking the weight pressing against his chest.

Then his eyes caught the rearview mirror.

And reality came crashing back.

The image was instant, vivid. The man on the sidewalk. The blood. The lifeless eyes staring upward. It all came back in perfect detail. The ringing from the gunshot still echoed faintly in his ears. The heat of the bullet that grazed his arm still lingered. His hoodie, torn and crusted with dried blood, was proof this wasn't some nightmare.

E sat quietly in the backseat, staring out the window like he was trying to disappear into the night. His leg bounced up and down like a jackhammer, a steady rhythm of nervous energy. Shadow caught a glimpse of E's reflection in the rearview mirror. His eyes were red and swollen, his lip trembling like he was holding back a scream or tears. There was a rawness in his face that Shadow had never seen before. But he didn't say anything. None of them did.

Ty had quieted down, too. He leaned his head against the window, chewing his thumb and blinking slowly. Whatever thrill he felt earlier had drained away. Now he looked like he'd aged ten years in an hour.

Shadow's grip tightened on the wheel again.

What the hell did I just get us into?

He looked up at his reflection in the mirror. Hollow eyes. Blood-stained sleeve. Nothing felt the same. Something had shifted, like they'd stepped across a line they couldn't uncross.

They had made it out of the Inner City alive.

But something had stayed behind.

And none of them were coming back the same.

CHAPTER 5

THE DOUBLE LIFE BEGINS

The air felt alive with energy as Elijah, Ty, and E sat under the old oak tree at the edge of the school campus. The sound of lockers slamming and students laughing carried across the courtyard. All three wore their caps and gowns, the fabric shifting slightly in the breeze. Graduation day had finally arrived, the moment they had talked about for years.

Elijah stretched out his legs, brushing his sneakers against the grass. A calm smile played on his lips as he looked over at his friends. He had big plans for the summer: chilling with the guys, getting in some extra training, and making memories before adulthood hit. For once, the end of the school year didn't feel like a deadline. It felt like the start of something new.

"You nervous?" Elijah asked, breaking the silence.

Ty gave a shrug and let out a dry chuckle, one that didn't match his usual attitude. It was the kind of laugh someone gives when they're holding back something real. "Nah, man. Just tired of school."

He motioned toward the campus, where other students were talking about college, jobs, and life after summer. Ty's words had a sharp edge, hinting at something underneath, maybe even a fear of being left behind.

Elijah had never fully understood Ty's home life. His parents had money, sure, but they were never around. Always off at meetings or events. It felt like they barely noticed their son.

Elijah had spent hours in Ty's huge house, walking through halls that felt more like a museum than a home. A grandfather clock ticked steadily in the background, the only sound in a place full of expensive furniture and empty space. Ty's parents came and went, exhausted from work trips, barely speaking to him. It was a life Elijah didn't relate to, one Ty had lived with for as long as he could remember.

"I'm just glad it's over," Elijah said, though his smile didn't reach his eyes. He glanced at Ty again, who was now staring off into the distance.

The three had grown up together. They were more like brothers than friends. But lately, Elijah felt something changing between them. He kept thinking about what Doc had told him, about what could come next. Elijah had always done what was expected: good grades, star athlete, solid future. His parents were proud, supportive, and always guiding him toward success.

But Doc offered something they couldn't: a taste of the Inner City life Elijah had only seen from the outside.

He looked at his phone. No messages yet.

Ty finally spoke, still sounding distracted. "So... what's your move after this? You doing college?"

E chuckled without much joy. "Man, Elijah's probably going pro. Don't even play."

Elijah grinned and shook his head. "I don't know yet. I just want to enjoy summer first."

But in his mind, the decision had already started forming. Doc wasn't just another big-time rapper: he was a legend. He ran more than the studio. He ran the streets. And now, he was offering Elijah a place in that world. It was tempting, maybe too tempting.

Elijah stared at the field for a second, his chest tightening with anticipation. Just as his fingers reached toward his pocket, his phone buzzed.

Doc: *Graduation party tonight. Come by the club, Jade will probably be there.*

Elijah's heart raced. He'd only met her once, but she had stayed on his mind. Seeing her again? That was reason enough to show up. But this wasn't just about a girl. This was about stepping into something bigger.

This wasn't just a graduation celebration. It was a velvet-roped night with flashing lights, booming music, champagne flowing, and the city's most important people either watching or getting watched. It was a world Elijah couldn't stop thinking about.

Ty's voice snapped him back. "You good, man?"

"Yeah," Elijah said with a smile. "Just thinking about what comes next. Big night ahead."

Ty gave him a look but let it go. "Don't forget about us when you're living that big-time life."

E nodded and smiled for the first time that day. "Yeah, don't leave us little guys behind."

Elijah laughed. "Y'all stuck with me."

They stood up together, walking toward the rest of their day. But Elijah's mind was already racing: to the club, to Jade, to Doc.

To the life that was calling him forward.

* * *

The snap of camera shutters, the scent of fresh flowers, and the buzz of families filled the air: it was graduation day. Elijah felt it settle on his shoulders, a mix of pride and nerves. The morning sun bounced off polished brass bells hanging from the stage, marking the end of one chapter and the start of another.

He stood in front of the bathroom mirror, adjusting his tie and brushing a hand across his face. His reflection stared back, dressed in a robe, suit, and cap, yet it all felt like a costume for someone else. Did he really look like the person everyone believed in? Was he ready for the future his parents had mapped out, or just going through the motions until tonight?

His cap sat slightly off-center. As he fixed it, his phone buzzed in his pocket. He pulled it out and saw a message from Doc.

Tonight's the night. You pullin' up?

A grin crossed Elijah's face. His fingers hovered over the screen before he replied:

I'm there. Let's do this.

A jolt of excitement shot through him. Graduation was just a milestone, but the real change waited beyond the stage, deep in the city, where Doc promised a different world: money, power, respect.

Outside, his mom, Vivi, walked toward him, her eyes glowing with pride.

"You look so handsome," she said, her voice tight with emotion. "We're so proud of you. Your father and I... we couldn't ask for a better son."

Elijah smiled, though a wave of guilt pulled at him. His parents had always supported him. Always shown up. But tonight felt like a line he couldn't uncross.

His father, Jules, gave a quiet nod. "You're a man now, son."

"I wouldn't be here without y'all," Elijah said. "You've always had my back."

His mom wrapped him in a tight hug, and for a second, Elijah let himself melt into the warmth. Let himself be her son. But the moment passed. The clock was ticking.

The stadium buzzed with life: teachers, friends, relatives, the whole town packed into the stands. Elijah slipped into the sea of caps and gowns and caught sight of Ty and E. Ty looked sharp in his suit, grinning wide, though something behind his eyes seemed unsettled. E scanned the crowd, silent, distant, still carrying the memory of the shooting.

Elijah's phone buzzed again.

Doc: *Don't be late. Bring your friends. It's going to be legendary.*

Elijah: *We'll be there.*

The ceremony passed in a blur. When Elijah's name was called, he stepped onto the stage, accepted his diploma, and waved to his cheering parents. But his thoughts had already drifted to the night ahead.

Ty walked the stage with confidence, soaking in the moment. E, tense and restless, looked like he wanted it to be over. Still, for just a moment, all three stood together, celebrating the same milestone in different ways.

As the event wrapped up, the weight returned, heavier this time. Not just the pressure of growing up, but the pull of something else.

Outside, graduates and families gathered. Elijah slipped away and checked his phone.

Ty and E found him again, and the three of them headed for the parking lot. Ty kept smiling, but he nervously tugged at the edge of his gown, a small tell. Elijah sensed something deeper behind the grin. Maybe even jealousy.

"You ready for tonight, man?" Ty asked, clapping Elijah on the back.

"Yeah," Elijah said, pushing the nerves down. "It's gonna be a big night."

They jumped into the car and drove toward the heart of the city. Elijah's chest buzzed with anticipation. The suburbs were safe. Predictable. But the life ahead?

That was real.

Doc was waiting.

Jade was waiting.

And tonight, Elijah wasn't just another graduate. That part of him was fading fast.

Tonight, he was Shadow.

As the club lights flickered in the distance, Elijah's phone buzzed one last time. A photo appeared: Jade, smiling. Something in her eyes dared him to follow through.

Doc: *See you soon, Shadow.*

Elijah stared at the screen, heart pounding. The name echoed louder in his head.

Shadow.

* * *

The club was jumping, its deep bass shaking the sidewalk beneath their feet as Elijah, Ty, and E stepped into the heart of the Inner City. Bright neon lights danced across the faces of the crowd waiting outside, buzzing with energy and excitement. But the three of them didn't wait. They weren't just anyone tonight. They were with Doc.

As they neared the entrance, the bouncer, a huge guy in a tight black tee with a thick gold chain, locked eyes with Elijah. Elijah gave him a cool nod, and just like that the bouncer stepped aside. No questions asked.

Inside, it was like another world. Smoke hung in the air, blending with the scent of cologne and spilled drinks. Lights flashed like lightning across the packed crowd. Elijah's heart raced. His eyes swept over the scene: people dancing, bottles popping, money tossed like it didn't matter. Every VIP table looked like something out of a music video: gold hookahs, sparkling champagne, stacks of cash.

And right in the center, like a king on his throne, sat Doc.

Doc leaned back in a booth, wearing a flashy designer tracksuit and thick gold chains that shimmered under the lights. A cigar dangled from his mouth, and his diamond-covered watch caught every beam. He was surrounded by rappers, street bosses, and beautiful women. This wasn't just a club: it was his kingdom. And walking into it felt like stepping into a spotlight Elijah wasn't sure he'd earned, but definitely wanted. It was like walking into a dream carved from smoke and noise, danger wrapped in velvet.

Elijah's eyes widened. This was the life he dreamed about, far from the polished homes and perfect lawns of the Outer City. This was raw. This was real.

Doc noticed him and lit up. He stood with the kind of swagger that pulled attention like gravity. Even in all the chaos, people paused. Heads turned. Whispers followed. That was the kind of pull Doc had.

"There he is! My nephew, Shadow!" Doc shouted, his voice cutting through the music. He stepped forward and wrapped Elijah in a strong hug, slapping his back.

Elijah grinned and shook Doc's hand. Ty and E followed, clearly stunned by it all.

"You made it," Doc said, blowing smoke to the side. He eyed Elijah with a smile. "Graduation day, huh? Big deal."

"Yeah," Elijah replied, looking around. "Thought we'd do it right."

Doc chuckled. "Now that's the mindset. And believe me, you're with the right people. Word's out, Shadow. You're on the map now."

Hearing the nickname lit something inside Elijah. Shadow. Here, in this world, that's who he was. Someone bold. Someone known.

They slid into the booth, and Doc poured drinks without hesitation. Elijah didn't even flinch. He felt a rush: not guilt, but excitement. No rules. No judgment. Just freedom. This wasn't about breaking the rules anymore. This was about rewriting them.

In Doc's world, the rules didn't matter. What mattered was who you were becoming.

And Elijah? He was becoming Shadow.

* * *

Shadow was mid-conversation with Doc when he saw her: Jade.

She moved through the crowd like she owned it. Heads turned as she passed, some offering subtle nods while others just stared. Her dark curls spilled over her shoulders, and the shimmer of her fitted dress caught every flicker of the strobing lights. She didn't have to command the room. She just did.

Shadow's breath caught. He couldn't look away.

Doc followed his line of sight and smirked, his voice low and amused. "Go on, Shadow. She's been asking about you."

Shadow's pulse spiked. He hadn't expected her to remember him, let alone ask for him. He nodded, more to himself than to Doc, and made his way to the bar where Jade was ordering a drink.

Sliding in beside her, he did his best to look composed, though his hands were clammy and the bass of the music seemed to thump in time with his heartbeat.

"Fancy seeing you here," he said, trying to sound smooth.

Jade turned, her eyes lighting up in recognition. "Hey, Shadow. You made it."

A slow smile curled across her lips. "You were a little nervous last time we met."

Shadow laughed lightly, rubbing the back of his neck. "Yeah… first time in a place like this. It was a lot."

She raised an eyebrow, playful. "You seem more comfortable now. What changed?"

He leaned against the bar, trying to play it cool. "Guess I'm adjusting. Besides, I heard you might be here. Figured I'd try again to make a better impression."

Jade laughed, a soft, melodic sound that made him want to hear it again. "Well, you're off to a decent start."

They ordered drinks and fell into a rhythm, their conversation flowing with unexpected ease. Jade was sharp, confident, and uninterested in surface-level charm. She pushed back, teased, and matched his wit. It only made Shadow lean in closer.

Then came the question he had dreaded.

"How old are you, Shadow?" she asked, tilting her head, her tone casual but her eyes focused.

He paused for a split second. The truth hovered at the edge of his lips, but so did the risk.

He smiled. "Twenty-one."

Jade studied him for a breath, then nodded like she bought it. Maybe she did.

Before her friends pulled her away, they exchanged numbers. Shadow stood at the bar afterward, staring down at his phone like it held more than just digits, as if it were the start of something. His heart was still pounding.

He didn't know if he was in over his head.

But it felt too good to walk away.

* * *

Shadow returned to the VIP booth, where Doc was waiting with a knowing smirk, his cigar now burned halfway down and resting between his fingers like a prop from a scene. The booth glowed with the soft flicker of neon lights reflecting off the velvet couch, casting shifting colors that made everything feel surreal.

"She gave you her number, didn't she?" Doc asked, his tone playful but layered with expectation. His eyes gleamed with amusement, like a teacher watching his student pass a test he always knew he could.

Shadow grinned, adrenaline still buzzing in his veins, heart pounding like a bassline in his chest. "Yeah. She did."

Doc leaned in closer, his playful demeanor melting into something more serious. His eyes sharpened, scanning Shadow like he was evaluating a diamond still rough around the edges. The smirk faded. He lowered his voice so only Shadow could hear, and when he spoke again, his words carried weight.

"You've got potential, Shadow. I see it in you. Always have. And I've got an offer for you."

Shadow's pulse quickened. A knot tightened in his gut, a swirl of excitement and uncertainty. The noise of the club, the laughter, the beat all faded. In that moment, it was just him and Doc.

"What kind of offer?" he asked, trying to keep his voice even.

"Work for me this summer," Doc said, his voice smooth and deliberate. "Run with me and my crew. Learn the game. Really learn it. Not just the shine, but the grind. See what this life is actually about."

Elijah paused, his mind racing. He knew this wasn't just a summer job. This was Doc handing him a key to a different life. A life where mistakes came with consequences, but the wins? The wins were legendary.

He pictured it: luxury cars with tinted windows and hidden compartments, late-night drives through the city under neon skies, wads of cash in gym bags, nods that meant deals were sealed. Designer clothes and street-level respect. Rooms where people listened when you spoke, not because they had to, but because they knew better.

But choosing that meant turning his back on what his parents had worked so hard to give him: his mom's late shifts, his dad's long hours in the studio, the private school tuition, the SAT tutors, the college acceptance letters. They had handed him a future lined with safety and opportunity.

He could already hear his mother's voice in his head: *You're not like them, Elijah. You were raised for more.*

The weight of that truth settled on his chest.

"I'll think about it," Shadow said finally, his voice quieter now. Unsure. Caught in the gravity of the choice. Was he Shadow now, or still Elijah?

Doc clapped him on the back with a heavy hand, his grin wide again. Now it felt official, the seal on a deal not yet made but almost inevitable.

"That's all I ask. Think about it," he said. Then, more firmly, "But don't take too long. This world moves fast, Shadow. And I don't want you to get left behind."

The music swelled again, the bass shaking the floor beneath them. The lights danced across the ceiling like stars trapped inside. Elijah's phone buzzed in his pocket: a signal from the life that waited outside these walls. But he didn't move. His eyes stayed fixed on the lights above, caught in a moment that could change everything.

* * *

As the night stretched on, Shadow lingered outside the club, his eyes tracing the electric sprawl of city lights. The air was cool against his damp skin, still slick with sweat from the heat and energy he'd just stepped out of. A faint shiver ran up his arms, and he shoved his hands deep into his pockets just as his phone buzzed.

Jade: *Good seeing you tonight, Shadow. Let's hang out soon.*

He smiled at the screen. The message made him feel wanted, like he belonged in this new world. But it also tugged at the edges of another life: the one filled with curfews, parent-teacher conferences, and expectations that never quite fit.

The club doors exploded open behind him, spilling bass-heavy music and raucous laughter onto the street. Doc stepped out, lighting a blunt with a flick of his lighter. The flame briefly illuminated his face: sharp, confident, in control. His stance radiated power.

He scanned the block, then turned to Shadow.

Without a word, Doc passed him the blunt. Shadow took it.

"Welcome to the Inner City, Shadow," Doc said, blowing a slow cloud of smoke into the air. "Summer's just getting started."

The smoke scraped down his throat, burning and bitter, before settling deep in his chest. He let it sit there, letting it change something inside him.

He wasn't Elijah Knight anymore. The kid with straight-A report cards and a future mapped out by someone else. He was Shadow now.

And this summer, he was stepping fully into the world that had only teased him before. A world of risk, freedom, and danger.

A world where he made the rules.

CHAPTER 6

SHADOW'S SUMMER

Elijah's bedroom looked like something out of a magazine: a king-sized bed with crisp white sheets, a sleek desk piled with books and a high-end gaming system, and a shelf full of trophies for basketball, football, track, and boxing, all gleaming under soft lighting. But the only thing that felt truly his was the sketchpad on the nightstand. Its pages held unfinished drawings and scattered song lyrics. That sketchpad was his escape.

From his window, he could see wide lawns and gated homes, the kind of place people dream about. But to him, it was starting to feel like a prison.

He stared at the ceiling for a while, lost in thought. The clock read 7:30 AM, but he didn't feel tired or ready to start the day. He had everything most people wanted: loving parents, a big house, straight A's, trophies. But it all felt fake.

With a sigh, he sat up and planted his feet on the cold floor. His mother's voice echoed down the hall, either on the phone or giving orders to the house staff, like always. Today, it grated on him.

He walked to the closet. Rows of neatly pressed clothes in blacks, grays, and whites lined the racks, each one a reminder of school events and family dinners where he had to look perfect. But behind them sat his secret stash: designer shirts, sneakers, distressed jeans. The kind of gear he wore with Ty and E the first time they ventured into the Inner City. A kid had complimented his Jordans. That moment had felt more real than any standing ovation or award.

He chose a clean white button-down and dark designer jeans. It was a look that was nice but casual. Limited-edition Jordan sneakers completed the outfit. It struck the balance he wanted, put-together without trying too hard.

As he zipped up his bag, he caught his reflection in the mirror. He looked like the perfect student, the perfect son. But that image didn't match how he felt inside. He wasn't Elijah Knight anymore, not the golden boy, not the future college athlete, not the son of a wealthy real estate mogul and a former street legend turned music mogul.

He looked away and grabbed his phone. No new texts or calls. Not that it mattered. He wouldn't have answered anyway.

He slid the phone in his pocket, grabbed his bag, and walked out. As he passed more mirrors in the hallway, he kept seeing a version of himself that looked polished and put-together. But inside, he didn't feel the same.

As he reached the stairs, a voice called out.

"Elijah, where are you going this morning?"

His mom stood in the kitchen, scrolling through her phone but still tracking his movements.

"Just going out," he replied, not slowing down.

"Elijah," she said again, looking up.

"I'm going to the pool house to meet Ty and E. I'll be back tonight," he said quickly, avoiding her gaze.

Vivi Knight's eyes softened briefly, but her tone stayed firm. It was how she kept order when she didn't know what else to do. "Don't forget about your college applications and summer plans. You need to stay focused. You're not like—"

"Like who, Mom?" Elijah interrupted, his voice sharper than he meant it to be. He could almost hear his dad's warnings about the streets echoing in his head. But he didn't want to hear it, not from her. Not now.

She didn't answer. She just exhaled and looked back at her phone. "I arranged a meeting with Dr. Williams at Princeton for you. Be careful. People talk in this neighborhood."

He didn't respond. He had no plans to stay here much longer. This world didn't feel like his anymore.

As he approached the front door, he heard his dad's voice from the study. Elijah stopped. Through the frosted glass, he saw his father's shadow. There was a time when that voice meant everything was under control. Now, it reminded him of everything left unsaid. His dad had left the streets and built a new life, but he never talked about what it cost. Elijah wished he could ask why. Why he never warned him how tempting the streets could be.

The door opened, and Jules stepped out, phone in hand. His voice was smooth and calm, but something about it made Elijah tense.

"Where are you going?"

"Just meeting up with Ty and E," he muttered, already feeling distant.

"Remember what I told you. You're a man now. Don't let anything or anyone throw you off course. Some people want you to follow the wrong path. Don't do it."

"I won't," Elijah replied, though he wasn't sure he meant it.

He stepped outside. The door clicked shut behind him, sounding more like a prison gate than a farewell. His Mercedes sat in the driveway, another gift, another symbol of the life laid out for him.

He got in and started the engine. The front gate separated him from the rest of the world. His phone buzzed.

E: *Yo, y'all still coming to the pool house?*

Ty: *Ready to roll.*

Elijah started to reply, but his mind drifted. They were chasing street cred, chasing respect. The risks made them feel alive. But the line between freedom and danger was getting harder to see.

For a second, he wondered if they could just keep life simple. Stay where it was safe. But then the car rolled forward, and the pull of that other world grew stronger.

As the mansion faded in his rearview mirror, one thought took over: *This is it.*

* * *

The summer heat pressed down on the Outer City as Elijah cruised through winding streets in his sleek, black Mercedes. His hands stuck slightly to the leather steering wheel. Even in a quiet, polished neighborhood like this, Elijah felt restlessness in the air. He wasn't alone: he and his boys were all hungry for something more.

When he pulled up to E's family pool house, the music was already pounding through the backyard. Ty never played anything low, and Elijah immediately recognized the beat: it was Doc's latest album. The hard-hitting rhythm and gritty lyrics didn't just fill the air; they demanded attention.

Ty was stretched out by the pool. He barely looked up as Elijah walked into the yard.

"Man, you still bumping this album?" Elijah asked.

Ty looked at him and smirked. "You already know. This one's fire. Doc speaks what most are scared to say."

The lyrics blared from the speakers:

You want power? That comes with some heat.
You want respect? It ain't free in these streets.

Elijah sank into one of the chairs by the pool. The words hit him harder than he expected, like a warning and a promise wrapped into one. Ty nodded to the beat.

E stepped outside, shaking his head. "Does he ever play anything else?"

"Only when something else is worth it," Ty shot back without looking away from the sky.

Elijah leaned back, letting his head rest against the cushion. He'd been feeling it for weeks now. That pull toward the Inner City. Not school. Not scholarships. Not what was expected. The closer their trip to the Inner City got, the more that itch grew into a craving.

"So, what's the move?" Elijah asked, eyes narrowing. "Doc's expecting us tonight. Said he's got something planned."

Ty cracked his knuckles, his whole posture changing. "We hit the Inner City. We meet up with Doc. And maybe, just maybe, we finally get an inside look at this life."

E crossed his arms. "Are we seriously doing this? We don't exactly blend in down there."

"You're right," Elijah said, pausing for a second. His old life of prep schools, neat uniforms, and careful routines flashed through his mind. "That's why we've got to change how we show up. Right now, we look like tourists."

Ty's grin grew. "Exactly. We need some gear, something that fits the life we're stepping into."

Elijah raised an eyebrow. "You think clothes are gonna make the difference?"

"Absolutely. You dress the part, you become the part," Ty said, dead serious.

E laughed. "What now? More designer clothes?"

"Not just designer," Ty replied. "We need fits that say confidence, that we're not pretending, we're built for this."

Elijah threw up his hands. "Alright, alright. So where to?"

"The mall," Ty said with a nod.

Elijah raised an eyebrow. "Same mall?"

E smirked. "Yeah, but maybe we skip the same clerk this time."

Ty let out a laugh. "Nah, she was cute. Bet she remembers us."

The boys all chuckled, the air filled with lighthearted banter.

Elijah sat quietly for a moment, his heart thudding under his calm surface. He was hyped, finally stepping toward the life that had called to him for so long. But in the background, a quieter voice warned him: once they crossed that line, they might not come back the same.

"We're getting some new gear."

* * *

Not long after, the trio pulled up to the same mall where they'd picked out their new clothes before. The Inner City still called Elijah's name, but for now, he was living the Outer City life: a place where image and reputation meant everything.

As they walked into the store, there she was: the same flirtatious cashier from their last visit. But this time, when she looked at Elijah, something had changed. He had money, sure. But it was more than that.

He came from the Outer City, but he was starting to carry the edge of someone who could belong to both worlds. She noticed.

Elijah stepped up to the counter and grinned. "You still got that pretty smile, I see."

She smiled back, bold and warm. "Well, if it isn't Mr. Shadow himself."

Elijah raised an eyebrow. "Shadow?"

She leaned in slightly. "Doc calls you that, doesn't he?"

The nickname hung in the air, sounding different coming from her lips. "Yeah, he does," Elijah said slowly. "But you still haven't told me your name."

She gave him a once-over, clearly impressed. "That's because you didn't ask," she said with a playful smirk. "I'm Lola. Lola Bryant."

Elijah met her gaze, leaning a little closer. "My real name's Elijah. But in the streets, they call me Shadow."

Lola's eyes sparkled with interest. "Why do they call you that?"

Elijah chuckled. "Because like a shadow, I never really leave. You might not see me, but you'll know I'm there."

Lola laughed softly. "I like that. There's something sexy about mystery."

Ty, who had been watching the whole exchange, let out a low whistle. "Man, you really know how to keep a girl's attention."

Lola shot him a look. "He clearly knows what he wants."

Elijah laughed. "Maybe I just want to see how far you'll let me push."

She leaned in just a little more, voice playful but bold. "Push me? I might just like that."

Her words lingered. Elijah wasn't used to this kind of challenge. Most girls melted under his charm. But Lola didn't. She played the game, and she played it well.

She moved behind the counter, pretending to busy herself with the clothes. "I think I can find something that'll really make you stand out," she said, glancing back at him.

"You think so?" Elijah asked.

"I'm sure of it."

She picked out a silk short-sleeve button-up with a black-and-gold floral pattern and held it up to his chest, her fingers brushing against him just a second too long.

"This would look great on you," she said.

Elijah smirked. "I'll take it."

Lola grinned. "I think you'll wear it even better than I could. But you can always find out."

While she rang up his three shirts and the $200 jeans, Elijah couldn't look away. Every move, every glance carried purpose, like she was performing just for him.

She wasn't just flirting.

She was studying him.

Right before they left, Lola leaned in close and said softly, "You know, Shadow… you might be worth the trouble."

Elijah grinned. "I'll make it worth your while."

As they walked toward the exit, Elijah could still feel the heat from their exchange. It clung to him, heavier than summer air. He'd charmed plenty of girls before, but this felt different. Like the first pull of something he shouldn't want but couldn't ignore.

Just as they reached the door, Lola called out, "You're really gonna leave without asking for my number?"

Elijah turned back, smirking. "I was getting to that."

He absolutely wasn't. The chemistry between them had him off his game.

He turned back and walked toward the counter, the moment pulsing with energy.

Lola leaned on the counter. "You sure? Or are you playing hard to get?"

Elijah chuckled. "Who said I'm playing?" He pulled out his phone.

She took it, typed in her number, and handed it back with a confident smile. "Don't keep me waiting. You know where to find me."

Elijah added his number to her phone too, their fingers touched.

"I'll call you soon," he said.

"Good," Lola replied, her smile both daring and sweet. "I'm looking forward to it."

As Elijah walked away, he realized he wasn't just interested. Lola had gotten under his skin. Maybe it was the way she said his name, like she already understood who he was. Or maybe it was how she blurred the line between temptation and connection, just enough to keep him wanting more.

* * *

The Mercedes cruised smoothly through the streets of the Inner City. Elijah gripped the steering wheel a little tighter. The car's interior smelled of fresh leather and black ice air freshener.

Tonight felt different. He wasn't just driving through the city; he was crossing a line. Leaving the safe, polished comfort of the Outer City for the unpredictable grit of the Inner City. The deeper they drove, the more the divide between his two worlds felt real.

Ty sat in the passenger seat, bouncing to the rhythm of Doc's latest album playing softly in the background. E sat in the backseat, arms crossed, his gaze fixed out the window, though his mind seemed miles away.

"Man, this night's gonna be fire," Ty said, grinning as he nodded to the beat. "Doc's on another level right now."

Elijah smirked, but his eyes remained focused on the road ahead. "Yeah, that track he dropped last week was crazy."

E leaned forward, his tone serious. "You both know we're not just here for the music, right? Doc's got more planned tonight."

Elijah gave a silent nod, picking up on the shift in E's mood. There was more to tonight than just new beats and bass drops.

As they drove on, the environment changed. Glowing billboards and spotless sidewalks were replaced by flickering streetlamps, boarded-up windows, and graffiti-covered walls. People lingered on corners. The road cracked beneath their tires, and a chill crept into the air.

Elijah watched it all unfold through the windshield. This was the Inner City. Rough around the edges. He had always heard stories, but now he was seeing it firsthand. It felt real in a way his polished life never had. There was danger here, yes, but also a kind of freedom. A truth.

Could he really walk both paths? Excel in school, smile for photos, be the golden boy, while also chasing something darker?

Ty suddenly turned up the volume, rapping along with Doc's lyrics like the world outside didn't exist.

"Yo, Doc's got us on a new wave. When we hit that club, they'll know we're in the building," Ty said, full of energy.

E let out a dry chuckle, but his words were clipped. "That's exactly what we need to avoid. Doc's watching. We can't be reckless."

Elijah met E's gaze in the rearview mirror. He didn't say it, but he heard the message loud and clear. This was bigger than showing up and showing off.

"I get it," Elijah said, a spark of adrenaline still buzzing under his skin. "But we still gotta live a little, right?"

E didn't crack a smile. "Just stay sharp. That's all I'm saying."

The car turned into a darker street. Elijah felt the shift instantly. The sounds of the Inner City surrounded them now: booming music from open doors, the echo of laughter, arguments bouncing off the walls. The night was alive.

Ty leaned back, tossing Elijah a playful look. Elijah returned a faint smile, though something had changed behind his eyes. Ty's excitement only reminded him how far they were from home.

"This is gonna be legendary," Ty said.

Elijah wasn't so sure. The closer they got, the more he felt the weight of what they were stepping into.

"You ready for this, man?" E asked quietly.

Elijah took a breath and nodded. "As ready as I'll ever be."

The city noise grew louder, a living current that surrounded the car.

As they rolled into the heart of the Inner City, Elijah felt something inside him shift. Whatever happened tonight, one thing was certain: this was the beginning of something he might not be able to turn back from.

* * *

The rumble of the engine faded as they pulled into the heart of the Inner City. Elijah, now going by Shadow, leaned against the window, taking in the view. Graffiti covered every building wall, each tag screaming defiance or telling a half-finished story. The air buzzed with energy, thick with the scent of gunpowder, exhaust, and smoke.

They turned onto a street lined with abandoned buildings, bass thumping through the car as they neared their destination: a warehouse plain and unassuming, except for the massive graffiti tags splashed across its walls.

Ty, riding in the passenger seat, grinned and tapped his fingers to the beat of Doc's latest album, which blasted from the speakers. The lyrics were raw, speaking of hustle, struggle, and rising from nothing. Shadow felt the pull. The vibe was starting to seep into his skin. But deep down, he knew. He wasn't fully part of this world. Not yet.

"Y'all ready?" Shadow asked, killing the engine.

E leaned back, glancing around. "Man, I don't know about this. We've never been this deep into the city before."

Shadow didn't answer immediately. His hands were clammy, pulse thudding in his ears. A part of him wanted to turn back.

But that part was shrinking. The fire in his chest, the need to prove himself, it was louder now. He had to stand tall, even here.

"We're good," Shadow finally said, unbuckling and stepping out. The screech of tires on cracked asphalt faded as they hit the sidewalk.

They passed through a gated entry, their footsteps echoing on the concrete. The atmosphere was electric. The warehouse towered above them. A security guard gave a quick once-over before nodding them in.

Inside, the walls were plastered with posters of legends: Tupac, Lil Wayne, Snoop, Timbaland.

They moved down a hallway, the pulse of music bleeding through closed doors. Some rooms were filled with people collaborating, others played dice in shadowed corners.

They stopped at Doc's office.

Doc sat behind a massive desk, leaned back in his chair, fingers drumming against the armrest. Behind him, a framed photo showed him onstage beside music legends. A diamond chain draped one corner of the frame, gleaming like a crown. Bass from a distant studio throbbed through the floorboards, like the building itself was alive with legacy. His eyes locked onto them.

He looked more intimidating than Shadow remembered. The fire in his gaze had only grown. Doc had seen everything and built this empire with Shadow's dad from the ground up. In these streets, his name meant power.

Shadow stepped forward, trying to stay cool. Doc was studying him.

Doc stayed quiet for a second then said, "What up?" His voice was smooth, confident, with a hint of amusement. "You used to run around this place when you were a baby. Before your dad went corporate."

Shadow shifted. "Yeah, well... I'm not a baby anymore."

Doc chuckled and leaned in. "Clearly." He narrowed his eyes. "So, you came for that job I told you about?"

Shadow hesitated. "Well, we not here for hotdogs and hamburgers."

Doc let out a slow exhale and nodded. "You think you're ready? This world's gonna test you."

"Test me how?" Shadow asked, his voice tense.

"You'll find out soon enough," Doc said, tapping the desk. "Lot of people want in. Only the real ones survive. But…" He paused, leaning back slightly. "You've got potential. Let's see if it burns bright or burns out."

Then, without breaking eye contact, Doc opened a desk drawer and pulled out a small slip of paper. He slid it across the table toward Shadow.

"This is the drop spot," he said. "You'll meet a guy named Ice. He's expecting you. Don't be late, and don't mess it up."

Shadow glanced at Ty and E. Ty was already grinning, eyes lit with excitement. E stayed quiet, soaking everything in.

Doc stood and walked to a shelf lined with vinyl records. He pulled one down and handed it to Shadow.

"You know this album?"

Shadow stared at the cover. Doc and his dad in their prime, young, untouchable, alive. He gave a small nod.

"Good. I see your old man let you hear some of our early stuff." Doc sized up the group. "We've got a private event tonight. You should come. It's not just about partying. It's about who you meet."

Shadow raised a brow. "And what's that supposed to do for me?"

Doc smirked. "It's your shot, kid. But you gotta make your move, or you'll get left behind."

Shadow's chest tightened. This wasn't encouragement. It was a warning. He nodded, feeling the moment. This was it. The start of something bigger. No turning back.

"People like us don't get handed things. We take 'em," Doc said.

The words hit hard.

"Alright," Shadow said firmly. "I'm in."

Doc nodded, something sparking in his eye. Respect, maybe. Or curiosity. "We'll see how you do. Just remember, it's not about what you know. It's about who you know."

As they left, Shadow looked back at Doc's office. The photo. The chain.

A swirl of nerves and ambition rose in his chest. This wasn't just another night.

This was the beginning.

His chance to prove he belonged.

* * *

Shadow leaned back in the driver's seat; his fingers draped loosely over the steering wheel. The leather felt cool and smooth beneath his hands, grounding him in a world that seemed to spin faster with every choice he made. Through the cracked window, the night whispered a symphony of city sounds: distant sirens echoing like warnings, a dog barking, and faint bass pulsing from somewhere deep in the district. The engine purred beneath him. A reminder that there was no turning back now.

He glanced at Ty, who stared out the window with a clenched jaw, and then at E, who looked like he'd rather be anywhere else. E's leg bounced restlessly, fingers tapping against the seat like a ticking clock.

"Let's make it quick," Shadow said, slicing through the silence. "Doc doesn't trust us yet. We get in, get the package, and bounce."

Ty nodded but glanced toward E, whose nerves were written all over his face.

"You good, bro?" Ty asked.

E blinked, forcing a grin. "Yeah. Let's just get it done."

They climbed out of the car. The streets were nearly empty, but the air thrummed with a low, electric tension. A bottle shattered somewhere in the distance. Muffled music leaked from a cracked door. A shadow flickered behind a curtain before vanishing again. It wasn't quiet; it was the kind of silence that crawled up your spine and warned you something was coming. An alley cat darted across their path, eyes glowing in the dark. The deeper they walked into the district, the more the city seemed to fold in on them.

The building ahead looked exhausted, its facade cracked and sagging, windows patched with crooked boards. A flickering neon sign buzzed above the door, casting a sickly green hue onto the warped sidewalk. This place didn't welcome you; it challenged you to enter. Elijah felt it in his bones. Every inch of it screamed that this was where the fake got exposed by the real.

He took a breath and stepped forward.

Shadow knocked on the door, firm and loud. The sound echoed through the night.

A moment passed. Then the door creaked open. A tall man stood in the shadows, eyes cold and watchful. He didn't say a word. Just stepped aside and let them in.

The hallway was dim and narrow. The air smelled of cigarettes, sweat, and something darker, maybe blood. Shadow didn't flinch.

The man led them deeper, each step creaking beneath their feet. Shadow kept his senses sharp. Something told him they weren't alone.

At the end of the hall was a cramped office. Ice sat behind a makeshift desk, a half-empty whiskey bottle by his elbow. The room was stripped down: two battered chairs, an overflowing ashtray, and a crooked newspaper clipping behind him. The article showed a younger Ice caught in a drug bust photo, the headline screaming about a major operation. A silent flex. Proof that he'd earned his place.

"You're Doc's boys?" Ice asked without looking up.

"Yeah," Shadow said. "We're here for the package."

Ice looked them over. His gaze lingered on Shadow.

"Doc's got guts sending you clowns down here," he muttered, grabbing a small package from the desk. "You sure you can handle this?"

Shadow met his eyes. "We don't back down."

Ice smirked. "Guess we'll see."

He slid the package across the desk.

E shifted behind him, twitchy, not built for this world.

The air felt thicker now. E's eyes darted around the room like he was searching for the exit. Shadow kept his voice calm.

"Let's get this over with," he said, stepping forward.

Just then, the door burst open. A tall, rough-looking man stormed in, eyes blazing. All three turned toward him.

"You think you run things now?" he spat, his glare bouncing between Shadow, Ty, and E.

Ty tensed, but Shadow gave him a sharp glance.

"We're here for business, not drama," Shadow said, his voice steady but cold.

The man cracked his knuckles. "You think Doc can protect you down here?"

Shadow stepped forward. "Try me."

The man lunged. Shadow reacted instantly, dodging the swing and landing a solid punch to the ribs. The man staggered back, gasping for air.

"Still wanna test me?" Shadow asked, his tone cold.

The man looked at Ice, who didn't move, arms folded and silent.

After a tense pause, the man stepped back. "Just remember who owns these streets."

Shadow didn't answer. He took the package and motioned for Ty and E to follow.

E let out a shaky breath. Ty looked back once, then faced forward again. Shadow kept walking.

This was only the beginning.

* * *

The car rolled to a stop in front of the trap house, a sagging two-story building hidden deep in a dead-end street where even the streetlights seemed to give up. Grass pushed through the cracked driveway, and broken glass from old liquor bottles glittered along the curb. The whole block looked forgotten, like it had been cut out of the city and left to rot.

E leaned forward from the backseat, squinting at the house. His hand hovered near the door handle. "Yeah, I'm good. I'll stay here."

Ty gave him a look. "You sure?"

"Got a weird feeling," E said under his breath. "Just don't take too long."

Shadow nodded. He stepped out of the car with Ty, a tightly wrapped package tucked under his arm. As they walked up the cracked front steps, the front door creaked open before they could knock. A skinny teen with tattoos winding up his neck leaned out and jerked his chin toward the inside.

"Follow me."

The hallway was narrow and dim, lit by one flickering bulb. The air was thick and stale, and the faint smell of weed mixed with something burning filled the trap. Music thumped from deeper in the house, heavy bass shaking the walls like a heartbeat. A couple of girls lounged on a torn couch, their eyes half-lidded and unfocused. The walls were stained with grime, and the floor felt sticky underfoot.

Shadow kept walking, his face hard and focused, his pulse steady but alert. Ty stuck close, his eyes scanning every corner.

They were led to a back room where a man sat at a folding table, a pistol beside a duffel bag. He looked up as they entered, sizing them up.

"You Doc's people?"

Shadow set the package down with calm precision. "We're not here to chat. You got the money?"

"Straight to business, huh?" the man said, cracking a grin. He popped open the duffel and turned it around to show neat stacks of cash.

Shadow gave a quick nod, scooped up the bag, and turned to leave without another word. Ty followed fast, exhaling once they were back in the hallway.

Outside, the night air hit them like a reset: cool, sharp, and full of tension.

But the relief didn't last.

Three figures stepped from the shadows near a busted fence. Hoodies up. Eyes sharp. One of them grinned, gold teeth catching the moonlight.

"Y'all look lost," the tallest one said, blocking their path. "Where y'all from?"

Shadow didn't slow down. "Just handling business. We're leaving."

Another guy smirked. "What's in the bag?"

The third lifted his hoodie just enough to flash a pistol tucked in his waistband.

Ty froze. "We don't want no problems, man. Just let us through."

Shadow raised a hand and stepped forward. His heart pounded, but his voice stayed even. "It's Doc's money. You want it, I'll tell him exactly who took it."

The gold-toothed guy tilted his head and looked closer.

"You that Shadow kid? Word is Doc got himself a new side kick."

A long pause followed. Then the guy stepped aside.

"Aight. You straight. Tell Doc we good."

They moved out of the way.

Shadow and Ty walked past without a word, tension unspoken but heavy in the air.

"I thought we were done for," Ty whispered. "That was wild."

Shadow muttered, "They needed reminding."

At the car, E unlocked the doors quickly. "Y'all good?"

"Better than good," Ty said as Shadow tossed the duffel into the backseat. "Your boy went full boss mode."

They drove in silence for a while, the city lights streaking past the windows.

When they reached Doc's building, E remained in the backseat.

"Yeah, I think I'll wait here again," he said, eyes scanning the block.

"Again? What's your deal?" Ty asked.

E shook his head. "I just don't like being around that dude more than I need to."

Ty got out, shaking his head.

Shadow paused, eyeing E. "We won't be long."

Then he followed Ty inside. The building door clicked shut behind them.

The elevator opened directly into the penthouse. Doc stood at the bar, pouring a drink. He looked up, immediately noticing something.

"Where's the other one?"

"E stayed in the car," Shadow said. "Didn't wanna crowd you."

He dropped the duffel onto the table. Ty collapsed into a nearby chair.

Doc grunted and nodded at the bag. "That all of it?"

"Every dollar," Shadow said.

Doc unzipped it, flipped through a few stacks, then zipped it shut again. He looked directly at Shadow.

"No short count."

He took a sip of his drink, studying the boy.

"Word is you handled yourself tonight."

Ty laughed. "Your name saved us, man."

Doc smiled faintly, but his gaze stayed locked on Shadow.

"My name opened the door," Doc said. "But your name made 'em move. That's power. Keep moving like that, and the city's gonna talk."

Shadow nodded. He held back the smile that threatened to surface.

Doc tapped his glass against the table. "You did good. Now go enjoy the rest of the night."

They stepped back into the night.

For the first time, Shadow didn't feel like an outsider. He felt like he belonged. Like he had passed the test and the city was finally starting to know his name.

* * *

Shadow and Ty strolled toward the car, their footsteps echoing off the walls of nearby buildings. The night air was thick with the pulse of the city: distant sirens, bass-heavy music from a passing car, the hum of a streetlamp flickering overhead. The adrenaline from their first job still buzzed in their veins. Shadow felt the weight of satisfaction settle over him. This was what he was meant for. The streets, the power, the respect. It all felt natural, like he'd been walking this path his whole life.

Ty elbowed him, grinning. "Man, if you'd seen your face when that dude tried to flex, you looked like you were born for this."

Shadow didn't laugh, but a faint smirk crept across his face. They reached the car, Ty still laughing as they climbed in, his voice bouncing off the alley walls. Shadow was quieter, lost in thought. He'd taken charge tonight, made the contact show respect. Every move, every word confirmed what he already knew: Shadow was in control.

The car's seats groaned as they settled in. Ty turned up the music, letting the beat shake the windows. The rhythm of the city wrapped around them like armor. But Shadow wasn't hearing it like before. The lyrics blurred. His mind was locked on the future, on what came next.

"You killed it tonight, man," Ty said, throwing him a quick grin. "I guess all those boxing lessons finally paid off."

Shadow nodded slowly. "I thought I'd be nervous... but I wasn't. I had that guy wrapped around my finger."

E chuckled in the back seat, his head leaning back. "You're not the same dude, Shadow. You used to be all about sports and school. Now? You're getting deep in this life."

Shadow's lips curled into a half-smile, but it never reached his eyes. "Things change," he muttered, eyes fixed on the blur of passing streetlights.

The car cruised through downtown, neon signs streaking across the windshield. Shadow felt a low burn of power in his chest. Everything about tonight had come too easy. Maybe this was what he was made for. Maybe the streets had always been calling.

Then his phone buzzed.

He pulled it out. One missed call. One text.

Vivi: *It's getting late. Where are you?*

His chest tightened.

His fingers hovered over the screen. He felt something stir in his gut, maybe guilt, but he didn't let it grow. He locked the screen and shoved the phone deep into his pocket.

Ty noticed. "Everything good?"

Shadow hesitated, then nodded. But that tug, that pull from the world he thought he'd left behind, it lingered.

"I'll deal with it later," he said.

Ty laughed, clapping his shoulder. "That's the spirit."

E gave Shadow a more serious glance. "Yeah... but don't forget there's still people who care about you back home."

Shadow didn't answer. Couldn't answer.

The phone buzzed again. Another message from Vivi.

He didn't even look this time.

He had a new identity now. A new path. Shadow was becoming real, and Elijah was fading.

Ty rubbed his hands together. "Next stop? The club, baby."

Shadow leaned back in his seat, locking eyes with the road ahead.

As they turned another corner, his thoughts flashed to the exchange earlier. The way that guy had looked at him, full of caution and respect.

Like someone important.

Like someone dangerous.

The phone buzzed again.

Shadow didn't flinch. Didn't move.

Summer had always meant freedom. But this year, freedom had a darker meaning, one that whispered a new name: Shadow.

And he was done whispering back. He was ready to answer loud.

CHAPTER 7

BETWEEN TWO WORLDS

— Vivi —

Vivi had always been the type to wake up early. Ever since Elijah was little, mornings had been her quiet time before the chaos of the day began. But something about this morning didn't feel right.

She tied her robe tighter and stepped into the hallway. Normally, she would have heard Elijah moving around by now: the creak of his bed, the shuffle of footsteps, maybe the sound of a basketball thudding against the floor. But today, there was nothing.

This wasn't the first time she noticed his absence. For the third or fourth morning this week, his room was empty.

Elijah's behavior had shifted lately. He barely looked at her when he came home. He used to joke with her, talk about his day, ask what was for dinner. Now, he mumbled a few words at most and vanished into his room. Some nights he came home smelling like smoke or liquor. He gave short, distant answers and stayed out of reach.

Vivi had thought that summer would give them time to reconnect. She pictured family dinners, movie nights, conversations that stretched long into the evening. But all of that felt out of reach now. Elijah was slipping away, and she didn't know how to stop it.

She walked over to his bedroom and slowly turned the doorknob. The room looked just as she expected: clothes on the floor, an unmade bed, no sign of Elijah. A few pairs of shoes were gone, along with his phone charger. She stepped inside briefly, looked around once more, then backed out quietly and closed the door.

Heading down the stairs, her worry grew heavier. She needed coffee. She needed to talk to Jules. This wasn't normal teenage rebellion.

In the kitchen, she went through the motions of making a pot of coffee, but her thoughts were far away. She couldn't stop wondering where Elijah was. Maybe he was just out with Ty and E, his usual friends. But part of her feared it was something more. She'd heard things: rumors about older boys from the Inner City. The kind of boys who didn't just hang out but got into trouble. Sex. Drugs. Gangs. She hated thinking like that, but the fear had rooted itself deep in her mind.

She didn't want to make a big deal out of it, but she couldn't keep this to herself anymore. She pressed the call button.

The phone rang a few times before Jules picked up.

"Yeah, babe?" he said. She could hear the familiar sounds of the studio behind him: machines, music, voices.

"I just checked on Elijah," she said. "He's not in his room again. This keeps happening. I don't know where he goes or what he's doing. He won't talk to me."

Jules paused.

"It's probably nothing, Vivi. He's a teenager. It's summer. He's probably out with Dumb and Dumber."

She clenched her jaw. "I know him, Jules. He's different. He barely speaks to me. He comes home late or not at all. This isn't normal."

Her voice trembled, but she didn't care. She needed him to understand.

"Maybe he's just growing up," Jules replied with a weak laugh. "You know how he gets. He has school, sports, all that."

"No," she said, more firmly now. "This is something else. He's sneaking out. Half the time I don't even know when he's home. I'm worried, Jules. Really worried."

There was another pause. When Jules finally spoke, his voice had changed.

"I'll talk to him when I get home," he said, though he sounded tired. "Just don't push him too hard. You know he shuts down when we do that."

Vivi lowered the phone and ended the call. It hadn't helped.

She stood in the kitchen, staring out the window as the early light broke through the sky. Her worry hadn't gone away. It had only grown deeper.

Something was wrong. And she was scared they were already too late to stop it.

* * *

It wasn't long before she heard the front door creak open, followed by the soft shuffle of footsteps slipping quietly into the house. Vivi held her breath, her ears straining for confirmation. How late was it?

She glanced at the clock. 5:53 a.m.

She hadn't meant to stay up this long, but worry had refused to let her sleep. Her mind spun in loops, playing every worst-case scenario. Was he in danger? Was he caught up in something he couldn't get out of? Every shadow outside the window became a threat. Every siren in the distance made her chest tighten.

Then the door opened, and there he was: Elijah. He slid in like a shadow, his eyes dull and shoulders slumped.

Vivi's heart sank. She had to confront him. It couldn't wait any longer.

"Elijah," she called.

His head jerked up, eyes widening at her voice. He froze in the doorway, like a kid caught red-handed.

"Where have you been?" she asked, trying to stay calm. "I've been waiting. You keep disappearing, and I'm done pretending not to notice. What is going on with you?"

He didn't answer. He just stepped inside and shrugged, gaze sliding away.

"Don't lie to me, Elijah," she said. "You've been off. Distant. I know you're hiding something. And you smell like alcohol."

He didn't flinch. He'd gotten good at this, at lying with silence, slipping into the role of Shadow when no one was watching. But his mom was watching now.

"I've been letting it go, but I can't anymore," Vivi continued. "You're barely ever home. And when you are, you move like a ghost. Where do you go, Elijah?"

Elijah shifted on his feet, the silence stretching between them like a tightrope.

"I've just been busy. With training... basketball... stuff like that."

Vivi frowned. "That's not it. You disappear for whole nights. You're not just busy. You're hiding something."

His heart pounded. He could almost hear it echoing in the room.

"It's summer. I just need space," he said, voice low.

Her eyes welled with tears, but she kept them from falling. "I know my son. I know when you're hiding something. You just won't let me in."

The front door opened again. Jules stepped in, taking in the scene: the tears brimming in Vivi's eyes, the way Elijah stood like a stranger in his own home. Tension rolled through the room like thunderclouds.

"What's going on?" Jules asked, voice steady but sharp.

"He's been out all night again," Vivi said, her voice cracking. "He won't tell me where he's been and he smells like liquor."

Jules turned to Elijah. "Is that true?"

Elijah clenched his fists. He couldn't hold it back anymore. "I'm tired of pretending like this house is perfect. Like we're perfect. I don't want this life!"

Vivi blinked, stunned by the sudden outburst.

"What the hell does that mean?" Jules asked, stepping forward.

"I mean this house, this picture-perfect life... it doesn't feel real!" Elijah said, louder now. "I feel more alive in the Inner City than I ever do here. At least out there, I'm not suffocating. At least out there, I can be myself."

"Be yourself?" Jules growled. "Out there with gangbangers, junkies, and killers? That's who you are now?"

"At least it feels real!" Elijah snapped. "You built this fantasy life and expected me to love it. But it's not mine. None of this is!"

"You think we did this for fun?" Jules shouted. "You think I clawed my way out of the mud, left behind people I loved, just so you could spit in our faces?"

"I didn't ask for any of this! You never gave me a choice!"

Vivi stepped forward, her voice trembling. "Elijah, we just wanted you to be safe. To have options. A future."

"I don't want your options!" he shouted. "I want my life. Even if it's messy. Even if it's dangerous. At least it's mine!"

Jules moved fast, his face inches from Elijah's. "You wanna be a man? Then act like one. You think those streets care about your feelings? About your dreams? The streets will chew you up and spit you out without a second thought."

"I'm not scared," Elijah said, chest heaving.

"You should be," Jules hissed. "I buried friends before I was your age. Watched cops beat my brother until he couldn't walk straight. I watched my own father rot in a cell for the rest of his life. That's what's waiting for you. You want that?"

Vivi stepped between them, voice trembling. "Please, stop."

Jules ignored her, voice rising. "You think you're grown? Fine. Go live your big, bad Inner City dream. But don't come running back to this 'fake life' you hate so much."

"Jules!" Vivi cried.

"And if you ever raise your voice to your mother again," Jules said, stepping even closer, "I'll show you just how real things can get."

Elijah stood frozen, rage and pain wrestling behind his eyes. He looked at his mother, her hands shaking, her lip trembling. He looked at his father, eyes burning, jaw clenched.

A thousand memories flashed: his mom's warm hugs after games, his dad fixing his tie before school, laughter in the kitchen late at night. He used to think those things would last forever.

But right now, all he felt was the break.

He turned without a word. The door slammed behind him, echoing through the house.

* * *

It was barely 7 AM. Elijah hadn't slept at all. After leaving his parents' house, he drove around the neighborhood for hours, aimlessly looping through old streets. At one point, he stopped at his old high school. He sat on a bench near the empty football field, staring at the bleachers and thinking back on the good times he used to have there, back when everything felt easier and he still felt like himself.

Now he didn't even know who that was.

As he walked back to his car, he pulled out his phone and typed a message to E and Ty: *Yo, meet me at Ty's. Some shit just happened.*

He hesitated, thumb hovering over the send button. His chest was still tight from the argument, his dad yelling, his mom trying not to cry. It was too much.

His phone buzzed.

E: *Yo, what's going on?*

Ty: *You good? It's 7 AM...*

Elijah didn't want to explain over text:

Just meet me, please.

A few seconds later:

Ty: *Aight, pull up. My parents still gone.*

Elijah walked back to his car and dropped his phone on the passenger seat and started the car again. His legs couldn't stop bouncing. His thoughts were running wild.

When he got to Ty's place, he parked, sat there for a second, then climbed out and rang the doorbell. Ty and E were waiting at the door, still half-asleep.

Ty rubbed his face. "Man, it's early. What's going on?"

"I need to talk," Elijah said, stepping inside without waiting for an invite.

They followed him into the living room. Elijah couldn't sit still. He was pacing, fists clenching and unclenching.

E sat on the couch. "What's up, bro? You good?"

Elijah stopped and looked at them. All the frustration he'd been holding in boiled over. "My dad kicked me out," he said. "I told him I wasn't trying to live this fake life anymore, and he told me to leave."

E blinked. "Wait... your dad? Are you serious? What happened?"

"I told him I been in the Inner City," Elijah muttered, dragging a hand down his face. "I told him I'm not the kid he thinks I am. I'm not that golden boy. I've changed."

Ty frowned. "What are you talking about, bro? You're still Elijah. You're just going through it. Don't act like this is who you really are."

"I'm not Elijah anymore," he snapped. He started pacing again, louder now. "I'm Shadow. I've been Shadow for weeks. I've been lying to everybody: them, you, myself. You don't get it. You don't know what it's like to live under all these expectations. To feel trapped in someone else's version of who you're supposed to be."

Ty looked confused and concerned. "So what, you're living some double life now? Is that why you been ghosting us? Man, this is wild. You're throwing everything away."

Elijah turned toward them, eyes intense. "You think I care? I don't want that perfect life anymore. I want to be in the city. Not this safe zone."

E leaned forward, voice low. "Come on, man. You're better than that. Don't do this to yourself."

"I can't fake it anymore. I have to be there. Even if it's risky. Even if it's ugly. I need to be Shadow, because Elijah? Elijah's falling apart."

Ty looked at E, who didn't say anything, then back at Elijah. After a moment he said, "You got a future, man. You got sports, school, both your parents in your life. That's more than some of us ever had. You really gonna walk away from all that?"

"I don't care!" Elijah shouted. Sports, school, none of it mattered. They don't see me. They never did. But in the city? I'm someone. I matter there."

Ty and E shared a look. Elijah's phone buzzed. He picked it up.

It was Doc: *Yo, got another job for you.*

Elijah stared at it, then typed: *Can I crash at your place for a couple of days?*

He hit send and lowered the phone slowly. The tension in the room didn't break.

"I'm staying here for little bit. I need to get some sleep," he said quietly to Ty.

Ty gave a slow nod, still confused but willing to let it go for the moment.

Elijah dropped onto the couch, his body finally giving out. "I'm sorry," he whispered. "I don't know what I'm doing. But I can't go back now"

No one said anything. Then Ty spoke. "Get some sleep, bro. We'll figure it out. But you can't keep living like this."

Elijah didn't answer. He just nodded.

His phone buzzed one more time.

Doc: *That's cool, see you soon. Stay dangerous.*

Elijah closed his eyes, sinking into the cushions. He didn't know what was coming, but he knew one thing.

He wasn't turning back.

CHAPTER 8
ELIJAH'S MORNING REALIZATION

The sharp sunlight pushed through the blinds, drawing crooked lines across the floor. Elijah squinted at the clock near the window, groaning as the brightness hit his eyes. 4:17 PM.

"I didn't mean to sleep that long," he mumbled.

Still stiff from the couch, he rubbed his eyes and sat up slowly. Everything from the night before felt like a blur: the noise, the drinks, the arguments, the adrenaline. He had turned off his phone to get some rest, but the second he powered it back on, it lit up with messages.

Doc: *Ay, Shadow. Come by the studio when you get a chance.*

Elijah stared at the message, then stood, his body heavy from sleep. As he walked slow circles across the living room, he tried to clear the fog from his mind. A part of him still clung to his old life in the Outer City: the clean streets, the private school, the easy future. But that world didn't feel real anymore.

His phone buzzed again.

Vivi: *Elijah, please come home. We need to talk. Please call me when you can.*

He stared at the screen, biting his lip. His mom would never understand why he was pulling away. To her, everything was fine. A good home. A good school. A safe life. But Elijah didn't want safe anymore.

He set the phone down, trying to shake the tight feeling in his chest. This wasn't about her. It was about him. About Shadow.

Another message came through:

Jade: *You should come to the club tonight.*

His heart jumped at the thought of Jade. There was something about her, the way she carried herself, like no one could tell her who to be. He was drawn to that. It felt grounding. She made him feel like he didn't have to explain himself.

Lola: *Dinner tonight at the steakhouse? I'll be waiting.*

Elijah smirked. Lola was bold, always kept things interesting. He liked that too. But something had shifted. It wasn't just about Lola anymore. The Inner City called to him in a way he didn't fully understand. It was messy, loud, and dangerous, but it felt more real than anything he'd ever known.

He felt a mix of anger and disappointment. His dad had lived that life once. Deep in it. And now? He was a star, living in a mansion, making music, and pretending like none of that past mattered. He had left it behind and never looked back. But Elijah couldn't do that. Not yet. Not when he still felt like a stranger in his own skin.

He sighed and rubbed his face. His eyes drifted over the messages again. Everyone pulling him in a different direction. Each text another reminder of how split his life had become.

He grabbed his bag, threw on his jacket, and headed to the door. This was it. He couldn't keep straddling both sides. He had to move. One way or the other.

He glanced at the time: 4:46 PM.

Still enough time to meet Lola before the studio.

He stopped at the mirror near the front door. Ty's mom's old hallway mirror, its corners chipped and the edges warped. A long crack ran through the center, splitting his reflection in two.

He stared.

Everything looked right on the outside. Fresh fade. Branded clothes. That practiced smirk he used in photos. But something in his eyes didn't match.

They didn't look tired. They didn't look excited.

They looked... different.

He tilted his head.

Was this what becoming Shadow looked like? Had the change already happened without him noticing? He couldn't remember when it started feeling more natural to be Shadow than Elijah.

Maybe it was that night of the first job, when Doc handed him the package. Or maybe it was the first time Doc called him "Shadow" like it was already his name. Or maybe it was when he first lied to his mom about where he was going. Back then, it felt thrilling. Now, it felt normal.

He leaned toward the mirror.

"Who the hell are you?"

The words hit hard. He'd heard them before. His dad had shouted them once during a fight when Elijah was younger. Back then, it hurt. Now, it echoed.

The mirror didn't answer. It just stared back.

A moment passed. Then Elijah grabbed his keys.

He walked out the door. But the question? That stayed behind.

And even though he left it in the silence, the consequences were already following him into his next move.

* * *

Elijah sat across from Lola at a small table tucked in the back of a fancy steakhouse. The air was rich with the smell of grilled steak, and soft jazz floated through the dim space. Their menus were open, but neither had really read them.

They'd gone out before, but tonight felt different. They weren't official, just two people who had hooked up once or twice. Their connection had always leaned more on flirting and fun than anything serious. At least, that's what Elijah kept telling himself.

Now, with Jade in the picture, being with Lola felt more complicated. She was confident, magnetic, and impossible to ignore. Being around her felt like standing too close to a flame.

Still, she made him feel seen. And that mattered.

"Look at Shadow," Lola said with a teasing smile. "I thought you were going to bail."

Elijah smirked as he looked up. "Wouldn't dream of it."

She leaned forward, eyes glinting. "Good. I like a guy who keeps his word. But I hope you're more exciting than last time, Shadow."

He shifted in his seat, the weight of yesterday pressing on his shoulders. He tried to push it aside. "I'm full of surprises, Lola," he said, faking a grin.

She laughed softly. Lola was always in control, and Elijah could feel that in the way she watched him. Still, something about her made him uneasy, like she saw more than he meant to show.

They talked while sharing an appetizer, the conversation light but charged with tension. Her fingers brushed against his more than once, each time sending a small jolt through him. Her eyes met his again and again, her smile teasing, daring him to keep up. She wore a low-cut top that made it hard for Elijah to focus, and despite his best efforts, his eyes kept drifting. He forced himself to maintain eye contact, but she noticed the struggle and smirked.

"So," she said, settling back in her chair, "what's your real story? We both know this bad-boy act isn't everything. What are you hiding?"

Elijah's chest tightened. He wanted to be honest, but his world was a mess. He was caught between the safety of how he was raised and the chaos pulling him deeper every day.

"I don't know what you mean," he said with a small smile.

"Oh, I think you do." She leaned in again, brushing his fingers. "But that's okay. It might be a mystery I'm willing to solve."

They locked eyes for a little too long.

After dinner, they stepped out into the cool night. Lola walked beside him.

"That was fun," she said, glancing up at him. "I had a great time, Shadow. But..."

She stepped in closer.

"You're being too good tonight."

Elijah gave her a tired smile. She sensed the change. Maybe it was how quiet he'd been. Or his posture. Either way, she wasn't wrong.

"But next time..." she whispered, kissing his cheek, her breath warm near his ear. "Next time, I want to see the Inner City you."

He froze, heart pounding as she pulled back. She shot him one last daring look, then turned and walked to her car.

Elijah stood there, unsure what to make of it all. He didn't love her. Wasn't even sure how much he liked her. But Lola had a way of pulling him into the moment and making him forget how lost he was.

She wasn't the girl he wanted most. He knew that. But she still made him feel something.

He got in his car and took a breath, then pulled out his phone.

Elijah: *On my way. Can I stop at your place first to drop my stuff off?*

A minute later, his phone buzzed.

Doc: *Mi casa es su casa, Nephew. You kickin' it with a legend. Come to the studio. My security will handle it.*

Elijah chuckled and slid his phone into his pocket.

Lola's words still echoed in his mind. He wasn't sure who the Inner City version of him really was.

But for now, he knew where he had to be.

The studio was waiting.

The Inner City was alive with noise and motion as Elijah pulled up in front of Doc's studio. Neon signs flickered above crumbling storefronts, casting flashes of color onto the cracked pavement. The air was heavy with the scent of fried food and exhaust. Music blared from a corner store nearby, mixing with the loud chatter of a group of guys holding down the block. A skinny dog darted past his headlights, slipping into the shadows. Everything felt alive, loud, and just a little dangerous.

Elijah turned off the engine and sat still, hands resting on the wheel. His heart was still racing from his time with Lola. Her words echoed in his head: the way she teased him, studied him, like she saw something buried inside that he hadn't meant to show. Part of him liked the thrill. Part of him wasn't sure if he liked the version of himself she was pulling out.

His phone buzzed in his pocket, but he ignored it. He needed a second. To think. To breathe. To decide who he was going to be when he stepped out of the car.

He glanced into the rearview mirror. The face staring back wasn't the clean-cut kid from the Outer City. His eyes were sharper now, more guarded. The easy smile he used to flash without thinking? Gone. His face looked leaner, like it had been shaped by things he hadn't told anyone. He didn't just look different; he felt different.

He drew in a breath, deep and steady, and opened the door.

The city sounds hit him instantly. His nerves faded. His posture straightened.

Elijah stayed in the car.

Shadow walked to the door.

* * *

The studio door opened into a scene straight out of a rap video. The air reeked of weed and alcohol, and the heavy bass made the walls throb. Girls in barely-there outfits danced around while men in flashy designer gear lounged with bottles, laughing and passing blunts.

Shadow paused in the doorway, his eyes scanning the chaos. The loud, wild scene clashed with the quieter moment he had just left. Part of him was drawn to the raw energy: it was exciting, unpredictable. But another part still echoed with Lola's teasing voice, whispering caution.

"Shadow!" Doc's booming voice sliced through the noise.

The crowd split as Doc made his way over, a dominant figure in a crisp tracksuit and diamond chains that glittered under the dim lights. His smile was wide, but his eyes were sharp, missing nothing.

"You made it," Doc said, pulling him into a quick hug. "I was starting to think you got lost."

Shadow smirked. "Just took the scenic route."

Doc laughed and gave him a firm slap on the back. "Well, you're here now. Come on, let me introduce you."

With a wave of his hand, Doc quieted the room. The music faded, and all eyes turned toward them.

"This right here," Doc said, his voice ringing out, "is my nephew: Shadow."

Murmurs moved through the crowd. Shadow stood a little taller, feeling the pressure of the name settle onto his shoulders.

Doc's eyes swept the room, cutting through the silence. Some guys dropped their gaze. Others sat up straighter. A few girls froze mid-laugh, suddenly alert.

"Let me make one thing clear," Doc growled. "Anyone who messes with Shadow? You mess with me. And you know how that goes. You don't question his place. You don't cross him. You ride with him. You die for him. Same way you would for me."

Heads nodded in unison.

Shadow felt pride swell in his chest. The room had accepted him. But deep inside, something tugged. A flicker of who he used to be, late-night talks with his mom, joking with Ty and E, reminded him this wasn't just a new chapter. It was a trade. Acceptance came at a cost.

The music blasted again, and the party resumed. Doc led Shadow to a private area stocked with more girls and bottles. He handed him a drink.

"Welcome to the family, Nephew. You been putting in work this summer."

Shadow raised the glass and knocked it back. The alcohol burned going down, but it dulled the noise inside his head.

As the night rolled on, Shadow drifted deeper into the scene. He smoked a blunt passed his way. The mix of weed and liquor swirled in his head. Strippers danced for him, drawn to his new status. They whispered sweet nothings in his ear as they ran fingers through his hair.

For the first time in a while, he felt free. No expectations. No rules. Just the thrill of the moment.

Later, he and Doc sat in a quieter corner. The noise buzzed behind them, but Shadow's thoughts felt heavier.

"Doc," he said, his voice low. "I need to talk."

Doc leaned back, unreadable. "What's up?"

Shadow hesitated, rolling his drink in the glass. "It's about my pops... and my moms."

Doc's expression darkened, but he stayed silent.

"They kicked me out. Well, my dad did." Shadow's voice softened, the edge he'd carried all night slipping away. "I feel like I been living a lie. They don't know what I'm doing out here. Sometimes I don't even know what I'm doing out here. I feel like I'm losing myself."

Doc nodded slowly, his gaze steady. "Sometimes you gotta leave who you were to find who you're supposed to be. I see a lot of your pops in you."

Shadow blinked. "What?"

"I know what you're dealing with," Doc said calmly. "That's how I felt when me and your pops started blowing up and spending more time in the Outer City."

Before Shadow could respond, his phone buzzed.

Jade: *Are you still coming to the club?*

He stared at the screen, then typed quickly.

I'll be there a little later.

Doc caught the exchange and grinned. "Girl got you moving, huh?"

Shadow chuckled. "Something like that."

Doc clapped his shoulder. "Go enjoy yourself."

Shadow stood. His head swam from everything: liquor, weed, emotions. As he walked toward the door, he pulled out his phone again.

To Ty & E: *Meet me at the club. Got us a booth.*

The cool night hit him as he stepped outside.

Tonight, he wasn't Elijah Knight. He was Shadow.

The Elijah his family knew was fading. And something darker, tougher, more dangerous was rising in his place.

The night was just getting started.

* * *

The line outside Vertigo stretched around the block, buzzing with energy and anticipation. Cars crawled by with their windows down, music blasting from every direction. People laughed, posed for pictures, and tried to catch the bouncers' attention.

Shadow pulled up to the curb and stepped out, the streetlights glinting off his designer jacket. His presence turned heads. He adjusted his collar, then glanced at his reflection in the car window. The glow from the club flickered in his eyes like neon fire.

Behind him, Ty and E appeared from the corner.

"Yo," Ty said, practically bouncing on his toes. "It's been a minute since we hit this spot. Man, this joint lookin' like it missed us."

E kept his hands in his pockets, eyes darting around. "There's a lot going on out here. Loud. Crowded. I don't know, man. Kinda intense."

Ty bumped him with a grin. "Exactly why we here. You been in that cave too long. Come on, live a little."

Shadow smirked and led the way to the front of the line. He approached the bouncer with calm confidence.

"Shadow," he said, chin lifted just enough.

The bouncer looked him over: designer fit, spotless sneakers, nothing but authority in his stance. Without a word, he unhooked the rope and waved them in.

Ty turned back with a wide-eyed grin. "We really just skipped, like, a hundred people."

Shadow shrugged. "That's what happens when you're with Shadow."

Inside, the club exploded with sound and color. Bass throbbed through the walls. Lasers cut across the dance floor. The crowd moved in waves, bodies packed shoulder to shoulder, the air thick with sweat and excitement.

Ty looked around, stunned. "Yo, Vertigo got even crazier. This energy is unreal."

E stuck close to them, eyes scanning everything. "Y'all got me out here about to get stomped on. This place is wild."

Shadow soaked it in. This wasn't just a night out. This was proof. He had arrived.

"Let's hit the VIP," he said.

Their booth sat behind a velvet rope, stocked with bottles and glowing in soft red light. Ty whipped out his phone, hyping them up for his story.

"VIP vibes! My boy Shadow came through tonight!"

E chuckled but stayed alert, still unsure about it all.

Time passed. Drinks were poured. The music kept pounding. Then, without warning, the atmosphere changed.

The lights dimmed near the entrance. The music slowed to a heavy pulse. Conversations fell to a hush as the entire room turned.

Doc entered like a force of nature.

A long designer coat trailed behind him. Diamond chains shimmered under the strobes. His cologne, a heady mix of smoke and spice, hit before he did. Flanked by bodyguards and hype men, he moved with slow, deliberate swagger.

The DJ killed the music. "Make some noise for the man, the myth, the legend: DOC!"

The club erupted. Phones flashed. Fans reached out. People parted like the red sea as Doc glided through the crowd, security carving a path straight to the VIP.

Ty gawked. "Yo... this man don't just own the room. He is the room."

Shadow didn't respond. He watched how Doc's presence bent the air around him. This was more than fame. This was control. Shadow stood, meeting him halfway.

Doc nodded at Ty and E, gave them a once-over, then clapped Shadow on the back.

"Come on. Let's grab a drink."

Shadow motioned to the table. "We got drinks right here."

Doc gave him a look. "Did I ask you that?"

Without another word, they moved to the bar. The bodyguards led the way. The bartender was already pouring before they arrived.

"To new beginnings," Doc said, lifting his shot.

"To new beginnings," Shadow echoed, clinking glasses and downing the tequila.

As he set his glass down, his eyes found Jade.

She stood near the dance floor, sleek black dress hugging her curves, long braids cascading over her shoulders.

"Go talk to her," Doc said with a smirk.

Shadow nodded and made his way over.

Jade spotted him and smiled. "Well, if it isn't Shadow."

"The one and only," he said.

The music shifted to a bass-heavy slow beat.

"Come on," she said, grabbing his hand. "Let's dance."

They moved through the crowd, finding a rhythm. Her body flowed effortlessly, and Shadow matched her step for step. For a moment, it felt like nothing else existed.

"So," Jade said near his ear, "why do you come around here?"

He paused. "What do you mean?"

"You don't move like the typical dude from here."

He smirked. "Guess I'm not typical."

Jade raised an eyebrow. "I'll give you that."

They danced on, lost in their own space. Shadow felt present. Like maybe this life, chaotic and raw, had room for him.

Until he saw them.

Near the bar, a group of guys stood huddled together. Shadow recognized two of them. The same guys who had tried to rob him and his friends the first time they came to the Inner City.

His body tensed, his mind flashing back to that night.

"What's wrong?" Jade asked, noticing the shift in his demeanor.

"Nothing," Shadow said quickly. "I just... need a minute."

He stepped away from Jade and made his way back to Doc, who was lounging in the VIP section.

"Those guys," Shadow said, nodding toward the group. "They tried to rob us."

Doc's expression darkened. He leaned in and whispered something to one of his security guards, who immediately disappeared into the crowd.

"Don't worry about them," Doc said. "I'll take care of it."

Meanwhile, Ty and E were watching everything unfold from the booth.

"Did you see that?" E whispered. "Those guys from before."

Ty nodded. "Yeah. And Shadow's telling Doc about them."

"This is getting out of hand," E said, shaking his head. "We shouldn't be here."

"Relax," Ty said, though his voice was laced with uncertainty. "It's just... part of the scene. Plus we are with Doc. We are untouchable"

But E wasn't convinced. Something about the way Doc might handle things didn't sit right with him.

Later that night, after the club's music faded into a distant throb and the lights dimmed to a dull glow, Doc led Shadow out the back through a heavy steel door that slammed shut behind them. They stepped into a narrow alley behind the club, the air thick with tension as the night pressed in around them.

Ahead, one of the robbers knelt on the cold ground, his hands bound tightly behind his back. Two of Doc's guards stood on either side, holding him in place. His face was badly beaten: one eye swollen shut, the other barely open. Blood trickled from his lip, and a soft moan slipped from his mouth.

Shadow came to a halt, frozen in place. His breath caught in his throat. His stomach clenched, twisting with dread.

Doc reached under his coat and pulled out a pistol. Without a word, he extended it toward Shadow.

Shadow stared at the weapon, his eyes wide. For a split second, he told himself this had to be a test, a sick joke. Maybe Doc would pull it back, laugh, and say it was all part of some initiation. But no one laughed. No one moved. The silence was too heavy. This wasn't a joke.

He looked at the gun like it was something foreign.

"I don't want to do this," Shadow said quietly, his voice cracking just enough to reveal the fear buried beneath his tough exterior.

Doc stepped closer, slow and deliberate. His eyes hardened. "You know what happened to the last dude who thought he could play this game halfway? That boy ain't breathing no more. Respect got rules, Nephew. And in this world, respect ain't given. It's earned. This? This is how you earn it." His voice dropped lower, more menacing. "You don't want to make me look bad in front of my people, do you?"

Shadow glanced over Doc's shoulder. Behind him, two of his guys exchanged glances. One let out a quiet laugh. The other leaned close and muttered, "Soft."

Shadow didn't respond, but the words dug into him. He felt the pressure, the eyes, the judgment. This wasn't just about Doc anymore. It was about all of them. About his place in this world. About the name he'd chosen.

"You're not just playing the part anymore," Doc said. "You are the part. This is the line, Nephew. You cross it, there's no going back."

From a narrow gap in the alley wall, Ty and E crouched, hidden in the shadows. They hadn't meant to follow, but something told them not to leave yet. Their faces were pale in the moonlight.

"Why is Doc doing this?" Ty whispered, barely audible.

E clenched his jaw. His eyes stayed locked on Shadow. "Because this is what he wants him to become."

"Yo," Ty said again, softer this time. "He ain't gonna do it, right?"

E didn't answer. Couldn't answer.

"This is your chance to prove you belong here," Doc said, his voice cold and sharp. "Pick up that gun, put it to his head, and paint the concrete with his brains. It's really that simple."

Shadow reached for the gun. His fingers wrapped around the cold metal, heavy and unforgiving.

He took a step forward. Then another. Each one heavier than the last.

The man on the ground whimpered. He tried to speak, to plead, but Shadow couldn't make out the words. The pounding in his ears drowned everything out. It felt like the whole world had gone numb.

Doc spoke again, his voice slicing through the static. "This is your name. Your power. You want to be Shadow? Make your mark."

He paused. Then, his tone shifted, softer, almost fatherly. "Your pops don't know who you really are. He raised you to be some golden boy. But I see it, Nephew. I see the fire he tried to bury. I'm the only one who'll ever give you the truth. You don't shoot? You walk away? Then you're always gonna be a puppet."

Shadow closed his eyes. He raised the gun. His hands trembled. His palms were soaked with sweat. His finger hovered over the trigger.

The man looked up, terrified. Whispered something. Shadow couldn't hear it.

Bang.

The gunshot cracked through the alley like a lightning strike.

The man collapsed, his body crumpling to the ground.

For a moment, silence returned.

Then Doc clapped, once, loud and slow. A wide grin stretched across his face. He stepped forward and slapped a heavy hand on Shadow's back.

"Now you're official like a whistle."

But Shadow didn't register it. The ringing in his ears drowned out everything else. His eyes were locked on the body. The stillness. The way it folded. He searched himself for something: remorse, rage, even pride. But there was nothing.

Only silence.

A flicker of memory surfaced. His mom's warm laugh. His dad cheering in the stands at his games. That first time he picked up a mic and felt invincible. It all felt like it belonged to someone else now. Someone far away.

Back in the alley gap, Ty reached for E's arm, pulling him gently.

"We don't know him anymore," Ty whispered, his voice shaky.

E looked at him, stunned. Then slowly nodded, his expression hollow.

They turned and slipped away.

The crack between Elijah Knight and Shadow?

It wasn't a crack anymore.

It was a canyon.

CHAPTER 9

EMOTIONAL FALLOUT

The smell of liquor, weed, and regret still hung in the air, clinging to half-empty bottles, crushed red cups, and the smoky curtains. Ashtrays overflowed on the coffee table, and faint footprints tracked across the floor, evidence of the chaos from the night before. In the distance, a car horn blared, but Shadow barely registered the sound. The silence in the penthouse was thick, almost too heavy to breathe through.

Shadow sat on the edge of the bed with his elbows on his knees, hands clenched so tightly his knuckles had turned white. He rocked slightly back and forth, his breathing shallow. He couldn't stop thinking about what had happened: the flash of the gun, the deafening crack, the stillness that followed. The blood. His hands were clean now, but they still felt stained.

Everything at the club had spiraled out of control fast. By the time the police arrived, the alley was empty. No gun. No shooter. Just a man laid out and bleeding. Doc's crew played it cool, claiming they heard a shot but didn't see anything. Shadow said nothing.

No one asked his name. No one pointed fingers.

The club got shut down for a few days. There were questions, but none came his way. Not yet. And somehow, that felt worse than being accused.

He hadn't told a soul. Not Ty. Not E. Not Jade. Not even Lola.

His eyes drifted across the room and landed on a basketball trophy sitting on a glass shelf. The gold surface caught the faint glow of the city lights outside. It used to mean something: a reminder of who he was, a kid with big dreams. Now it felt like a relic from a life that no longer belonged to him.

He stood up slowly and walked over, his fingers brushing against the base. As he stared at it, his dad's voice echoed in his mind. At first, it was just a faint whisper slipping through the cracks of memory. A mix of warning and wisdom.

The walls of the penthouse seemed to close in. His heartbeat pounded in his ears. The shooting replayed in his mind again and again: the body falling, the sound of footsteps on pavement, the taste of fear rising in his throat. Sweat clung to his back, his shirt damp against his skin. He pressed one hand against the glass and leaned his forehead on the window, staring out at the city below, a maze of streets, lights, and shadows.

A voice deep inside reminded him: he wasn't supposed to be here. Not like this. Not hiding in someone else's luxury while everything inside him came undone. He gripped the trophy tighter and sat down as if it could somehow hold him together.

He remembered the moment he'd won one. The roaring crowd. His coach clapping him on the back. And Jules, his dad, standing in the back of the gym, eyes full of quiet pride. Shadow had been MVP, the star player, the kid with the bright future. That was before the betrayal. Before the streets took over. Before he became a version of himself he no longer recognized.

A breeze stirred the curtains, carrying with it the familiar scent of sandalwood and his father's cologne. The smell hit so hard it made his eyes sting. His thoughts slipped into the past, into a conversation that had etched itself deep into his memory.

He could still hear Jules' voice, clear as day.

* * *

It was a quiet Sunday afternoon. Pops sat on the couch with a glass of whiskey in his hand. He looked calm on the outside, but his eyes were sharp, focused, like something heavy was sitting in the back of his mind. The room was dim, sunlight sliding through the curtains and painting long shadows across the leather furniture.

I had just come home from practice. Still in my gear, jersey soaked in sweat, shoes slung over my shoulder. My legs ached, but I felt good. Really good. That kind of high you get when everything clicks. Every play tight, every sprint sharp. It wasn't just about the game. It was about momentum: about believing I was heading somewhere big.

That's when Pops started in on leadership again.

"Being a leader means taking responsibility for yourself and for the people who count on you," he said. His voice was steady, the kind that didn't ask for attention; it demanded it. "You can't afford to let them down, Elijah."

Shadow wasn't even a thought yet. That version of me didn't exist.

"You're the one they look up to," he said. "You set the tone. Whether you like it or not, people follow what you do."

I nodded, heart pounding with a mix of pride and pressure. I hung on every word. I wanted to be that leader for my team, my boys, my family... for him. I needed him to believe I had it in me. I needed to believe it myself.

But now?

Now those words felt like echoes.

Back when I thought I understood what leadership meant. Back when I thought I was on the right path.

How did I mess things up this bad?

The shooting. The silence. The lies I chose to carry. Everything Pops warned me about... it wasn't some theory anymore. It was real. Right here. Right now.

I wasn't leading anybody. I wasn't lifting anyone up.

I was following my dad's path.

And I didn't even know where it would take me.

* * *

The flashback faded as quickly as it had come, but the heaviness stayed, sinking deep into Shadow's chest. He stood up abruptly, the motion too sharp, too desperate. He needed to move, to breathe, to do something, anything to escape the pressure building in his head. He put the trophy down and stepped towards the door, hand twitching toward the knob like he might actually leave. But where would he go? Instead, he turned back, paced the length of the room, and put the trophy on the shelf. His fingers brushed the cold metal, then recoiled.

Without thinking, he grabbed his phone and unlocked it.

No new messages.

He scrolled to Ty's name. The thread was still there, frozen in time, full of old jokes, inside references, memes, links to songs and plans that once felt like a blueprint for the future. One message stood out: a video of them racing shopping carts through an empty parking lot, laughing like they didn't have a care in the world.

His thumb hovered over the keyboard.

What up?

He stared at the words.

Then deleted them.

He opened E's thread. Same story. No unread bubbles. No reply waiting to save him. Another wall between him and the people who used to feel like home.

With a sigh, he tossed the phone onto the bed, screen down. Then he dropped beside it, arms spread out, eyes fixed on the ceiling.

He didn't even know what he wanted them to say, maybe something to erase the guilt. Maybe a joke to make him feel normal again. Maybe he just wanted to believe that someone still saw him the same way, like he hadn't already crossed the invisible line that couldn't be uncrossed.

The penthouse was quiet, but it didn't feel peaceful. It wasn't comforting; it was loud in its emptiness.

Somewhere out there, someone was dead because of him.

A siren wailed in the distance, shrill and sharp, slicing through the stillness like a blade. His body tensed. He tried to tune it out, but the sound wormed its way beneath his skin.

He brushed the inside of his sleeve with his fingers, settling on a familiar rough patch. A small scar. It wasn't big, but it had never gone away. It stayed. A mark that reminded him who had his back. A time when proving himself meant scrapes and bruises, not guns and drugs.

That old feeling came rushing back, that burning need to be more than just another kid fronting like he had it all figured out. That hunger had lived in him for as long as he could remember.

And now, it stirred again. As another memory rose to the surface, uninvited but vivid, pulling him backward into a moment he hadn't thought about in years.

* * *

I was ten when it happened. Some older kid at the rec center shoved me during a game. I had just hit a three-pointer right in his face, and we were up by fifteen. He got in my face, shouting, and I laughed a little too loud. Then bam—he knocked me down. My shoulder hit the court hard. The sting came fast. My skin burned, but it was my pride that hurt more.

Before I could even get back on my feet, Ty jumped in. He didn't hesitate. His fists flew like he was fighting for something bigger than just me. I remember sitting there, stunned. Part of me was scared, yeah, but mostly, I was proud. Proud that someone cared enough to stand up for me like that.

He landed two solid hits before the other kid clipped him in the mouth. Blood came quick. A coach came running and pulled them apart. The whole gym fell quiet, just the squeak of sneakers and a voice from the back saying, "Yo, Ty crazy."

Later, we sat on the bench, cooling off. Ty pressed a crumpled paper towel to his split lip, still grinning like he didn't have a care in the world.

"You're the golden boy. Can't have you scarred on my watch," he said. I didn't know what to say. I looked at him, shirt stretched, lip bleeding, and he still smiled at me like I was worth it. In that moment, I felt seen. Safe. Like maybe being the golden boy wasn't the worst thing in the world.

"Next time, swing first," he added. "But if you can't, don't worry. I got you."

And he did. At school, on the field, at the court, Ty always had my back. Even when it was risky, even when it didn't make sense. Loyalty wasn't something he talked about. It was just who he was.

Golden boy. That name stuck. Back then, it meant promise. Potential. I was the one teachers pointed out, the one people said was going places. I wore that name like a shield. Like it could keep all the bad away.

But now? Now it really feels fake. Like a part I was given in a story I didn't audition for. Like I was pretending to shine when everything inside me was dim.

That version of me is gone.

Or maybe he never existed.

Maybe I made him up because I needed to. Because I wanted to believe I was something more.

If I really was the golden boy, then maybe the things I've done wouldn't feel so heavy. Maybe I wouldn't feel like I've fallen so far.

But laying here now, all I feel is the distance between who I was and who I thought I was supposed to be.

And that distance? It feels endless.

* * *

Shadow sat alone in Doc's guest room, shoulders heavy, thoughts spinning like a broken record. The shooting. The blood. The silence. It all played over and over in his head, stuck on a loop he couldn't escape.

His phone buzzed on the bed, breaking through the noise in his mind. He reached for it without thinking. Jade.

"Hey," he said, his voice low and scratchy.

"Shadow." Her voice was sharp, but it carried something else, something fragile. Like she'd been crying, but wasn't ready to admit it. "I can't sleep. Can we meet?"

His stomach tightened. There was something off in her tone. Something distant. But he couldn't figure it out, and right now, he didn't have the energy to try.

"Yeah. Come by Doc's place. He's still out. I'll text you the address."

"I'll be there soon," she replied quickly. But her words were cold, stripped of their usual warmth.

The line went dead.

Shadow sat frozen, phone still in his hand. That tight, hollow ache in his chest returned, like guilt was coiled around his ribs, making it harder to breathe. No matter how much he tried to push it down, his mind kept circling back to the alley. The shot. The aftermath.

Jade was the last link to the person he used to know. The only piece that still felt real.

But even she seemed to be slipping away, like sand through his fingers.

Shadow paced back and forth in Doc's penthouse, waiting for Jade. His thoughts were a mess, still spinning from the shooting. He hadn't eaten. He hadn't slept. Every step he took echoed with memories he couldn't silence: the look in that man's eyes before the gun went off, the way the world seemed to stop, the sound of his heartbeat louder than the shot itself.

A knock at the door pulled him out of it. He froze for a second, then walked over and opened it.

Jade stood there. She looked exhausted, like she hadn't rested in days. Her face was hard to read, guarded, like she was holding something in that she didn't know how to say.

"Hey," Shadow said, stepping aside.

She nodded and walked in quietly, her movements slow and careful. Her eyes scanned the room, but her mind seemed far away.

"You okay?" he asked, closing the door behind her.

She shrugged, crossing her arms over her chest. Her silence spoke louder than words.

"Talk to me," Shadow said, his voice low and steady.

Jade didn't sit. Her eyes landed on the trophy sitting on the shelf in the guest room.

"You ever think about how things could've been different?" she asked, her voice soft but tight, like she was holding back something sharp.

Shadow followed her gaze. His jaw tightened. "Every damn day."

She nodded slowly, still staring at the trophy. Then she turned to face him. Her arms stayed crossed, but her voice dropped.

"You ever feel like... no matter how hard you try to change, people still see you for who you used to be? Like your past just sticks to you, no matter what?"

Shadow took a breath. "Yeah. Every time I look in the mirror, I see who I was. It's like no one believes I can be different; sometimes I can't either."

Jade stepped closer, finally meeting his eyes.

"That's how it starts," she said. "You tell yourself you've got control, that you're still choosing your path. But the streets? They don't care what you think. They take from you, piece by piece, until you're nothing but a version of the person you were trying to escape."

Her voice cracked. Shadow noticed her hands were trembling.

"You don't have to go through that again," he said gently. "Whatever it is, you can tell me."

She looked away. "It's not about me anymore. It's about making sure no one else leaves me again."

She inhaled; her breath unsteady.

The memory crept up on Jade like a shadow she couldn't shake.

* * *

Flashback: —*Jade*—

Jade was sixteen, sitting on the front steps of her apartment building. The concrete was warm beneath her, and distant sirens echoed through the neighborhood. She was waiting for Leo.

He'd promised they would leave this place. "We'll start fresh," he had said, his eyes full of dreams that felt too big for the block they grew up on. Jade wanted to believe him. She had to. Everything at home was falling apart. School felt like a dead end. But Leo made it sound like they could be something more than what the streets had already decided for them.

But dreams like that didn't get far around here.

The sun kept sinking. She checked her phone again and again, even though she knew there was nothing new. She bounced her knee, tugged at a loose thread on her jeans, and kept looking toward the corner like he might show up out of nowhere. She told herself he was just late. That he would still come.

But the longer she waited, the more that hope drained away.

It wasn't Leo who gave her the news. It was Ms. Rosario, the neighbor always camped out on her porch with her little radio. She told Jade Leo had been arrested. A drug deal gone bad. He wasn't coming.

Her stomach dropped. She froze. For a second, she thought if she didn't move, maybe it wouldn't be true. But it was. The heat built in her chest: anger, shame, and that quiet pain that never hits all at once. Disappointment. She should have known. But she let herself believe anyways.

She didn't cry. Not then...

Because it wasn't just about Leo. It was about every promise she had ever heard. Every one that broke before it could be kept.

That was the day she stopped trusting words and started watching actions.

The day she promised herself she would never sit around waiting for someone to save her.

* * *

Jade blinked slowly, like she was surfacing from a dream she hadn't meant to fall into.

"I trusted him," she said quietly, returning to the present. "I really thought he'd get us out of here. That he meant it. But he didn't. He couldn't."

Shadow studied her. He sensed the depth of her pain, a pain she rarely let anyone see.

"I'm not him, Jade," he said, his voice low but steady.

"I know," she replied, though a flicker of doubt clung to her words. "Still… you're walking a dangerous line, Shadow. And I've already lost two people to these streets. I can't lose another."

Shadow's hands curled into tight fists. Frustration stirred beneath his skin. He wanted to argue, to push back. But deep down, a part of him understood. Maybe even agreed.

"I'm trying to save you from becoming another name on a T-shirt," Jade continued, her voice cracking under the weight of emotion. "I've seen too many good people swallowed up by this life."

The silence that followed was heavy. It pressed down on both of them, thick with memories and fears neither was ready to voice. Shadow turned away, his eyes fixed on a distant point across the room.

Jade took a breath, steadying herself. "Come with me tomorrow," she said. "To the vineyard. Let's get out of the city for a while. Maybe we both need that."

Shadow looked at her, caught off guard. "The vineyard?"

She nodded, a faint smile forming at the edges of her lips. "Yeah. It's in the Inlands. Real quiet out there. Peaceful. You'll like it."

For the first time in a while, something in Shadow shifted. The tightness in his chest loosened, just a little. Her offer felt like a lifeline, something honest in a world that kept twisting.

"Alright," he said, voice soft. "I'll go."

Jade's smile widened, but her eyes still held a flicker of sadness, the kind that lingered even through good moments. Shadow saw it and knew it mirrored his own. The grief. The regrets. The unspoken things that hung between them.

"Good," she whispered.

She stepped forward and wrapped her arms around him.

At first, Shadow didn't move. But slowly, he let himself return the hug. It wasn't just comfort. It was permission. Permission to be vulnerable.

Maybe he didn't have to weather the storm alone after all.

* * *

The morning came quietly: no gunshots, no shouting, just the hum of tires on pavement and the low thrum of the radio. The city shrank in the rearview mirror as Shadow and Jade cruised down the highway, heading toward the Inlands.

It felt strange to Shadow. The shift from the gritty, fast-paced city to the slower rhythm of the Inlands was jarring. Everything felt cleaner, calmer. Jade leaned back in her seat, humming along to a mellow track on the radio, clearly in her element. She belonged here. Shadow felt like a visitor.

He shifted in his seat, uneasy. Peace made him feel exposed. How could Jade move between these worlds so easily? How could she leave the chaos behind like it was nothing?

"You ever feel like you just don't belong?" Shadow asked, his voice low.

Jade turned her head slightly, a knowing smile tugging at her lips. "In the city? Or here?"

"Here," he said, drumming his fingers on the steering wheel.

She looked out at the vineyards as they passed, the green stretching for miles. "Yeah, I get it. It's slower. But out here, I can breathe. I remember there's more to life than the city grind. It's not about running away; it's about choosing peace when I can. I just want something less broken. You know?"

Shadow gave a small nod. Her words sank in, heavy and unfamiliar. His life had been broken for so long, he didn't know if there was another way.

They pulled into the vineyard, and a warm, golden light bathed the rows of grapevines. A hush settled over them, thick and unfamiliar. Shadow felt like he'd stepped into a world built for someone else.

Inside, a clean-cut employee greeted them with a polite smile. "Can I see your ID?" he asked Jade. She handed it over without hesitation.

The employee nodded and turned to Shadow. "And you, sir?"

Shadow tensed. His chest tightened. He patted his pockets like he was searching, buying time.

"Do you need a minute?" the employee asked, clearly growing impatient.

"Uh... might've left it in the car," Shadow mumbled, avoiding eye contact.

Jade gave him a puzzled look but didn't say anything.

Then, his phone buzzed. Shadow glanced down: Doc.

He stepped aside and answered on speaker, raising his voice just enough. "Yo, what's up Doc? I'm at the vineyard with Jade."

Doc's voice rang through the speaker. "Oh, word? Hit me when you're done."

The employee's eyes widened.

Shadow took his shot. "Did I leave my ID in your car last night?"

Doc caught on. "Yeah, it's in the cup holder."

The employee's attitude shifted instantly. He stepped aside. "You're good. Go ahead."

Shadow exhaled and slipped his phone back in his pocket. Jade stifled a laugh.

"That... worked," he said.

"Guess your uncle's more useful than I thought," she teased.

"Yeah," Shadow said, a bit too fast. "Guess so."

They found a secluded spot outside, overlooking the vineyard. Shadow sat down stiffly. The silence felt loud. The air smelled like earth and wine and something else: freedom. He didn't know if he liked it.

Jade crossed her legs under her and looked out at the vines. "There's something about this place," she said. "Like the world still makes sense out here. Like maybe there's a future beyond all that noise."

Shadow didn't answer. His fingers tapped against the chair.

"I don't know if I can just walk away," he finally said.

Jade turned to him. Her eyes were steady. "You don't have to be who they say you are."

"And who do they say I am?" he snapped, more defensive than he meant to be.

"A boy trying to be a man in a world that will chew you up and spit you out," she said gently.

Her voice was soft, but the truth in it was hard. Her hand brushed his on the table, a quiet invitation. A lifeline.

Was he ready to take it?

Then came the sharp sound of heels clicking against the stone.

"Well, if it isn't the prince of the city," a familiar voice teased.

They both turned.

Lola stood confidently on the vineyard path, designer sunglasses pushed up on her head and a smug grin curling on her lips. Her eyes moved slowly between Shadow and Jade.

"Didn't expect to see you out here, Shadow," she said, raising an eyebrow at Jade. "This your sister?"

Jade stood up calmly, her expression even and measured. "No. Just a friend. Showing him there's more to life than bottles and bass."

Lola smirked. "Adorable. You should bring him around more often. Good place to chill, or cause a little trouble."

Shadow rose to his feet, his muscles tight. "Lola, what are you doing out here?"

"Business," she said vaguely, then gave him a wink. "And maybe a little pleasure now."

Her gaze lingered on Jade just long enough to send a message. No words needed. Then she turned, heels tapping away like a slow drumbeat.

Jade watched her leave, then looked at Shadow. "That kind of thing happen a lot?"

He paused. "Depends on the night."

Jade sat back down, her voice softer now. "You gotta choose, Shadow. One of these lives won't wait forever."

The peace that once blanketed the vineyard felt like it had thinned.

"My dad..." Jade said quietly. "He meant everything to me."

Shadow didn't say anything.

"They came for him. I didn't get it at the time. He was supposed to protect me, but that day, he couldn't even protect himself."

She looked down. "That life doesn't just take people you love. It takes little pieces of who you are."

Before Shadow could respond, his phone buzzed.

Ty: *I can't take this anymore. We need to talk, face to face.*

Shadow stared at the message.

The city was calling, and with it, everything he thought he'd escaped.

The decision wasn't getting any easier.

And he wasn't sure he could face his friends.

CHAPTER 10
A WAY OUT

Shadow hadn't planned on stopping at the park. He was just cutting through the neighborhood after making a quick drop. One of those fast exchanges that left your heart racing and your palms damp. His head was down and his thoughts still tangled in everything that happened. But then he saw her. Jade.

She was sitting alone beneath a tree, arms folded tight across her chest, her gaze drifting across the park like she was trying to solve a problem too big for words. She looked the same, but something about her energy felt different. That was enough to make Shadow stop.

The park stretched out before him, worn and tired like the Inner City itself. A crooked sign hung lazily on the gate, its paint chipped and peeling. The grass was patchy, sun-scorched in some places and bare in others. Benches sagged under the weight of years and weather, covered in layers of graffiti that told a story of their own. The old playground groaned in the breeze, its rusted swings swaying slowly, as if haunted by laughter from another time. Kids raced across the cracked basketball court, their sneakers slapping against the pavement, shouts echoing over the rumble of distant traffic. The neighborhood was rough, no doubt, but there was still life here.

Shadow got out of his car and leaned against one of the old benches, its paint chipped and metal warped from age.

He stared at Jade. She looked like she didn't want to be seen, but also didn't want to be alone. Like she was searching for something, or someone, and hadn't found it yet.

He took a step forward. Gravel crunched beneath his sneakers. Her head turned quickly, shoulders tight, until she saw him. Then her posture softened.

"Hey," he said, voice low but steady.

Jade gave a small nod. "Hey."

"You good?" he asked, his tone light but sincere.

"Same as always," she replied, but it came out hollow.

He moved closer, watching how her arms stayed crossed, like she was holding something in.

"You seem off," he said.

She leaned back against the tree, sighing. "It's nothing. Just... stuff."

"Stuff? That's vague, even for you."

She let out a small laugh, the kind that doesn't quite reach the eyes. "It's my brother. Kian."

Shadow didn't interrupt. He just waited.

"He's getting older," she said quietly. "Too smart for his own good. Asking questions he shouldn't be. I try to keep him away from it all, but... you know how it is. Around here, kids see too much. Hear even more."

"And start to think that's just how life is," Shadow finished for her.

She nodded, eyes on the ground. "I don't want that for him. I don't want him to end up like..."

Shadow stepped beside her, resting against the same tree. "You always looking out for everybody else. But who's looking out for you?"

She shook her head. "I've never needed anyone to."

"Maybe that's the problem."

Jade turned toward him, her expression guarded but honest. "It's not that simple. It never is."

"It could be. If you let it."

The wind kicked up, rustling leaves and lifting a swirl of dust around their feet. The heat of the day had softened, the sun dropping low behind the buildings. Neither of them spoke for a moment. Jade closed her eyes, breathing in deep. When she opened them again, Shadow was still there, still watching her, but not like everyone else.

"Why do you always make me forget everything else?" she asked, her voice soft.

Shadow gave a faint smile. "Because I see you for who you really are."

"You think you know me?"

"I know enough," he said, stepping a little closer. "And I want to know more."

She hesitated. Then lowered her eyes. "I'm scared, Shadow. Scared that no matter how hard I try, I'll never get out of here. That Kian won't either."

Shadow reached out, his fingers brushing against hers, just enough to let her know he was there.

"Then we'll figure it out," he said. "Together."

She didn't flinch. Didn't pull away. She let the moment stay.

"Together," she repeated.

The sun dipped lower behind the skyline, casting long shadows across the park. Somewhere, a siren screamed and faded into the city's heartbeat. But here, beneath the orange haze of a dying day, two souls stood quietly, side by side, caught between the world they knew and the one they hoped to find.

"Let me take you home," Shadow said as they walked toward his car parked up the street.

* * *

They pulled up to Jade's apartment just as the sun dipped behind the rooftops, throwing long shadows across the cracked sidewalk. The streetlights buzzed to life, casting a soft orange hue over the neighborhood.

Shadow leaned back in the seat, staring out the window, still thinking about the vineyard, the weight of what Doc asked him, and the silence that followed. He hadn't planned on coming this way, but after a drop-off nearby, he saw her outside and offered a ride. Something told him he needed this.

Jade glanced at him. "You hungry? I was thinking about cooking."

Shadow nodded. "Yeah, I could eat."

She gave a faint smile, then got out. They walked up the creaky steps to her unit on the second floor. The building showed the Inner City's wear and tear: brick faded by time, stair rails rusted, and doors that didn't quite shut all the way. But inside, her place felt different. Lived-in. Loved, even if it was rough around the edges.

The apartment was small and worn but spotless. Wallpaper peeled slightly at the corners, and a single flickering bulb hung in the kitchen. A breeze drifted through the cracked window until Jade closed it tight.

Kian sat at the table, head down, eyes locked on his homework. His pencil scratched the paper in short bursts.

"Almost done?" Jade asked as she walked past him to the stove.

"Yeah," he mumbled, not looking up.

She stirred a pot, steam curling into the air. The smell of something familiar and warm filled the room.

"You need help?"

"Nah. Got it," Kian replied, still scribbling.

Shadow stood by the doorway, taking it all in, unsure of what he was feeling. Part of him felt comforted, like he was witnessing the kind of life he used to have. But another part felt like an outsider, like he didn't belong in something this peaceful. He watched Jade stir the pot and Kian scribble at the table. For a moment, it felt normal. Domestic, even.

Kian suddenly looked up at Shadow, curiosity in his eyes. "So... are you a rapper or a gangster?"

Shadow blinked, caught off guard. "What?"

Kian shrugged. "I mean... you dress like the guys in the streets and you look like you've been through some stuff."

Shadow opened his mouth but didn't know how to answer. He wasn't sure which version of himself to give the kid.

Jade stepped in quickly. "Kian, worry about your homework. Don't be asking grown folks questions like that."

"Just asking," he muttered, going back to his paper.

Then came three sharp knocks at the door.

They all froze.

Another knock, louder this time.

Jade wiped her hands and glanced toward Kian. "Stay here."

She stepped to the door and looked through the peephole.

"Damn it," she whispered.

She cracked the door an inch, just enough to meet his eyes. Her voice was low but steady. "What do you want?"

Marcus stood there, arms crossed, his gold tooth catching the hallway light. His tone was casual. "Kian's getting older. Time for a talk."

"He's not interested."

"Smart kid. Could be useful."

"He's got a future. In school."

Marcus leaned in a little more, voice dropping. "School won't keep him safe. The streets always come knocking."

"Not if I get him out."

"You think you can protect him forever? Someone's always waiting."

"You're not taking him."

Kian peeked around the corner, his voice low. "Why do you always fight for me?"

Jade's voice didn't waver. "Because no one else will."

Marcus smirked. Raised his hands in mock surrender. "Time runs out fast."

She slammed the door. Locked every bolt.

Then turned to Kian. "We're getting out. You're gonna have a future."

He looked at her, skeptical. "You think we can?"

"I know we can. One step at a time."

Later, after dinner had been started, Shadow was helping set the table when Jade's phone buzzed. She glanced at it, eyebrows raised, and stepped into the hallway to answer.

"Hello?"

Shadow stayed near the kitchen, only catching fragments of her side of the conversation. Her voice tensed.

"Wait, what? We just saw her at the vineyard."

A pause.

"Yeah... I got it," she said, her tone clipped.

Another pause. Then, "Thanks."

When she walked back into the kitchen, her expression was tight. Her shoulders stiff. She folded her arms across her chest.

Shadow looked up. "Everything good?"

Jade's voice was calm. Too calm. "I heard some things. You been messin' with that Lola girl?"

Shadow froze. The fork in his hand hovered mid-air.

"Jade, it's not—"

"Don't lie to me."

He tried to play it off. "She's just someone I know. Nothing more."

Jade stepped closer, eyes searching his face. "You think I didn't see the way she looked at you back at the vineyard? You think I don't know what it is?"

Shadow looked away. He wanted to tell her everything. About Doc. About Lola. About how deep he was in it already. But he couldn't pull Jade into that darkness.

"It's not like that," he said, even though it was.

Jade's voice dropped, cracked with pain. "I thought I meant something to you. But you're just like every other guy around here."

She turned away.

Shadow didn't follow. He couldn't. Not when he didn't even recognize himself anymore.

And just like that, the voice in his head wasn't Shadow's anymore.

It was Elijah.

* * *

The night felt still, like the calm before the storm. Shadow didn't even remember agreeing to meet Doc, he just knew his feet kept moving, and this is where they led him. After the mess with Jade, he should've stayed away. But the Inner City didn't let go that easily. It pulled you back in, step by step.

He and Doc walked side by side, their footsteps echoing on the cracked pavement. Neon signs flickered from corner stores and liquor shops, casting broken reflections in the puddles. The air reeked of oil, fried food, and smoke: grimy, loud, and very much alive. A heavy silence stretched between them, thick enough to choke on.

Shadow's jaw was tight, his fists buried deep in his pockets. Doc, in contrast, looked like he was out for a casual stroll, grinning like he ran the world.

"You ever worry walking around here this late?" Shadow asked, breaking the silence.

Doc laughed, loud and easy. "Worried? Out here?" He stretched his arms out, spinning slightly like the block was his stage. "This is my city. I don't gotta watch my back. I am the back."

Shadow didn't respond. Just kept walking, every step grinding his teeth further down.

"You know," Doc said, slipping into that familiar smirk, "I been out in the Inlands a lot lately. Met this young thing with legs for days. She threw that number at me like a Hail Mary. You ever mess around out there, Shadow? You'd clean up. They love a little danger."

Shadow said nothing, but the way his shoulders stiffened was answer enough. Doc caught it and grinned wider.

"Something about those girls, man. I think they can smell when you've survived something. Makes 'em curious. Makes 'em want to touch the fire."

Shadow stopped in his tracks. "What's your point, Doc?" His tone was flat, but there was fire behind it.

Doc turned, still smiling. "No point. Just sayin', you gotta enjoy what's yours while it's yours. Like Jade."

Shadow's eyes locked on him.

"I mean," Doc continued, unbothered, "if I wasn't tight with her old man, who knows? She's got that classy thing. Always respected that."

Shadow's fists curled at his sides. "You don't talk about her. Ever."

Doc tilted his head, like he was studying a painting. "Relax, Shadow. It's a compliment."

But Shadow wasn't relaxing. He wasn't armed, but in that moment, it didn't matter. He'd throw hands if it came to it.

The tension sparked in the air like a downed wire. Then Doc's hand drifted toward his waistband.

Shadow's eyes tracked the movement, his body coiled.

"You sure you want to do this, kid?" Doc asked, his voice still smug, but sharper now. "Because I promise, it won't end well."

Just before Shadow could speak, a voice cut through the night.

"Hey, are you Shadow?"

Both turned sharply. A man stepped from the shadows, slim, ski mask on his face. There was something about the way he moved: smooth, confident, dangerous.

Shadow narrowed his eyes. "Who's asking?"

The man didn't blink. "You killed my best friend."

Everything stopped. Even the wind held its breath.

Shadow heard the scrape of Doc's boot, the faint hum of traffic, the click of a safety being released.

The first shot cracked the night open. Then four more followed, rapid and loud.

Shadow stumbled, heart pounding, thoughts spinning. His ears rang. Time warped.

Am I gonna die today?

Jade's face flashed in his mind: her laugh, her eyes, the way she looked at him like he was still redeemable.

Does she know what I've done? Would she even care if I disappeared?

Everything he'd done crushed down on him. The lies. The blood. The blind loyalty to Doc.

Was it all for this?

The streetlights flickered above him, throwing shadows across the pavement. The gunfire stopped, replaced by silence.

Shadow laid there, breathing hard.

For the first time, he wasn't sure if he would live or die.

* * *

Shadow's eyes cracked open to the sound of muffled voices and the distant wail of a siren. For a moment, he didn't know where he was. A sharp chill crept through his clothes, mixing with the grime of the pavement and the sting of panic. Confusion clouded his thoughts, his mind sluggish, like he'd just been pulled from the bottom of a deep, dark pool. His chest felt tight, and a sour taste clung to the back of his throat. The rough texture of concrete scraped against his palms as he pushed himself upright. Pain shot through his ribs, but when he looked down, there was no blood. He wasn't dead.

The memory of gunshots slammed into him, and his heart pounded. His surroundings sharpened: the faint glow of streetlights, the bite of the cool air, and the shuffle of fading footsteps. Distant, but not distant enough.

"Doc?" Shadow rasped, barely above a whisper.

A figure moved at the mouth of the alley. Doc stood there, back turned, phone pressed to his ear. "I handled it," he said, voice low and hard. "Clean up the mess. Now."

Shadow's stomach twisted. He staggered to his feet, each muscle aching. "What... what happened?"

Doc turned slowly, his face unreadable. His eyes lingered on Shadow, weighing him like a problem that hadn't solved itself yet.

"You're lucky I was here," Doc said, slipping the phone into his pocket. "That guy wasn't playing."

Shadow's thoughts raced: the stranger, the gun, the shots. He tried to put it all together, but it felt like trying to hold water in shaking hands.

"Did you...?" The question died in his throat. He wasn't sure what scared him more, if Doc had pulled the trigger himself, or if he'd made someone else do it.

Doc smirked, his hands buried in his pockets. "What do you think?"

Shadow wanted to demand answers, to yell, to push back. But everything weighed him down: his limbs, his guilt, the realization that none of this was a game anymore.

"What happened?" he asked again, his voice sharper now, tinged with something close to fear.

Doc stepped in close, his presence heavy. "You think this is a game, Shadow? The streets don't care about your guilt. They don't care if you freeze up or break down. All they care about is power, and whether or not you've got enough of it to keep breathing." He paused. "That guy wasn't looking for me. He was looking for you. Maybe next time, don't leave loose ends."

Shadow's blood turned cold. "Loose ends?"

His fists clenched. "You're saying this is my fault?"

Doc tilted his head, the smirk fading into something harder, darker. "I'm saying, if you're gonna live this life, then be ready for everything it throws at you."

Shadow didn't answer. Couldn't. The knot in his chest was too tight. Doubt flooded his mind like a broken dam.

A blacked-out Suburban rolled up to the curb. Shadow watched as two men jumped out, their movements quick and practiced. They lifted a body from the pavement and loaded it into the trunk without a word. Doc took a step toward the vehicle, then paused. He glanced back over his shoulder, his expression unreadable. "Let this be a lesson, kid. In the Inner City, the moment you let your guard down might be your last."

Shadow stood frozen, every muscle rigid with disbelief but the questions stuck in his throat, too heavy to speak. Guilt swirled in his stomach. Someone died because of him. Again?

He didn't want the answer. Not really. But he already knew.

Sirens pierced the night, closer now. Shadow turned away from the street and slipped deeper into the shadows of the alley, his steps slow and unsure.

Doc's smirk. The stranger's words. The chaos.

Am I even in control of my own life anymore? The thought punched through him.

He didn't know.

All he knew was this: whatever just happened wasn't the end.

It was only the beginning.

ACT II
NAMES LIKE GHOST

CHAPTER 11
INTO THE CROSSFIRE

Shadow paced the length of Doc's high-rise penthouse. Outside the floor-to-ceiling windows, the city lights sparkled like shattered glass. He was still buzzing with adrenaline, his thoughts tangled and sharp. Doc sat at ease on a leather couch, a glass of cognac in hand, watching him with the stillness of a predator.

"You're wasting energy, kid," Doc said, swirling his drink. "Sit down."

Shadow stopped, but he didn't sit. "You don't get it, Doc. Someone just tried to kill me."

Doc smirked slowly. "Welcome to the Inner City, Shadow. You're not just some spoiled kid pretending anymore. You made enemies. Now you need to be ready."

Shadow's stomach churned, but he masked the fear. "Who were they?"

Doc took a long sip before answering. "ICS. Inner City Soldiers. These boys aren't like the small-time crews you've bumped into before. They don't have rules. No loyalty. No code. Just violence and death."

The name hit like a warning siren. "And now I'm their target," Shadow said.

Doc nodded. "You're still breathing because of me. Don't forget that." He leaned forward, setting the glass on the table. "So, you've got two options. Run back to your cushy life and hope they don't find you, or stand your ground. Show them who you really are."

Shadow squared his jaw. "I'm not running."

Doc reached into his jacket and pulled out a sleek black Glock 19. He placed it on the table with a dull thud. "Then you'll need this."

Shadow stared at the gun. His reflection warped across the cold metal. His pulse kicked up. The alley came back in flashes: the panic, the chaos, the deafening crack of gunfire.

"I don't need a gun," he said, though his voice faltered. He wasn't just afraid. He was in denial. Taking that weapon meant admitting he was in too deep, that he wasn't a visitor in this world anymore. He was part of it.

Doc chuckled, dry and cold. "That's what you think? Out here, it's kill or be killed. ICS won't care that you're new. In fact, they'll think you're and easy target. You better be ready."

Shadow's hand hovered above the gun, fingers twitching. Every part of him wanted to walk away, to prove he could resist being pulled in deeper. But then he saw the alley again. Remembered how close death came. Thought about Ty. About E. About Jade. About everything he hadn't yet lost.

Slowly, he picked up the gun. It was heavier than he expected. Cold. Solid. Real. And it felt too natural in his hand.

Doc nodded. "Smart move. Keep it close."

"How do I find them?" Shadow asked.

Doc leaned back, eyes calculating. "You don't. Not yet. Let them come to you. And when they do? You show them they picked the wrong one."

Shadow clenched his teeth. Doc was always so calm, always in control. It made him furious. But deep down, he knew Doc wasn't wrong. ICS wouldn't stop until they finished the job.

"I need to see my friends," Shadow said suddenly.

Doc frowned. "That's a bad idea. If ICS is watching, going back to the Outer City might lead them straight to your people."

"They're already in danger because of me," Shadow said. The moment Doc mentioned ICS knew who he was, a horrible realization had hit. If they knew he was Elijah, they could find Ty and E. One photo, one tag, one careless moment was all it would take. "I can't sit here while they're out there."

Doc studied him for a long moment, then shrugged. "You still don't see the full picture. But go ahead. Be the hero. Just remember, every choice you make comes with a cost."

Shadow said nothing. He turned and walked to the door, the gun now tucked tight into his waistband. He knew the risk. But Ty and E were his people. And he had to warn them.

* * *

Shadow kept his head low as he grabbed a set of keys from Doc's valet drawer. The garage was lined with luxury: Bentleys, Lamborghinis, even a bulletproof SUV. He skipped them all for a matte black sedan with dark windows and no vanity plates. It still whispered money, but not the kind that screamed headlines. That was the point. He didn't want attention, just protection. And driving one of Doc's cars carried weight. People recognized them. They knew better than to test whoever was inside.

He slid into the driver's seat. The leather hugged him, soft and deliberate. The engine purred when it came alive, low and smooth, like it expected the road to move aside. Shadow gripped the wheel tighter, breath measured. Mirrors checked once, twice, three times before he pulled out. Every shadow felt like it had eyes. Every car behind him made him wonder if this was the one. He wasn't just leaving the Inner City; he was dragging danger with him.

The skyline fell away as he drove. Towers gave way to broken sidewalks, corner stores, cracked windows. With each mile, another layer of him shifted.

By the time he crossed into the Outer City, his pulse had slowed, but the tension stayed wired beneath his skin.

He eased down a narrow street. Same storefronts. Same chipped paint. Same crooked mailboxes. But it all felt different now. The block that once brought him peace now pressed in on him, like the past itself was waiting at the curb, arms crossed, ready to ask what took him so long.

Passing the old corner store, a memory blindsided him. Sharp, vivid, impossible to ignore.

* * *

We were sixteen, playing in the semifinals. The gym was packed. I was one foul away from getting benched, and we were down ten with three minutes left. I was in my head. Coach knew it. He was watching me like I was already out of the game.

Then, out of nowhere, Ty dropped to the floor. "Hamstring!" he shouted, holding his leg. "I think I pulled it!"

The crowd went silent. Coach and the trainers rushed over. Ty winced like it was serious, but when he leaned in close, he whispered, "Three minutes, bro. You got this."

He limped off the court so I could stay in.

That was Ty. Didn't care about stats. Didn't care about being the hero. He cared about the team. About the win. About me.

And E? E was always there. Every single game. Rain or shine. Didn't matter what was going on at home or at school. I could look up and see him in the bleachers, yelling like I was in the NBA.

He didn't even play ball, but he studied the game like it was homework. Drew up plays on napkins. Broke down every move I made. He believed in me when I didn't believe in myself.

We weren't just friends. We were brothers.

Watching Ty fake an injury for me, hearing E scream from the top row like it was life or death, that was the moment I knew I'd ride for them. Always.

That kind of loyalty doesn't fade.

That's why I came back.

Not because it was smart.

Because it was right.

* * *

Elijah pulled up to Ty's house, the weight in his chest growing heavier with every block he passed. As he stepped inside, he was surprised to see Ty's mom sitting at the kitchen table, flipping through a magazine. The smell of something warm and familiar hung in the air. She didn't even look up.

"Hey, Mrs. Foster," he said.

She looked up with a small smile. "Elijah! Haven't heard that name in a while."

He paused. It felt strange hearing it again. "Yeah... I don't really hear it much either."

She gave him a long look, like she saw something in him. Maybe it was how tired he looked. Or maybe she saw how much he had changed. He wondered if she could still see the same kid who used to sit at that table laughing about nothing.

"Ty and E are out," she said. "Probably at their usual spot."

He nodded. He already knew.

Elijah walked back out and drove a few blocks down. When he turned the corner, he spotted Ty and E sitting where they always did. For a second, it looked like nothing had changed. But deep down, he knew better.

"Yo, Elijah!" E called out, waving.

Ty gave him a nod. "What's up, man? Been a minute."

"Yeah, it has," Elijah said, sitting down with them. Soon they were talking like old times.

"Yo," Ty said with a grin, nudging Elijah. "Remember when we snuck into the rec center and blamed E for getting caught?"

E rolled his eyes. "Man, that was your idea! You ripped your pants jumping the fence, and I got grounded for a week."

Elijah laughed. "Coach made you run suicides. Like, every day."

Ty grinned. "Still dropped twenty the next game."

Their laughter echoed through the quiet neighborhood, and for a moment, it felt like they were just kids again. Elijah leaned back, letting the memory sink in. His guard lowered. He let himself believe, just for a second, that everything was okay.

But it wasn't.

A black car rolled down the street with no headlights, gliding through the shadows. Elijah's eyes locked on it, his stomach tightening.

"Yo, you see that car?" he asked.

Ty and E turned to look. Ty shrugged. "Probably just someone lost. Don't trip."

But Elijah couldn't let it go. The car circled the block again, creeping by at the same slow speed. The hairs on his neck stood up.

"I don't like it," Elijah said.

E tried to laugh it off. "You're paranoid. We're good."

Still, Elijah couldn't stop watching. The car rolled away again and disappeared around the corner.

Ty leaned back and stretched. "Yo, remember when we tried to build that treehouse in E's backyard?"

E laughed. "You mean the death trap? Y'all left me on the roof when it started raining!"

Elijah smiled. "We thought we were engineers with nothing but two hammers and a dream."

Ty added, "And a box of stolen nails from my dad's shed."

The laughter faded, but the warmth lingered. Elijah let himself relax.

Then the car came back.

"There they are again," Elijah muttered.

This time, the car slowed even more.

A single shot rang out, loud and sharp.

Everything stopped.

Then the back window dropped, and a man leaned out. Muzzle flashes lit up the dark as more shots tore through the night.

Elijah dove behind a dumpster. Ty yelled and ducked behind a tree. E scrambled behind a car. Bullets smashed into walls, glass, and metal. Screams filled the air.

Elijah's hand went to the gun Doc had given him. He hesitated. This wasn't the Inner City. This was his block. But he had no time.

Shadow took over.

He dropped to one knee and returned fire. The car sped off as Elijah fired again and again, hitting the rear window and side. The car didn't stop.

The taillights flared for a second, then vanished.

Shadow's heart pounded. He stood up fast, scanning the street.

Then he saw E.

He was lying on the ground. Still. Too still.

"No, no, no," Shadow whispered, stumbling over. His legs barely worked.

Ty was already there, kneeling beside E. "He's not waking up, man." His voice cracked. His hands were red with blood, pressing against E's side.

"This is my fault," Shadow said. "They were after me."

Ty didn't speak. His mouth opened, then closed. He looked at Elijah, then E. He shook his head and pressed harder.

He fumbled for his phone, dialing 911 with shaking fingers.

Shadow dropped to his knees and saw the wound just below E's ribs. He yanked off his shirt and pressed it against it.

"Stay with me, E," he whispered. "Come on."

But the blood kept coming. E's face was pale. His lips were turning blue.

The sirens were coming. Still, they felt too far away.

A sprinkler ticked nearby, still doing its job.

A camera blinked quietly from a porch.

A luxury car sat untouched at the curb, catching the flash of red and blue.

And Shadow just kept pressing, whispering E's name, hoping it wasn't already too late.

* * *

The waiting room was cold and sterile, the kind of place where time felt like it didn't move. The low hum of machines was the only steady noise, broken occasionally by the shuffle of footsteps or the soft murmur of nurses passing by. Elijah sat still, his hands trembling in his lap.

Hours had passed since the shooting. The police had questioned them relentlessly, over and over again. Different officers, same story. The detectives didn't seem convinced, but with no proof and Doc's car off the books, they let them go. Maybe they didn't care. Maybe they just wanted to clock out. Whatever the reason, they weren't in cuffs.

Now it was sometime after midnight. E had been in surgery since they arrived. No updates. No news.

Ty paced back and forth in front of him, every movement sharp and tense. His fists were clenched, and the veins in his neck stood out like wires ready to snap. Every few seconds, he shot a look at Elijah, like he was trying to figure out if the boy he once knew was still there or if Shadow had taken over completely.

Elijah could feel the tension building. He knew what was coming, but it didn't make it any easier when Ty exploded.

Ty stopped pacing and turned on him, voice tight with rage. "You brought this here!"

Elijah flinched.

"You wanted to play gangsta, and E paid for it!"

The words hit hard, knocking the breath from Elijah. Ty's eyes were full of fire, the kind that came from betrayal. "You had chances, man. Real chances. Stuff we only dreamed about. You threw it all away. For what? Fake respect?"

Elijah didn't have the words to defend himself. He hadn't meant for any of this to happen.

"You think this is worth it?" Ty said, voice low and sharp. "You think throwing away your life and putting ours in danger was worth it?"

Elijah stood, fists clenched. He felt split down the middle. Shame pulling one way, anger pulling the other, and everything he couldn't say pressing down on him.

The weight of Ty's words dragged him lower. A memory bubbled up through the hurt.

* * *

I was ten, maybe eleven, standing next to Ty on the cracked blacktop at the neighborhood park. That's when we first saw E.

155

He was small. Way smaller than us. Getting pushed around by three older boys who looked like they had nothing better to do. E didn't fight back. He just kept getting up, his tiny fists clenched, backpack sliding off his shoulder like it had given up, too.

"We should step in," I told Ty.

Ty didn't even blink. He picked up a big tree branch, nodded, and started walking. We didn't have a plan. Just that feeling in our gut that this wasn't right. Shoulder to shoulder, we stepped up. Ty puffed his chest out like he was six feet tall. I stuck close, trying to look tougher than I felt.

"Y'all done?" Ty barked at the older boys.

One of them took a step forward, then paused. Maybe they weren't looking for a real fight. Or maybe they saw something in us, something that said we weren't scared.

They backed off. Tossed a few curses our way, but they left.

E just stood there, stunned. He looked up at us like we were superheroes. Didn't say a word. Just followed when we walked off. He stayed close all the way to the corner store.

Ty cracked a joke about one of the bullies' busted sneakers, and E laughed. Real quiet at first, like he wasn't sure he was allowed to. But by the time we were all sharing a bag of chips on the curb, it felt like he'd always been one of us.

That day, we weren't just three kids from the same neighborhood anymore.

We became brothers.

We made a promise that night. Not with words, but with scraped knees, shared snacks, and sticky juice stains. A silent vow to always have each other's backs.

And for a long time, we did. Through fights. Suspensions. Detentions. Wins and losses on the court. Everything.

But tonight... I broke that promise.

* * *

The memory faded, but the ache stayed. The flashback had cracked something open. Ty's words hadn't just made him angry. They'd made him feel exposed. Hollowed out.

His eyes dropped to his waistband and his heart jumped.

The gun.

He hadn't realized it was still there. Tucked away like a secret he couldn't let go of. The police never searched him. In all the chaos, he'd forgotten it.

His hand brushed the cold metal, and a thousand thoughts ran through his head. Could it protect him? Was it the only power he had left?

Ty noticed.

"What?" Ty said, voice bitter. "You gonna shoot me too? Like you did that dude in the alley?"

Elijah froze.

How did he know?

The memory of that night surged up again: the blood, the look in the man's eyes.

He wanted to say something. To explain. But his throat closed up.

Ty shook his head, disgusted. "I can't deal with this. Not right now."

He walked out, leaving Elijah standing there alone.

The silence in the waiting room swallowed him whole. Elijah stared at the empty seat where Ty had been. The ghosts of their brotherhood haunted that chair.

Then the door opened. A nurse walked in, calm and collected. She gave a polite nod. "Mr. Knight, we have an update on your friend."

But Elijah didn't hear her.

His mind was somewhere else.

What if the ICS came for his parents?

The thought hit hard. His heart pounded. If they found out where he lived. If they went after the people he loved...

"I need to check on them," he muttered.

His phone buzzed in his pocket. He didn't check it. Didn't care.

He stood and walked toward the door, mind racing. He had already brought too much darkness into their lives. He couldn't let this spiral any further.

He had to protect them.

Whatever it took.

* * *

Elijah stepped out of the hospital. The night air hit his face, cool and sharp, but it did nothing to settle the dread in his chest. He glanced down the empty street. The world was quiet. Like it knew something was coming.

He moved on instinct, feet fast, eyes wide. Every sound made him flinch. The city around him felt off.

That's when he saw it.

A car, parked across the street. Engine running. No lights. No movement. Just sitting there.

It could've been nothing.

But his gut said otherwise.

Elijah's hand moved to the gun at his waist.

The metal of the gun was cold against his skin. It reminded him that this wasn't some nightmare. This was his life now. And someone was watching.

The shadows shifted. He couldn't see anyone clearly, but the feeling was unmistakable.

Eyes were on him.

His heart thudded harder. His fingers gripped the gun tighter.

He took one step towards the car, then froze.

What if they were already there?

The car's headlights flashed once. Then off again.

He turned sharply, planning to circle around. To come in from the back, maybe. But that's when he saw it.

A figure.

Still as stone, half-hidden in the shadows across the street. Watching.

Elijah's breath caught.

That was the moment Shadow took over.

The version of him who didn't hesitate. The one who didn't panic.

His back straightened. His jaw tightened. He let the fear settle deep inside, where it couldn't get in the way.

But his thoughts kept racing.

Doc.

Had he really been on Elijah's side?

Or had this been the plan all along?

The things Doc said. The gun. The pressure to become someone else. To become Shadow.

Then came Jade.

And Lola.

He'd been split between the two of them, and now it all felt connected in ways he couldn't explain. Doc, the girls, the lies. It was like someone had been pulling strings behind the scenes.

He closed his eyes for a second, tried to steady his breathing. It didn't help.

He thought about his parents again.

They were the only real thing he had left.

He couldn't lose them.

He wouldn't.

The car across the street shifted slightly, engine revving low. Shadow didn't move.

He was done running.

Not tonight.

Worried about his parents and Jade, Shadow drove straight to his parents' house. As he steered through the quiet streets of the Outer City, his mind raced with worst-case scenarios. He pulled out his phone and dialed Jade's number.

No answer.

He tried again.

Still nothing.

His pulse quickened, a knot of panic growing tighter in his chest.

He left a voicemail, his voice low and urgent: "Jade, it's me. I need you to call me back. It's important. I think... I think they might be coming for you."

He stared at the screen, hoping it would light up with her name.

Nothing.

The Outer City rolled by, quiet and calm on the surface. But inside, Shadow was spiraling. Since leaving the hospital, every moment felt like borrowed time.

When he turned onto his parents' street, he slowed the car. Their house came into view, the porch light glowing faintly through the haze. It looked the same as always. But something about it felt off.

He eased into the driveway, eyes sweeping the neighborhood. Every shadow, every idle car felt like a threat.

He stepped out and stood at the curb beneath a flickering streetlight. The hum of the night filled the silence around him.

He checked his phone again.

You safe?

Still no reply.

He called once more.

Voicemail.

His heart thudded in his chest. The idea of losing her. Of being too late. It gnawed at him.

He looked up at the sky. The stars were drowned out by the city's lights, but the weight of the moment made it feel darker than usual.

This wasn't just about surviving anymore.

It was time to become something more.

Not just Shadow.

But a weapon they'd never see coming.

He walked slowly toward the door, nerves on edge. Every rustle of wind, every creak of the neighborhood made him tense. He scanned the area, his instincts screaming at every movement.

His hand moved toward the gun tucked at his waist. Then it stopped.

He crouched and reached beneath the flower pot. His fingers brushed the metal of a spare key.

He slid it into the lock.

One quiet click.

Then, with a breath held tight in his chest, he stepped inside.

NO LOOSE ENDS

The smell of rust and gun oil clung to the concrete walls. The room, a maintenance bunker beneath an abandoned warehouse, felt cold and forgotten. Overhead, the lights buzzed like lazy lightning bugs. Shadows gathered in the corners, listening.

Serena "Slick" Morales leaned against a battered metal table, her gloved fingers tapping a spent bullet casing. Each tap echoed like a message only ghosts could read.

Across from her, a girl sat still in a folding chair. Younger. Tough. But not yet forged.

Slick didn't face her at first. Instead, she looked toward the shadows behind her and said, calm and deliberate:

"Call Doc. Tell him the chicken's back in the barn."

The girl didn't move. Her fingers stayed wrapped around the phoenix pendant at her neck. Scratched gold, still warm from her skin.

Slick turned back to her. "Doc appreciates the tracker you planted earlier. Worked like a charm. Just like he planned."

A beat passed.

"He say who it was?"

"Whoa, slow down now," Slick said, a smirk tugging at her lips. "He said you ain't ready yet. Said you got more to learn."

The girl's fingers traced the pendant again. *My brother gave me this.* His laugh echoed in her memory. Gentle, out of place in a world like this.

Her eyes drifted to a burn mark scorched across the far wall. She didn't speak.

Slick let the bullet casing go. It clinked, rolled, and settled.

"You're quiet."

"I'm thinking."

"About your brother?"

A flicker passed across her face. "He wasn't meant for this."

"No one is. Until they are."

Silence settled again, heavy and thick.

Slick turned to face her fully now. "You're emotional," she said. "That's your weakness. But it's also your fire. Shape it right, and it becomes your weapon."

The girl shifted. The pendant rose and fell with her breath, resting over her heart like a second pulse. The soft part of her, the one that still hurt, began to harden.

"You think I'll be ready?"

Slick's smirk returned. "Not yet. But you will be. People like us? We don't fade. We burn down what came before. Then we rise."

She flicked ash onto the floor.

"And next time someone comes for you… or your new family…"

She exhaled slowly. Smoke curled around her words like a whisper.

"They won't see the fire until it's already on them."

The pendant gleamed.

And this time, it looked like it remembered.

CHAPTER 12
SHATTERED PEACE

The door creaked shut behind Elijah as he stepped into the foyer of the house he once called home. He stood still for a moment, his hands buried deep in the pockets of his jacket like he needed to anchor himself to something solid. The night chill still clung to his clothes, but it was the warmth of the foyer, the soft lighting and the smell of his mom's cooking, that hit him the hardest. Everything looked exactly the same: clean, quiet, untouched. But to Elijah, the calm felt artificial. The warmth only made the guilt twist deeper.

Faint neighborhood sounds filtered through the closed door: kids laughing down the block, a car humming past, the creak of the porch swing next door.

His eyes drifted to the staircase, then down the hallway where framed photos lined the walls. One caught his attention: seventh grade, honor roll, smiling wide like he still believed he could be everything his parents wanted.

That version of Elijah was gone. In his place stood someone colder. Someone who had made decisions that couldn't be taken back.

He took a deep breath and stepped further into the house. Memories hit him from every direction: birthday parties in the living room, holiday mornings full of laughter, quiet nights by the fireplace. They felt distant now, like scenes from a movie about someone else's life.

Still, something pulled him closer.

The scent of his mom's cooking lingered in the air. It should've made him feel at home. Instead, it cracked something open inside. A memory he'd tried to bury beneath anger and regret came rushing in.

* * *

It was a regular evening. I was fifteen, sitting at the dinner table with the scent of roasted chicken and potatoes hanging in the air. My father's voice cut through it. Sharp. Cold.

"You think this is a game, Elijah?" he snapped, his eyes locked on mine. "Do you even understand what it means to carry this name? This legacy?"

My jaw tightened. I stared down at my plate, my fork frozen midair. "I didn't ask for this," I muttered.

"Speak up," he barked. "You want to act like a man? Speak like one."

I looked up, anger burning in my throat. "I said I didn't ask for this. I didn't ask to be your son, or to carry your stupid legacy."

The room went dead quiet. My mom, sitting at the other end of the table, reached forward just a little, trying to defuse what was coming. "Jules," she said gently.

He didn't flinch. "Stupid legacy?" His voice dropped, low and dangerous. "You think this just landed in your lap? You think you can throw away everything we built?"

I shoved my chair back so hard it screeched. "I don't want it!" I shouted, my voice cracking. "I don't want any of it!"

And I ran out of the dining room, past my mom's voice calling after me, and up the stairs. I slammed my bedroom door and collapsed onto my bed.

Lying there in the dark, staring at the ceiling, I made a decision. If he wanted that legacy so badly, he could keep it. I'd make a name of my own, even if it meant leaving everything behind.

* * *

The memory faded.

Elijah stood in the foyer of his family's home, fingers brushing the wall for balance. His legs felt weak. The anger from that night still lived inside him. He'd followed through on what he said. He left. But what had it really cost him?

From the kitchen came the sound of dishes clinking, and his mom's voice humming. He stood frozen, caught between who he was and who he used to be. Then, with a breath, he stepped forward, ready to face whatever was waiting.

When he stepped into the kitchen, the scent of lemon and roasted vegetables drifted through the air, mingling with the scent that still lingered from the foyer. The chandelier's golden light poured across the polished floors, casting long, dramatic shadows that stretched toward his feet.

He hadn't called ahead. The surprise on his parents' faces told him all he needed to know.

His mother's hand flew to her chest. "Elijah," she said, part gasp, part sigh. Her voice trembled with a blend of relief and disbelief. "You're here."

Jules looked up slowly from his plate. His eyes locked onto Elijah's, the familiar hardness forming, but something flickered beneath it first. Disappointment? Fear? Maybe even concern. Whatever it was, it disappeared beneath the steel of a clenched jaw.

Elijah shifted, keeping his hands tucked in his jacket pockets. Part of him wanted to turn around and walk out before things soured. But the smells, the warmth, the echo of laughter from years ago, all of it rooted him. "I thought I'd stop by," he said, aiming for nonchalant, though his shoulders stayed tight.

His mom moved fast, motioning to the table. "Come, sit. You must be hungry." She turned toward the cabinet, grabbing another plate with urgency.

"No need, I'm fine," Elijah said, but she was already laying out a place for him. Typical. That was her love language. Acts, not words.

He sat down reluctantly, hyper-aware of the silence that followed, and of Jules's stare pressing into him.

"Decided to remember where you come from?" Jules asked. His voice cut through the air like a blade.

Elijah stiffened, but didn't bite. Same old Jules. No welcome, no warmth. Just a test.

"Jules," his mother said, her voice soft but pleading. She lowered herself into the seat across from Elijah, offering a tired smile. "It's good to see you, honey."

Elijah stared at the tablecloth, tracing its pattern with his fingers.

"Why are you here?" Jules leaned forward. "Last time you stepped foot in this house, you made it pretty clear you were done with all of this."

"I—" The words he had rehearsed on the way over, the speech he'd recited in his head, vanished into the heat of the moment.

"Jules, please," his mother said again, this time more firmly. "Let's just eat. Can we do that? As a family?"

Jules leaned back in his chair. He didn't say another word, but his silence was sharp enough.

His mother moved dishes around, trying to push the evening forward with clinking plates and forced conversation. Elijah took a small bite of the pasta. The garlic, olive oil, and lemon took him back. Back to nights when this house still felt like home.

But nostalgia was fleeting.

His mom tried to keep things light. She asked about the weather, his routine, anything to create a current strong enough to carry them past the tension. Elijah offered nods, a few quiet answers. But he wasn't really present. He was wondering if this had been a mistake.

Jules broke the silence. "You think you can walk in here and everything's fine? That's not how this works. You're still avoiding what you owe."

Elijah dropped his fork. The metal clinked sharply against the plate.

"I didn't come here to fight," he said. "I came because I thought I owed it to Mom. Maybe even to you."

Jules scoffed. "You owe more than that. But I guess respect's still too expensive for you."

"Stop it, both of you!" his mother said, her voice cracking as her hand trembled near her plate. Her eyes were glassy. "Can't we just have one meal without tearing each other apart?"

Elijah's anger faded. Guilt took its place.

"I'm sorry, Mom," he said, voice low.

A long silence followed. Jules didn't speak. His mother wiped her eyes discreetly.

"I've lost my appetite," Jules muttered.

His mother reached across the table, her hand warm and steady over Elijah's. "He'll come around," she said, though her eyes weren't so sure.

Elijah nodded, but didn't speak. This wasn't the reunion he'd imagined. But deep down, it felt like the one he deserved.

* * *

The air in the dining room was tense and quiet. Dinner had ended a little while ago, but no one had moved. Jules sat stiffly, tension radiating off him. Vivi kept trying to make small talk, her voice light but shaky. Elijah sat silently, his nerves on edge. Something felt wrong, though he couldn't explain what.

Then came the noise, a low, steady rumble outside. At first it was barely noticeable, but it grew louder and more aggressive.

"What the hell?" Jules muttered, standing up fast. His chair scraped loudly against the floor as he turned toward the window.

Suddenly, gunfire erupted, loud and fast. Bullets tore through the front windows, spraying glass across the room. Vivi screamed and dove under the table. Elijah's body moved on instinct. He lunged to cover her.

"Stay down!" he yelled, heart pounding.

Through the shattered window, two masked men leaned out of a black sedan. Muzzle flashes lit up the street as they fired into the house. Bullets slammed into the walls and furniture.

"Elijah! Vivi!" Jules called out. He was already on the move, heading toward the back. Within seconds, he returned holding a black pistol. His movements were sharp, practiced, like someone who had been through chaos before.

That's when the shift happened. Elijah wasn't Elijah anymore. Something hardened inside him. The fear turned to focus. From that moment on, he moved like someone else. He moved like Shadow.

Shadow crawled out from under the table, glass crunching beneath his knees. He looked back. Vivi was still crouched under the table, arms over her head, trembling but alive. Outside, the rapid gunfire stopped, replaced by distant shouts and the distinct sound of reloading.

Shadow reached for his waistband and pulled out his Glock. He took a breath and looked at his father. Their eyes met. It was time.

"You good?" Jules asked, calm but intense.

Shadow nodded.

They moved together, crouching near the broken window. Outside, one of the masked men stepped into view, just behind the car door.

Jules fired. One clean shot.

The man dropped.

Panic followed. The others unleashed another wild volley of bullets before the sedan screeched off, tires peeling as they vanished into the night.

Shadow and Jules stood and stepped out onto the lawn, guns still raised.

"Stay there, Mom!" Shadow called over his shoulder.

He scanned the street: dark, broken, and buzzing with whispers. Neighbors peered out of windows and stepped onto porches, phones in hand.

Jules was already pacing the yard, phone to his ear.

"This wasn't random," he muttered. "No one comes at my family."

Shadow could hear Doc's voice through the line, gravelly and calm. Jules' expression darkened.

"You know who it was? Find out. Now."

The front of the house looked like a war zone: glass glittered across the lawn, bullet holes riddled the siding, and flashing lights from neighbors' phones cast eerie glows.

Shadow's thoughts churned. He been questioned by the cops about the last shooting. But now? This could change everything.

Jules ended the call and climbed the steps to the porch. Vivi was standing in the doorway now, pale and dazed.

"Pack a bag," Jules said. "We're not staying here."

Shadow's fists clenched. This wasn't just about him anymore. His choices had pulled his family into the line of fire. Someone was going to pay for that.

Inside, the dining room was wrecked. Shattered glass blanketed the floor. The scent of gunpowder lingered in the air. Vivi sat in the corner, her wide eyes locked on her son.

Jules lowered his pistol, gaze fixed on Shadow, who still held the Glock that Doc had given him.

"What the hell are you doing with that?" Jules snapped.

Shadow gripped the gun tighter. "I needed it," he said. "The streets aren't safe."

"The streets? Boy, I'll smack the hell outta you," Jules barked, stepping forward. "You been wearing cardigans and loafers your whole life, and this what you've sunk to? Running around with a gun like some common thug? I ain't never seen a thug in Sperrys and a damn sweater tied around his neck. Yo ole private school going, honors class having, country club membership, privileged-ass kid."

Shadow said nothing at first. He looked to his mother, her lips barely forming a whispered, "Careful."

Jules stepped in closer. "I would've given anything to have the life we gave you. You never had to struggle, not once. So, where'd you even get it?"

Shadow's jaw set. "A friend."

Jules laughed coldly. "A friend? Got a name, or are we playing dumb now? Is that how deep you are in this?"

Shadow's chest rose and fell. "Why does it matter? I needed protection."

"You think this is protection?" Jules shouted, gesturing around the room. "This is what that gun got us: chaos. And don't act like they weren't here for you. I saw your face. You brought this into our home. Don't lie to me."

Vivi stood abruptly, stepping between them. Her voice trembled but held strong. "We just survived a shooting. Please, try not to fight."

Jules took a hard breath, still staring at his son. Then he extended his hand.

"Give it to me."

Shadow didn't move. His grip tightened. "I can't. Not yet."

Jules stared for a beat longer, his fury shifting to something harder to read. Then he turned and walked toward the kitchen.

Vivi stood in front of Shadow. Her eyes glistened.

"Please," she whispered. "Try not to fight."

Shadow turned away. Her words weighed heavy, but they didn't change what had been set in motion.

The wail of sirens closed in. Red and blue lights flickered against the walls.

Shadow slowly lowered the gun and tucked it into his waistband.

But deep down, he knew one thing for sure:

The war had followed him home.

CHAPTER 13

A HOUSE DIVIDED

Elijah stood in the doorway of his old bedroom. He hadn't planned on going upstairs; his body had moved on its own, searching for something that felt familiar. The room looked untouched, frozen in time, full of reminders of who he used to be. Posters were still pinned to the walls, a cracked trophy sat on the shelf, and his worn basketball shoes rested beneath it. Looking at it all made his heart race. This place held a version of him that felt like a lie now.

He noticed his lucky hoodie draped over the edge of the bed, the one he always wore on game days. He put it on. It felt snugger than before. In the mirror, he smoothed his jeans and stared at himself. For a second, he looked like that same hopeful kid people believed would go far.

But that wasn't who he was anymore. He took a breath. Outside, the real world waited.

He walked downstairs with slow, heavy steps. The house still smelled like spices and old wood, but something in the air had changed. Through the shattered front windows, flashing police lights spilled across the floors. Engines hummed outside. Voices mixed with the crackle of radios.

Outside, his father Jules stood just beyond the doorway, calm and collected. His hands stayed in his pockets, his shoulders loose, his voice low and steady while he spoke to the police.

Elijah stepped onto the porch. Cold air hit him instantly. He scanned the street: four police cars were parked out front. Two officers stood near Jules, while two more were talking to neighbors. A woman held up her phone, recording. Another just stared. Elijah's eyes drifted from the broken windows to the yellow tape going up around the yard.

Guilt tingled through his body. Again. He wondered what the neighbors saw when they looked at him. A victim? Or a warning?

"Random act of violence," Jules told an officer, calm but firm. "Drive-by. Wrong place, wrong time."

The officer, short and broad, looked at the bullet holes in the house. "That so? You got enemies, Mr. Knight?"

Jules gave a dry laugh. "I run one of the biggest record labels in the country. Jealousy makes people stupid."

The cop didn't look convinced, but Jules had a way of making people doubt themselves. Elijah watched closely. Jules wasn't just explaining; he was steering the story.

"Elijah?"

Elijah turned. A younger officer approached, recognition on his face.

"No way, man. You used to play for St. Francis, right?"

Elijah hesitated. Part of him wanted to deny it, stay invisible. But he nodded. "Yeah."

"Knew it. You were cold on the court. What happened? Thought we'd be watching you play for Duke. That scholarship was all over the local news."

Elijah forced a weak smile. "Life happened."

The older cop nearby smirked. "Bet scouts are still watching."

The younger one pulled out a small notebook. "You mind signing this? Just in case you make it big. Gotta get in early."

Elijah's hand trembled as he took the pen. He'd held a gun just minutes ago. It felt unreal. The cops still saw him as a success story, not a kid standing in the middle of a crime scene. He signed the page and handed it back.

"Appreciate it, man. Seriously."

Elijah just nodded. Jules was watching him, measuring him. Elijah didn't know if it was pride or disappointment behind that look.

Before going inside, Elijah had to answer some questions. He gave simple answers: he didn't know who did it, didn't see anything. The truth wouldn't help him here. As he turned to leave, the older cop spoke up.

"That's two shootings you've been connected to this week. That's not normal for this neighborhood. We'll be watching you."

The words hit harder than Elijah expected. Fear knotted in his gut, but he kept his face calm. Defending himself wouldn't change anything. Around here, what people believed was more dangerous than the truth.

He didn't argue. Just nodded and walked away.

Inside, his mom Vivi sat stiffly on the couch, hugging herself like she was trying to stay in one piece. She flinched when she saw him but softened quickly.

"Stay, Eli. Please."

Her voice was quiet, pleading. She wanted to believe this was just a bad night, that things could go back to normal. But Jules was already moving.

"Get your bag," he said flatly.

Elijah started to speak, but Jules cut him off, his tone sharp.

"You brought this here."

The words hit like a punch. Elijah clenched his jaw, not out of anger but shame. Jules was right. His presence had shattered their peace. But the way his dad said it, like it was just one more mess to clean up, made something twist in Elijah's chest.

He didn't respond. He let the silence speak for him. Jules turned away like it meant nothing. But Elijah felt it deeply.

Vivi looked from one to the other. She wanted to say something but couldn't. Her eyes softened when she looked at Elijah, but he wouldn't look back. He wanted to tell her everything: the gun, the danger, who was really behind all this. But he couldn't. Not yet. Not if it meant shattering what little image she still had of him.

He shifted his weight, stuck in the silence. Something in him softened when he looked at her, reminding him of a memory.

* * *

I was thirteen, the night before tryouts for the middle school track team. I couldn't sit still. I kept pacing my room, back and forth, the floor creaking beneath me. The air smelled like old books and the lavender-scented polish my mom used every Saturday. Posters on the wall shifted slightly from the breeze sneaking in through the window. I was biting my thumb, overthinking everything. I was convinced I wasn't fast enough. I kept imagining myself tripping or freezing up when it mattered. Every bad scenario played on repeat in my head.

My mom walked in quietly, moving like she didn't want to wake anyone, carrying a mug of chamomile tea. She handed it to me with both hands, her fingers warm against mine. Our eyes met for just a second. They were calm, like she saw everything I was feeling. She didn't give a speech. Didn't try to fix it. That was her way of saying, I see you. I've got your back.

"I saw you run at field day," she said, settling on the edge of my bed. Her voice was soft but sure. "You've got fire in you, Eli. Don't let fear outrun it."

That helped. A little. I nodded, took a sip of the tea, and let her words settle into me like warmth. The next morning, I gave it everything I had. I didn't mess up. I made the team.

After that, she was at every single meet. No matter the weather: rain, wind, or cold, she was in the bleachers, screaming my name like I was a star. She even brought a foam finger when nobody else did. She tracked my race times, knew my biggest rivals, and clapped just as hard when I didn't win. Sometimes I caught her wiping away tears when I crossed the finish line first. Other times, I saw her smiling even when I didn't.

Now she was in that same house, arms wrapped around herself like she didn't know how to hold me anymore. That memory of her felt far away. Cold. Like it belonged to someone else. I wanted to speak, to reach out, but the words got stuck. The silence between us pressed in.

It felt like I was remembering a different version of myself: a kid who still believed in safety nets, in moms who showed up with warm tea, in talent being enough to carry you forward, in futures that didn't shift under your feet. That kid believed the people cheering for him would always be there.

And just like that, the memory faded. Replaced by the now, where none of those things felt certain anymore.

* * *

That memory belonged to someone else now.

Jules stepped aside, pulling out his phone. Elijah overheard just enough as Jules passed.

"Tell me you heard about this. No? Then you should have. I want names when I get there."

Elijah's chest tightened. Jules was going to meet with Doc.

The air felt heavy. Vivi looked between them. "This isn't how it's supposed to be."

Elijah had no words. He ran a hand over his face. He needed answers, and he wasn't waiting around for them.

"I'll call you when I'm on the way," Jules said as he ended the call.

When Jules walked off, Elijah slipped into the hallway shadows. Without a word to Vivi, he cracked open the door and stepped outside.

The lights were still flashing. Cops were still around. Neighbors were still watching.

No one stopped him.

As he passed his car. The one he drove there. His breath caught. Two bullet holes were in the driver's side door. The window was cracked like a spiderweb.

He swallowed hard and got in. Whatever was coming, he wasn't going to wait for it.

He was going to face it head-on.

* * *

Elijah gripped the steering wheel, speeding through the city as the lights smeared into blurs around him. His thoughts ran just as fast, looping Jules' words in his head. His dad's voice echoed, sharp, cold, unrelenting.

But Jules didn't know everything. He didn't know about Doc. About the war rising beneath the surface. About the blood that had already been spilled. Shadow clenched his jaw. If Jules thought he could control everything: steer the streets, protect the family, and still pull Elijah's strings, he was dead wrong.

Elijah needed answers.

The stereo crackled on, breaking the silence. A familiar beat thumped through the speakers, the bass heavy in his chest. One of Jules' old songs, back from his days in the trenches, before the suits and boardrooms. Elijah's grip tightened as the lyrics came flooding back.

He found himself rapping along before he even realized:

See I came from the dirt, had to grind for the crown
Now when I speak, they all writin' it down
But I'm built from the pain, ain't no breakin' me
And if you ain't talkin' money, don't talk to me

That was Jules. Still echoing through the streets, even now.

Elijah turned off the stereo, but the lyrics stuck. Jules had survived all this once. But now the past was back, and this time Elijah wasn't facing it as his father's son. He was stepping into it as Shadow.

The Inner City swallowed him fast: neon signs flickering, sidewalks cracked, people moving with purpose and paranoia. He pulled up to Doc's penthouse, its dark windows towering over him like eyes watching.

He didn't pause. He got out, slammed the door, and walked straight to the entrance. One of Doc's men recognized him and buzzed him in without a word.

The air inside was thick with smoke, liquor, and low music pulsing in the walls. Two girls lounged on the couch laughing. Two of Doc's men stood by the windows, eyes on the street. Another guy, half-asleep in a chair, held a burned-out blunt. Doc sat in his usual spot, a leather chair with a drink in hand and an unreadable expression. Calm in the chaos.

"Look what the cat dragged in," he said, smirking. "Didn't think I'd see you tonight, Nephew."

Before Shadow could respond, Doc snapped his fingers. "Alright, ladies. Party's over."

The girls groaned, dragging themselves up.

"Sorry, ladies," Doc added, flashing a grin. "Baby boy here's in his feelings. Come to the club later, and we'll finish this there."

One rolled her eyes. The other blew him a kiss as they walked out.

Doc glanced at Shadow. "You're such a cock block."

Shadow didn't blink. "You knew something."

Doc raised an eyebrow. "You're gonna have to be more specific."

"The drive-by," Shadow said, stepping closer. "ICS. My parents' house. My dad called you like he expected answers."

Doc sighed and set his drink down. "If I had planned it, they wouldn't have missed. You'd be laid out, not walking through my door."

Shadow's heart pounded.

Doc leaned forward. "I know a lot. Hear more. But that's not the point. The point is this. What are you willing to do about it?"

Before Shadow could speak, the intercom buzzed.

One of Doc's men checked the screen. "It's Jules."

Shadow's stomach dropped.

Doc turned to him. "Back room."

Shadow hesitated, torn.

"Now."

The tone made it clear. This wasn't optional. Shadow backed into the hallway, blending into the shadows. From where he stood, he could see a sliver of the room: what he couldn't see, he could hear, every word landing like a punch.

Jules entered. The shift in the room was instant. Even here, in Doc's territory, Jules owned the space. The music faded. No one said a word.

Doc leaned back, smiling. "Wasn't expecting you, Jules."

Jules closed the door with calm precision. "I don't have time for games. You knew I was coming."

Doc shrugged. "And yet, here we are."

Jules stepped in, sharp and controlled. "I don't like surprises. Especially not when they involve my family." He narrowed his eyes. "Was this Lucien?"

Shadow froze. A name he didn't know, but one he wouldn't forget.

Doc's smile stretched wider. "That's the thing about trust. Hand it out, they use it. Keep it close, they call you paranoid. Me? I trust leverage and opportunity. And I've got plenty."

He held Jules's gaze. "Word is, Lucien's trying to start a war."

Jules didn't flinch. "Give me names. Give me locations. If this leads to you, I won't protect you. Don't forget who built this."

Doc chuckled, but it was dry. "Still playing the hero, huh? I don't need saving. I'm not the sidekick from back in the day. I'm the king now. The streets made me. Paid me, too."

Jules turned to leave. "You've got twenty-four hours."

Once the door clicked shut, Shadow stepped back into the room.

Doc took another sip of his drink. "I'ma be at the club later. Blow off some steam. Your girl Jade might even be there."

Shadow's face hardened. He hadn't seen Jade in days. The fact that Doc was keeping tabs made his stomach twist.

Outside, the city roared. But Shadow felt like the only one left in it.

He leaned against his car, trying to catch his breath.

He should call her. Just check in.

But what if they were watching? What if that simple call put her in danger?

He pulled out his phone... and then locked the screen.

If he reached out, he might drag her into all of this. If he didn't, he might lose her completely.

Jade's laugh echoed in his mind. The way she looked at him. Like she still believed in the boy beneath the shadow.

That memory of her hurt worse than the silence.

But the streets didn't care about memories. Or love.

He had to choose:

Shadow's war.

Or Elijah's heart.

* * *

The club throbbed with life: bass pounding like war drums, lights flickering like muzzle flashes. Shadow wasn't supposed to be here, not tonight. Not after the shootout. Not after Jules confronted Doc. But his instincts had brought him anyway. He needed clarity. Answers. Proof that his gut wasn't lying to him.

Doc had said Jade might be around. Shadow had brushed it off then, figured it was just Doc being messy. But the way he said it was like a trap wrapped in silk. That, and the timing. Everything was spiraling. And if Jade really was mixed up in all of this, if she was anywhere near Doc's orbit, Shadow had to know.

He didn't go through the main entrance. He parked two blocks away and slipped in through the kitchen loading dock, unnoticed. He climbed the back stairwell, sweat beading at his brow. The air buzzed with smoke, spilled liquor, and perfume. The sound of muffled bass and laughter pounded through the walls, scraping against his nerves. He wasn't here to party. He was here for the truth.

On the second floor, the hallway to the private lounge stretched ahead. Shadow crept along the wall, shoes sticking slightly to the stained floor. He kept his breathing low, controlled. Every muscle tight.

A cracked door near the end leaked golden light and the sound of conversation. He recognized the voice first: Lola. Instinct made him freeze.

She wasn't alone.

From his spot in the shadows, he could just make out her silhouette. She stood with Zico, one of Doc's most dangerous lieutenants. The kind of man who didn't blink before pulling a trigger. His face was partly turned, but the vibe was unmistakable: serious business. And then Lola spoke.

"I like him a lot, but I can't lose focus on my job," she said, swirling a drink with one hand, her posture casual but alert.

Zico grunted. "You got him playing the role. Doc thinks the kid might be useful."

"If it helps me find my brother's killer," she said with a faint smile, "I'll keep him close. Boys like him? Show a little skin, they stop thinking straight."

Shadow went still. The hallway felt colder. She was talking about him. That was how she saw him?

But then it got worse.

"That Jade chick?" Lola added, flicking her hair back. "She might have to be handled too."

Zico didn't flinch. "Clean?"

Lola shrugged. "Only if necessary. But if it comes to that? Yeah. I'll make it look like an accident."

Shadow's heart hit his ribs like a drum. Jade. They were talking about Jade. He stepped back instinctively, but his heel caught a loose bottle.

Clink.

Silence.

"Who's there?" Zico barked.

Shadow didn't wait. He spun and sprinted down the hall, lungs burning. He flew down the stairwell, footsteps echoing in chaos behind him. His whole body felt like it was vibrating.

He burst out into the alley, ducked behind a dumpster, and pressed himself into the shadows. Every breath was like fire in his chest. He yanked his phone from his pocket, thumb shaking as it hovered over Jade's name.

But he hesitated.

What if they were watching her already? What if calling her put her in more danger?

Before he could decide, headlights flared at the alley's mouth. Car doors opened. Footsteps crunched. They were coming.

Shadow stuffed the phone into his pocket and ran. He reached his car, yanked the door open, and threw himself inside, locking it fast. His fingers gripped the wheel like a lifeline.

He stared into the rearview mirror. His eyes were wild. His jaw clenched. Fear. Rage. Betrayal. All of it warring in his gut.

He hadn't just lost control.

He'd pulled Jade into it.

He looked back at the glowing club sign one last time.

Everything was unraveling.

And this time, there might be no pulling it back together.

CHAPTER 14

BLOOD TIES AND BLIND SPOTS

The morning after the shooting at his Doc's penthouse was quiet. The kind of quiet that made your skin itch. No birds, no horns, just the dull whisper of wind brushing against the glass. Shadow could hear his own breathing, slow and uneven, and the faint ticking of a wall clock inside. Even the city, usually a constant backdrop of chaos, seemed to be holding its breath.

Shadow stood alone on the balcony, his hood pulled low over his eyes as he stared out across the Inner City skyline. He found a half-smoked blunt left on the coffee table from the night before. He didn't usually smoke, but right now, his nerves were frayed and his thoughts tangled. The acrid scent calmed him in a strange way.

Last night had changed everything.

He had driven around for hours after leaving the club, mind racing, thoughts churning. The things he'd overheard: Lola's voice, the way she spoke about Jade. It haunted him. He couldn't go home, couldn't call anyone, and definitely couldn't sleep. So he kept driving, looping around the Inner City until the sky began to fade from black to gray. When he finally pulled into Doc's underground garage, it was close to sunrise.

That's when he realized something was off.

Doc hadn't told him anyone would be there. But when he stepped into the penthouse, Lola was already inside. She didn't live there. She hadn't come with him. And yet, she was there, like she'd been waiting.

Now, inside the kitchen, the morning light spilled through the tall windows. Shadow sat stiffly at the counter, untouched eggs and toast growing cold in front of him. The hum of the refrigerator filled the space between them. Across the island, Lola leaned lazily against the counter in an oversized tee that clearly wasn't hers, sipping from a ceramic mug. Her eyes followed his every move, too curious to be casual.

He frowned. "How'd you even get in last night?"

Lola smiled over the rim of her mug. "Doc let me in," she said, tilting her head like it was no big deal. "Said I could wait for you. Figured you'd be back sooner or later."

Shadow's jaw tightened. Doc had given her access without saying a word to him. After everything he'd overheard, that felt like a betrayal. Not just from her, but from Doc too. Was Doc pulling strings and keeping secrets? His stomach turned, but he kept his face blank.

Lola had passed out shortly after he arrived. Champagne. Games. Sex that once ignited something in Shadow but now left him hollow. There had been a time when he craved her attention, convinced himself that her touch meant something real. But after everything he'd heard, the illusion was gone. Her body felt like armor he no longer wanted to wear. Each kiss, each moan, it all felt rehearsed, a performance in a script he was no longer willing to play along with.

He couldn't even look at her the same way. And the more she acted like nothing was wrong, the more it burned.

"You went to the club last night, didn't you?" she asked suddenly, watching him closely.

Shadow didn't blink. He set his fork down, calm and deliberate. "Yeah. I was looking for Doc. He said he'd be there. Didn't see him, so I left."

Lola tilted her head, the corners of her mouth curling. "You sure that's all you saw? You didn't happen to catch anything... unusual?"

His chest tightened, but he kept his tone level. "Why? Something I should've seen?"

A sly smile crept across her face. She swirled the coffee in her mug. "Just asking. Things move fast around here. Better to know who's watching."

He leaned back in his chair, matching her tone. "You think someone's watching me?"

"I think you're not as invisible as you think," she said, her voice a sugary blade. "And if you start sniffing around where you don't belong... people start asking questions."

There it was again. The threat wrapped in sweetness.

Shadow met her gaze evenly. "I only go where Doc tells me to."

Lola nodded slowly, but something flickered in her eyes. "That's good. I guess you're not all looks."

She turned and walked toward the guest room but paused at the doorway. Her tone stayed light, but the weight of her words was anything but.

"Oh, and Shadow? If Jade keeps popping up... she might find herself on the wrong end of somebody's patience. Just saying."

The door clicked shut behind her.

Shadow sat frozen, her words sinking like stones in his gut. His fists curled in his lap. That was it. She knew something. And now, she suspected he did too. And if she was throwing Jade's name around like that, then things were worse than he thought.

He stood, the chair scraping against the floor. He walked to the hallway, staring after the door Lola disappeared behind. His breath came hard and slow.

It was time to stop waiting.

It was time to find out the truth himself. Before someone else used it against him. This wasn't just about survival anymore.

This was about protecting the only thing left that still felt real. Jade.

* * *

The low hum of the city barely reached the tall windows of Doc's penthouse. Shadow moved through the hallway like a ghost, cautious and quiet. The living room was dim, empty, but still carried the leftovers of the night before: half-finished drinks on the table, a faint trace of expensive cologne in the air, and the soft thump of music leaking from a speaker somewhere deeper inside.

To Shadow, the place didn't feel like home. It never had. It felt like a mask, slick and smiling, hiding everything underneath. A space dressed up in power and flash, but heavy with secrets.

He hadn't planned to snoop. But ever since that conversation with Lola, and everything he'd overheard, something had been gnawing at him. Like there was a piece missing in a puzzle he didn't even know he was solving. Doc was hiding something, and Shadow was done being a pawn in someone else's game.

He made his way toward the office, the one room Doc always kept locked. Tonight, the door stood cracked open. Was it an accident? A setup? Shadow didn't care. He stepped in.

The office was clean, but it felt lived in. Trophies lined the walls: plaques, framed magazine covers, photos of Doc shaking hands with mayors, rappers, producers. It was a gallery of power. But to Shadow, it looked more like a stage.

As he moved toward the desk, his foot knocked against the leg of a chair, scraping it loudly against the floor.

"Smooth," he muttered under his breath. "Real smooth."

He bent to reposition the chair and paused. *What am I even hoping to find?* A confession? A clue? A reason to finally walk away?

Shadow opened the desk drawers, rummaging through paperwork: invoices, receipts, manila folders. Most of it looked routine. But tucked under a folder labeled *Southside Vendors*, something caught his eye.

A phone.

A burner.

He stared at it for a moment before picking it up. His heart thudded harder. It was the kind of phone you used when you didn't want to be found.

This was a line, he thought. *And I'm crossing it.*

Then a voice cut through the quiet.

"What are you doing in here?"

Shadow froze.

Lola stood in the doorway, hair tousled from sleep, Shadow's T-shirt barely covering her thighs. She rubbed her eyes, blinking at him. "Shadow?"

He slipped the phone into his hoodie pocket in one smooth motion, trying to stay calm.

"I heard noise," she said, stepping into the room. Her voice sharpened. "What are you doing in Doc's office?"

He noticed her eyes flick to the desk.

"I was looking for Doc," Shadow replied evenly, gently closing the drawer. "Didn't see him out there. Figured maybe he was in here."

"Really?" she said, arching a brow. "You thought he might be hiding in that drawer?"

He didn't answer.

His eyes caught on her necklace: a small gold pendant shaped like a phoenix in mid-rise. He had seen it before.

Not on her. In a photo. One of the many frames on Doc's wall. A younger Doc, arms around two people. A man and a little girl. The girl wore that same necklace.

A memory hit hard.

"I don't got kids. Closest I came was my boy Darrell's little girl. He died in a turf war years back. I made a promise I'd look after her."

She wasn't just some girl from the Inlands. She was *his* girl. The one Doc had sworn to protect. Which confirmed everything Shadow thought they had: every laugh, every touch, every moment. None of it was real.

He wasn't the prize.

He was the play.

"You're acting different," Lola said, stepping closer. "Like you're about to disappear."

He kept his eyes off her. "I got somewhere to be," he said, brushing past.

She leaned in the doorway with a pout. "You're already leaving?"

He didn't stop moving.

Her voice followed him, now low, syrupy, and edged. "Be careful, Shadow. People in this world? They'll lie straight to your face... and smile while they do it."

He didn't turn back.

The door clicked shut behind him. The burner in his pocket felt heavier now than when he'd found it. His fingers brushed the grip of the Glock Doc gave him, tucked inside his jacket.

Whatever was on that phone. It was worth hiding. And maybe dying for.

* * *

It had been hours since the sun dipped below the horizon, and Shadow hadn't slept in over twenty-four hours. After leaving the penthouse earlier, he'd driven aimlessly, too wired to rest, circling the edge of the

Outer City. At one point, he even drifted near Jade's neighborhood just to make sure no one was watching her place. He didn't stop, didn't go in. Just kept moving. Now he was back on foot. His car sat locked in a garage a few blocks away. Something about being on the move, able to duck and weave through the shadows, made him feel safer. In a car, he was a target. On foot, he had an edge.

He crossed the street and slipped down a narrow alley behind a shuttered corner store. His footsteps echoed off the concrete walls, a reminder that he was alone but still being watched. He reached into his hoodie pocket and pulled out the burner phone he'd taken from Doc's office.

His thumb hovered over the power button. He took a breath. Then pressed it.

The screen lit up. No password. Just a plain interface. Built for quick texts, nothing fancy. A burner, just like he thought. But now, with Lola likely to tell Doc what happened, this phone might be the only leverage he had.

Messages loaded.

Shadow scrolled. The words hit harder than bullets.

Text Thread: Jules↔ Doc

Jules: *Make it clean. That boy's the son of the ICS leader. Don't leave any room for mistakes.*

Doc: *It's done.*

Jules: *Good. No ties back.*

Shadow's stomach turned. *No ties back?* He *was* the tie. The one they used, manipulated. Jules, his own father. Doc, the man who claimed to look out for him.

Text Thread: Doc ↔ ICS Contact

Doc: *I'm giving you what you want. You take the heat off me.*

ICS: *You want Jules gone. We want revenge. Win-win.*

Doc: *His kid's still in the dark. But not for long.*

His pulse thudded in his ears. He had stumbled into a war that started long before he came around. And they were using him to finish it.

Text Thread: Doc ↔ Lola

Doc: *Keep him close. Keep Jade off balance.*

Lola: *If she starts getting to close?*

Doc: *Then end it. Quietly.*

His grip tightened. Lola. Her touches. Her lies. The way she made him feel like he mattered. It was all part of the play. A setup.

And Jade?

She was in the middle of it now, caught in a game she never asked to play.

He started to put the phone back in his jacket when it buzzed again.

New message. No name. Just a number.

Unknown (ICS): *The kid's on the move.*

Shadow froze. His chest tightened.

He looked up. The street was still.

He started walking fast. His heart pounded in his ears. His instincts screamed. They knew. Lola must've told Doc. Or someone else did. Now ICS was tracking him.

He reached for the Glock tucked into his waistband.

SCREECH.

A black sedan whipped around the corner, headlights slicing through the dark like blades.

Shadow's fingers brushed the grip of the gun but the shots came first.

Gunfire exploded from the back seat. One, maybe two shooters. Their muzzle flashes lit up the block like fireworks.

Shadow dove behind a parked car. A bullet caught his shoulder mid-dive, ripping through hoodie and skin. He hit the ground hard, a shout stuck in his throat.

The burner phone flew from his hand, clattering across the pavement. It landed inches from his face.

Sirens wailed nearby. Police were already closing in. The sedan sped off, tires screeching.

Shadow gritted his teeth. He rolled to his side, pressing a hand against his shoulder. The pain was blinding. He looked down and saw blood soaking his hoodie, running down his arm. The tear was deep. Clean but brutal. Blood pooled fast, hot and slick on the concrete.

But his expression didn't show fear.

Just fury.

They played him. Lied to him. And now they were trying to end him.

He reached out, grabbed the phone again. Held it tight.

His voice was low. Fierce.

"You watching me?"

He rose slowly, jaw clenched, shoulder burning. His figure cut sharp against the streetlight behind him, blood dripping onto the pavement.

"Then I guess I'll put on a show."

* * *

The world tilted as Shadow stumbled forward, clutching his bleeding shoulder. Each step sent sharp pain shooting down his arm. Blood soaked through his hoodie and dripped onto the pavement with every movement. He still hadn't been to sleep. The exhaustion weighed on him like chains. His vision blurred, thoughts cloudy, but he kept moving, driven by a mixture of fear and fury.

Somewhere nearby, he thought he heard footsteps, maybe a voice, but it could've been the blood loss playing tricks on him. He hugged the shadows, staying close to the buildings. Across the street, headlights flashed. A police cruiser crawled by. He ducked his head and turned into a side alley, heart thudding.

The garage. It wasn't far now. Two turns. Just two.

He gritted his teeth and pushed forward, dragging his hand along the wall for balance. When he reached the entrance, his knees buckled, but he caught himself on the railing, barely holding on. Level two. Row B. His car waited like a lifeline.

Fumbling with his keys, he finally managed to unlock the door and collapsed into the driver's seat. His body sagged against the leather, the adrenaline wearing thin. He gasped through the pain and twisted around, reaching into the back seat. His fingers closed around a crumpled T-shirt he'd left behind weeks ago.

He pressed it to his shoulder, biting down to stop himself from screaming. Blood quickly soaked the fabric. His hands trembled as he tightened the makeshift bandage. For a few minutes, he just sat there, listening to the hum of the city above and his own ragged breathing.

Eventually, the chaos in his chest slowed. His heart steadied. The pain dulled into a background throb.

He reached into his jacket and pulled out the burner phone. The same phone that had nearly gotten him killed. He stared at it for a moment, then unlocked it and tapped into the media folder.

First file: a picture of him and Jade walking down a sidewalk. She was laughing, her face turned toward his, her arm linked through his. He remembered that day.

Next: Blurry footage from outside the club. Jules standing alone. Doc's voice offscreen: "Keep him close. Let Jules keep thinking he's in control."

Another file: security cam footage from the mall. Shadow entering. Lola at the counter. She smiled up at him like she hadn't known he was coming, but clearly she had.

He scrolled.

Audio File.

Doc: "If he figures it out, he becomes a liability."

Lola: "He won't. I don't know what you're planning, but I'll help you. Until you help me find my brother's killer."

Silence.

Shadow leaned back against the seat, every breath shallow. His muscles trembled. Rage simmered beneath his skin, but it couldn't mask the truth: he'd been used. Played by everyone.

His phone buzzed.

Ty: *Yo. E's stable for now. He been asking about you.*

Shadow let out a breath. Finally, some good news. E was alive.

But relief didn't last long.

He couldn't go to the hospital. That was off the table. Too many questions. Too much exposure. But he knew someone, someone who could patch him up, no questions asked. It wasn't safe, but it was his only option.

Doc had once told him, in that gravel-and-iron voice of his, "If you ever get hit and can't go to a hospital, go there. Ask for Rico. Say nothing else."

He gritted his teeth, stuffed the burner phone back into his jacket, and started the car.

As the engine rumbled to life, Shadow caught a glimpse of himself in the rearview mirror. Blood streaked his hoodie. His eyes were sunken, rimmed with exhaustion. But somewhere behind that, fire still burned.

He tapped the wheel with trembling fingers.

"Let's see how deep this rabbit hole goes."

CHAPTER 15

NEUTRAL GROUNDS

Blood still covered the side of his hoodie, warm and sticky against his ribs, but Shadow didn't stop driving. Every second hurt. The kind of pain that reminded him he was still alive. Still in the game. Still a threat. Barely. He could feel the blood still leaking. He wasn't sure he'd make it before blacking out.

But he pushed forward.

The night felt like it was pressing in on him. Shadow didn't stop until he saw the flickering red light over a dented metal door. It looked like nothing important, just another run-down building in the Inner City.

He knocked: twice fast, then once more after a pause. Exactly like Doc told him. Shadow didn't question it. Not out loud. But as his hand hit the door, doubt crept in. Doc knew too much. He knew Shadow was hurt. He knew where he'd end up. It was starting to feel like Shadow was playing into someone else's plan.

The door slit opened. A tired, red eye stared at him, scanned him, and then disappeared. The door clicked open slowly.

Rico stood in the shadows. His face was lined with years of hard living. He didn't say a word, just tilted his chin toward a beat-up leather chair under a weak ceiling light.

Shadow stumbled inside. His legs weren't injured, but the blood loss made them shaky. Every step felt like he was dragging bricks.

The place smelled like oil, old metal, and smoke, like a mechanic's shop that had been forgotten. Shadow didn't know if this was an old garage, a safehouse, or just Rico's personal hideout. It didn't matter. It felt dependable in a rough, underground way. The single bulb cast a dull yellow light over the room. A scratched-up radio crackled with static on a metal table. Next to it sat a bottle of gin and a greasy toolkit. This wasn't a hospital, but it looked like it had patched up plenty of people.

Shadow dropped into the chair, his breathing rough. Blood soaked through the rip in his hoodie and into the seat, but Rico didn't react. He moved quickly, grabbing an old first aid kit, some tweezers, and a rag that had seen better days. No warning. No talking. Just action.

He poured clear alcohol on the wound.

Shadow clenched his teeth and took the burn without flinching.

"Doc still vouchin' for you?" Rico asked, his voice rough and scratchy.

Shadow hesitated. He thought about the phone. The shots fired. Doc's name in all of it.

"Yeah," he said. "Something like that."

"Man, you remind me of your father," Rico said.

That hit a nerve. Shadow's eye twitched. His stomach tightened. Being told he was like his father didn't feel like a compliment. Every time someone said it, it reminded him of the legacy he was trying to break free from.

The tweezers went in. Sharp pain shot through him.

Shadow clenched his jaw and breathed slowly through his nose. The room spun a little. He tasted blood. But he didn't move.

Rico dropped the bloody fragment into a metal tray with a clink. Then, with steady hands, he threaded a needle.

"You boys think you're untouchable until you start bleeding," Rico said as he stitched. "Everybody bleeds."

Shadow stayed quiet. He looked around the room. Shelves stacked with ammo boxes. A wall covered in old Polaroid pictures. One caught his eye: a younger Rico standing with two other men, rifles in hand and dirt on their faces.

Rico saw him looking. "That was before everything changed. We fought for a purpose. Now it's just for turf."

"Can you keep this quiet? I don't want Doc to worry," Shadow said.

"Doc don't worry about anything but Doc, money, and women. But don't worry, I keep things quiet. I don't want people knowing you were here either. I heard ICS is hunting you. And it's not because they like you."

He tied the last stitch with a tug.

Rico slapped a fresh bandage on the wound. "You'll live. But don't stay long. This place isn't as low-key as it used to be."

Shadow nodded. He stood up, shaky, vision still a little blurry, but his mind was clear. He had a plan now. Whatever Doc was up to, Shadow wasn't going to keep playing along. While Rico cleaned up in the back, Shadow scanned the room. No cameras. But his eyes landed on a picture on the wall: Rico, Doc, his father, and Darrell. He recognized Darrell from the photo in Doc's penthouse.

His stomach turned.

Shadow slipped a hand into his hoodie pocket and pulled out the burner phone.

He turned it on. The screen glowed.

Four unread messages. No names, just one number, over and over.

Of course. Doc probably knew he had the phone. Probably knew he got shot. If the shooters had followed him, Doc definitely knew where he'd go. This place. Rico's. It wasn't just a hiding spot; it was a checkpoint on a route Doc probably helped design.

He didn't open the texts.

Instead, he whispered, voice low and sharp:

"Time to flip the board."

Then he walked out the door and disappeared into the night.

* * *

The Inland night air was colder than Shadow expected. Not the kind of cold that sank into your bones, but sharp enough to keep you on edge. Every gust through the grapevines, every distant bark or screech of tires made him tighten up. He stayed hidden near a shipping container. Doc had once told him about this spot during a late-night talk. But Shadow hadn't come blindly. After slipping out of Rico's, he circled the area, checking for exits, blind spots, and any signs of recent activity. Doc's advice led him here, but Shadow made sure it was still good ground.

"If you ever need to disappear," Doc had said, smoke curling between them on the penthouse rooftop, "go to the Inlands. There's a small shipping yard behind the old vineyard. Nobody asks questions out there. You lay low till things cool off."

That felt like a lifetime ago. Back when Shadow believed Doc was just a mentor. Not a manipulator.

He was running on fumes. He hadn't slept since before the shooting, and now the adrenaline was wearing off. Every blink came with the risk of closing his eyes too long. But this wasn't over. Not yet.

His shoulder still ached from the graze. The bandage Rico had slapped on it itched, but the pain kept him alert. He leaned against a rusted fence post, eyes on the dirt road. This was his one shot at getting answers.

Crouching lower, Shadow kept watch on the road leading into the lot. The stitched wound in his shoulder pulsed beneath the bandage. He cracked his neck, trying to stay loose. Headlights flared in the distance.

Earlier, just after leaving Rico's, Shadow had pulled out the burner phone. Pretending to be Doc, he sent a message to the number that had texted earlier. He hesitated before pressing send, wondering if they'd see through the act. Could they trace him? Would Doc find out? It didn't matter now.

Shadow (as Doc): *Meet me. Inlands. Old ship yard. Come alone.*

He didn't know if they'd show. Or worse, if they'd bring backup. But he couldn't wait around. Not after being shot. Not after finding out both Jules and Doc had lied to him. Not after realizing ICS might be chasing something that had nothing to do with him, until now.

Nearly forty minutes passed before anything happened. During that time, Shadow shifted positions to keep blood flowing through his legs. He scanned the gravel for fresh tire marks and used his phone screen as a mirror to check the tree line behind him. His shoulder burned, but the sharp pain had dulled to a steady throb. He flexed his fingers now and then to keep the arm mobile. One gun. Fully loaded. No extras. Every move from here had to count.

Finally, a black SUV rolled into view. Its engine purred low as it crept across the gravel. Dust followed in its wake. No second vehicle. No shadows in the brush. Just one figure stepping out under the flickering floodlight. Tall. Fit. Dressed in black. An ICS soldier. And not just any soldier. Shadow's jaw clenched as the man stepped into the light. Recognition hit hard.

It was him.

The shooter from that night. The one who dropped E.

Shadow rose from the darkness, calm and locked in. The man had a gun tucked at his waist but hadn't drawn it.

"Took you long enough," Shadow said.

The man narrowed his eyes. A smirk crept across his face. "Wait a second... you're not—"

He reached for his gun.

Shadow lifted his own, aiming fast.

The man froze.

Then his expression changed as he studied Shadow more closely. The smirk faded.

"You set me up," he said, his voice tight with anger.

They began to circle each other slowly. Gravel shifted underfoot.

"So what is this? Loyalty test? Trying to make a name for yourself?"

Shadow's voice was low. "I want to know who thought they could shoot up my block like it's nothing."

The man scoffed. "Your block? Last I checked, your dad's the one wearing the crown. This is war. Boundaries blur."

Shadow moved.

He didn't shoot. Not yet. Killing him would be easy. Too easy. But answers? Those had to be taken.

A sharp step forward. Elbow up. He struck fast, brutal. The man's head snapped to the side, body twisting with the momentum. Shadow didn't give him time to recover. Another blow to the gut, a swift knee to the back of the leg, and the ICS soldier collapsed.

Before the man could get his bearings, Shadow had him face-down, zip-ties tightening around his wrists. The soldier grunted, trying to twist out of it, but Shadow drove a knee into his spine. Click. One zip tie. Then another. Shadow yanked them tight with his free hand and teeth, keeping his gun arm locked at the elbow. The injured arm was good for nothing but balance now, but adrenaline made up the difference. The man thrashed, but Shadow had pain, rage, and determination all working in sync.

"You were at the park," Shadow said, low. Not a question.

"Clearly," the man spat, face brushing dust.

Shadow dragged him upright and shoved him against a rusted support beam. The moonlight caught the side of the soldier's face. A thin scar ran along his jawline, too clean to be accidental.

"What's your angle here?" the soldier growled.

"You're going to talk," Shadow said.

Shadow reached into his pocket and yanked the man's burner phone out, more to confirm what he already suspected than to learn something new. The screen lit up. Same number from Doc's burner.

He crushed it under his boot.

"So it was you," Shadow said. "The park. Outer City. You shot my boy."

The soldier stared back with cold, empty eyes.

"Wrong place, wrong time," he muttered. "Bullets don't have names on them. My gun's rated E for everyone."

The words cut deep. Shadow's body went still. He pictured E on the pavement, blood spreading fast, eyes fixed on nothing. That moment had never left him.

He stepped in close.

"Say that again," he whispered.

The soldier smirked. "Don't go soft now. Not after all this. You chose this life."

Shadow's fist flew.

The punch wasn't clean or precise, just pure rage. Pain and exhaustion bubbled over. The jolt lit up his injured shoulder, but he didn't care. The soldier slumped, blood dripping from his lip.

Shadow stood over him, breathing hard. His body trembled, part anger, part fatigue, part blood loss. For a second, he nearly lost himself.

But he caught it.

"Who gave the order?" he asked.

The soldier spat blood. "I don't get names. Just targets."

"You're lying."

"Think I'm scared? Pull the trigger."

Shadow didn't.

He crouched low, face close.

"I want Lucien," he said. "I heard his name at Doc's place. He's involved. Don't act like he's not."

He raised the gun slightly.

"Is he running things now? Or is he just hiding behind the curtains?"

A twitch. A subtle shift in posture. The name had weight.

"You don't want Lucien," the man said. "You don't even want to know what table he sits at. You're just a rich kid playing gangster."

"Then why are you working with Doc? Why does Lucien care about me?" Shadow asked, shoving the barrel closer.

The soldier's tone dropped. Cold. Bitter.

"This war started before you were born. You're just a fuse."

The words landed hard. Shadow didn't fully understand them, but that was what made them worse. It hinted at something bigger, older, messier. He wasn't just being hunted. He was being used.

"Ask your dear old dad," the man added.

Shadow's jaw clenched. "Tell Lucien I'm coming. Not with warnings. Not with threats. With fire. If E dies... I'm not just lighting up your corner. I'm burning it down."

No response.

Shadow turned and walked to the SUV.

"What are you doing?" the soldier called.

No answer. Shadow opened the door and paused. Something about the man's calmness didn't sit right. He searched the backseat and found a duffel bag under the seat. Inside: a second burner phone, a velvet pouch of small blue pills, opioids or maybe ecstasy, a loaded gun, and a stack of dirty cash.

Shadow let out a breath and dialed.

"Yeah. Black SUV. Shipyard behind the vineyard. Plates are..." He read them off. "Saw him dealing."

He hung up.

The sirens weren't close yet. But they would be.

He walked back to the soldier and crouched.

"Next time you show up in my world," he said, voice like steel, "you don't leave it."

He leaned closer.

"And tell your boss..."

He paused.

"I'm not my father."

The words cut through the air. Jules would've pulled the trigger or sent someone else to do it. No hesitation. No warning. That was his way. Shadow didn't know if holding back made him stronger or weaker, but it made him different. He wasn't here to be a copy of the man who raised him. He wasn't here to be feared like his father.

This was about control.

And about choosing who he would become.

* * *

The Inlands faded behind Shadow as he drove, but the soldier's words kept echoing. *You're just a fuse.*

Every twist of the steering wheel sent pain tearing through his wounded shoulder. The face of the shooter wouldn't leave him: cold smirk, empty eyes, the way he talked like E's life was just collateral damage. Shadow hadn't slept. Hadn't stopped. Couldn't. Not now.

The phone rested on the passenger seat, cracked and streaked with dried blood but still powered on. He glanced at it, then back at the dark road ahead. There was one more move left tonight. One more name he had to call.

He pulled into an old rest stop off the freeway. A lone streetlamp buzzed overhead, its flickering light barely cutting through the night.

The world around him was still. Eerie. The kind of quiet that only comes before everything falls apart.

Shadow leaned back in the seat. He was running on fumes: blood loss, no sleep, and a storm of thoughts tearing him apart. He'd zip-tied a man. Punched him. Threatened to kill him. And in the end, he still didn't have all the answers.

He scrolled through his contacts until he found the name.

Jade.

His thumb hovered over the screen. Then he tapped it.

The phone rang.

Once. Twice.

"Hello?"

Her voice hit him like a punch to the chest.

"It's me," he said.

"Shadow? Are you okay? I heard about the house, your friend... Shadow, talk to me."

Her voice cracked on the last word. He could hear the fear laced behind it.

"I'm okay. Not great, but alive. I need you to listen. Carefully."

She sucked in a breath.

"Something's going down. Bigger than I thought. Doc and my father... I don't know if they're against each other or working together. And ICS? They're not just moving, they're watching. I think you're already on their radar."

Silence.

Then she asked, "So what do we do?"

"You and your brother disappear. Tonight. Go somewhere safe, somewhere you trust. Don't go back to your apartment. Don't talk to anyone. Don't call me after this. Not until I say it's safe."

"No. I'm not running."

"Jade, please. This isn't about being tough. It's about surviving. If you stay out in the open, they will find you."

Her voice dropped.

"I think they already did."

His heart stopped. "What?"

"Two men and a woman. Parked outside my building last night. They never got out. Just watched. I felt it. I stayed with my cousin after that. I didn't want to tell you until I knew what it meant."

Shadow shut his eyes, jaw tightening.

"It means I was too late."

"No," she said, stronger now. "You're right on time. We just have to move smarter. Together."

He swallowed hard. Wanted to believe that. Needed to. But after everything, he didn't know if being together made her safer or put a target on her back.

He said nothing.

But she wasn't finished.

"Don't shut me out. Not again."

Then, softer: "And this isn't just about ICS or Doc. I haven't forgotten that call, Shadow. The one from my friend. About you and Lola. I never got the truth. I'm not asking you to be perfect, but if you want me with you, if we're going to survive this together, you can't lie to me anymore."

It hit hard. Not because she was wrong. But because she was still here. Still answering his call. Still offering a chance.

He didn't deserve her.

But he needed her.

"Where can I meet you?" she asked.

He looked out the windshield into the night. He thought about the safehouse. The vineyard. The bridge over Parker Creek.

"I'll let you know once I'm sure it's safe."

"Okay," Jade said, her voice full of worry. "Just... be careful. I'll see what I can find out."

Before he could say anything else, the line went dead.

Shadow sat in the driver's seat, phone in his lap, heart pounding.

One shot left. One shot to figure out who he could bring into the war, and who was already waiting on the other side.

CHAPTER 16

QUIET BLEEDS

The city felt colder when you had something to lose: family, friends, the girl who still picked up when she had every reason not to. Shadow felt all of it now, the weight of it sinking into his bones, chilling him in ways the wind never could. It was the next day, though everything blurred together into one long stretch of pain, fear, and regret.

After catching a few hours of sleep, he'd stopped by Rico's shop. Rico didn't ask questions. He just patched up Shadow's shoulder with fresh bandages, slid a couple of pain pills across the counter, and muttered, "Make this the last time, unless you're dying. I'm only doing this because me and your dad go way back. I ain't tryna get mixed up with ICS."

Rico handed him an extra roll of gauze and a small bottle of pills for the road. Shadow nodded his thanks and left without another word.

Now, he sat alone on a crumbling rooftop near the edge of the Inner City. The rooftops used to feel like freedom. Now they just felt like distance, distance from E, from Jade, from the version of himself that hadn't wrecked everything.

Below, the city buzzed with sirens wailing in the distance and faint music from a party echoing between alley walls.

His phone buzzed once in his pocket. Then again.

He didn't move. Just stared at the screen: an old thread with E. A meme from a dumb late-night text. A video of E roasting Ty's hairline. Their half-baked plan to turn Shadow's room into a recording studio. His throat tightened.

Buzz.

He finally answered.

Ty's voice came through low and strained, like he was barely holding it together. In the background, Shadow caught the sound of beeping machines, the shuffle of nurses, someone yelling for a crash cart.

"They're prepping him for another surgery," Ty said. "Third one since he got in. Bullet tore through a major artery. They stopped the bleeding last time, but… they're saying it might not hold."

Shadow's grip on the edge of the roof turned his knuckles white. He shut his eyes and let the pain swirl inside him, physical and emotional, all of it bleeding together. He could still hear the soldier's voice from yesterday: "Wrong place, wrong time. Bullet doesn't have a name on it."

But E's name might as well have been carved into that bullet.

Ty exhaled. "Just thought you should know."

Click.

Shadow stayed frozen, the phone still pressed to his ear even after the line went dead. A sharp gust of wind caught the edge of his hoodie, slicing through him. It wasn't the cold that made his eyes sting.

It was the image of E. Pale and broken, lying in a hospital bed, cut open again… maybe for the last time. And he was up here, hiding from it all, pretending he had more time.

No more.

He stood. His shoulder screamed with pain, but he ignored it. Every step toward the fire escape felt heavier than the last. He didn't know what he'd find when he got there. He just knew one thing:

If this was goodbye. He had to be the one to say it.

* * *

The hospital room was dim, lit only by the steady glow of machines: green pulses and red numbers blinking like life had been reduced to math. E lay motionless beneath too-white sheets, his skin pale, lips cracked, IV lines branching out from both arms like delicate spiderwebs. He looked smaller than Elijah remembered. Fragile in a way that made Elijah's chest tighten.

Elijah pulled a chair close and sat, elbows resting on his knees, hands clasped like a prayer, not because he believed in it, but because it gave his guilt somewhere to go.

"I found the guy who pulled the trigger," he said, his voice low and steady. "He's locked up. Might talk, might not. Depends how loud he wants to sing."

He looked down at his hands, fingers laced tight.

"I'm ending this. All of it. No more people bleeding because I didn't know when to walk away."

It had only been two days since E was shot, but it felt like weeks. Time moved differently now, stretched and twisted by regret, by sleepless nights, by memories that refused to sit still.

E stirred. His eyelids fluttered. Then slowly, they opened, hazy but locked on Elijah.

Elijah straightened, startled by the sight of E awake. A mix of relief and dread surged through him.

"Eli...jah," E rasped. His voice was barely a whisper. "Don't."

Elijah didn't respond right away. His body was rigid, but his eyes gave away the storm inside.

"You think vengeance fixes this?" E asked, his breath thin.

A long pause.

"No," Elijah admitted. "But maybe it stops the next one."

The door creaked open.

Ty stepped into the room, breathless like he'd run the whole way there. His hoodie clung to his back, and his eyes, bloodshot and puffy, narrowed when they found Elijah.

"I know that look," Ty said, voice low but sharp. "You're about to do something dumb. Again."

Elijah rose slowly, the weight of his body sinking into his bandaged shoulder.

Ty shook his head. "You wanna act hard, cool. Go chase danger. But keep that energy away from us. Last thing we want is more bodies."

The words hit like fists. Elijah flinched, but said nothing.

Ty brushed past him, intentionally clipping Elijah's wounded side. Elijah winced but didn't react.

"They shouldn't have let him in," Ty muttered to E. "That's not the Elijah the Outer City knew."

E didn't reply. His eyes drifted shut again, breath shallow but steady.

Elijah lingered.

E's voice returned, a soft whisper through cracked lips. "Whatever you're turning into... don't forget who you were."

The words hit deep. Elijah looked at them. His brothers. One fading, the other fuming.

He gave a small nod.

"Don't worry," he said, his voice barely above a whisper. "I'll make this right."

Then Shadow turned and stepped into the hallway, where the fluorescent lights felt colder than the winter air outside.

He walked alone. Carrying the weight of a promise. And the chilling sense that he might not get another chance to keep it.

* * *

Shadow sat hunched in a corner booth, hood pulled low over his head, hands clasped tightly on the table. Earlier that day, he'd finally opened one of Jules's messages:

Meet me at the old pool hall on the border 2pm.

It was a place neither of them had been to in years, but its memory hadn't faded. His phone sat face down beside him, hiding dozens of unread texts from his mom. She'd been trying, calling, messaging, but he hadn't answered. Not yet.

He didn't look up when the door creaked open.

Jules stepped in, coat drawn close to block out the cold, his eyes sweeping the room with practiced awareness. That same alertness. Like muscle memory. Like the part of him that had never stopped looking over his shoulder. He nodded at the bartender like he still belonged, and a drink was already waiting for him.

Watching his dad enter brought everything rushing back.

* * *

I remember the times my dad brought me here. I must've been around nine or ten. It was always after basketball practice, just the two of us. He called it our secret hideout, a place where the pressure couldn't follow us. Said we needed somewhere to think, to breathe. And it really felt like that. Like all the noise outside stopped the second we stepped in. It was just him and me, and in that moment, nothing else mattered: not the expectations, not the pressure of school, not even the secrets I hadn't yet learned to question. Just the quiet understanding between a boy and his dad, held together by the click of billiard balls and the rare feeling that I could just be a kid.

My mom would've been pissed if she ever knew. She hated this side of the city, called it poison. But with Dad, it felt safe.

Back then, this place wasn't a pool hall. It used to be a small storefront. Dad told stories about the woman who ran it, Karina. Said she reminded him of Mom when he was tipsy, though he never said it directly. Karina ran a tight shop in the front, but in the back? That was where the guy who owned it made the real moves. Shipments, strategy, coded calls. He made it sound like a command center disguised as a corner store.

One day it was just gone. I asked him why. He stared at nothing for so long I thought he didn't hear me. I never brought it up again. But every time he mentioned Karina, his voice dropped, like she was more than just someone who ran a store.

* * *

The pool hall was dead quiet. Dust hung in the air like the memory he just had. One light buzzed above a scratched table.

Jules slid into the booth across from Shadow, his eyes drifting across the room. They stopped on the old pool table in the corner—their table. Shadow caught the flicker in his gaze as it brushed over the carved initials, JE. He said nothing, but he noticed.

"You got my message," Jules said, settling in. "This place brings back a lot of memories. Feels like a different life."

He took a sip of his drink, but his eyes stayed sharp. Then the edge came back to his voice. "ICS is heating up. I've been feeding them fake info, trying to stall them, but it's not working anymore. They're moving like they know me: like really know me. Every step I take, they're one ahead. Makes me think they've been watching for years. And I don't know who to trust. My whole crew? Might already be in Doc's pocket. It's just us now, Lij. Whether we like it or not."

Shadow didn't respond at first. His face stayed still. "While you were pretending to stay clean, keeping secrets from me and Mom, you made it sound noble. You made it seem like you were better than this. Like staying away made you noble."

Jules's jaw tightened, guilt breaking through the surface. "Don't tell your mom about any of this," he said, almost pleading. "I just handle the books."

Shadow gave a dry chuckle. "Yeah? Well, Mr. Book Keeper... I don't know if I can trust you."

Jules's eyes sharpened, but he stayed quiet.

Shadow leaned in. "First time I ever bled in the Inner City, I was with Ty and E. We got rushed by two guys who pulled guns on us. One shoved a piece in Ty's face. E froze and peed on himself. I got grazed. Someone else down the block caught the bullet. We ran."

He kept his voice low and even. "Later, I saw those same guys again. Told Doc. Thought he'd handle it." He paused, then continued. "He took me out back. One of them was already there. Bloodied. Barely breathing. Doc gave me a gun. Told me it was time to stop being Elijah. Said I needed to become Shadow."

Shadow caught it. His father's hand clenched against the edge of the booth.

"I pulled the trigger," he said. "Didn't even ask about the guy's family. Didn't matter."

Jules didn't flinch. But Shadow saw the shift in his posture. The way his chest stopped rising for a second.

"That was your hit, wasn't it?" Shadow asked, calm but sharp. "That was the job you ordered."

Jules finally spoke. His voice was tired. "I make the call. I don't shoot the ball."

Shadow shook his head. "You didn't just let this happen. You helped build it."

Jules stood up like the truth was too heavy to sit with. "Then don't trust me," he said. "But move smart. Stay alive."

He turned to leave.

Shadow watched him walk away. Just as Jules reached the door, Shadow said: "I met your friend Rico."

Jules froze mid-step. His shoulders tightened. Every part of him went rigid, like the name had knocked the wind out of him.

He didn't turn around.

After a long pause, he just said, "Call your mom. She's worried sick." And then he disappeared into the cold.

Shadow stayed seated in the quiet. And the name Elijah felt like a story someone else used to tell.

* * *

Shadow stayed at the pool hall longer than he should have. It was quiet, out of the way. A place nobody would expect to find him. He ate, had a couple drinks, and played a few games of pool. Tried to act like he wasn't being hunted. But he knew better. The clock was ticking. Every second, the walls closed in tighter.

Now he sat in the driver's seat of his car, parked behind a building in a narrow alley. The sunset bled through the windshield, painting everything in orange and gold. It made the world look tired, like it had seen too much. His gun lay across his lap, safety off. He watched the street like a hawk, body still, finger near the trigger. In this life, hesitation could mean death.

His phone buzzed.

He didn't move. Just glanced down.

Unknown Number: *Is this Shadow?*

His brow furrowed. Another unknown name.

He typed back:

Who wants to know?

The phone rang.

He didn't say a word. Just answered, lifting the phone to his ear with one hand while keeping the other on the gun.

A calm, confident voice came through the speaker.

"I'm an old friend of your father's," the man said. "He saved my life once. I owe him. And I've got information you need."

Shadow said nothing.

"If you want the details, meet me tomorrow. One o'clock. Steakhouse. Back of the Inlands."

Shadow's voice was quiet, but sharp. "The last so-called friend of my dad's I trusted left me bleeding. What makes you any different?"

The man let out a low chuckle. Not smug. Almost like he pitied him.

"Because if I meant to hurt you, you'd already be hurt."

Shadow went still.

His eyes scanned the street through the windshield. Empty.

Then suddenly, an engine roared to life. Tires screeched. A car peeled off down the block and vanished into the night.

He raised the gun slightly, breath held. Waited.

Nothing.

A moment passed. Then another. He slowly lowered the weapon.

He didn't trust the man. Didn't trust anyone. But he needed answers.

He was going to that steakhouse. Not for peace. For the next piece of the puzzle. And maybe, if it turned out to be a setup. To end it.

Shadow loaded a fresh mag, checked the spare clip, and slid the burner into his waistband. Then he pulled onto the road and disappeared into the dark.

CHAPTER 17
FUEL TO THE FIRE

The steakhouse sat at the edge of the Inlands like a memory that wouldn't fade. Its red bricks were worn, the neon sign buzzed and flickered, and the smell of old grease clung to the air like smoke from a long-dead fire. It was the kind of place people went to disappear. Or get caught slipping.

Shadow parked three blocks away and walked the rest, hoodie up, gun tucked into the back of his jeans. He had noticed the silver sedan trailing him earlier, then saw it again parked a few spots from the steakhouse. He didn't stop or slow down. Just kept moving.

Inside, the place was dim. Torn booths lined the walls. Lights buzzed overhead. Three older customers sat scattered around, drinking coffee. None looked up when he walked in.

A large man sat alone in the back booth. Shadow didn't recognize him. He paused. Maybe he expected someone smaller, someone who knew his father. But this guy? He was massive. He filled the booth like it had been built around him. Not even close to being "tiny."

Shadow didn't know whether to feel relieved or more on edge. But something about this felt important.

The man, Tiny, was broad and bearded, with a beat-up leather vest stretched over his frame. Tattoos snaked along his arms and under his sleeves. He stabbed a piece of steak with his fork like he had a grudge against it.

He didn't stand when Shadow approached. Just gave a nod and kept eating.

Shadow hovered beside the table, unsure whether to speak or sit. His eyes scanned the exits and corners.

He started to say something, but Tiny raised a thick finger without looking up. He kept chewing. The message was clear: wait.

Shadow sighed and slid into the booth.

Eventually, Tiny spoke.

"Your father ever tell you about Jakarta?" he asked, still chewing.

"No," Shadow said, his gaze fixed on Tiny's hands.

"Didn't think so. He saved my life out there. That's why you're here. I owe him."

"So talk."

Tiny wiped his mouth with a napkin. His eyes flicked toward the front, then back. "Lucien and Doc's alliance? It didn't start with blood."

He leaned forward, lowering his voice. "Way before your time, your dad, Doc, and a guy named Darrell ran their own crew. Real tight. This was before ICS got big. Back then, ICS was just backup muscle. No brains. But your dad had bigger plans. He left, took a bunch of info, and built something different."

Shadow furrowed his brow. Trying to picture Jules and Darrell on the same team felt off.

Tiny kept going. "Darrell got caught in the middle. Word is, he died in a turf war. Not long after, the name 'Lucien' started spreading. No one's seen him. No photos. No voice. Just whispers and fear. Folks say he's a ghost. But ICS moves like someone's calling shots."

He tapped the table with a finger. "Doc acted like he could keep the peace. Then he started playing sides: ICS, city officials, your dad. Feeding everyone just enough to keep them hungry."

Shadow narrowed his eyes. "What changed?"

Tiny leaned back. "Something called the Hawthorne File. Last I saw it, it was locked in your dad's safe. Then it vanished."

Shadow's pulse jumped. He remembered seeing the name. "What's in it?"

Tiny gave a dark chuckle. "Depends who you ask. Some say it's a kill list. Doc calls it leverage. Your dad? He said it was a blueprint: everything they built, and everyone they burned to build it."

Shadow stayed quiet, mind racing. How did this guy know so much?

"There's names in there. Old ones. New ones. One stands out: Cambria. Goes by Phoenix now. Young. Smart. Deadly. Works behind the scenes for Doc. Rumor is she cleans up messes. They say she's looking for whoever killed her brother. They also say if you cross her path, turn around. Fast."

Tiny leaned in. "She wears a gold phoenix pendant. Wings out, mid-rise. Pretty little thing. You see it, you'll know."

Shadow's mind flashed to Lola. The necklace. The way it shimmered when she laughed. The way she touched it when she thought he wasn't watching. A knot tightened in his gut. Had he already met Cambria without knowing it?

Tiny slid a folded slip of paper across the table.

"Storage yard. Inlands. Near the docks. A quiet place. You want answers? Start there."

Shadow took the paper and stood.

"One more thing," Tiny said, still not looking up. "You were followed. Woman. Silver car. You better hope it wasn't her."

Shadow blinked. "How do you know that?"

Tiny looked at him for the first time. "It's my job to know. Nobody in the Inner City follows someone without me noticing. And she's still parked outside."

Shadow stared at him. He hadn't expected this guy to be this sharp. He wasn't just muscle. He was connected. Dangerous in a quiet, calculating way. Maybe this wasn't just a favor. Maybe it was the start of something bigger.

Shadow gave a slow nod and turned to leave.

Before he reached the door, Tiny called out, voice low and firm. "You better be ready, kid. You're in the big leagues now."

Shadow didn't look back. He gave Tiny a small nod and walked out of the steakhouse.

* * *

Shadow slipped out the side door. The silver sedan was still there, engine idling up the street. He didn't head toward it. Instead, he circled the block, cut through an alley beside a hardware store, and crept up from behind.

Gun drawn.

He grabbed the door handle... then yanked it open.

Jade.

"Why are you following me?" Shadow barked.

She flinched hard. "Damn, Shadow. You almost gave me a heart attack," she said, clutching her chest.

Shadow didn't lower the gun.

"Give me one reason not to pull the trigger."

His heart was racing. *What the hell was Jade doing here?* A setup? Doc's move? Or worse? She was working with someone else. His pulse thundered in his ears. One hand stayed tight on the grip of his gun.

She didn't look away.

"Because I'm not your enemy," she said calmly. Then, after a pause, "And because I found something... something called the Hawthorne File."

Shadow blinked. He hadn't expected that. Especially not from her. How could Jade have found out about it? Shock. Fear. Frustration. It all churned in his stomach.

His grip on the door tightened. He looked her in the eye, searching for any hint of a lie. But Jade just stared back.

"I told you to lay low," he said finally. "Not go digging for answers. You're going to get yourself killed. How long have you known?"

"I just found out," she said. "I've been trying to tell you, but you don't stay in one place long."

Shadow's stomach turned. There was fear in his eyes. Not for himself, but for her. She knew too much now. And that made her a target.

"I just found out about it too," he admitted. "And I've got a lead I need to check out. Don't follow me, Jade. If they find out you're digging, you'll end up on their list."

Jade gave a small nod. "Be careful. Whoever's behind this... they're dangerous. They don't want that file getting out."

Shadow hesitated, then pulled her into a quick, tight hug.

"I have to go," he said.

He shut her door, tucked his gun away, and started walking back to his car.

Behind him, her voice rang out, soft but serious.

"Lose the car, Shadow. If I found you, they can too."

* * *

Shadow rode along the edge of the Inlands, a motorcycle rumbling under him. He didn't have a helmet, so he wore a ski mask to avoid being recognized. The wind was cold, but riding made it easier to move fast through the streets. He had grabbed the bike from a quiet side street, easy to steal and already full on gas. The crumpled note Tiny gave him sat in his jacket pocket.

In the Inner City, stealing wasn't unusual. Most people didn't even blink.

"It's only a crime if they catch you," Doc always said.

His backpack was tight against his shoulders, packed light but ready. Just the basics: his phone, a burner phone, gloves, and bolt cutters. Tools meant to break in and disappear fast. That said everything about where his head was. This wasn't just curiosity. This was recon.

Shadow stuck to side streets, staying one move ahead of anyone who might be watching. At a red light, he tapped his chest. The paper was still inside his jacket.

He didn't need to pull it out.

Storage Yard. Docks. Unit #19.

The sun had dropped behind the skyline, casting the Inlands in rusty and purple light. Long shadows stretched over fences and sagging power lines. This part of the city looked forgotten, buildings falling apart, wires drooping like they carried too much weight. It was the kind of place where people didn't ask questions, because they didn't want the answers.

Shadow parked two blocks away and walked the rest, slow and alert. The air smelled like iron and burnt rubber.

Then a thought hit him: the phoenix necklace. He'd seen it on Lola. In Doc's office. Even in an old photo.

Doc's voice echoed in his mind: *Closest I came to a kid was Darrell's girl. Promised I'd look after her.*

Lola.

Shadow pushed the thought aside.

The yard was exactly like Tiny described: quiet, locked up, remote. Shadow tested the gate. Locked. He grabbed the bolt cutters from his bag and snapped the chain easily. It hit the ground with a loud clang.

The gate creaked open. Inside, the storage units looked like tombs. He found Unit 19. New padlock. He cut it, too.

The smell hit first: dust, old paper, and cold metal. A flickering light came on when he flipped the switch. The place looked like a bunker. Shelves lined the walls, filled with crates stamped with ICS logos, By Knight Records labels, bundles of files, and loose wires. But it was the safe in the far corner that grabbed his attention.

Black. Waist-high. Digital keypad and mechanical lock. It gave off a faint hum.

He stepped closer. No keyhole. Just a blinking pad.

A label was taped to the front, yellowed with age.

CLASS 7 ACCESS ONLY.

Shadow's stomach tightened. Whatever was inside wasn't just private; it was top secret. This was bigger than the streets. His fingers itched to open it, but his instincts told him to be careful.

He snapped photos of everything: the lock, the label, the serial number. Jules once told him, "The fastest way to get caught is to rush into something you don't understand." Shadow wasn't about to forget that.

He pulled out Tiny's note and unfolded it.

The light hit it just right. Something shifted. He flipped it over. There, faint in the corner, was a four-digit number. *Has it always been there?*

He started to punch it in then he heard a noise outside.

A scuff.

Shadow pulled his gun and ducked behind the door.

Footsteps.

He waited. Silent.

The door creaked, and a figure moved.

Shadow jumped out, grabbed the person, and shoved him against the wall, gun pressed into his ribs.

"Who sent you?" he demanded.

"I...I just do drops! I don't know who they are!"

The voice was young. The kid looked about fourteen. Thin, shaking, eyes wide with fear. ICS was stitched on the front of his denim jacket.

Just a kid. But already branded. Born into it, probably.

"Why this unit?"

"The boss... said this drop was urgent..."

Shadow's grip tightened. "Where does he operate from?"

The kid shook his head quickly. "Nobody knows. They say only Doc... and some guy named Jules ever saw him in person. They know everybody. You know Jules, right? Big-time record label guy. Made that song *Outta Your League*. You kinda look like him. That's all I know. I swear."

Shadow lowered the gun and stepped back. "Yeah, I know Jules. I used to look up to him."

Was it the music? Maybe. The man? Hard to say. Back then, Jules was a name you trusted. Now? Shadow didn't know what to believe.

He'd heard the track a few nights ago, blasting through his car stereo, muffled by static as he crossed the line between the Outer and Inner City.

Didn't think much of it.

But hearing it now. Like it was common knowledge. Hit different. The city didn't know whose story that song really told.

The words sank deep into his chest. Jules. That song. That night.

His thoughts spun out, dragging him backward into memory before he could stop it.

A dog barked nearby. A train rumbled in the distance.

But all of it faded.

A familiar piano riff echoed in his mind.

And just like that, he was back there.

* * *

I used to love that song. I remember the first time I heard it: Jules played it in the studio, eyes closed, nodding like he already knew it was going to be a hit.

That was before it played on every station. Before it blew up.

My dad wrote *Outta Your League* when I was in eighth grade. Back when I couldn't miss a shot and coaches were showing up to watch me play. I was dominating every sport I touched.

He told me it was mine. Said it was inspired by how I moved. How I saw the world like a chessboard, always thinking two steps ahead.

"Nobody out there can touch you, son. You're already outta their league. A man among boys, with the bloodline to prove it."

I tried to record it.

But my voice kept cracking, skipping like a scratched CD. I couldn't land the hook or keep the rhythm in the verses. I was smooth on the field, but the booth? It was another world. I froze. And deep down, I knew why.

I hadn't lived the story I was trying to tell. Not yet. I grew up in the Outer City. Clean streets, quiet nights, schools where the heaters worked and the teachers knew your name. No gunshots at night. No flashing lights through the window. In hip hop, if you haven't lived something real, people don't think you've got anything worth saying.

That's part of why I kept looking toward the Inner City. It wasn't just curiosity. It was hunger. I wanted to prove myself. I wanted to earn the right to speak.

My dad told me it was fine. Said, your time will come. Said the song was still ours.

But a month later, it was his voice on the radio.

Same beat. Same hook. Just a few tweaks.

And yeah... he made it sound better.

I wasn't mad. Not really.

But sometimes, when that chorus came on and hit just right, I'd hear his voice in my head. The version from before the fame.

"Don't ever let anybody write your verses for you."

And I'd wonder...

Did he forget? Or did I?

* * *

"Go," Shadow told the kid. "If you see me again, keep moving."

The kid took off running.

Shadow waited a few seconds, scanning the area. His heart was still racing. He couldn't relax. Not yet.

He returned to the safe and typed in the code. There was a soft click, then a hiss as it opened.

Inside were stacks of folders and papers.

He grabbed his phone and started taking pictures. Anything that might come in handy.

The folders were marked with classification stamps. Most of the documents were blacked out: old ICS operations, heavily redacted.

He worked fast, snapping photos of everything he could before someone else decided to check this place out. He didn't take anything. That felt like the smarter move.

As he turned to leave, he bent down to tie his shoe. That's when he noticed it. A folder partially wedged underneath a box.

He pulled it out and opened it.

The first page said:

PRIMARY SUBJECT: E. BLAKE

Elijah Blake? His pulse spiked.

Was that him?

His stomach dropped. His breath caught. Everything else in the file was blacked out. Names. Dates. All of it.

He took a few pictures and slid the folder back exactly where he found it.

But that name... it wouldn't leave his mind.

Like something he'd been chasing for years. Or trying to escape.

It didn't feel like a file. It felt like a grave.

Suddenly, memories he hadn't touched in years came flooding back.

* * *

She was tucking me in. I couldn't have been more than six. Her hands trembled as she brushed my hair back.

"You're special, Eli," she whispered. "Don't let anyone else tell you who you are."

Was my whole life just a test? A project passed from one person to the next? My mom and dad always acted like they were shaping something. Like I was a blueprint, not a person.

They told me to "rise above," to "lead with your mind," to "be better." I used to think they were just pushing me to succeed. But now I wondered if those words were part of a plan I never knew I was part of.

I used to think she meant talent.

Now I wondered if she meant design.

* * *

His stomach twisted.

He thought about E bleeding on the pavement. Ty's eyes filled with hurt. His mom's pain. Jade's disappointment.

He didn't feel like Shadow. Didn't feel like Elijah. He just felt... used.

E. Blake.

Was that really his name? Elijah Blake?

He turned off the lights. Stepped out. Closed the storage unit behind him like nothing had happened.

Whatever came next, one thing was clear.

Doc, Jules, and Lucien. They didn't build him. They buried him.

Now, with his mind sharp and his heart steady, he wasn't running anymore.

He was digging himself up.

* * *

Shadow crouched on the rooftop of a forgotten warehouse. The Inland skyline carved jagged edges into the night behind him. Wind cut through his hoodie, but he didn't care. He wasn't here for comfort. He was here to think.

He pulled out his phone and opened the photo he'd taken at the storage yard.

He stared at the image like it might shift. Like the letters might blur and resolve into something else. Something that made more sense.

"Elijah Knight," he whispered, testing the name on his tongue. "Son of Jules. Vivienne's boy. That's me."

But the words didn't land the way they used to.

E. Blake.

Why that name?

He slipped the phone back into his pocket, but the thought wouldn't leave him. That name wasn't a mistake. It was a breadcrumb in a twisted trail of lies.

He pulled the phone back out.

Someone had written it for a reason. Filed it. Sealed it away.

"If that's who I was," he muttered, "then what the hell did they turn me into?"

The wind pulled harder now. Below him, the city murmured: alive and restless.

They gave him a name.

Now he was going to steal it back.

He pulled out the second burner, the emergency phone. No messages. No missed calls. A clean slate.

He copied the photos of the files onto it, encrypted the folder, and locked it behind a fail-safe password. If everything went south, someone needed to know. Even if it wasn't him.

The wind shifted again.

Shadow rose to his feet and looked out toward the docks.

A memory flashed: ten years old, bare feet smacking against the pavement, lungs full of wind. Vivi clapping from the porch, her voice lifting with joy. Jules laughing from behind the grill, a beer in hand. For one bright moment, the world had been whole. Before the lies. Before Shadow. Back then, there were no secrets.

That boy was dying now.

Only Shadow remained.

"But they forgot what happens when the weapon starts thinking for itself," he said aloud.

His phone buzzed in his pocket.

Blocked Number: *They know you're looking. Get ready.*

He scanned the streets below. Maybe Tiny was out there: watching, silent, ready to move.

Shadow slipped the phone into his backpack, pulled his hood tight, and disappeared into the night.

A mystery chasing names. A son chasing truth.

He didn't know where the next bullet would come from.

But this time?

He was ready.

THE CUTS THAT DON'T HEAL

CHAPTER 18
PING

It had been a few days since the warehouse rooftop. Since then, Shadow had been laying low in the Inlands, switching out burner phones, using fake names, and dodging ICS eyes at every corner. Jade had reached out once. So had his mom. Even Ty told him he should stop by and see E. But Shadow couldn't. Not yet.

Finding Jared took time. Shadow had been laying low for weeks, switching burner phones and ducking ICS eyes, chasing rumors through the underbelly of the Inlands. Jared was off the grid, practically a ghost. Shadow had to meet a guy who knew a guy, follow dead ends, trade favors, and wait. But eventually, the trail led here. And now, he was standing in front of the van, ready to dig for answers.

This part of the Inland didn't sleep. It just changed shape. Not rich enough to matter. Not poor enough to fear. Just stuck in the middle.

He needed help making sense of the name "E. Blake" and all the mystery surrounding it. And Jared? Jared was the only guy he knew who could trace someone in the digital world.

By day, this neighborhood looked tame: police patrolling, white picket fences, and older folks just getting by. But at night, it changed. The shadows took over. It felt like the whole place held its breath, hoping trouble would pass on its way to somewhere worse.

Shadow walked with his hood low, hands buried deep in his jacket pockets, the burner phone warm against his thigh. The hairs on the back of his neck stood up. Like someone was watching. He didn't look around. He didn't need confirmation. Paranoia wasn't just a feeling anymore. It was a lifestyle. He moved like eyes were always on him. Because to him, they were.

He slipped behind the old barbershop on 108th, scanning the alley before stopping beside a rusted-out van squatting between two busted dumpsters. Satellite dishes poked out at odd angles, tangled wires drooped along its sides like vines, and mismatched metal panels were duct-taped on with zero concern for style. Antennas jutted out from the roof like broken insect legs, while a soft electric hum pulsed underneath it all. A solar panel tilted toward the sky. This wasn't just a van. It was a Frankenstein fortress on wheels. Jared's hideout. Part hacker den, part surveillance hub, part fallout shelter. Jared was a tech genius with a shady history, the kind of guy who could disappear from the grid and still know what everyone else was Googling. Shadow hadn't seen him since high school, back when they faced off in the state finals. But now? Now he needed Jared more than ever.

The van's side door creaked open before Shadow could knock.

Inside, Jared typed one-handed, an energy drink in the other. The interior was cramped. Gear lined the walls: signal boosters, coiled wires, radios, soldering kits.

Chaos, but intentional. Like a hacker's war bunker on wheels.

"You really did all that work just to dig up a guy like me?" Jared grinned, his face lit by the glow of three mismatched monitors. "I mean, I'm flattered. But you know they got therapists and support groups for that kind of obsession, right?"

Shadow stepped inside, ducking the low ceiling. The van smelled like sweat, burnt wires, and stale chips.

Shadow tossed a folded note onto Jared's lap. "Name. Run it."

Jared unfolded it and squinted. "E. Blake? What, like the poet or something?"

Shadow didn't answer.

"Alright, chill." Jared cracked his knuckles and started typing. "You know, I still have nightmares about that tournament. You lit us up in front of the whole school. I lost my scholarship over that game."

"Maybe you should've guarded me better," Shadow said, leaning against the wall.

Jared snorted. "Touché."

The screen flashed. Data scrolled fast.

"Yo..." Jared muttered. "This kid's flagged as dead. Like, seventeen years ago. Outer District Medical Center. Fire. No remains. Case closed as 'presumed.'"

Shadow's breath hitched. Seventeen years ago? He would've been a baby. The hum of the hard drives filled the van, but all he could hear was the pounding confusion in his head.

"Says the mom was someone named Vivienne Blake. Father not listed. There's a sealed custodial file filed a few days later. Weird."

Shadow's jaw tightened. Vivienne. That name cut through everything.

"What's the play here?" Jared asked.

Before Shadow could answer, his phone buzzed.

DOC - Incoming Call

He hesitated, then picked up.

"You didn't happen to come across a burner phone in or around my office, have you?" Doc's voice was calm, but there was tension under the words. Tight. Dangerous.

"No. Why?"

"Because it's missing. And I keep what matters on what don't look like it matters."

Click.

Shadow stared at the phone. His gut twisted. Doc wasn't just asking. That was a warning. A threat dressed up like concern. Shadow's grip tightened around the burner. Real fear crept in.

"I don't wanna sound nosey," Jared said, "but was that Doc Blackwell?"

"Yeah."

Jared let out a low whistle. "Man... music's dope, but word is he's grimey. You trust him?"

Shadow paused. "I thought I did."

A beat passed.

"Can you run something else?" Shadow asked.

Jared raised an eyebrow. "Another dead baby?"

Shadow pulled the burner from his pocket. The same one he'd taken from Doc's office. He didn't know what he expected Jared to find, but something told him it mattered. The device felt like a key to a bigger story.

"Can you hack into this?"

Jared blinked. Then grinned. "Now we're talkin'."

* * *

Dream Fragment

I've had this dream before. Smoke sneaking through the cracks in a car window. Red and blue lights flashing behind the glass. A woman's voice breaking apart like static. But this time was different. This time, the dream had names. It felt sharper, like it wasn't just a memory. It was a message.

I was in the backseat of a car, holding a toy lion with a missing tail. My fingers were clenched so tight around it. The engine rumbled beneath me, the warmth pressing up through the seat like the car itself was alive.

"You like speed, little man?" the driver asked. His voice was smooth and low, warm like something from a memory I couldn't quite catch. "We don't stop until we're safe."

The woman in the front seat turned around. It was Vivi. Her hair was longer then, pulled back in a scarf, curls still wild at the edges. Her eyes were wide and wet, darting to the road, to me, to the mirrors.

"Darrell can't find us," she snapped, her voice high and strained. "Drive. Now. Before it's too late."

Then—pop. The sharp crack of something tearing. The tire exploded. Burning rubber. Screeching tires. A trail of fire in the side mirror.

The man's arm reached back, fingers blackened and outstretched.

Reaching for me.

I jolted awake, heart racing, lungs dragging for air.

Darrell.

The name stuck in my chest like a nail. I didn't know what it meant. But something inside me did.

* * *

As Jared dug into the data, Shadow stepped outside to clear his head. He sat on an old plastic crate, elbows on his knees, just breathing. Trying to let the dream dissolve.

He saw it all over again.

Darrell.

It stuck with him. Like it wasn't just a dream but a memory trying to claw its way out. Was it real? Or just another piece of his cracked mind playing tricks?

He didn't know. But the deeper he dug into his past, the more it felt like the answers were hiding in plain sight.

After a while, he stood and knocked twice on the van's rusted side.

Jared cracked the door. "Took you long enough. What happened, you had some kind of epiphany?"

"Something like that."

"You good?" Jared asked, not looking away from the screen.

Shadow leaned against the wall. "Not sure. Think I remembered something... or maybe I just dreamed it."

Jared raised a brow. "You forgetting how to tell the difference?"

Shadow shrugged. "Lately, yeah."

The van hummed around them as Jared pulled up a new screen. Lines of code flew by, then stopped.

"Okay, so your burner? It's bouncing off ghost towers. Someone set it up to disappear. But..." He tapped a line on the screen. "One number repeats. Six times last week. No ID. Just a letter."

L.

Shadow's stomach tightened. A wave of unease crept up his spine.

"You know who that is?" Jared asked.

Shadow stared at the screen. "Maybe."

He copied the number into his phone, hand steady even though his mind was racing.

Jared glanced at him. "You ever stop to think maybe you don't want the answers you're chasing?"

Shadow paused. Just for a second.

Then he pocketed his phone. "Too late for that."

* * *

By the time Shadow stepped out of Jared's van, the Inland sky had already darkened to a heavy gray. His mind was spinning: names, pings, half-truths all tangled together. He had leads now, sure, but nothing solid. Nothing that could hold under pressure. He needed something else. Something that could tie it all together.

He kept his head down, ignoring the endless buzz of his phone. Dozens of missed calls, probably more. He couldn't bring himself to answer any of them. Not until he knew more. Not until he had something to show for all this running.

Auntie Relle's walk-up looked just like it did when he was a kid. Same cracked bricks, same crooked gate, same porch light flickering like it was about to die.

He stood on the steps for a long moment before finally pressing the buzzer.

The door creaked open. Auntie Relle squinted at him through the screen. "You finally come by to check on an old woman, or you duckin' your parents?"

"Bit of both," he said with a faint smirk.

Inside smelled like warm wax and sandalwood, just like he remembered. A faint gospel tune played low from a scratched-up radio in the kitchen. He didn't sit. "I need to ask you something," he said. "About my mom. And the fire."

Her smile faded. "Lord, you don't waste no time."

She lit a stick of incense and placed it in front of a worn photograph in a cracked frame. Then she lowered herself into her chair with a soft groan.

"What about the name Blake?" he asked. "E. Blake?"

She froze, the incense smoke curling between them.

"That name don't belong in the world anymore," she said quietly. "But... it used to."

Shadow said nothing, waiting.

"Vivienne didn't want to let it go," she continued. "But Jules said they had to bury it. Said if Darrell ever found out that boy was still breathing, it'd be war all over again. Said Darrell would use that boy to take back the Inner City."

Shadow's chest tightened. She didn't say Lucien.

She said Darrell.

It landed heavier. More real. Like a ghost finally stepping into the light.

"And the fire?" he asked.

She waved her hand like swatting away smoke. "Not all my story to tell. But what I will say is this: being with Jules nearly got Vivienne and you both killed. That feud with Darrell? It's been burning a long time, baby."

She got up and shuffled toward the kitchen. Shadow figured that was his cue. He turned toward the door.

"I should go. Thanks for talking with me."

She walked with him, slow but steady. Auntie Relle rested her hand on the doorframe. "Elijah, if you keep digging, make sure you're ready for what's still breathing under all that dirt."

Outside, dusk had settled in. The streetlights flickered, caught between staying on and giving up.

Shadow stepped off the porch, pulled out his phone, and scrolled until he found the number Jared had flagged.

L.

He stared at the screen. His thumb hovered over the call button.

He didn't press it.

But he didn't delete it either.

* * *

The ride through the Inland was quiet. Shadow had taken Jared's car this time. Beat-up, anonymous, forgettable. It rattled over the uneven concrete as he stayed off main roads. His mind churned with everything Auntie Relle had said. There were still too many missing pieces, but something about the letter "L" made his gut twist.

He parked in the alley behind the safehouse, an abandoned house he'd been using while lying low. This was the only place that felt remotely safe.

Inside, it smelled like overheated electronics. Three fans buzzed in different corners, barely moving the heavy air. A cracked window was sealed with duct tape. Power cords tangled like jungle vines around towers of stolen routers and hard drives. Paranoia seeped from the walls. Jared had helped him rig the place to send out signals, but nothing could get in.

Shadow dropped onto the creaky couch and pulled out his phone. He scrolled to the contact: L.

His thumb hovered over the button. His chest tightened.

Call.

One ring. Two.

Then a voice came. Calm, deep, dry like sunbaked concrete.

"Elijah."

Shadow froze.

The voice didn't wait.

"You still trying to figure out who you are?" A pause. "Tell Jules the past is circling again."

Click.

Silence.

Shadow stayed still, the phone pressed against his ear even though the call was over. His grip tightened, jaw clenched. The voice echoed in his head.

It felt like the whole city had just turned to look at him.

Around midnight, a knock.

Three sharp raps. A pause. Two more.

Shadow opened the door just a crack. "You alone?"

Jared stood there, hands raised. "Always."

Inside, Jared looked uneasy. Not tired, but rattled. "That number you asked me to trace? It lit up again," Jared said.

Shadow tensed.

"Someone else is chasing the same signal. Same towers. Same path. Someone else is in the dark with you now." He hesitated, then added, "You've got maybe a day before this stops being your secret. I spoofed the signal, but I don't know how long it'll hold."

Shadow didn't call Jules. He thought about it, but he wasn't ready to get brushed off. He didn't even know if the trust was still real. So, he started packing. It was only a matter of time before it all caught up to him.

At a red light, Shadow stared into the cracked side mirror. The reflection didn't look like him. Tired eyes. Dirty clothes. A mouth that hadn't smiled in days.

Who am I really?

The voice on the other end had barely said anything.

But it had known him.

Shadow didn't call again.

He sat in silence, staring at the screen, thinking about the files. The fire. A boy who'd died seventeen years ago, and the shell who may have taken his place.

He gripped the wheel. Then he drove faster.

Not to run.

To move before they found him first.

He didn't know exactly where to go next. But his mind kept drifting back to a place he'd once heard mentioned on the radio.

Doc's old gym.

If anything about the voice, the files, or this whole mess tied back to Doc, that's where he'd start.

* * *

He didn't know where the gym was, only the part of the city where he'd heard whispers about it. Still, it felt like his best shot at finding something. Maybe a clue. Maybe closure. So he drove for hours, cutting through back alleys and old neighborhoods until something finally clicked.

The building appeared through the morning haze, tucked behind a row of boarded-up shops. He pulled over and just sat there, staring.

The place had shut down shortly after opening, some supposed code violation. But Shadow remembered the rumors from back when he first started hanging around Doc's people. This gym wasn't just for training. It was a meeting place. A hiding spot. A trap house. Deals went down here, and so did people. That memory alone was enough to make him trust his gut.

The chain on the front door was rusted shut, but Shadow didn't bother with it. When he circled the building, he noticed the side entrance was still loose.

He stepped inside.

It smelled like dust, mold, and untold secrets. A heavy bag hung from the center beam, torn in places. He ran his fingers along the walls until he found the corner locker. Something felt off about it, so he opened it.

Inside was almost what he expected: Cash. Rolls of it, bundled tight with rubber bands. Ammo. Fake IDs and passports, boxed and covered in dust. But there were fresh fingerprints on the lid of the box.

His breath hitched. It wasn't just what was there. It was what it confirmed. Doc had been here recently. This was real.

He found a key ring that jingled softly in his hand. A flash drive sat beside it, scuffed but intact. He pocketed them both. When he turned around, his breath caught in his throat.

"Snooping around again?"

A chill ran down his spine.

Lola.

She stepped out from the shadows, arms crossed. Her stance wasn't defensive.

"How long you been trailing me?" Shadow asked, voice sharp.

"Since you left that abandoned house," Lola replied, cool but distant.

Shadow narrowed his eyes. If that was true, why wait until now to show herself?

He let out a bitter laugh. "You working for Doc? Or Lucien? Or are you just following your own rules now?"

She didn't answer. Just stared.

"Cambria," he said. "That's your real name, right? Phoenix girl. Cleaner."

Her eyes flinched, just a little. But it was enough.

"I don't know who Cambria is." She didn't deny being Phoenix. Just stepped closer. "You think you're the only one who lost something?" she whispered.

He stared at her.

"You used me," Shadow said.

"No. I was looking out for you. You just don't see it yet," Lola said.

Shadow raised an eyebrow. "Looking out? That's what you call it?"

Lola stepped closer. "If I wanted you dead, you would be. I've had plenty of chances."

Shadow took a step back, cautious.

"That was never the goal. My job was to keep tabs on you," she said, moving a little closer.

"So what, you're my babysitter now?" he snapped.

She shook her head with a faint smirk. "Babysitters don't do the stuff we've done. And... I kind of like your dumb ass. Don't ask me why."

He gave her a skeptical look. "So what. Flirting with me, getting close. That was just part of the job too?"

"I didn't plan for that part," she said, voice softer now. "But I wasn't gonna let you walk into something blind either."

"You protected me? When?"

"You remember that meeting with Ice down by the pier? He was ready to pull something. I texted Doc to pull you out before it went sideways. And when you met with that guy at the corner store, I trailed behind to make sure you weren't being followed."

Shadow's expression shifted, unsure whether to believe her or not.

"Why?" he finally asked.

She shrugged, half-playful, half-serious. "Like I said... I kind of like your dumb ass. And my mission isn't to kill you. It's to watch you. That's it. But I still need to find out who killed my brother."

His eyes searched hers, trying to catch a lie. "Then why not just tell me the truth from the start?"

"Doc told me not to. He said I had a job to do, and you had a role to play."

He stared at her in silence, then finally said, "So the whole time, you were just playing me?"

"No," she said, more serious now. "I really was trying to protect you. I still am. And I still need to figure out who killed my brother. You and I are in two different fights, Shadow. Yours is just going to cause more destruction."

Shadow pushed past her, anger in every step.

"Shadow, you need to go see Doc. He's pissed, and I don't want to keep following you."

"Then don't," he said, spinning to face her. "Go find something better to do. I'm sure Doc's got someone else he wants taken out."

He saw it land. Just a flicker of pain in her eyes. Even with Doc pulling her strings, they'd built something. Something almost real. And if she truly wanted him dead, she would've done it already.

But Shadow couldn't afford feelings right now. Not when he was this close.

* * *

He drove for more than an hour, looping through side streets, jumping on and off the freeway, and squeezing into alleys so narrow his mirrors nearly scraped the walls. He couldn't tell if he was really trying to shake a tail or just outrun his own thoughts. The city stretched endlessly around him, neon lights flashing against cracked asphalt, each turn making him question what he was even chasing. The only thing he knew for certain was that he needed space, room to settle his nerves, room to breathe.

When the streets finally quieted and the noise fell away, he turned back toward the gym. His chest tightened as it came into view. He'd been here plenty of times, but tonight it looked different, hollow, like the building itself was bracing for something it didn't want to face.

There was still one place left to check.

After Lola vanished, he forced himself down the dark hallway until he reached the back office. The door leaned off its hinges, crooked like it had nearly given up. Inside, the air was thick with dust, coating everything in a dull gray. The single bulb overhead flickered once and died, leaving only a thin strip of streetlight spilling in through a cracked window. In the corner sat a sagging metal desk, rust creeping along its edges. He tugged at the top drawer, but it was jammed tight. Sliding a small brass key into the bottom lock, he twisted until it gave way with a tired groan.

Inside was another key, cold and heavy in his hand. Beside it lay a folded slip of paper, an address scribbled in rushed, uneven handwriting. The kind you leave behind when you hope no one will notice what you're really trying to say.

* * *

Later, Shadow pulled up to a weather-worn storage unit near the water. He checked the number. This was it. The key turned with resistance. The steel door groaned open.

Boxes. Binders. Photos. Bolted against the far wall stood a filing cabinet, its paint chipped and drawer handles dull with age.

He crossed the concrete floor, gripped the top drawer, and pulled. Inside, centered like it had been waiting for him, was another folder marked with the initials: E.B.

His chest tightened.

He opened it.

DNA reports. Medical records. Police files. A photo of the car from his dream: burning. The back seat was empty, but you could see the remains of a burnt toy lion.

He turned to the last page. A memo read: *"Primary subject E. Blake has been relocated, last name changed, and cleared. All connections to the name Blake erased."*

At the bottom, it said: *"File Prepared By: D. Maddox."*

Shadow froze.

"D. Maddox?" he said under his breath. "Is that Doc... or Darrell?"

The names spun in his mind like loaded dice. His grip tightened around the folder.

"Nobody died in the fire," he whispered. "This was a cover-up."

CHAPTER 19

WHERE THE LIES LIVED

Shadow stood outside the door for a full minute before knocking. Three short knocks. Footsteps. A click. Then the door opened.

Jules didn't look surprised. He actually looked like he'd been expecting him. He stood in the doorway, eyes sharp but tired, like he hadn't slept in days.

"Didn't think I'd see you again," Jules said calmly.

Shadow didn't blink. "Was Blake your real name?"

Jules didn't answer. He just turned and walked back inside, leaving the door open.

Shadow followed him in.

The apartment was clean but cold. No pictures. No decorations. Just a half-empty glass of whiskey on the windowsill.

The lights were off, but it wasn't completely dark. The curtains were half-closed, and shadows sat in the corners like they paid rent. A slow, moody jazz record played quietly in the background. It didn't fill the space. It just gave the silence weight.

Jules sat down in the chair he used to crash in after long studio nights. Shadow stayed standing. He took the burner phone he found in Doc's office from his pocket and set it on the table between them like a threat.

"I called one of the numbers. Contact name was just 'L.'"

He looked up. "Pretty sure you know who that is."

Jules didn't respond.

"He knew my name. My real one." Still no response. "Elijah," Shadow said softly. "He called me Elijah."

Jules's eyes didn't move, but his jaw tightened.

Shadow watched him. Elijah still hoped. "Are you going to tell me everything? Or do I have to wait until someone else tries to kill me?"

He pulled out his phone, swiped to a picture, and laid it face-up on the table. It was a document from the storage yard.

Jules didn't touch it.

Shadow swiped to another photo. This one read: CLASS 7 ACCESS.

"Your handwriting," Shadow said. "You didn't just change our names. You had a whole system. Backups and plans..."

Jules exhaled. "Not like that, fool. I didn't know what would happen if you ended up on the wrong side of a barrel," he said. "And I wasn't raising a weapon."

Shadow scrolled through the messages and held the phone out. "Funny thing about weapons," he said. "They can point both ways."

On the screen:

Jules: *Make it clean.*

Doc: *It's done.*

Jules: *Good. No ties back.*

Jules stared at the phone. Shadow stared at him.

"That night in the alley... you heard about it, didn't you?"

Jules didn't say anything. Didn't deny it. He just looked smaller somehow. Like the image of the man Elijah once believed in had faded. He didn't look like a legend anymore. He looked like someone who thought his actions would never catch up to him.

"He's the son of a dangerous man. The word on the street was it was either him or you. But now, I don't know. Maybe I got played too." Jules threw up his hands. "You ever seen a movie? Bad guy shows up and says, 'I got your family.' Then the hero has to do something reckless to save them all." He raised his eyebrows. "You get it now? Or do I need to draw it out for you?"

Shadow stepped forward. "Yeah... and in those movies? It's always the one trying to 'protect' everyone who ends up destroying everything. If you had just prepared us instead of hiding the truth, maybe I wouldn't be caught up in a war I didn't even start." His voice dropped. "Did you love us at all? Enough to walk away from all this?"

Jules looked at him. Not with anger, just exhaustion. "You think I liked making those decisions? That's the price you pay in this game."

Then—

"Don't make him dig for what he already knows."

Elijah turned.

Mom.

He hadn't heard that voice in weeks, but it was still familiar. It had called him in for dinner, hugged him tight, promised he was safe. Now it felt different. He froze as she stepped from the shadows. Unsure if it was really her.

She walked in like she had never left. Hair tied up. Same kind of cardigan she always wore. Her eyes locked on Elijah and didn't let go. She looked just as tired as Jules. She moved slowly and sat in the other chair. Her eyes scanned him, head to toe. Like she needed to be sure he was whole.

"I thought we lost you," she whispered. "And I didn't know if I had the right to cry about it."

Jules looked down, his jaw tight. He didn't say he was glad Elijah was safe, but his tapping foot and clenched fists said he'd been scared.

She looked at Elijah again. He stayed standing, stuck between the people who made him and the lies they told to protect him.

"Start talking," he said. "Both of you."

Jules leaned back and crossed his arms. The burner phone sat between them like a ticking bomb.

Silence.

"It was my name," Jules finally said. "Before all this. Before I gave it up."

"Jules Blake?" Elijah asked, testing the name.

Jules nodded. "Yeah. That was me. Before Lucien. Before ICS. I dropped the name a long time ago. Just not officially."

Shadow began to pace.

"So what was I? A backup plan? A lie?"

He shook his head. "You didn't just change my name. You changed my life. You decided who I got to be. And you never even told me."

His voice cracked. "Did you ever stop to think about who I could've been if you had just told me the truth?"

Jules didn't respond.

Vivi did.

Her voice was calm but steady. "My family didn't like your father. They said he'd get me killed. That the Blake name was cursed. But I knew who he really was. So we left. Came here. To this place."

Elijah clenched his fists. "And after?"

"After," she said, "we got married and had you. This place felt like the safest spot."

Jules added, "She was trying to run. This apartment was from my dad. It was for emergencies only."

Silence filled the room. Heavy but necessary.

"So we all died... technically," Elijah said. "In the fire? That was the story?"

"Lucien found out about the Blake name," Jules said. "He would've hunted us down. Didn't matter if you were my wife or my kid. I didn't even know the guy. He just showed up one day. So I changed all our last names to Knight."

Elijah looked at his mom. "And you agreed?"

She flinched. "I thought I would lose either way. At least this way, we lived."

Jules spoke again, quieter this time. "Lucien was taking out anyone he saw as a threat. He came after me a few times, always made it personal. I knew I had to step back and let Doc be the front man while I stayed behind the scenes. He had a list. Blake was at the top. He built ICS fast. No face. No case. I only ever talked to him on the phone, always with some voice changer."

"When did he show up?" Elijah asked.

Jules rubbed the back of his neck. "You were still a baby. Things were getting too dangerous. I had you and your mom to think about." He let out a breath. "I don't know where I'd be without you two."

Elijah felt a tear try to form, but it vanished quickly, burned away by the truth they'd been hiding.

"So you made me into Shadow," he said.

"No," Jules said. "The world did that. Your choices did that. I just gave you a name no one could trace. At least, until now."

He didn't say anything else. His hand twitched, like he wanted to reach for something but didn't know what. He looked at Elijah, not as the man standing in front of him but as the boy he once tried to protect.

Vivi said softly, "He never trusted himself to raise you, Elijah. He trusted plans more than people."

Elijah's voice cracked. "I trusted both of you."

He raised his voice. "You told me to stay away from trouble. To be better. But you never told me what I was running from."

He pointed at the burner. "And now those people are coming for me. Not you. Me."

He looked between them, voice steady now. "You made the choices. I'm the one paying the price."

He turned toward the door, then looked back at them over his shoulder. His voice lowered. "Now I have to decide if I can forgive you... or just keep walking and never look back."

He snatched the burner off the table on his way out. It was his now. And so was the truth.

* * *

He didn't slam the door. Didn't storm out. That would've made it seem like they still had control over him.

Instead, Shadow walked to the door with slow, steady steps. The apartment felt smaller now. Tighter. Like the walls had closed in around the secrets they'd kept hidden.

No one followed him.

Jules took a step, then stopped. Vivi reached out like she might say something, might stop him, but her hand dropped to her side. Some truths are too heavy to carry for someone else. And some paths have to be walked alone.

Shadow kept moving.

He didn't pause. Didn't look back. But the silence behind him said more than any apology ever could.

They hadn't just hidden him. They had erased who he used to be. Changed his name. Changed his story. All in the name of protection. But love shouldn't erase someone just to keep them safe.

And now, for the first time, he understood. He finally saw why they did what they did. Why they ran. Why they lied.

That understanding should've brought peace.

But it didn't.

It hollowed him. Because knowing they were right didn't take the pain away. They had protected him, but they had also erased him.

He opened the door and stepped into the hallway.

Vivi took a small step forward. Just one. Not enough to stop him. Just enough to show she wanted to.

She opened her mouth to speak, but nothing came out.

"Elijah," she whispered.

But the door was already closing.

CHAPTER 20

THE CHECK-IN

Shadow walked through the gates of the Outer City graveyard, his phone still warm in his pocket from Ty's message.

Meet me at the graveyard. 45 mins. By my brother's stone.

Ty had only mentioned his brother a couple of times, always quiet, always brief. Asking Shadow to meet here wasn't random. It was intentional. A message.

The graveyard sat quietly on the edge of the city, bordered by manicured hedges and a tall iron fence. Rows of polished headstones stretched out in perfect lines, some decorated with fresh flowers in glass vases, others bare and forgotten. Solar-powered lanterns lit the paths with a soft, steady glow.

Shadow wasn't here to mourn. He came because Ty asked. But as he stood there, hands buried in his pockets, the peacefulness of the place felt like a slap. Everything here was clean, quiet, cared for. The exact opposite of the life he'd been running through.

The wind stirred dry leaves along the walkway. Above him, a fogged-up billboard flickered faintly. It was an ad for Princeton. The Latin words, etched in glowing gold, loomed above: *Dei Sub Numine Viget.*

Shadow had seen it before. Never knew what it meant. Never cared. Tonight, though, it landed differently.

Below the Latin: *Your future begins here.*

He stared at the words longer than he meant to. He thought about his old high school counselor practically begging him to apply. He'd laughed it off back then. But maybe if he'd made better choices, things would be different. Maybe there was still time to change where this road led.

Ty showed up late. Not too late, just enough to make a point.

He didn't say anything at first. Just nodded at the headstone a few rows away, *his brother's*. The silence between them was tight and heavy, like a wire pulled taut.

Shadow finally spoke. "You good?"

Ty let out a dry chuckle. "You really asking that? After everything?"

Shadow held his ground. "I didn't know what else to do."

Ty's jaw clenched. "You didn't just disappear. You shot someone, then dipped. Left us in the middle of that storm."

A train rumbled somewhere in the distance, the sound low and dragging.

"I was trying to protect y'all," Shadow said quietly. "After E got hit... I knew I had to move different."

Ty folded his arms but didn't look away. "You walked away from the people who cared. We saw what you did. And we can't unsee it."

Shadow lowered his eyes. "My whole life... my name... it wasn't even real. I just found out everything I thought I knew was fake."

Ty didn't move, but his voice softened, just a little. "Then why come back?"

Shadow looked up. "Because I don't want to run anymore."

Ty studied him for a second. "So who are you now?"

Shadow hesitated. Then: "I don't know yet. But I'm figuring it out. One truth at a time."

Ty nodded slowly. "If you want trust again, stop disappearing every time things get hard."

"I hear you," Shadow said. "I've been trying to clean up my part. Stay low. Keep y'all out of danger. I ain't perfect. But I'm not hiding either."

Ty let the silence stretch a little. Then he muttered, "Next time you go digging through the past... bring backup."

He paused, his eyes shot back onto the headstone. "I ever tell you how he died?"

Shadow shook his head. "No. I don't think so."

Ty kept staring. "He got mixed up in Inner City stuff. Started being home less. Thought he could handle it. Thought he was smarter than the streets."

Shadow's stomach tightened.

"They used him," Ty said. "Then dropped him when they got what they wanted. My mom got the call... he was already gone."

The silence grew heavier. It wasn't just about the two of them anymore.

Ty looked over at Shadow. "So yeah... I don't do well when people I care about go ghost."

Then he turned and walked away, hands shoved in his coat, shoulders squared like he'd been carrying the weight alone for too long.

Shadow watched him go. Then his eyes shifted to something nearby.

Three headstones. Two large. One small.

Julian Blake

Vivienne Blake

Elijah Blake

No dates. No flowers. Just names.

Shadow stared at the stones. Not with anger. Just a heavy ache. He was looking at the version of himself that never got to exist.

He took a deep breath and turned toward the city.

The burner buzzed again in his pocket.

This time, he was ready.

* * *

Lola had texted him last night: she wanted to talk. The message carried an edge, tight and urgent, like it couldn't wait. Shadow hadn't replied. This morning, he sent her a location. No explanation. No follow-up. Just a time and a place.

The campus made sense. Cameras. People. Distractions. Pulling something here wouldn't be easy. That gave him the advantage. And right now, he needed every one he could get.

His shoulder itched. He scratched it absentmindedly, and his fingers brushed the scar Rico had stitched weeks ago. The skin had mostly healed, but the ache still came and went. That scar reminded him: he wasn't safe then, and he wasn't safe now.

He picked a table with his back to the wall, where he had a full view of every exit. His eyes scanned the space, tracking movement and memorizing faces.

Lola showed up five minutes late, looking like this was a date. She wore a gray crop top and tight jeans, moving with the same casual confidence that had once pulled Shadow in. Every step said she belonged here, like this was her world and she'd invited him into it.

She smiled like nothing had changed between them. Like no lines had been crossed. He used to like that about her.

A memory blindsided him. Lola laughing in Doc's penthouse during a blackout, the two of them wrapped in a blanket, candles flickering. She had whispered against his chest, *"If the world burns down, you and me still got this."*

It had felt real back then. Now it only felt rehearsed.

"You've been real quiet lately," she said, sliding into the seat across from him. "That got anything to do with Doc's burner going missing?"

Shadow didn't blink. "Nah. Just not in the mood to be social."

She nodded, like that made sense. But her eyes said something different. Her fingers toyed with the edge of a sugar packet, though she never pulled her gaze from his. Behind her smile was something else: alertness, calculation. The kind that made her dangerous in a room full of strangers.

"Didn't think much of it at first," she said. "But I caught you in his office that night. You were jumpy. Like you were hiding something. I was half asleep, so I can't be sure. But it doesn't look good for you."

Shadow shrugged. "I don't mess with things that aren't mine. Especially not Doc's."

Lola leaned in, arms crossed. "I ain't dumb, Shadow. But you better hope Doc is."

He didn't respond. His phone buzzed.

Jade: *Got something you need to see. I know you said leave it alone, but I couldn't. We need to talk. Don't trust them.*

Lola's eyes flicked to the screen. "Jade? Thought she was out the picture."

Shadow slipped the phone back into his pocket without a word.

That killed the mood.

He stood, a quiet pressure building in his chest.

"Appreciate the concerns," he said. It wasn't warm. It was final.

Lola didn't move. Just watched him walk away.

* * *

—Lola—

She waited until he disappeared down the path, then pulled out her phone. Doc's number wasn't saved. Never had been. She knew it by heart. Safer that way. Whether it was fear, caution, or just instinct, she'd never let that number live in her contacts.

She tapped it in and held the phone to her ear.

"She reached out," Lola said, voice low and controlled. "Jade. She thinks she knows something."

She leaned back in her chair, eyes following the direction Shadow had gone. He hadn't said much. But she saw the way he reacted. The way his body tensed.

"He read the message," she added. "Didn't say a word. But I know he felt it."

A pause.

"You want me to handle it?"

Click.

* * *

Shadow moved fast through the Outer City, hood up, head down. Not running. Not strolling. Moving like a problem looking for a door to kick down.

He had options. Plenty. But when your name might be on a hit list, every ride started to feel like a setup.

He found a bike left unattended near a corner store and rode it most of the way. A ski mask tugged low kept his face off cameras. His hand stayed near the gun in his hoodie pocket, ready if anybody got bold. When the streets started to look familiar, he ditched it.

He wasn't walking blind. He was headed to a flagged address he'd pulled from the burner's log, one of the last pings in a long trail of encrypted texts. It could be nothing. Or it could be the whole damn story.

It could be a setup. Either way, he had to find out.

He was two blocks out when his phone buzzed.

Jared: *Don't go where you're going. Eyes up. Meet at the safehouse. Come now or don't come at all.*

Shadow cursed under his breath and pivoted, cutting down a narrow alley and disappearing behind a dry cleaner. His pulse spiked.

Jared didn't do panic texts. That shift in tone? That meant something was really wrong.

* * *

Shadow slipped into the safehouse and froze. Against the far wall, a board stretched from corner to corner: photos, scraps of paper, strings linking faces: Lola, Doc, and his father. Two spots bore only question marks where Darrell and Lucien's faces should have been. Marker circles surrounded dates and places, some slashed through, others underlined twice. Weeks of quiet digging, his off-camera hunt to connect the dots between them, sprawled out in a web only he understood.

Jared paced in front of it, hair wild, eyes bloodshot. A laptop blinked on the floor beside an overturned crate, cables snaking across the concrete.

"Took you long enough," Jared muttered, not looking up. "Sit. Shut up."

Shadow dropped onto a crate, elbows on his knees. Jared's shirt was soaked under the arms, his breath uneven. Fingers hammered the keyboard in a nonstop rhythm.

"Everything you gave me, the burner logs and the pings, bounced off a dead tower string," Jared said, spinning the laptop toward him. "They even know I pulled those death records. You get what that means?"

The screen was chaos: heatmaps flaring, encrypted thread routes sprawling like lightning.

"They spoofed the line. Routed it through a dead hub. It was bait. They followed the trail right here."

Shadow's eyes narrowed. "How close?"

Jared stopped. His hand shook as he rubbed his temple. "Close enough I'm not betting on sunrise. I don't do this. I fix signals. I bury trails. I don't run from hit squads."

The router hummed. Shadow's jaw tightened. "Then we burn it all. But not before you do something for me."

"Yeah, sure. What now?"

"Copy the burner's data. Load it onto mine. Then I ditch it. Trail ends."

Jared kicked aside a pile of power bricks and yanked a hardline from the router. "You're gonna get me killed."

"Only if they catch you."

Jared's eyes flicked to the trace feed, his jaw tightening. "We've got five minutes, tops. After that, this place lights up like a beacon."

Keys rattled. Data streamed, encrypted mid-flight. Red shifted to green, then the burner buzzed.

Jared froze.

Unknown: *We see you.*

Shadow's spine locked. "Transfer done?"

"No time. Take it."

Shadow pocketed both burners and gave the room one last sweep. "Burn it."

Jared didn't hesitate. He ripped out cables, stomped hard drives, swept photos and tangled string into a bin. Shadow found a half-empty bottle of rubbing alcohol on a shelf and poured it over the pile. One flick of his lighter, and the flames jumped high, tearing through paper, plastic, and fabric. The sharp stink of burning wires and melting plastic filled the air, smoke curling thick toward the ceiling.

"Go," Jared snapped, voice cracking.

They didn't stick around to see it all go. Fire was already climbing the walls as they slipped into the alley.

* * *

The car was one Jared had lined up earlier. Borrowed from a contact. Not stolen, but far from legal. Its engine trembled, tires thinner than Shadow liked, and the interior reeked of mildew under a tired pine air freshener that couldn't hide the age. Still, it moved.

Jared sat in the passenger seat, clutching his laptop like a lifeline. Both the burner and Shadow's phone rested on his knees, screens glowing as his fingers flew, transferring the last of the data.

"Left. Now."

Shadow cut hard onto a side street lined with boarded-up warehouses and flickering traffic lights. A black SUV tailed them, lights off.

"They're still on us," Jared muttered.

Gunfire tore through the air.

The back window shattered inward, glass spraying across the seats. Jared shouted. Shadow jerked the wheel, fishtailing into the next block. Tires screamed. A trash bin toppled as they clipped the corner.

Another shot smashed the passenger mirror.

"Move! Move! Move!" Jared yelled, ducking behind the glove box.

They looped east, weaving through tight streets until the SUV lagged near a construction yard. Sirens wailed somewhere distant. Shadow spotted a narrow, greasy alley and swerved in. The tires scraped the curb, jolting over potholes.

A fire escape ladder screeched against the roof as they passed. The SUV didn't follow.

They burst out the far end into another stretch of the construction site, gravel crunching under the tires. Shadow killed the lights and slid the car behind a stack of cement barriers.

They waited, listening in the silence. Shadow's grip tightened on the wheel, one hand hovering near the gun in his hoodie pocket. His pulse pounded. He weighed his options: keep running, or strike before they did.

Silence.

Jared straightened, hands trembling as he finished the transfer. "Done," he said, handing the phones back.

Shadow didn't respond.

"You always pick shootouts for fun, or is this new?" Jared asked, voice thin with adrenaline.

Shadow stepped out, stared at the burner for a long moment, then smashed it against the ground.

Jared leaned against the car, breathing hard. "This better be worth it."

* * *

They ditched the car six blocks from the construction site, heading toward an old laundromat Jared had rigged years ago. Shadow wiped the steering wheel, door handles, and even the inside of the rearview mirror, just in case the cops decided to check for prints. Jared mirrored the motions, stiff and pale, sweat streaking down his neck.

They moved quickly into a narrow service alley. On the cracked sidewalk, a busted vending machine hummed under a drooping awning.

Jared paused to dig for change. "You ever think about just… bailing? Disappearing?" His hands trembled as he fed coins into the slot.

Shadow's gaze swept rooftops, alleys, and corners. "Used to. Back when I thought disappearing fixed things."

"And now?"

"Now I know it just makes more problems."

The can dropped. Jared reached for it. Shadow caught movement. A black SUV rolled into view, lights off.

"Move," Shadow barked, yanking Jared by his laptop bag just as a gunshot cracked. The soda burst in Jared's hand, spraying foam. Another round slammed into the vending machine.

They bolted, sneakers hammering pavement. A brick exploded by Shadow's head as they cut left, weaving between trash bins and rusted fire escapes. The SUV's engine snarled behind them.

They slipped through the laundromat's back door. Keypad hidden behind a soap dispenser. Blackout curtains sealed the windows. Inside, the air reeked of mildew, steel, and stale detergent. A single bulb flickered over a folding table cluttered with surveillance gear, energy drinks, and three burner phones.

The two of them stood still for a moment, catching their breath. The sound of their own breathing felt loud. Jared's hands shook as he set his bag down. That small pause, hearts still racing and muscles tight, made the shift from flight to focus feel like balancing on a knife's edge.

Shadow dropped into a metal chair.

Jared wiped soda from his shirt. "You owe me a soda, by the way."

Shadow stayed silent, eyes on the door. After a beat, Jared unzipped his bag and powered up his laptop.

"You need to see this," he said, connecting a hardline drive.

The screen glowed with a red trace map: pings, towers, encrypted strings. One pulsed yellow.

"She's the one who…" Jared started.

"Don't," Shadow cut in, voice sharp. "You don't need that name in your head."

Jared hesitated, then turned back to the screen without pressing further.

Shadow already knew who.

He crossed to an old payphone Jared had rewired into a one-way relay. The line crackled. No ring. No tone. His words would bounce through a chain of blind drops until they landed with one of Phoenix's contacts.

"Message for Phoenix," he said into the static. "Tell her the weapon's out the holster. And now, it's firing back."

He hung up.

Jared leaned against the wall, wide-eyed. "You just lit a fuse."

Shadow's voice stayed even. "Good. Let's see who burns first."

Outside, the wind shifted. Distant sirens wailed. Far, but close enough to remind them. The night was never still.

And in the still, every truth will be revealed.

CHAPTER 21

CRACKS IN THE GLASS

The rooftop hadn't changed much since the last time Shadow had stood there with Jade. The same rusted railing, the broken antenna, and even an old soda can kicked into the corner served as a reminder of the night she laughed so hard she couldn't breathe. Back then, the city below had seemed small and manageable, like it could be reshaped into something better.

Now it looked like a battlefield. Every light below felt like a threat. Every building looked like a possible grave.

Shadow kept his hood low, his eyes scanning the horizon. He didn't move. He didn't fidget. Meeting Jade here was risky, but he couldn't ignore it.

Jade arrived just after sunset, a backpack slung over one shoulder. She moved like someone was watching her, even if she hadn't said it out loud. Shadow watched her approach, his hands deep in his pockets, jaw clenched.

She stopped a few feet away. "You still like rooftops?" she asked, her voice softer than he remembered.

"I like the altitude," he replied.

There was a pause between them, thick with memory. The city buzzed below with life and danger, but for a moment, it all felt far away.

Shadow walked to the railing and gripped the cold metal. Jade joined him, their shoulders barely touching. Close enough to remember. Far enough to remind.

"I used to think this was the only place I could breathe," she said.

"Is that right?"

She nodded. "And you told me rooftops weren't for breathing. You said they were for jumping."

He didn't smile. "I meant that."

She looked down at the street. "I think you just liked the quiet."

He turned to face her. "Why'd you call me?" His voice was low, sharp. "I told you it wasn't safe to be around me right now."

She opened her mouth but hesitated. Then she reached into her bag and pulled out a folder.

"I found this last week," she said. "My cousin works cleanup at one of the precincts. Thought you should see it."

She held the folder a moment longer, like giving it to him made her part of whatever came next.

That caught his attention.

Shadow opened the folder. Inside lay a heavily redacted data file. One section was labeled: Project Phase Three. Two names had been blacked out, then manually overwritten in pen:

ELIJAH BLAKE

CODE NAME: SHADOW

His vision narrowed. The edges of the paper seemed to curl inward like they might catch fire.

So I've been Shadow all along. Not just a nickname. Not a reputation. A label.

Jade leaned closer, her voice low.

"I thought I was done," she said. "Done with you. Done with this life. But then I heard someone was looking for you. A girl wearing a phoenix necklace. She's been tearing the city apart trying to find you."

Shadow froze.

A foggy memory surfaced from a night with Lola. They were both drunk.

"He gave it to my mom. His name was Darrell. Died when I was little. This is all I got left."

She'd clutched that pendant like it could keep her anchored.

Shadow took a step back without realizing it. His breath caught in his throat. That moment belonged to a memory he had buried.

Now it was real.

And it was right in front of him.

Maybe it was proof. Maybe it was a warning.

The folder slipped from his hands.

He bent down, fingers just brushing the edge—

CRACK.

A gunshot ripped through the air, passing through the space where his head had been moments earlier. But it didn't hit him.

It hit Jade in her side.

She gasped and stumbled. Her mouth opened like she wanted to speak.

Shadow caught her before she fell.

Sniper.

The rooftop erupted into chaos. Shadow dragged her behind the rusted HVAC unit. His heart pounded. Adrenaline surged.

She groaned. Still breathing. Still alive. But hit.

"Stay with me," he muttered, tearing off his overshirt and pressing it to her side. He pulled out his phone.

No signal.

Another shot rang out, striking the metal nearby. Shadow curled tighter around her, shielding her with his body.

He didn't look back at the city.

It had already made its move.

They bolted for the emergency stairwell. Shadow half-carried, half-dragged her down four flights. She cursed at him. *That's a good sign.*

They reached her car. He started the engine.

His hands trembled. He tightened his grip on the wheel and floored it.

Every turn felt like life or death. Backstreets blurred past. Red lights became tests of nerve. Each brake squeal reminded him how fast the time was running out.

Jade's breathing was shallow, short ragged pulls like each inhale fought to survive. Blood soaked through the shirt he had pressed to her wound.

She groaned again, low and breaking.

"Don't close your eyes," he said, not looking away from the road.

She didn't answer.

He ran a stop sign. Swerved around a delivery truck. Passed a police cruiser without flinching.

At one point, her lips moved. Just a whisper.

"Elijah…"

His throat tightened. "I'm here," he said. Not loud. Just enough.

The cracked concrete of the Inner City gave way to the cleaner, wider streets of the Outer. Billboards looked newer. Trees lined the medians. The world changed around them, but inside the car, time stood still.

Shadow pressed harder on the gas.

The hospital came into view like a fortress.

He slammed to a stop out front. Didn't wait. Ran around, yanked open the door, and lifted her in his arms.

Nurses saw the blood and moved fast. Shouts. Stretchers. Gloves snapping. Paperwork waived.

Shadow stood frozen until the sliding doors closed.

He breathed. Once. Then again. Looked down at his hands.

Red.

Everything around him spun: nurses rushing, voices yelling, blood everywhere.

He didn't follow her.

He stepped into the lobby and sat down.

He wiped his hands on his jeans, but the blood didn't come off. It was caked under his nails, sticky and deep in the creases of his skin. The lobby went quiet. People stared. A woman pulled her child closer. A security guard emerged from behind the desk but didn't move.

Shadow leaned back in the plastic chair and stared at the ceiling lights. The buzz was dull and constant, growing more unbearable the longer it droned on.

A nurse walked by with a clipboard. She slowed when she saw him. "Family?" she asked.

He nodded. "Yeah."

She gave him a polite smile and moved on. But the word echoed in his mind.

Family.

What was he to Jade now?

Across the room, a father cradled a small child in his lap. A bandage wrapped around the kid's wrist. The man's eyes were red, worn.

Shadow looked away.

He couldn't hold that gaze. Not tonight.

He tugged his hoodie down over his face, trying to disappear. The fluorescent hummed above him.

And just like that, he wasn't in the hospital anymore.

He was back on the rooftop.

With her.

* * *

Back then, it was just me and Jade.

She sat cross-legged on the rooftop, tracing invisible lines into her jeans with her fingertip, like she was sketching thoughts she couldn't say out loud.

It's strange what your mind holds onto when someone you care about is bleeding out, maybe dying. Not the big, dramatic moments. The quiet ones. The ones that seemed small until they come back to you. Like the night Jade taught me how to lie.

"Eye contact," she said. "People believe you if your eyes don't twitch. Doesn't matter what you're saying if your stare holds steady."

She wasn't playing. She said it like someone who'd had to learn that the hard way. This wasn't about tricks. It was about survival. Maybe she'd had to lie to stay safe. Maybe more than once.

She practiced with me like it was training. Made me lie about harmless things. My favorite color. Favorite song. Who kissed who first.

Every time, she spotted the lie. Called me out without hesitation. Until one night, I got her.

"That one was good," she said, flashing a grin. "Scary good."

I kissed her after that. Not because I fooled her.

Because something in me couldn't hold back any longer. Her smile made the world feel warm again, if only for a second...

* * *

The rooftop was gone.

Jade's warmth. Her grin. The way she'd said "scary good." All replaced by harsh hospital light and the sharp scent of disinfectant.

He couldn't sit still any longer.

Shadow pushed up from the waiting room chair and drifted through the halls without asking for directions, hoping he might stumble onto something familiar.

He moved like a ghost, hood up and head low. Cameras tracked him, but no one stopped him. Then he glanced across the hall, through a glass window.

E laid in bed, an IV in his arm, chest rising slowly but steadily. Ty sat slouched in the corner, hood shadowing his face, hands pressed together as if he were praying or plotting.

Shadow froze.

He wanted to go in, to speak, to do something. But the door felt miles away.

Two uniformed cops appeared from the far wing. A nurse pointed straight at him.

Shadow didn't wait.

He walked quickly but steadily down the hall, turning a corner before they could reach him. They'd questioned him twice already. A third time, tied to another shooting, wouldn't end with questions.

There was nowhere safe. Not for him. Not anymore.

He didn't go far.

He was parked in a crumbling underground garage on the south side of the hospital. Engine off. Lights out. Only the tick of cooling metal filled the silence.

The hospital had pushed him out. Jade was in surgery. Nurses said, "we'll update you," like the words could hold off the worst, like they could keep her heart pumping.

The burner buzzed.

Jared: *Hospital cams flagged your face. You need to disappear. Now.*

Shadow: *Already gone.*

He let the phone fall onto the passenger seat and stared at himself in the cracked rearview mirror. His eyes looked older. Harder.

He pulled the USB from the glove compartment, the one he'd found at Doc's boxing gym. He'd avoided it, dreading what it might reveal. But after the hospital, after Jade, he couldn't wait. The car wasn't his, and Jade's perfume still lingered faintly in the air. He had the universal adapter he'd taken from Jared before the safe house burned. He plugged the USB into it, then into the dash port.

A loading bar blinked on the screen, followed by a simple, clinical file tree.

PHASE ZERO: SEED FILE

He opened it.

Names. Dozens. Codenames. Dates. Assignments.

BLAKE, ELIJAH — STATUS: ACTIVE

PHOENIX, CAMBRIA — STATUS: REINSTATED

His stomach dropped. The word pulsed like a warning.

Cambria.

He'd known the truth, but seeing it confirmed still hit hard. The pendant. The way she moved. How she was always one step ahead, never caught off guard. This was proof.

He sat back, lungs tight. The darkness inside the car seemed to press in.

Was anything real? He heard her voice: "I don't ask twice." That wasn't flirtation. That was protocol.

He opened another folder. Inside was Cambria's dossier, partial and redacted.

Affiliations: Heir

Handlers: Lucien / Doc

Last target cleared: [REDACTED]

Status: Field active. Unstable bond with subject.

Motive: Revenge for her brother's death.

His hands clenched. *Unstable bond.* That's what they called it.

He yanked the USB out. It was hot to the touch.

He let his forehead rest against the steering wheel. One breath. Two. Then he straightened, eyes cold. He grabbed the burner and dialed the encrypted number tied to her real name.

Not Lola. Not Phoenix.

Cambria.

The line buzzed.

"Message for Phoenix," he said, voice low and rough. "Tell her to catch me if she can."

He started the engine and hung up. The air inside the car thickened.

He stared at the phone as if it might speak again. But the screen went dark.

Leaning back, he let the silence wrap around him.

He should have felt anger. Or relief. Instead, he felt empty.

He thought of Jade's weight in his arms. Her faint voice. The way she'd looked at him with trust after the shot. He thought of E, unconscious. Ty, simmering with barely contained fury. And Lola. No. Cambria. Smiling in his face.

He glanced at his reflection in the smudged side window. Not a face. Just a shape.

He didn't look like a man anymore.

He'd made the call. Whatever came next, he'd face it head-on. The engine roared to life, and Shadow sped out of the garage without looking back.

CHAPTER 22
THE ONES WHO SEE THROUGH YOU

Two days after Jade was shot, the first thing Shadow noticed was the silence in the hospital. He slipped in through a side entrance, avoiding the main halls. But it wasn't Shadow who walked into that room.

It was Elijah.

The moment he stepped inside, the world seemed to stop. Every sound from the hallway faded. No machines beeped. No nurses bustled past. Just Jade, awake but changed, her golden skin dulled by bruises, her eyes sharp like glass. Even the air felt heavy.

She didn't smile. She didn't move.

"You brought flowers?" Her voice was rough, almost brittle.

Elijah looked at the daisies in his hand, plucked from the vending stand downstairs because they were the only ones left. They felt small, almost foolish, against the tension in the room.

"Yeah," he muttered. "Figured it was the least I could do."

She didn't take them. Her gaze never wavered.

"You could've told me," she said. "About her."

He froze. She didn't need to say the name. It was already there between them, heavy and unspoken.

"I didn't know how," he said, lowering himself into the chair beside her bed. "It didn't start like that. Lola just… kept showing up."

"You let her," Jade said.

"I didn't know she was connected. Not like that."

Jade tilted her head slightly. "You knew enough to lie."

Elijah's jaw tightened. His fingers curled against his knee. The air seemed thicker.

"I figured it out later," he said. "Tiny told me the Phoenix pendant belonged to someone named Cambria. Even when I knew for sure, I didn't tell you. I thought I could keep you safe. I wasn't ready to face what that meant for us."

Jade flinched, just enough for him to notice.

"I saw Lola wearing it," he continued. "And one night at Vertigo, I heard her tell someone, 'If Jade gets in the way... take her out.'"

Jade was silent for a long moment. She blinked once, slow, not with anger but with exhaustion.

"Do you think she pulled the trigger?" she asked.

"I think she made sure someone did," he said. "Cambria doesn't get her hands dirty." His voice trembled. "I didn't mean for any of this to happen."

"You didn't mean to get me shot," Jade said, staring up at the ceiling. "But you didn't mean to stop it either. Meaning doesn't change the result."

"I thought I was building something real."

"You were. Just not with them."

The silence between them pressed in like a living thing.

"I thought if I was careful, I could protect you from it," Elijah said. "I wanted us to be above all of it. Separate from the mess. Untouched by the games being played around us."

"You're not above it," Jade said. "You never were. You're knee-deep in it, still acting like you can win."

He looked down at his hands, faint stains still marking them from choices he couldn't undo.

"I didn't lie to hurt you."

"No. You lied to protect the image you had of yourself."

He blinked, the truth landing heavier than he expected.

"You think you're a good man stuck in a bad system," Jade said. "But you didn't just get stuck in it. You ran it. You gained from it. You excused it every time someone got hurt."

"I've been a pawn this whole time," he said quietly.

"You're worse. A prince pretending to be a pawn. That's how people die."

Her words cut deep, but he didn't look away. He stood, nodding slowly. "I'm done being moved."

At the door, he paused. "You think there's a way back from this?"

"Not unless you destroy the whole board."

Her words stayed with him. *Every piece.* Doc. Jules. Lola. Even Jade. All part of the game.

He thought of the boards he'd stood on. Jules' polished tables. Doc's velvet lounges. The cold concrete yards where survival was the only rule. Different places. Same cost.

Maybe the only way to win was to make sure no one else could play.

He stepped into the hallway, the sharp scent of antiseptic fading into the low hum of life beyond.

And he left the silence behind.

* * *

—*Jules*—

The Inland sky hung low, a dull sheet of gray pressed against the horizon. Jules approached the storage unit, pushing through the rusted gate like a shadow slipping between time and memory.

He crossed the cold concrete floor, his steps slow and deliberate. The latch resisted under his hand, but he eased it open. The creak of the door echoed like a warning.

Inside, he went straight to the filing cabinet bolted against the wall. He crouched, pulled the drawer open, and there it was: the Hawthorne file, untouched.

But the dust told another story.

A footprint. Size 11.5. Basketball sole.

And near the edge of the cabinet, tucked behind a loose tile, a keychain. Torn leather. Faded logo of Elijah's high school.

Jules picked it up as if it were a piece of his own heart.

His thumb traced the cracked edge, following the faded logo. Cheap vinyl, worn thin, but weighted by memory. Not for what it was. For who it belonged to. A boy who spent evenings shooting free throws until night claimed the court. A boy who used to knock on his studio door just to sit quietly and listen.

He had never told Elijah the full truth.

How do you explain hiding someone's identity to save their life, while also keeping them bound to you? How do you admit you were protecting and controlling them at the same time?

Lowering himself onto the edge of an end table, Jules leaned back against the wall, clenching the keychain until the cracked leather bit into his palm.

"Should've told you," he murmured into the empty room. "Before they did."

His eyes drifted back to the open drawer. The Hawthorne file lay there.

He wasn't sure what frightened him more: if Elijah had found it… or if he hadn't found enough.

The moment pulled him backward into a memory. Soft around the edges. Creeping in uninvited.

* * *

Elijah at seven, sitting cross-legged on the studio floor, headphones far too big for his head. Jules had just finished a mix, his shoulders tight from hours of work, his mind still buzzing with the frustration of the day. Elijah looked up, his wide eyes older than they should have been, a knowing smile curling on his lips.

"That beat sounds like running," he said. "Like when you're scared but go anyway. Like you don't stop 'cause stopping's worse."

The words hit Jules in a place he avoided. Back then, he only nodded, pretending it was just a kid's remark. But the truth stayed with him long after the track ended.

The kid had always been able to see straight through him, peeling back the layers Jules thought were impenetrable.

And still, Jules kept lying, adding new layers even though Elijah could read the truth in the silence.

* * *

He stood for a long moment before pulling out his phone.

Three rings.

"What?" Elijah's voice was sharp.

"You been by the unit in the Inlands where the Hawthorne files are kept?"

A pause.

"Yeah," Elijah said. "And what's it to you? You hiding something else from me?"

Jules's voice dropped, low and rough. "Listen close. That file was never just insurance. It's the blueprint for a war that started before you were born."

Silence.

"You want the truth? You think you're ready?"

"Then meet me."

"Where?"

"Our old house. Outer City. Tomorrow night." Jules let the words hang heavy. Meeting there was risky, a step back into history and into danger, but some things couldn't be said over the phone. "And make sure no one follows you."

He ended the call, his gaze lingering on the dark storage unit before lifting to the gray sky. For a fleeting moment, he thought he saw Elijah as a boy, sprinting down that same hallway, laughter echoing in the dark.

That boy was gone.

A shadow had taken his place.

CHAPTER 23

THE HOUSE WE BURIED

The Outer City didn't shine here. It hummed low and steady, like something forgotten. Streetlights flickered weakly, their glow barely cutting the dark. Houses leaned into themselves, sagging from years of standing.

Shadow stood outside the house Jules had always acted like didn't exist. The yard was a tangle of weeds climbing the rusted fence. The middle of the house sagged, siding warped, windows cloudy with years of neglect. The porch light was out. It always had been.

He pushed the gate open, its hinges squealing in protest. Inside, the air was thick with dust and damp wood, heavy with old secrets. The floor creaked under his weight, a reminder that time moved on, even if the past refused to leave.

The house didn't welcome him, but it didn't push him away either. It just stood there, hollow, like something once sacred turned into a tomb.

Every step felt like trespassing through someone else's memories. His fingers brushed along the chipped hallway molding, pausing at the dent by the closet door, the one from when he used to bounce a basketball until Jules yelled. It was still there, like it had been waiting for him.

The living room sagged under the weight of years. Dust coated the bookshelf like a burial shroud. On the mantle, the only picture faced backward: a portrait of his mother holding him when he was about three. She was laughing, not posing, just alive in a way he hadn't seen in years.

He picked it up, wiped the glass with his sleeve. A crack split her smile. Somehow, it felt right.

He lowered himself onto the old couch. It groaned like it remembered him. He stared at the ceiling until his vision blurred.

Why this house? Why now? Was Jules bringing him full circle… or trying to bury him here?

The back door creaked.

He walked into the kitchen, dragging his fingertips through the dust on the countertop. The cabinets were still closed, drawers still full of things no one needed but couldn't throw away. Same cracked tile. Same burn mark near the stove. Jules had called it a grease fire, but Shadow had always suspected a bullet. A cold draft slipped through a broken windowpane, brushing the curtain like a ghost testing the air.

He knew it was Jules by the rhythm of his steps, that slow, steady walk, like nothing could catch him unless he allowed it.

Shadow took a seat at the old table. It still wobbled, legs uneven, truth never sitting quite right. He ran his hands over the wood, feeling familiar grooves, knife marks, burn spots. He remembered watching Jules clean his gun here.

A sound behind him.

Jules stepped in through the back door, quiet, dressed in all black as if the past still hung from his shoulders.

"Didn't think you'd come," Jules said.

Shadow didn't look up. "Didn't think you'd finally talk."

Jules set a bottle of Hennessy on the table. The same kind he used to pour when he thought Elijah was asleep. The amber liquid caught the dim light, and Shadow stared at it. He'd never shared a drink with his father before. The thought pulled at him. Half curiosity. Half caution.

"You ever wonder why I kept this place?" Jules asked, settling into the chair. "It ain't for nostalgia."

Shadow raised an eyebrow. "Then what is it? A grave?"

Jules nodded slowly. "Something like that."

Silence spread through the room like fog.

"I looked through the Hawthorne file," Shadow said.

"I know."

"You labeled me as a primary subject."

"You were always at the center of this," Jules said. "Even when you didn't know it."

Shadow leaned forward. "Then tell me what I didn't know."

Jules studied him, really looked. For the first time in years, he didn't see a boy. He saw a man: scarred, dangerous, demanding the truths Jules had spent years locking away.

He opened his mouth.

"Alright," he said.

* * *

Jules took his time opening the bottle. The sharp click of the cap echoed in the stillness of the kitchen. He poured two glasses: one for himself, one left untouched in front of Shadow. Shadow didn't move.

"Let's start with Darrell," Jules said, his voice low, like the name weighed too much to carry. He kept his gaze fixed on the amber liquid.

Shadow sat motionless, silent, waiting.

"Back then, it was me, Doc, and Darrell running our the city. Doc was the face: smooth talker, loud, always in front. Darrell was the muscle, the one people feared. And I was the brains, keeping the books clean and making sure we stayed out of jail."

He rubbed a hand along his jaw, as if trying to scrub away the memory. "Darrell changed. Started moving product we never agreed on.

Cutting deals with people we couldn't trust. And Alex Hawthorne? Internal Affairs. Came in pretending to be a buyer, but he was playing both sides: ours and the feds."

"So you snitched?" Shadow said sharply.

Jules shook his head slowly. "I tried. I told Bishop I'd give him what he needed: ledgers, meeting spots, drop points. In return, he'd give me a way out. A new name, a clean slate, protection for you and your mother."

His eyes met Shadow's, tired and worn. "I was ready to leave it all behind just to get y'all out."

Shadow's voice was flat. "But that didn't happen."

Jules nodded again, slower this time, each movement heavy with thought. "Darrell found out. I don't know how. Maybe Doc told him, maybe Bishop slipped. Either way, we met in this house. Right here."

He tapped the table, the sound sharp in the still air. "He had a gun. So did I. We argued. He said I was selling out my family."

Shadow's breath caught. Heat crept up the back of his neck, and his pulse hammered in his ears. His stomach twisted, a tight knot forming as his eyes dropped to the tabletop. He traced the worn grooves with his gaze, like maybe there was another version of this story carved in the wood, one that didn't end the way Jules was telling it.

"Then he came at me. I pulled first. Shot him twice, close range. He was dead before he hit the floor."

The walls seemed to lean in on Shadow, making the room feel smaller. His fingers curled into fists against his knees, nails biting into his palms until it hurt.

"I wrapped him in tarp, took him to an alley off Sixth. Burned the clothes. Made it look like a hit. No body was ever found. No funeral. No goodbyes. To the world, Darrell just... disappeared."

Jules took a sip from his glass, the amber liquid catching the light, but it didn't seem to loosen the weight in his chest.

"That was the point. A clean slate. But ghosts don't stay buried, son. They wait."

Shadow finally looked up. "You killed your brother."

Jules stood slowly. "No. I killed a man who was going to kill me. A man who would've sold you out to the same streets I bled to escape."

He walked to the sink, turned the tap on, then off again. "It was either him or me."

Shadow leaned back in his chair. His fists loosened, but his jaw stayed tight.

"And now what? You think telling me this is supposed to make it better?"

Jules turned, leaning on the counter. "No. I think it makes it yours. You carry the name. The blood. The reputation. Now you know why."

* * *

Shadow sat frozen in that chair, as if it were gripping him to the floorboards he'd walked on since he was a kid. Everything in the house felt smaller now.

He kept his eyes on the table, avoiding Jules. "So you thought hiding all of this would keep me safe? That if I didn't know who I really was, I'd never become what I am now?"

Jules leaned against the sink, moving like every step cost him. His face stayed steady, but his voice carried a crack. "I thought if I could give you peace, maybe you wouldn't have to live through the same things I did. I didn't realize that peace could turn into its own kind of prison."

"You mean lying." Shadow's fists tightened on the table. "You lied to me. To mom. To everyone."

Jules gave a slow nod. "That too."

The quiet pressed in. Shadow's gaze drifted to the burn mark near the stove. He couldn't remember when he first asked about it, just that Jules had given him a story, and he'd believed it. Like all the other stories. Like all the other lies.

"All this time I thought I was choosing who to be," Shadow said, his voice low. "If I'd gone to college instead of chasing the Inner City, maybe things would've been different. But it turns out I've been following a script other people wrote: Darrell, you, Doc. Everyone shaping me into what they wanted."

Jules pushed off the sink and stepped forward. "That's not true. You're more than what's been done to you. You're what you choose to become, even when others try to pull you off course."

Shadow's eyes snapped up, his words sharp. "Don't talk to me like I'm some second chance." He caught the twitch in Jules's jaw, proof the words had landed.

A pause.

Then Jules nodded once. "Fair."

The room felt heavier, as if the past were seeping through the walls.

Shadow stood slowly, the chair scraping back like a blade leaving its sheath. "So what do I do with it?"

"You strip away the parts that were never truly yours. And keep the ones that feel right. The ones that make you stronger and happier."

Shadow gave a short, bitter laugh. "And how do I know which is which?"

"You don't," Jules said. "Not until you're tested. That's when you'll know."

Shadow's phone buzzed. Ty's name glowed on the screen.

He answered. "Yeah?"

Ty's voice was scratchy but steady. "They say E's might be able to go home soon."

Shadow closed his eyes briefly. "That's good," he said, and meant it.

He hung up, slid the phone into his pocket, and looked at Jules. Not as a father. Not as a killer. But as a man who couldn't undo what was done.

"This house isn't a grave," Shadow said, heading for the door. "It's a mirror. And I'm done looking at it."

He left the chair where it stood, without a backward glance.

* * *

—*Lola*—

Shadow wasn't here to see it. This was Lola's world now. What happened tonight would set a fire between them that couldn't be put out.

Lola stood at the window in Doc's penthouse, arms crossed, staring out at the city like it had betrayed her. Below, traffic moved in glowing red streams, unaware of the truth that's about to shatter her.

Doc poured himself a drink, setting another glass on the counter but leaving it untouched. "Why are you so quiet?"

She didn't turn around. "I don't feel like talking."

He leaned against the bar, his tone easy but sharp. "Remember what you asked me when you came to the club?"

Her jaw tightened. "Who killed my brother."

"I told you we'd find him. We did."

Her eyes narrowed. "Who?"

"Shadow. Elijah. The boy with two faces."

Her fists clenched. "You're lying."

"I don't lie. I plan."

He slid a folder toward her. On top was an envelope stamped with Jules's name and a coded order: *Sparrow*, circled in red.

"That's the hit Shadow's dad signed off on."

Her chest tightened, a mix of rage and disbelief crashing over her. She'd been sleeping beside her brother's killer. Trusting him. Letting him close.

"Why didn't you tell me sooner?" she demanded.

"The timing wasn't right," Doc said.

Her eyes burned. She grabbed her phone, turned for the door, and didn't look back.

Outside, the cool night air stung her face. She scrolled to his name. Shadow, not Elijah. And hit call.

Three rings.

"Lola?"

"Twenty minutes. Back lot of the mall. If you're not there… I'll find you."

She hung up, pulse pounding, each step away from the building sharpening the storm inside her.

CHAPTER 24

ASHES DON'T BURY THEMSELVES

Across the city, Shadow stared at his phone screen. He remembered the warning whispered at Vertigo, one that had never left his mind: *"If Jade gets in the way… take her out."*

His phone buzzed again. It was Jade.

"I'm out," she said. Her voice was shaky but determined, like she was holding herself together with sheer willpower. "They're letting me go soon. I just… wanted to hear your voice."

He closed his eyes for a moment, listening to her breathe. "Lay low. Don't try to find me. I've got a safe place for you. Take your brother to an old laundromat in the Inlands. Ask for Jared and tell him I sent you."

"Elijah—"

"Please. I don't want you to get hurt again."

He hung up before she could argue.

Some truths were still too dangerous for her to know.

The parking lot behind the mall felt like an open wound in the city. Weeds pushed through cracked pavement, and broken streetlights flickered, throwing restless shadows across the ground. Somewhere far away, a siren wailed, then faded into the low hum of freeway traffic.

Shadow leaned against a pillar covered in layers of graffiti. This was where he'd first seen her. Not as an enemy. As a girl whose eyes could make him lose his cool.

Footsteps broke the silence.

He turned.

Lola stepped out from the darkness, her shape strong but lined with pain. Her jacket pulled tight across her shoulders, and the click of her boots echoed in the empty lot. Each step was slow and deliberate.

She stopped a few feet from him. "I thought you might not show."

"Thought about it," he said. "But I knew you'd find me either way."

"You always this bold with women who might kill you?"

"Only the ones I cared about."

Her face didn't soften. "Don't. Not tonight."

He nodded.

"I need to ask you something face-to-face," she said, her voice sharp. "Did you kill a boy outside Vertigo? His name was Sparrow."

"I didn't know him."

"You didn't need to." Her tone was full of anger. But underneath was something else. Uncertainty.

"Yeah," he said quietly. "He tried to rob me. I pointed him out to Doc. Then… Doc had his guys grab him. They beat him up, dragged him into the alley. That's when Doc handed me the gun and told me to pull the trigger."

Lola froze. The light above them buzzed louder in the stillness. "He… didn't tell me that." Her voice was thin. "Doc told me your dad ordered it. Said you did it without hesitation."

Shadow met her eyes. "He didn't tell you everything."

She turned slightly, as if hiding her reaction. "Why would he keep that from me?"

"Maybe so you wouldn't know who was really giving the orders."

Her eyes snapped back to his, still sharp but less certain. "You pulled the trigger," she said.

"And I've never forgotten it."

She stepped closer. "He was my brother." The words slammed into him like a hard punch, stealing his breath for a second. His hand gripped the edge of the pillar, a tightness building in his chest he couldn't shake.

"I didn't want to do it."

"But you did. You touched me with the same hands that killed him."

He looked away. "I'm sorry."

"That doesn't bring him back."

"I know. But it wasn't my plan. It came from the people we both trusted."

Her gaze was like a blade. "And my whole life since then has been built on what he told me."

"Then we were both being used."

"Don't try to connect with me. You don't know what I'm thinking of doing to you." Her words made his stomach knot. A flicker of fear crossed his eyes before he could hide it.

"You think I didn't lose anything? I've been paying for that night every day since."

"You're still alive."

"Barely."

The wind pushed dust and scraps across the lot. She looked toward the skyline, her hair whipping across her face.

"So am I next?" he asked.

She stayed quiet for a long moment. When she finally spoke, her voice was rough, like sand dragged across stone. "I haven't decided yet." She turned and walked away, her steps slower now, like she wasn't sure about the ground she was walking on.

Shadow stood still, watching her fade into the darkness. His breathing was slow and heavy. Then, out of the corner of his eyes, he spotted headlights creeping into the far end of the lot. A dark car turned the corner, moving too slowly to be passing by. His pulse jumped. He scanned the area: two exits, both partially blocked. No cover except the pillar and a rusted dumpster twenty feet away. The hairs on his neck stood on end.

Time to move.

He pushed away from the pillar, keeping low as he slipped into the shadows. His steps were silent and quick, his eyes darting for threats, disappearing before the car could get close enough to see his face.

* * *

—*Jules*—

Jules Knight sat in his study, sipping a glass of Macallan 18-year-old whiskey while soft jazz drifted lazily through the room. The record needle traced the final groove, clicking quietly at the end of a forgotten tune. It was late. Jules figured Shadow was out somewhere in the city. Knee-deep in trouble that would end up at his doorstep again.

His phone rang.

"Jules."

A voice smooth and familiar slid through the line. "Been a long time, Jules. I hear your armor's cracking."

Jules froze, setting his glass down slowly. The voice was a ghost from the past. "Darrell?"

"That name's buried," the voice replied. "Call me Lucien. You know the name. We've been playing chess from opposite corners. And you seem to have lost your touch."

Jules rose from his chair, one hand braced on the desk. "You're supposed to be dead."

"I was supposed to be a lot of things."

Silence stretched between them, broken only by the soft pop of the record needle.

Jules kept his voice steady. "Word is, someone named Phoenix has been tracking my son."

Lucien's tone coiled tight, like a snake ready to strike. "I've seen your boy pretending to be a thug. He's getting good at it. Takes after you."

"Your problem's with me. Leave him out of it."

"Can't do that. You took someone from me."

Jules's eyes narrowed. "Sparrow."

"Your son took mine. So I'm taking yours."

Jules's grip on the desk tightened until his knuckles turned white. "You calling to warn me, or just to hear yourself talk?"

Lucien's voice cut sharper. "And Vivi? Still the prettiest thing you never deserved?"

The chill hit instantly.

"Tell her I said h—"

Click.

Jules ended the call.

The silence that followed wasn't calm. It was the sound of a loaded chamber. An old war had just been reignited. Somewhere out in the city, while Shadow walked the streets, another move was already in motion. Jules knew it would come fast.

* * *

Shadow sat on the front steps of Ty's house, hood up, a cigarette dangling from his fingers. He didn't usually smoke, but the stress tonight made him need to watch something burn. His eyes kept sweeping the street, alert for any sign of trouble. A few cars rolled past without slowing, but he didn't trust the quiet.

Ty emerged from the shadows. "So this is where we're at now? Cigarettes and bad choices?"

Shadow didn't smile. "Fitting, right? If this doesn't kill me, ICS will."

Ty glanced toward the street before lowering himself beside him. "You better not be bringing that heat to my place."

"Relax. I checked the block twice before I sat down."

They sat in silence for a moment.

"Lola knows," Shadow said finally. "About the alley. About the guy I killed. He was her brother."

Ty's shoulders sagged. "Damn."

"She thinks I did it on purpose, like it meant something. But it didn't. Not until she gave him a name."

"You tell her?"

"Didn't matter. She doesn't want the truth. She wants blood."

Ty tapped his shoe against the step. "You think she's coming back?"

"She said she hasn't decided if I live or die yet."

"That's romantic."

Shadow let out a bitter laugh. "You should've seen her eyes. It wasn't rage. It was betrayal. That's what broke me."

He pulled his hoodie tighter.

"Jade called. She's safe. Out of the way. I told her to keep it that way."

"You going after her?"

Shadow looked up at the sky. The stars blinked like dying promises. "This ends when someone stops pretending this city still plays by rules."

Ty stood, offering his hand. "Then stop pretending."

Shadow clasped it and gave him a nod while Ty helped him up.

Before heading inside, Ty paused. "E's getting out of the hospital in three days. You should visit him."

"I will."

When Ty disappeared inside, Shadow stayed put. The cigarette burned down to the filter, and still, he didn't move. The embers glowed faint, like memories you couldn't outrun.

He wandered to the far corner of the backyard.

Years ago, they buried things there: sneakers, dead phones, even Ty's report card once. Like if they buried it deep enough, the world would forget it ever existed.

Ty's voice drifted from inside. "You should leave before someone decides to pull up shooting."

No destination. Just forward. Away from the version of himself that let others write his story.

Tonight, that ended. He decided no one would control his fate again, no matter the cost.

Some names were meant to be whispered.

His would be the one they screamed.

CHAPTER 25
BROTHERHOOD IN THE BALANCE

It was two boys in a small room that held more memories than space. The air smelled faintly of rubbing alcohol mixed with something cooking down the hall. An old box fan hummed in the window, slow and steady, like it had been there forever. The curtains didn't match, one floral and one striped, stitched together with a grandmother's stubborn care. Faded posters curled at the corners, and a leaning stack of old video games rested against the dresser.

E lay on the bed, wrapped in tight bandages, his back propped up by pillows. He looked stronger but quieter, like pain had spoken through him and left him empty. His hair was a little longer, and there were dark circles under his eyes.

"You didn't have to come," E said, staring at the ceiling instead of at Elijah.

Elijah stood with his hands buried in his hoodie pocket. "I know. But I wanted to."

E rubbed his jaw. "They're sending me to college. Orientation. Rehab. Whole reset."

Elijah's chest tightened. A mix of pride and sadness. It was great news, but it reminded him how much had changed and how far apart they'd drifted.

"That's good."

"Yeah. Weird though. I thought all three of us would go."

Elijah didn't respond. The silence stretched between them, full of things neither wanted to say. Outside, a car rolled by slowly.

E finally looked at him, his eyes steady. "You know they weren't aiming for me, right?"

"I know."

"I was just there. Just trying to be there for you guys. Next thing I know, I'm on the ground. Didn't even see it coming. Heard Ty scream. Then nothing."

Elijah's jaw tightened. "I saw it. I see it every time I close my eyes."

The fan clicked, its gears skipping. A dog barked twice outside, then silence again.

"I'm not mad at you," E said. "Not like Ty is."

"You should be."

"Maybe. But getting shot changes things. Makes you realize what matters. Who you still have."

Elijah moved to the corner chair. The cushion sighed under his weight, and the wooden frame creaked.

"I never wanted this to touch you."

E shrugged and winced. "Didn't matter what you wanted. The streets always find your people. That's the real GPS. No matter how far you get, it finds you."

Elijah leaned forward, "You think I can come back from this?"

E didn't answer right away. He looked at his leg, flexed his toes, then stared out the window where the wind swayed a hanging plant with brittle leaves. Finally, he said, "I think you already left. You just don't know where you landed yet."

He reached for a framed photo on the nightstand. Three boys outside the rec center, laughing like they understood and trusted the rules of the world. The frame had a crack in one corner, like it had been dropped and put back together.

"You remember this?"

Elijah nodded, his throat tight.

"Back then," E said softly, "we thought loyalty could protect us. We believed if we had each other's backs, nothing could touch us."

Elijah held the frame like it was a confession, his thumb brushing a smudge from E's smile.

"It didn't."

"No," E said, meeting his eyes. "But it still means something. Maybe even more now."

* * *

The court behind the Outer City rec center was still in pieces. Shadow stopped at the corner a block away, scanning both ends of the street and checking the rooftops. He waited ten long minutes. No cars passed. No movement where there shouldn't be any. Only then did he cross, knowing full well the risk of being out in the open. The chain net was rusted. The pavement cracked like tired hands refusing to let go. The front of the building had been refreshed with new paint, bright lights, and even a mural no one asked for. But back here. This was the real memory. The part untouched by time or city funding.

He slipped through the rear gate, its hinge bent, the peeling sticker that once read NO DUNKING now simply saying NO. The court still carried the echoes of rough, personal games and friendships forged through game winners and fouls nobody ever called.

Ty was under the rim, headphones hanging around his neck. The ball hit the blacktop in a steady beat. One-two. One-two. A heartbeat on concrete. He dribbled, pivoted, and released. Clang. The rim groaned.

Shadow lingered by the fence, remembering when Ty's handles made grown men stop mid-step and when E could drain corner threes like it was nothing. Back when he was still Elijah, not the shadow he'd become.

He stepped forward.

Ty kept shooting.

"I didn't see you at E's grandma's," Shadow said.

"Didn't have anything to say," Ty replied. "But now? Now I got words."

Ty missed another shot and let the ball roll back to him. He turned, eyes sharp. The kind of look you give someone you used to ride for but can't face without heat in your chest.

"We were at the park, laughing. Then chaos. Gunfire. Blood. All because you been living two lives and kept us at arm's length."

"I was trying to keep you out of it."

"Out of it?" Ty's voice rose. "You made us targets. Extras in your story. And when the plot flipped, we took the hits." He tossed the ball aside. "You brought heat to our neighborhood."

Shadow stepped closer, hands in his jacket. Not defensive. Not relaxed. Just contained. "It wasn't supposed to happen like this."

Ty scoffed. "But it did. You think E's gonna be the same just because you meant well?"

Shadow said nothing.

"I didn't know it would go that far," he admitted.

"Nah." Ty stepped in. "You didn't care if it did."

That one stung.

"I care. Always have. That's why I'm here now."

Ty picked up the ball, palming it like nothing. "Yeah? Well, don't be. Everyone's safer that way."

Shadow took a step. "If I don't make it back—"

"Don't give me that shit," Ty cut him off. "Don't start with your martyr speech. You ain't a hero. You're a ghost. You died the day you chose the dark."

He brushed past Shadow.

"You ain't Shadow to me," Ty said over his shoulder. "You're just somebody I used to hang with."

Then he was gone.

* * *

The sedan sat just beyond the last streetlamp, headlights dimmed, engine rumbling low like someone holding their breath. The lot around it was empty. An abandoned strip mall with boarded-up windows. Cracked pavement. Shards of glass glinting under the faint light. Even the wind seemed to know to stay quiet.

Shadow spotted it from half a block away and slipped into the narrow shadows between two buildings, scanning for movement. No shapes in the seats. No one leaning on the hood. But its stillness said it was waiting for him.

He circled wide, hand resting near the grip of his gun beneath his jacket. When he finally stepped into the open, he approached from the driver's side, gun raised just enough to make his point.

The window slid down, revealing a broad man with a scar running along his jaw and a smirk that didn't touch his eyes.

"Get in," the man said. "Doc wants a word."

Shadow glanced into the back seat, expecting to see Doc. It was empty. He slid his gun back under his jacket and opened the passenger door.

The driver handed him a phone. "For you."

Static crackled in his ear. Then Doc's voice slid through. Smooth. Cold.

"Where you been hiding, boy?"

Shadow stayed silent.

"We not friends anymore? Can't call your old pal Doc?"

His grip on the phone tightened.

"That's alright," Doc said, his voice like ice. "You've got twenty-four hours to come see me. Don't make me have to come find you again."

The line went dead.

The driver shifted into gear, but Shadow was already stepping out. He stood in the empty street, watching the taillights disappear into the dark.

His pulse pounded. Tomorrow, he'd face Doc.

And it might be the last thing he ever did.

CHAPTER 26
DOC'S REVEAL

Shadow paused in the alley across from the unmarked door. He pulled the burner from his pocket, typed Jared's number, and sent a pin drop.

If you don't hear from me in two hours, call the cops. This is where I am.

He slid the phone away, took a slow breath, and crossed the street.

He stared at the screen for a second longer, thumb hovering over the send button. If he was walking into a trap, at least someone would know where to find the body.

The place wasn't what Shadow expected. Not a warehouse. Not a trap house. It was an old jazz lounge, tucked on a quiet block just outside the Inner City. The windows were blacked out, the entrance unmarked. You wouldn't find it unless someone told you where to look. This wasn't a place for casual visitors. It was built for secrecy.

Inside, the air was still, the silence feeling intentional. The wood floors held a muted shine, the velvet booths sat empty but spotless, and the tables were set as if guests might still wander in. A slow, mournful horn drifted from hidden speakers, wrapping the room in old memories.

Shadow moved carefully, each step echoing. He passed the empty stage with its untouched mic, then the long mahogany bar where a single glass waited, almost like part of a ritual. Every detail felt chosen.

Doc sat in the back under a lone spotlight at a round table. Black slacks. Black turtleneck. No jewelry. Just a quiet authority that didn't need volume.

Shadow stayed standing.

"You made it," Doc said, voice low and steady.

Months ago, those words might have filled Shadow with pride. Now, they scraped against the truth he knew. His face stayed unreadable.

"You sent for me."

The walls were lined with black-and-white portraits: Darrell in his prime, leaning against a black Charger; Jules, younger, caught mid-verse at a mic, defiance in his eyes; and a few faces Shadow didn't recognize. Men whose names lived only in whispers.

One frame was empty.

Doc nodded toward it. "That one's for a future legend. Someone still writing their story."

Shadow finally sat, slow and tense. "You always this theatrical?"

Doc smirked. "Only when it matters."

The horn kept playing. The ceiling fan spun in lazy circles.

"You ever wonder why I let you get this close?" Doc asked.

Shadow didn't answer, but his gaze didn't waver.

"Because I saw what you were before you did," Doc said. "Your father had fire, sure, but you? You move like smoke, slipping in and out without a trace. You didn't just end up here by chance, Elijah. You were shaped for this, piece by piece."

Something flickered in Shadow's eyes: not fear or anger, but recognition. Another piece of the puzzle slid into place.

"I didn't bring you close out of pity," Doc continued. "I need a successor. Someone who can live in both worlds, light and dark."

He leaned back, letting the words settle.

"I brought you here to stop pretending. Pretending you have a choice. Pretending you're not already waist deep in this shit."

Shadow's gut tightened. He wasn't sure the old version of himself even existed anymore. Part of him resented the trap Doc was setting. Another part, the part shaped by survival, felt the pull of acceptance.

"And this is?" Shadow asked, his voice edged with caution.

Doc reached under the table and set a pistol on the surface with deliberate care. "Your final offer," he said evenly. "Your place at the table: everything you wanted, and what you never saw coming."

The light buzzed overhead, one flicker from darkness.

"Then let's stop pretending," Shadow said. "Tell me what I don't know."

Doc poured two drinks from a crystal decanter, the liquid inside a rich gold. He slid one glass toward Shadow without asking, then lifted his own.

"To inheritance," he said.

Shadow didn't touch the drink.

Doc smirked. "Still holding on to that part of yourself. The part that thinks you can keep your hands clean in this world. That won't last."

He took a slow sip and leaned back in the booth, looking like a man watching the empire he built run itself. The low, sorrowful horns in the background played like a confession set to music.

"I've been watching you for years. Long before you ever stepped foot in my world. The way you moved, the way you planned ahead. Your pops never saw it, too busy chasing second chances and melodies."

The light above the bar hummed, a faint buzz that cut through Doc's words. Shadow shifted in his seat, feeling the room press in like the walls were listening. Shadow stayed quiet, his fingers curling against the table's edge. The drink remained untouched.

"The second time you came to the Inner City, you hit that store in the mall. You thought you were just showing off for your boys, but I saw the way you looked at her, and I knew you'd return. I wanted to see what you'd do, so I made a call. Placed her behind that counter, already primed with your name and one job: watch you, learn you. That wasn't fate, Shadow. That was me pulling the strings."

He set his glass down, the soft click against the wood sharper than it should have been.

"She wasn't supposed to fall for you," Doc said. "She was supposed to report back. But feelings? That was her weakness."

He tapped his glass, eyes sharp. "Maybe if I'd told her more, she wouldn't have broken the rules. Maybe she wouldn't be hiding right now."

Shadow's voice was low. "So she was just another piece."

Doc shrugged. "Everyone's a piece. I just know how to play the game better than most."

He leaned in, his voice slowing like a storyteller just before the twist.

"Ever ask Jade where she's from? Who her father was?"

Shadow didn't move. "No, but she told me he died in a turf war."

Doc gave a short, mocking laugh. "Her father helped build ICS. Sat beside Lucien when they laid the foundation. She acts clean, but she's from the same dirt as the rest of us, just knows how to make it look good."

The thought twisted in Shadow's gut. Jade's fire, her edge, the way she seemed to know too much: it all made sense now. And none of it felt right.

Doc smiled knowingly. "You think you know the people around you. But everyone's got a mask, Shadow. Even you."

Doc stood, lifting the pistol from the table, and moved slowly to Shadow's side. He let the weight of his words settle, studying Shadow's face like an artist judging a finished piece.

"They say what doesn't kill you makes you stronger. You? You've dodged death more than once. That's not luck. That's evolution."

Shadow looked up. Something in his eyes had gone still.

"Sparrow? That was a sacrifice. I knew Lucien would bleed for his boy. He'd either retaliate or fold. Either way, I win."

Shadow's brow furrowed, a mix of confusion and dread shadowing his face. He couldn't decide what was worse: Doc treating people like chess pieces or how well his plan worked.

Doc laced his fingers together, elbows on the polished wood, his voice calm but heavy. "If Lucien kills Jules, I get the streets through Lucien. Blood buys loyalty. If Jules kills Lucien, I get his people, his muscle, his reach. And if they kill each other?"

Shadow's mouth opened slightly, but no sound came. His mind was already connecting the dots, and the picture made his stomach turn.

Doc paused, a faint smile playing at his lips. "I get the kingdom. All of it. You could've figured that out yourself if you'd followed the trail. The moves. The hits. The whispers in the alleys. All pointed to me setting them up to collide."

Shadow's jaw tightened, but he didn't blink.

Doc tapped a folder on the table. "That war? You didn't start it. But you sure as hell pulled the trigger that set it off again."

He leaned forward, eyes narrowing. "You think I didn't notice when you took that burner from my desk? That I wouldn't realize you were following the breadcrumbs I laid out for you?"

Shadow stayed silent, but his shoulders shifted, bracing.

Doc chuckled. "I left it for you. Planted it like bait. I wanted you to see your father for who he is. Not the man he pretended to be."

He stood and walked to the far end of the room. While Doc's words sank in, Shadow's hand dipped to his pocket under the table. He slid the phone out just far enough to type a single message to Jared.

Come get me.

He hit send and slipped it back, eyes never leaving Doc.

A door creaked open, revealing dim light and a concrete floor. Inside, a chair was bolted to the ground. Thick rope bound a man's wrists and ankles, and a strip of cloth was tied tight across his mouth. Dried blood marked the corners of his lips. Shadow recognized him, the other guy from the robbery, the one who got away. Cold realization gripped him: this wasn't just a captured enemy, it was proof that Doc tied up every loose end. The sight twisted in his gut, a warning of how close he'd come to ending up in that chair.

Doc stepped into the doorway. "He thought he could sell scraps of info. Move behind my back."

One shot rang out, cracking through the room, echoing off the walls and blending with the mournful jazz overhead. The man slumped sideways, a bullet to the head.

Doc returned to the table as if nothing had happened. He wiped the gun with a handkerchief and set it down.

"I don't reward disloyalty."

He stepped in front of Shadow, his silhouette cutting across the table. "You either walk with me: keep doing jobs, stay at my side, let me pull you deeper into this. Or you end up in a chair like that. I can keep you safe, but only if you're under my protection."

Shadow's mind flashed to all the times Doc's name had opened doors or stopped trouble cold. That kind of power could keep him alive, but it could also cage him.

He swallowed. "And if I turn you in?"

Doc's eyes didn't waver. "Then you'd better pray someone else can protect you."

A pause. A breath. The final truth.

"No one's safe on the way up, Shadow. Not even you. So make up your mind. Fast."

With slow, steady steps, Doc walked out. The door clicked shut behind him, leaving Shadow alone in a room full of ghosts, blood, and the suffocating silence of choices already made.

The room felt colder now, not from the body, not from the gun resting on the table, but because Shadow had finally seen the full picture of what's been developing all along.

Doc hadn't just played the game: he was the game. And Shadow? He'd passed every test, played every role, carried out every task like a weapon forged without knowing.

He rose slowly, took a step toward the door, then stopped.

In the far room, the body sat slumped, the overhead light flickering like a failing heartbeat. Shadow didn't look away. He let the moment sink in, not just the violence, but the design behind it. The cold strategy in every move Doc made.

The burner phone buzzed on the table. A single message lit the screen:

I'm outside.

It wasn't part of some master plan, but it was his lifeline, proof he wasn't leaving alone.

Shadow picked it up, eyes lingering on the words before shifting to the empty glass frame on the wall: the one with no picture, no name.

The reflection staring back wasn't Elijah, the boy who dreamed of music, college, and freedom. It was someone hardened, shaped by betrayal and fire.

He slipped the phone into his pocket, straightened his jacket, and walked out of the lounge alone. The door clicked shut behind him, trapping the silence inside.

Outside, the world was alive. Sirens wailed in the distance. A car backfired. Somewhere else, a gunshot cracked through the night.

Shadow stood at the curb, scanning the dark. A black sedan rolled to a stop.

Jared sat behind the wheel; computers stacked in the back.

Shadow climbed in, closing the door with finality. The engine roared.

And the reckoning began.

THE RECKONING

CHAPTER 27
HOUSE OF CARDS

He hadn't been back to the apartment in a while. Not since the night everything fell apart. But when Vivi called, he answered.

Not to beg. Not to cry. Just to ask.

"Please. Just come."

He'd already been thinking about going there. Jules had answers he couldn't get anywhere else, answers about Doc. Vivi's call didn't change his mind; it just gave him an excuse to walk through the door.

She didn't say why, but he had a feeling. Maybe it was about E. Or maybe she already knew what was coming: how danger follows you even when you try to leave it behind, how changing your name doesn't erase the past.

On the way there, a green sedan slowed beside him. The driver leaned out, pretending to be lost. "Hey, you know how to get to—"

Shadow spotted the gun in his hand before the words finished. His own came up faster. Two quick shots. The man slumped against the wheel, motionless. Shadow didn't wait to see if he was dead.

By the time the echo faded, he was already gone, heart steady, breath even. Just another reminder: you can't outrun this life. Not even on your way to your family's door.

The door was unlocked. It gave with a soft click, like even it wasn't ready to keep him out.

Inside, the air felt thick and still. Jules sat at the table, hands folded, unmoving. His eyes didn't follow Shadow, but his presence filled the room.

Vivi stood near the counter, arms crossed like she was holding herself together. A single photo lay between them on the table. Fresh print. Black-and-white. Its edges curled slightly, still drying. Shadow didn't need to get closer to know what it showed.

A still from a parking lot security camera. Him. And Doc.

Vivi didn't look at the photo. She looked at him.

"I spoke with E," she said, her voice steady. "He's scared for you. Says he doesn't recognize who you're becoming."

Her eyes searched his face. Not angry. Not hurt. Just searching, like she was trying to find the boy she once called son.

"We didn't raise a liar, Elijah," she said softly. "So tell me, what have you been doing?"

He didn't flinch at the name. He'd heard it plenty of times before, but now it felt different, like hearing an old voicemail from a number you don't call anymore.

"Why? So you can act surprised? Pretend this didn't start with you?"

Vivi's arms tightened around herself. Jules stayed still.

"I'm going to protect what matters," Shadow said, stepping forward. The room seemed smaller now. "Doc's been moving behind the scenes this whole time."

He looked at them both. "You want the truth? He used me. Watched me. Put people in my path: Lola, maybe Jade, the jobs, ICS. He planned it all. I thought I was choosing this life. But I was just playing his game."

He nodded toward the photo. "That's not just a message. It's a warning. He's not finished, maybe not until I'm dead or standing next to him. If I don't move first, he will. That's why, on my way here, I had to pull the trigger before someone else could. This is the life he's boxed me into."

Jules' voice finally broke the silence. "Then what do you plan to do?"

"I need what you know," Shadow said, voice low but sharp. "You've been in the trenches with him longer than I've been alive. You know his moves, his tells. I'm not here for a reunion, I'm here because that's the edge I need to put him down before he puts me under."

The room stood still.

"I can't lose another man in this family to the Inner City." Vivi's voice cracked.

Shadow's face softened. "You already lost him, Ma. Elijah died the night he pulled a trigger for someone else. All that's left is who I had to become."

Her eyes glistened. She stepped forward, placing her hand on his chest.

"You don't have to come back whole," she whispered. "You just have to come back alive."

For a moment, the weight lifted. Just enough for a crack of light to push through.

She stepped back without a word, slipping into the back room. The soft click of the door sealed her grief away like a secret.

Shadow and Jules were alone.

Shadow didn't sit. Jules didn't stand. Their eyes locked. Jules shifted his weight, rubbing the back of his neck before letting his hand drop. His jaw tightened, holding back words he wasn't sure he could speak.

"You don't have to do this," Jules said finally, his voice worn and tired. "There's still a way back."

Shadow's gaze was steady but hollow, stripped clean by years of lies.

"This isn't who you are, Elijah. You still have time. You can walk away. Let me handle it."

The back-room door eased open. Vivi stepped out, lingering near the doorway, her eyes darting between them.

Shadow shook his head. "I don't want to walk away," he said, his voice sharp. "I want to end it before someone else I care about gets caught in the crossfire. I'd rather be judged by twelve than carried by six."

Vivi's breath caught, her arms folding tighter.

Jules exhaled through his nose, pressing his fingers to his temples before dropping them. "Doc's not just a man. He's a system. A virus. He's survived more than you know. You think you're ready to take him on?"

Shadow's fists curled. "I'm not ready," he said. "But I'm done waiting."

Vivi stepped forward, lips parting, but she stayed quiet.

"This isn't about proving I'm tough," Shadow said. "It's about stopping this before it kills me and everyone I care about. I came here because, whether I like it or not, you're the only one who can keep me from walking in blind. I don't think I'll ever forgive you. But I'm doing this. So either help me, or stay the hell out of my way."

Vivi's eyes glistened, but she stayed still.

Jules's shoulders sagged. His hand twitched like he might reach for his son, but he didn't move.

Shadow headed for the door, each step quiet but heavy. The talk with Jules burned in his chest like a slow fire: contained, but dangerous. Nothing more could be said without tearing open wounds too deep to close.

"Elijah..." Jules said, like a final attempt to save him.

The hallway stretched ahead, a tunnel between past and future. At the end, Vivi stood with her arms crossed, shoulders curled inward, eyes wet with truth.

"Elijah... please," she whispered.

"He won't stop. Not until someone stops him," Shadow said.

"Let your father handle it. Please, Elijah... don't go out there."

He stepped closer, the hallway narrowing with every move. His voice softened, touched with something that used to be love.

"He had his chance, Ma. You know he did. But this is mine."

Her fingers brushed his arm, fragile and desperate. "You don't have to become this."

Shadow looked at her. Not past her. Not through her. At her. And for a heartbeat, Elijah surfaced.

Not the soldier. Not Shadow. Just the son.

"I'm sorry," Elijah said, rough but honest. "For what I became. For what I'm about to do. But I can't keep running from it. Not anymore."

Vivi's lip trembled. She looked like she wanted to scream and collapse all at once. Then she broke: shoulders shaking, breath uneven, tears spilling like they'd been waiting years.

He pulled her close, arms wrapping around her like a son, not a weapon. He held her until her sobs slowed.

Let it last, he thought. Let her remember this. Let me remember it too. Then he stepped back.

She reached for him again, but he turned away. He opened the door. Behind him, Vivi dropped to her knees, hands to her face, sobbing as if she were reaching for something already gone.

Elijah couldn't stand to see his mother cry, but it was better than her putting roses on his casket.

* * *

The night air cut sharper than it should've, stinging his lungs with every breath. Shadow kept moving, his steps quick, his mind still burning from the conversation with Jules. He didn't slow. Didn't look back. That heat inside him needed somewhere to go.

Two side streets later, he spotted a corner bodega glowing like an island in the dark. He stepped inside, bought a burner phone, dropped cash on the counter, and gave the clerk a single nod. No words. No expression. Just business.

The bell over the door jingled as he stepped out. That's when he saw them.

Three young guys leaned against the wall, ICS colors tucked in their shoelaces and caps for anyone who knew where to look. They'd been waiting.

One pushed off the wall, smirking. "Yo, what's in the bag?"

Shadow didn't answer. Kept walking.

Another stepped in front of him. "Don't be rude. Just your phone, your cash... and that watch."

Shadow's eyes swept over them, measuring angles like a fight already playing out in his head. "Look, I'm not in the mood. You should walk away." His stance shifted, feet set, shoulders loose.

They laughed. The first lunged. Shadow slipped the punch and snapped a jab into his nose. The second swung wide; Shadow took a shot to the ribs, gritted his teeth, and answered with a hook that sent him stumbling. The third came from the side, throwing wild punches.

They hit him all at once, grabbing and swinging, trying to pull him down. Shadow moved in tight, blocking, countering. Elbows and short punches landed heavy. His knuckles split on a cheekbone. A fist clipped his jaw. He slammed one into the wall, ducked another swing, and drove his shoulder into someone's chest.

Steel flashed. The ringleader now held a knife, the blade catching the streetlight.

Shadow stepped back, chest rising and falling. His hand went inside his jacket and came out with something colder.

"Haven't anyone told you," he said, voice low and steady, "play stupid games. Win stupid prizes."

The knife froze midair. All three backed up.

"Run."

They scattered into the dark.

Shadow lowered the gun, ribs aching with every breath, adrenaline still coursing hot through his veins. The city pressed in from all sides, but this time Shadow wasn't shrinking. He was coiled, ready to swing back.

CHAPTER 28

LOVE ON THE LINE

Shadow went to the safehouse where Jared had hidden Jade, a quiet, tucked-away place wired with enough traps to make any intruder think twice.

A moment passed before the lock clicked.

She opened the door slowly, leaning against the frame like the pain was still hanging on. Her crop top revealed the edge of a scar, a sharp reminder of the cost of loving someone too close to danger. It hadn't fully healed, but her stance said she wasn't waiting for permission to get strong again.

Shadow's gaze lingered, guilt tightening in his chest until his breath felt shallow. He shifted his weight, jaw set.

"Gotta let it breathe," she said.

He gave a small, tense smile.

"So why are you here?" Jade asked.

He didn't answer right away.

She didn't push. She simply stepped back.

After glancing down the street to make sure no one had followed him, he crossed the threshold.

The safehouse was dim but warm. A folded blanket rested on the couch, a cup half-full sat on the table, and a faint hum came from the back bedroom where Kian was likely asleep. Shoes were lined neatly by the door, and a sweater lay draped over a chair. These were the quiet signs of someone trying to live a life that refused to be silenced. He wondered how long it had taken her to make this space feel like hers.

They stood in stillness, caught between tension and familiarity.

"You look like hell," Jade said softly.

"I feel worse."

Her lips curved, not into a smile but into a silent acknowledgment. Survival had a look, and they both wore it.

Shadow's eyes moved around the room.

"Say it," she murmured. "Whatever it is."

He nodded slowly and stepped closer.

He told her everything: Doc, ICS, Lola, the lies, even the truth about his age. His voice started steady, but by the end it was barely above a whisper.

Her eyes flickered at the name. "Lola?"

He nodded again.

"She wasn't supposed to fall for me… but she did. And I let myself believe it was real. Until it wasn't."

Jade didn't answer right away. She studied him like she was separating truth from pain.

"I lost myself trying to play a game I didn't know was rigged," he said. "People are dead. Doc's still pulling the strings. I'm going to end it."

He stepped closer. Not to plead, but to be honest.

"I didn't want to bring this to you. I didn't want you in it."

"But I was," she said firmly, her hands curling at her sides. "I am. I took a bullet, remember?"

He looked away, jaw locked. That memory still burned. Her blood on his hands. Her gasping for breath.

"Then run with me," she said, stepping toward him. "Tonight. Right now. We leave and never come back."

He wanted to. God, he wanted to. The thought of waking up beside peace was almost too much.

"Doc knows who we are. He won't stop. We run; he finds us. And if he finds us…"

Jade didn't flinch.

She placed a hand over his heart. Her fingers trembled, but her eyes stayed steady.

"Then go finish it," she said. "And if you make it out… we run."

They stood there, close but incomplete. The air between them felt thin, ready to snap.

She kissed his cheek. Soft and quick. Not a promise, just a breath of hope.

He turned to leave.

"Elijah," she called.

He looked back.

Her eyes were fierce, though fear glimmered beneath.

"Come back to me."

He didn't answer. Just gave a single nod. Hope was alive, but never guaranteed.

He left in silence. But not alone.

* * *

—*Jade*—

Jade stood in the middle of the apartment long after the door shut. No tears this time. There was none left to cry.

She crossed to the couch, picked up her mug, and sipped the cold tea. Soft footsteps broke the quiet.

"You should be asleep, Kian."

"I heard voices." His tone was calm, just curious. "It was Shadow, wasn't it?"

She nodded, eyes still on the streetlights outside.

"Is he in trouble?"

"Yeah," she said. "The kind I try to keep you out of."

Kian folded his arms, something too old in his young eyes. "You think Dad would've helped him?"

That made her pause. "Dad helped build the kind of trouble Shadow's in."

He took that in, then asked, "Is that why we don't talk about him?"

"Some names are safer left in the past," she said, crouching to meet his eyes.

He nodded, satisfied enough. She hugged him once, firm. "Go to bed."

His door clicked shut a moment later, leaving her alone with the hum of the city and the echo of questions she didn't want answered.

* * *

The Inner City streets were quiet this late. Not the kind of quiet that meant peace, but the kind that came after something breaks. Traffic hummed far away, like the city was breathing slow through failing lungs. Streetlights flickered overhead, as if tired of pretending they could keep the dark away.

Shadow walked alone. Head down. Heart heavy. Not hiding. Just thinking. Jade's words echoed with every step.

If you survive… we run.

It sounded simple. Almost beautiful. But survival wasn't about wanting it. It was about odds. And in those odds, someone else's blood was the only way to get even.

He passed a busted bus bench, stopped, and sat like maybe he could hold time still. Pulling the burner phone from his pocket, he scrolled past threats, plans, and ghosted numbers until he reached the one that never left his mind.

Lola's last voicemail.

He didn't play it. Just stared at her name glowing on the screen. Lola: still somewhere out there, off the grid, moving in silence like she'd been trained. Every hour she stayed missing pressed heavier on his chest, the kind of weight you don't feel until it cracks something inside.

Sliding the phone back into his pocket, he kept walking. Turned a corner. Slipped into a shadowed alley he knew better than he wanted to. Crouching beside a rusted dumpster, he pried open a metal lockbox hidden behind the bricks: a stash point.

Inside: a handgun, a roll of cash, and enough space for the things he couldn't say out loud.

He tucked the gun into his waistband and stepped back into the street. The burner buzzed.

Unknown number. One message:

You didn't create this alone. So I won't let you handle it alone. —JK

Shadow stared at it. Didn't reply. Couldn't. This wasn't just about forgiveness; it was about trust, and he wasn't ready to risk his life on a father he hadn't forgiven.

He opened a new text to Jared, a precaution he couldn't ignore. Just one line, meant to make sure the one person he couldn't lose stayed out of the fire:

If anything happens, keep Jade out of it.

Under the flickering streetlight, the buzz of the bulb matched the beat of his thoughts.

Elijah would have asked for help. Would have waited for a sign. But Shadow only needed silence and a loaded gun. He wasn't walking away from love.

He was walking toward the storm, ready to end it once and for all.

THE DEVIL'S HAND

"The devil doesn't need a throne.
Just a room full of believers."

The music thumped low through the floor of the old jazz lounge, deep bass and smooth rhythm wrapped in shadows and lies. Upstairs, the party swayed and shifted. Around fifty people filled the space, their voices and laughter weaving over the music.

Lola slipped away from the crowd, moving down a plush hallway toward a half-open door glowing red at the far end. The noise of the party faded behind her, replaced by the low murmur of voices from inside. She stopped just outside, blending into the shadows, lifting her glass as if to sip while angling herself to listen.

Inside, Doc sat in a windowless back room. The leather chair at the center might as well have been a throne. Around him, a tight circle of five young lieutenants leaned forward, hanging on his every word. They laughed, drank, and studied him with a mix of respect and ambition.

"You ever see a man build his own kingdom out of borrowed bones? That was Jules. Thought he could escape the trenches just because he wore a suit. And Lucien? He let grief and revenge make him soft."

Doc took a slow pull from his cigar.

"But me? I played them both, like I dealt them two losing hands— giving just enough to make them hate each other, then sitting back to watch the fire spread." He leaned forward, the cigar tip glowing. "The devil doesn't need a throne, just a room full of believers."

Laughter rippled through the room. Glasses clinked. A toast rose in the air.

Lola's grip on her glass tightened.

Doc kept going, bragging about how he had manipulated everyone. Shadow, Lola, Jules, and Lucien were pieces on a game board only he could see. "Set up that robbery like a stage play. Put Shadow right in the spotlight. Had Sparrow bleed for the sins of his father." His grin was razor sharp.

A knot formed in her chest.

She stepped back from the doorway, heart pounding. She'd known for a while he was using her, but hearing him gloat hit like a punch. Memories flashed: his orders, her reports, every time she told herself she was doing it for her brother.

She slipped into an empty room down the hall and locked the door.

Her hands shook as she dug through her purse until she found her phone.

One ring. Two. Click.

"Shadow? It's me. It's Lola. I didn't know who else to call. He's out of control. Please, you have to believe me. I didn't know what he was planning. What he did. It's Doc. He—"

A loud bang hit the door.

She gasped and dropped the phone. It landed face-down on the carpet, still connected. Still recording.

A voice called, "Lola?"

She snatched the phone back up. "You were right about Doc," she whispered, voice shaking but eyes burning. "He's not the person he claimed to be."

The door burst open. Two of Doc's men stepped inside. Doc followed, calm as ever.

"That was disappointing," he said. "After everything I gave you."

Lola shook her head, breathing fast.

Doc nodded to his men. "Take her somewhere quiet. She needs time to remember who she belongs to."

They grabbed her arms, the phone flying from her hand again. She didn't scream, just locked eyes with him one last time.

The phone lay on the carpet, still connected. Still recording.

NEUTRAL GROUND

—Jules—

The pool hall was a place where grudges were paused, deals were struck, and old enemies could breathe the same air without reaching for a weapon. Tonight, muffled music played under the thud of pool balls and the low murmur of conversations that stayed clear of trouble.

Jules sat alone at a small corner table, posture loose but eyes fixed on the front door. A half-finished drink sweated in front of him.

The door opened. Conversations dipped, the air shifted, and the bartender froze mid-pour.

Lucien.

Broad-shouldered under a black coat, his presence was heavier than the bass from the speakers. The bartender slid a glass of amber liquor down the bar without a word. Lucien caught it mid-stride, lifting it in silent thanks.

Their eyes met: a collision of years without words, betrayal still fresh, history still raw.

Jules stood. Without speaking, he nodded toward the back.

The bartender caught the cue. A quiet hand signal sent the regulars gathering their things. Chairs scraped the floor, cues hit racks, conversations ended mid-sentence. Within a minute, the place was nearly empty. Only the echo of balls settling in pockets remained.

They passed a pool table near the rear wall, the one Jules and Elijah had claimed as theirs. The carved initials *JE* still marked the wood. Before it was a pool hall, this place had been a small corner store. Karina, Jules's girl back then, ran the front, the legitimate side. Jules worked the back, moving shipments, taking coded calls, running strategy. It was their command center. Until the day Lucky came for Jules.

Beside the table, a rack of pool cues stood ready. Jules took one, pressed it against a certain panel, and a hidden door clicked open. The bartender looked away.

Inside, the low-lit back room was all concrete and history. A single round table waited, a relic from when Jules, Lucien, and Doc ran the Inner City Hustlers. ICH. They had been brothers out of high school, building something from nothing.

Jules poured a drink. "This is our ground. No blood, no heat. That still stand?"

Lucien sat, swirling his glass. "For now. But don't forget who kept it that way."

"We did," Jules said. "Back when it was me, you, and Doc. ICH."

Lucien's smirk was cold. "ICH died the night you put two in my chest."

"You went rogue," Jules said evenly. "Brought the feds down on us. I had to make a choice. A player's choice. And you made yours."

"No," Lucien replied. "You made yours when you sold me out. Thought you killed me. I crawled out of that dumpster, Jules. Been waiting ever since."

"I want a truce. Leave my wife and son out of it."

"This isn't about touching them," Lucien said, voice low. "It's about taking everything from you, piece by piece. And now your boy's in it too."

Jules leaned forward. "You missed your shot years ago. You won't get another."

Lucien's smile was thin. "Difference is, I'm patient. ICS isn't a knockoff. We're the upgrade. I make the calls you never had the guts to make."

A flicker of the old fluorescent light filled the pause.

"You cross the line, you won't walk away," Jules warned.

"I'm not walking away," Lucien said, rising. At the door, he looked back. "You might want to check on your wife."

Then he was gone.

CHAPTER 29
THE BREAKING POINT

The burner phone buzzed once. Shadow recognized the number, though he'd never saved it.

He answered without hesitation. "Yeah."

Jules' voice was tight, urgent. "It's your mother. I just called her. She said someone's following her. I'm too far away to get there in time."

Shadow was already standing, jacket in hand. "Where is she?"

"I told her to meet me at the corner store off 9th, right by the laundromat. She's on her way there now."

"I'm on it."

"Elijah—" Jules paused, then said quietly, "She's scared. Don't make her bury you."

The line went dead.

Shadow moved on instinct. Hoodie on, burner in pocket, the cold weight of steel tucked at his waist. No strategy. Just urgency. He'd lost too many people. He wasn't adding his mother to that list.

At a gas station, a car sat idling, keys still in the ignition. Without a second thought, he slid in, shifted to drive, and hit the road. The city blurred past in streaks of neon and cracked concrete, his pulse syncing with the hum of the tires.

Voices and faces flashed through his mind: Doc's schemes, Lola's empty charm, Jade's searching eyes. None of it mattered now.

Only Vivi.

He stopped one block from the store, engine still running. Stepping out, his gaze swept the shadows. Calm, focused. Fear had no place here.

Then he saw her.

Vivi stood beneath a streetlight, keys in hand, glancing over her shoulder every few seconds. Her body was tense, ready to move but frozen in place until she spotted him.

From the alley behind her, a figure emerged.

Shadow's hand gripped the steel. He moved.

Not as Shadow. Not as a soldier.

As a son.

The figure stepped fully out of the alley, moving with the easy swagger only someone with bad intentions could carry. He wasn't hiding. He was waiting, like he already owned this moment.

Shadow moved fast but low, every step measured. Vivi saw him and froze, her breath catching.

The man turned, a slow grin spreading across his face. "Well, well. Look who showed up."

"Step away from her," Shadow said, voice flat and cold.

"Relax," the man replied, lifting his hands as if to show he meant no harm. His stance stayed loose. No weapon in sight. No rush to hurt Vivi. That was the tell. She wasn't the target. She was bait. "I was just keeping her company."

Shadow stepped in front of Vivi, the tension between them like a live wire. "Elijah…" she whispered, her voice trembling.

"Get behind me," he told her, eyes locked on the man.

The man laughed, sizing him up like a predator reading prey. "You ain't built for this, kid. You act hard, but your hands… yeah, they shake."

Shadow's grip stayed firm. He raised the gun, steady as stone.

"You don't have it in you to pull that trigger," the man taunted.

The silence thickened.

Then the man moved. Fast. Hand diving into his jacket.

Shadow fired.

One shot. Center mass. The man collapsed hard.

Vivi screamed, hands flying to her mouth. The parking lot went still, the world holding its breath.

Shadow stood over him, chest heaving, gun still aimed.

The man coughed, blood bubbling at his lips, but a faint laugh slipped through. "Doc's gonna kill you. Nobody's safe."

His eyes went still.

Tires screeched. A car flew into the lot.

Jules.

He jumped out, scanning the scene. Vivi trembling. Shadow rigid. The body cooling on the pavement.

Jules' face shifted. Not anger. Not shock. Recognition. Like seeing his younger self caught in the same deadly cycle his own father couldn't escape. The curse that clung to the Blake name.

"Elijah…" Jules said, voice low but sharp.

Shadow stayed silent.

"Take her. Get to her car. You parked close?"

Vivi nodded.

"Then go. Don't make me say it twice."

Shadow tucked the gun and guided Vivi toward the car. Her legs wobbled, but he kept her moving. He never looked back.

The car door shut with a solid click. The engine turned over. Taillights cut through the dark.

Jules stood over the body, the silence pressing in.

Shadow wasn't fazed.

Not this time.

* * *

Shadow kept one hand on the wheel, the other resting against his thigh. Vivi sat beside him, shoulders hunched, as if she could shrink small enough to disappear. The only sound was the low hum of the tires rolling over the cracked pavement.

He reached for the radio, needing something. Anything to cut through the silence.

Static hissed, then a slow, heavy beat began to pulse through the speakers.

A voice slid over it.

"Brand new from Doc. 'Smoke & Mirrors.' Just dropped an hour ago."

Vivi flinched. Shadow didn't move.

The lyrics rolled in, calm like a confession, sharp like a blade.

He runnin' from the man in the mirror that I framed

But the name that he hates is the one that I gave

Got ghosts on his back and a trigger in his hand

But the devil already drew up the master plan.

You think you made choices? Nah, you move where I say so…

And that girl that you loved? She was on my payroll.

They always come back. Even the firebird. Don't forget it.

And your daddy? He's a bitch. You can tell him that I said it.

The hook crept in:

You can't run from the smoke, even when the fire's gone.

Vivi's voice broke the silence. "Is that… him?"

Shadow nodded once, eyes still locked on the road. He didn't touch the dial.

She swallowed hard, her voice trembling. "We didn't raise you to end up like this."

"I wasn't raised for it," he said quietly. "But that doesn't matter now."

The song kept playing, Doc's voice bleeding through the speakers like a sermon.

Shadow's thoughts twisted. *I thought I was caught between two lives. Truth is, I never had one. Just the name. Every step I've taken, every move I've made, it was all laid out before me. I've just been walking the path they built.*

His grip on the wheel tightened until his knuckles went white.

"He said he was gonna kill me," he muttered.

The hook came again. *You can run from the smoke...*

Shadow's reply was low. "He's welcome to try." The words weren't just tough talk. They carried the weight of someone who despised the life he was in but knew walking away meant giving Doc everything: the streets, the power, the control. And that was something Shadow couldn't allow. "Better him than me."

CHAPTER 30
NO MORE NAMES

The burner buzzed once.

Shadow didn't know the number, but he didn't need to. The message was short, sharp, and heavy enough to say more than a name ever could.

Southside stash. Doc's slipping. Lucien already hit two spots. Jules is next. Move quiet. —Tiny

Tiny. The guy from the steakhouse. A man with ties buried deep in the city. If he was sending a message, it wasn't just talk. It was a warning.

Shadow stood in the safehouse kitchen, frozen. The fridge hummed. The light above flickered like it couldn't decide if it wanted to live or die. Even the air felt different, thinner, like it knew what was coming. He had already sent Jade and her brother away, set them up in the Inlands near the vineyard she loved. At least she'd be safe.

He read the text again. Then once more. Not because he doubted it, but because reading it twice made the truth sink in. Lucien wasn't circling anymore. He was closing in.

This was it. The end of the maze.

Shadow moved quickly. Gun. Jacket. Burner. Extra clip. Gloves. Every action sharp, practiced, automatic. His hands didn't shake. They worked like they'd been trained for this moment, each decision stamped into his body long before tonight.

On the way out, he stopped at the mirror near the door. Looked hard. What stared back wasn't Elijah. Wasn't Shadow either. It was both. A man shaped by two names, two bloodlines, and every bad choice along the way. For a second, the reflection almost looked alive, like it wanted to speak back but stayed silent.

He tapped the glass once with his knuckle. "It's time."

Outside, the city stretched wide and quiet. But quiet here never meant peace. It meant trouble was on the way, and people were smart enough to stay out of it.

The car waited under a broken streetlight. A black-on-black sedan, its rearview mirror cracked like a spiderweb, a dented fender telling its own story of old fights. A scar on wheels. It smelled of old smoke and close calls. Shadow slid into the seat. His hand hovered on the key, knowing that once he turned it, there was no undoing what came next. He sat still a second longer, breathing slow and steady. The kind of breath you take when you know you've got nothing left to lose.

Then he started the engine.

He popped the glove box. Inside sat the second burner, the one he had copied everything from Doc's phone onto. Still untouched. He opened it, typed a message: If I don't make it, check this phone. You'll understand why.

No name. No reply expected. Just facts. A truth left like a trap, waiting to go off. For a moment, he wanted to crush the phone, erase the risk. Instead, he let it rest in his palm before shutting it back in place.

The skyline burned with gold and smoke as he drove out. The horizon looked like a fuse already lit. Traffic lights blinked on empty corners, glowing like warnings. Each turn of the wheel felt permanent, like the city itself was pulling him toward an ending it had planned all along. The streets looked deserted, but Shadow felt eyes on him, like the city was watching to see how this story closed.

Faces flashed in his mind: E laughing too loud at something dumb, Ty clowning him after a spar, Jade's eyes cutting through him, Vivi's quiet worry hidden in her smile. Lola's fire. Doc's lies. His father's shadow, stretching further than he ever wanted it to. They were all on his back now, heavier than the gun on his hip, heavier than the weight in his chest.

The wheel shook under his grip as he pressed the gas harder. Tires hummed against the broken pavement, carrying him closer with every spin.

This wasn't vengeance. This wasn't survival. This was judgment, and Shadow held the gavel.

He drove on, chasing the horizon, chasing the ending written in blood long before tonight. The city's pulse thumped with his own, fast and unrelenting. Each block blurred past. There was no turning back now. Only forward. Into the fire. Into fate. Into whatever was waiting at the Southside stash.

Tonight, the scales would finally balance.

* * *

The burner hadn't stopped buzzing all day.

First it was Big Drew. Then Keke from the east corner. Even Chedda called. And he never touched a phone unless someone was already in a coffin.

Everyone sounded the same: nervous, uncertain, afraid.

"Doc's looking for you."

"He's saying you're moving funny."

"You good, fam?"

Shadow silenced the ringer. He knew what this was. Not a warning. A trap. Doc was throwing lines across the city, testing to see who Shadow would trust enough to answer.

He parked three blocks from the stash house, engine still ticking with heat. His mind was ice-cold. Every streetlight and broken sidewalk felt like it was watching him. A dog barked behind a fence, then cut off, like it knew to stay quiet.

The Southside air carried a mix of gunpowder, grease, and gasoline. A cop car crept past, lights off. Just watching. Just waiting. Even the law wanted a front-row seat to whatever was about to break loose.

Shadow didn't run.

Each step he took felt like walking through his own past, like stepping into a version of himself already dead. Back when stash houses were safe, not traps. Back when loyalty wasn't questioned.

Every step was heavy. Not with regret, but with consequence. It was like the city had already written his role, and he was only acting it out.

He passed a mural of kids killed by gunfire. Eighteen faces, names scrawled in marker. He paused for a breath. A cigarette butt smoldered on the ground, proof someone else had stopped to remember too.

The stash house leaned on a block of dying homes, three stories tall and tired. Porch light flickering. A busted camera dangled above the door, useless. Paint peeled away in strips. The mailbox gaped open with old mail stuffed inside. The place didn't look like a fortress. It looked like a grave.

He didn't knock. He walked in.

The smell hit first: sweat, rot, copper.

Blood.

He moved low, muscle memory taking over. Gun loose in his hand. Eyes cutting through dark corners. Careful. Quiet. The only sounds were his breathing and the creak of floorboards.

The first floor was wreckage. Bottles. A cracked TV. A single sneaker by the couch. A chair broken in two, as if someone had fallen hard.

The second floor stretched long and narrow, like a throat. The hall carried whispers of bad deals, broken promises, and names already buried.

He stepped over a body slumped by the wall. A face he almost knew. Marcus, maybe. One of Jules' security. Throat cut. Eyes open. A shattered phone still clutched in his hand. Whatever warning he tried to send had died with him.

Shadow didn't flinch. At the end of the hall, a photo was taped to the door. Graduation day. Elijah, Ty, E. A knife stabbed through Elijah's face.

Shadow stared. The blade left a rust stain across his printed smile.

"Was wonderin' when you'd show."

Lucien stepped from the shadows. No crew. No gun. Just a grin that never touched his eyes. "Here to take back what's yours? Or just to see how much of your daddy's kingdom already got carved up?"

Shadow said nothing.

Lucien smirked, pacing slow. "Ah, one of the quiet types. Do-as-you're-told. You ever get tired of being everybody's project? First Jules. Then Doc. Always stuck in the middle."

Shadow stepped closer. He wanted to speak. But silence felt safer.

Lucien circled him. "I heard a rumor. Heard your name ain't even your name anymore. You're Shadow now, right? Street-made. Club-blessed. Doc's little prodigy."

Shadow's eyes narrowed. His pulse hammered. The name cut into him, part pride and part curse. He felt Elijah and Shadow both pressing down, fighting for space inside him. His grip on the gun tightened.

Still no answer.

Lucien leaned in close. "You know what's funny? Even shadows can bleed."

Shadow drove a fist into his jaw, then another into his ribs. "That's for E and Jade."

Lucien stumbled, blood running down his lip. He laughed. "There he is," he coughed. "Jules' little shadow."

Shadow lifted the gun. Lucien raised his hands. "Oh, now you wanna be the big bad wolf? Kill me and you're just another headline. Another body for ICS. And trust me, they're watching."

Lucien reached into his coat.

Shadow didn't fire. His chest felt like stone. Maybe he wasn't here to kill Lucien. Maybe the real play was to tell him the truth, to drag Doc into the light. Elijah's voice pressed through, wanting to explain, to clear his hands of blood he never meant to spill.

Lucien pulled out a phone, showing his palms first. "Easy, cowboy. I'm just getting my phone." He dialed, put it on speaker. Two rings.

Then Jules' voice: "Darrell."

Lucien smiled, teeth red with blood. "I've been thinking. Talking to people. Turns out Doc's been hiding the truth this whole time. I know what happened to my son." Silence. "So I changed my mind."

Jules let out a shaky breath, fragile, almost hopeful.

Lucien's voice dropped. "I won't kill your boy." A pause. "But I do hope he likes roommates."

Click.

Shadow froze. His breath locked in his chest. His stomach twisted.

Lucien wiped his mouth. "You don't have many doors left, kid. And one of them leads straight to a cell."

Sirens wailed closer, echoing against the walls. He was out of time.

Shadow turned and ran. Out the back. Down the stairs. Through the alley where rats scattered. He vaulted a fence, lungs burning. Behind him, red and blue lights splashed across the brick like paint. His heartbeat thundered like a war drum. He didn't stop until the skyline blurred and the streets no longer knew his name.

* * *

The sirens still echoed in his skull long after he escaped the stash house. Shadow ran until the noise behind him faded into nothing. Only then did he duck into a hideout. The silence inside was heavy, and for the first time since Lucien, he could breathe.

The room was bare. Four walls. No windows. Just concrete and dust. The kind of place people went when they wanted to disappear. The kind of place where memories came to die quietly.

Shadow sat on the edge of a rusted cot. His hoodie was damp with sweat, not from heat but from the rush of adrenaline that still hadn't faded.

He scrolled through old photos on his phone. Baby pictures. Family shots. Smiles with Ty and E back when things felt simple, back when the future seemed possible.

He stared at one picture like it might move. Like if he looked hard enough, he could see the exact second everything broke apart. Deep inside, a voice rose up: *We were supposed to stick together.*

But memory was cruel. It only showed you highlights after the game was already over.

He looked away and lit a cigarette he didn't even want. Elijah still lingered somewhere inside him, but Shadow's voice was louder now.

The silence pressed against him. He thought this room was safe, but the quiet felt staged, like someone holding their breath just outside the walls.

His burner buzzed in his pocket. One new message.

TY: *Rooftop. Tomorrow. Outer City. Midnight.*

He took a long drag, ash falling onto the floor. He could ignore it. He could stay hidden. But Lucien's words clawed at him, and Doc's reach grew longer by the hour. Trust wasn't free anymore. It had to be tested.

Shadow crushed the cigarette under his heel. His chest tightened. Elijah whispered caution. Shadow drowned it out.

He stood, pulled his hood over his head, and walked to the door.

If this was a trap, better to step into it with his eyes open than sit in the dark waiting for it to find him.

* * *

They met on a rooftop that didn't belong to any of them, but it always felt like it did. When they were kids, they would sneak through a side door, climb twelve flights, and stretch out on the rooftop like they owned the world. From up here, the city looked smaller, almost manageable. They used to trade stories, dream about life after high school. Back then, it felt untouchable. Safe. Shadow remembered the smell of tar on hot nights, the wind cutting sharp and clean, the sound of their laughter drifting farther than it should have.

That was why he came now. Not because it was safe. He knew better. But because it was theirs. If he couldn't trust this spot, then nothing was left. After Lucien's words, he needed to see his boys face-to-face. Words could lie. Eyes couldn't. He knew it was risky being out here, but the bigger risk was not knowing who was still loyal when everything closed in.

The concrete still held the day's heat even though night had already taken the sky. The air was dry, filled with midnight silence.

E leaned against the ledge, arms crossed, eyes tired. Not from lack of sleep. From knowing too much.

Ty bounced a pebble in his palm, letting it slide between his fingers like a nervous habit.

"You good?" E asked, voice low.

Shadow nodded. Didn't speak.

He glanced at E again, softer now. "How you been holding up??"

E gave the smallest shrug, like even admitting pain was too much. "Getting there."

Ty stepped forward, his smile cracked at the edges, his words tight. "Crazy thing, that night in the alley... it's blurry, you know? People talk like it was nothing. Sometimes I wonder if I even remember it right."

Shadow let the silence hang. He smirked faintly, like Ty's memory was failing him. "C'mon, you really don't remember how that night went?"

"I mean, I think I do. People been talking. Said somebody moved like a shadow. Sparrow didn't even blink."

E cut Ty a sharp look, a warning to stop. Ty ignored it.

"What was it like?" Ty pressed, softer now, coached. "When you pulled? Was it instinct, or a choice? You knew, right? Like really knew."

Shadow exhaled, steady. "Why you asking all that?"

Ty laughed without humor and scratched his neck. "I don't know. Just... trying to get it. You out here living in a movie, and we're still stuck watching the trailer."

Shadow's eyes stayed on Ty. He wasn't listening to the words, but watching his face. Lucien's voice echoed in his head:

Everyone's project. Always the middle.

Shadow needed to know who would stand with him when everything fell apart.

Ty swallowed hard. His voice dropped. "You think if nobody pulled the trigger... we'd all be dead?"

* * *

Three blocks away, inside a van, two officers hunched over a console. A receiver blinked, synced to the tiny wire clipped under Ty's shirt.

"Got him on Sparrow," one whispered.

The other tapped the waveform. "No confession yet. Let it ride."

Static hissed across the feed.

* * *

Back on the roof, E shifted, like words were clawing at his throat. His jaw tightened, hands clenched and unclenched. He opened his mouth, then closed it again. Whatever he wanted to say never came out.

Sirens started low. Grew fast. Too fast.

Ty froze. Shadow saw it: the flicker, the sudden shift, the stutter in the pattern.

"I gotta bounce," Shadow muttered.

He didn't wait for a reply. Just vanished down the stairwell.

* * *

The city bus rattled and groaned like it might fall apart any second. Shadow sat in the back row, hood pulled low, face hidden. He had never taken a bus before. Usually, he drove or walked. But after what happened last night, his car was too risky, and the streets even worse. The bus wasn't comfort. It was cover. A way to keep moving without drawing eyes.

Outside the scratched windows, the city slid past in streaks of neon and bricks. Storefronts shuttered, sidewalks cracked, corners that never slept. It all looked alive, but it was a lie. A mask stretched over decay. Hours blurred together as the bus rolled on, until the night thinned and the first pale colors of dawn leaked into the sky.

Across the aisle, a younger boy leaned against his older brother. Both were knocked out, shoes scuffed, laces mismatched. They didn't have much, but what they had, they shared. Shadow's eyes lingered on them, then fell to his lap. He clutched the faded photo again, edges creased, faces half-worn. E. Ty. Him. Three kids who once thought the future was theirs.

His head drifted against the cold glass. The steady hum of the engine rocked him into a shallow sleep, one foot in the past, one in the blur of now.

The violent screech of brakes snapped him awake. Bright morning light flooded the windows. The bus hissed to a stop. Outside, red and blue lights cut across the rising sun. *A police checkpoint.*

Passengers stirred, whispering. No one moved. The front doors groaned open, and a uniformed officer climbed aboard. He started down the aisle slowly, gaze heavy, scanning every face.

Shadow's chest tightened. His pulse hammered. Sitting still wasn't an option.

The officer's shadow stretched toward him. In one quick motion, Shadow grabbed the red handle above the emergency exit and yanked. The alarm shrieked, sharp and accusing.

The window burst open. Shadow shoved himself through. Cold morning air slapped his face as he hit the pavement running, hood snapping back in place. By the time the alarm echoed behind him, Shadow was already gone.

* * *

—Vivi— Present Day

The apartment was still. Cool air from the a/c brushed against Vivi's silk robe as she stared out across the skyline.

Behind her, Jules stood restless, hands buried deep in his pockets, jaw tight. "He's not a kid anymore," he muttered.

"He's still yours," Vivi said softly.

Jules looked away. "He chose this."

"No," she replied. "You chose not to stop it."

She turned to face him. Her eyes were tired but sharp. "If there's anything left in you worth saving... go find our son. Bring him home."

Jules didn't answer.

"I know you, Jules. You'll try to fix it the only way you know how. I just hope he survives that too."

He stepped forward, almost ready to speak, but the words died before they left his mouth.

Vivi didn't press. She'd lived with his silence too long to expect more.

He nodded once, jaw locked tight, then walked out.

* * *

—*Ty— Five Days Earlier (Before the Meeting)*

They didn't even cuff him. Just told him to come in for a few questions. Said it wasn't a big deal. Said his name barely came up.

The room was beige and freezing, the kind of cold that got into your bones and made it hard to think.

A detective in plain clothes sat across from Ty, tapping a folder against the table. "Look, we're not trying to arrest you. We just need context. Help us connect dots."

Ty folded his arms. "I already told y'all everything. I ain't see nothing."

The detective opened the folder and slid a photo across the table. Grainy. Timestamped. It showed an alley. Two boys running. One looked too much like him.

"You're not in trouble. Yet. But Sparrow's dead. And someone's gotta pay."

Ty's pulse hammered in his neck, equal parts fear and guilt.

"We know who did it. We just need someone to confirm. Help us tie the loose ends. You've got plans, right? College? You want to keep those?"

Another officer stepped in, dropping a black wire on the table. Thin as a shoelace. Cold. Empty.

"This isn't a confession, Ty. It's just a conversation. Keep him talking. That's all."

Ty stared at the device. "You want me to wear that?"

"You want a future?"

The detective slid another object across the table, a tracker small enough to hide in a pocket. "Slip this on him. We'll do the rest."

For a long time, Ty didn't move.

He thought of Elijah's laugh. How it used to sound before the streets weighed him down. He remembered summer nights on the court, when the three of them believed life could still be simple.

Then he looked back at the wire. At the tracker. At his own future slipping away.

His throat closed. His fists tightened on the table.

"I didn't betray him," Ty whispered. "I just don't have a choice."

* * *

—Tiny— 30 Minutes Earlier (Before the Message)

The steakhouse back door swung shut behind him. The alley was cold. Doc leaned against the wall, two men at his side. One smoking, the other cracking his knuckles like a metronome.

Tiny froze. His throat went dry.

Doc stepped forward, voice low and sharp. "You know why I'm here."

Tiny nodded. "I been loyal. You know I have. But Jules... our loyalty's generational. He's the godfather to my daughter. He saved her life and mine."

Doc's eyes cut into him. "Then don't be the reason y'all die."

Tiny flinched. His mind drifted back to the day his daughter got really sick. Jules had paid the hospital bill before the ambulance even showed. No questions asked.

He looked at the burner in his hand like it was a weapon.

The screen already displayed the message:

Southside stash. Doc's slipping. Lucien already hit two spots. Jules is next. Move quiet. —Tiny

Tiny read it. His thumb hovered. "I ain't choosing sides."

Doc's stare didn't waver.

Tiny pressed send. "Forgive me, Jules."

Then he walked back into the kitchen like a man heading toward his own funeral.

* * *

—Lucien— 10 Minutes Earlier (Before the Rooftop Sirens)

Lucien sat in the backseat of a black car, engine humming low. A soft buzz filled his ear. Ty's voice leaked through the wire: shaky, rehearsed, heavy with nerves.

Lucien smiled to himself. Not wide. Not warm. Just enough to show teeth.

"Kid sounds shook," the driver muttered.

Lucien didn't answer. He pulled out his phone, dialed, and waited one ring.

"Move in," he said.

Outside the window, city lights shimmered against the glass.

"This city don't know it yet," Lucien whispered, "but tonight's the start of the end."

* * *

The rec center rooftop hadn't changed. Same rusted chain-link fence. Same broken glass. Same busted corner where they used to stash snacks after games. Out here on the edge of the Outer City, the place felt forgotten, like the world had already buried it.

But to Shadow, it felt like a grave.

The court below stretched like an old scar. The paint was faded. The backboard was cracked. The air was heavy with memories of who they used to be.

Shadow stood near the ledge. Hood up. Gun tucked but not drawn. His hands were steady, but his mind raced. He had called Ty here for answers, ones that couldn't come in a text. Footsteps scraped behind him. Ty. Late, like always.

"You remember when we played E for pushups?" Ty's voice was too light, too careful. "You beat us both. You always did."

Shadow didn't smile. He padded him down for a wire.

Ty stepped closer, empty-handed. No weapon. Just guilt. He put a hand on Shadow's shoulder. His jaw twitched, the same nervous tic he had back when he lied about breaking his parents' window. "I didn't know what to do. I didn't think they could catch you anyways."

"You didn't think at all."

"I didn't say your name."

"You didn't have to."

Ty's shoulders sank. "They showed me a picture of me running from the alley. Said someone had to pay. I froze."

Shadow turned slowly, eyes burning beneath his hood. "So you gave them the alley. And the rooftop?"

Ty swallowed. His voice cracked. "That day we talked... I had a wire on me."

Shadow's gaze cut sharper, cold as steel. "I knew. Every word out your mouth wasn't yours. It was theirs."

"I thought if I kept you talking, they'd back off."

"You thought wrong."

Ty drifted back to the railing, their old spot where they once leaned and talked about dreams, girls, and who would dunk first. His voice wavered. "I didn't want this."

"You wanted out," Shadow said. "So did I. So did E."

Silence pressed between them, heavy and final.

"We were brothers," Shadow said. "But you made me choose between loyalty and betrayal."

Ty stepped forward, chest heaving. "Then finish it. If you came here to end me, do it."

Shadow studied him. Really studied him. Long enough to see the kid who snuck out for sour gummies, who cried when he almost got cut from varsity, who swore he'd never leave.

Then Shadow stepped closer. "I already did."

He turned and walked for the exit, leaving Ty alone on the rooftop.

* * *

45 Minutes Later

Rain pattered against the hood of Shadow's jacket, each drop steady as a ticking clock. Far off, the city hummed. Sirens crying, neon buzzing, the hunger of streets that never slept.

He pulled a cheap burner from his pocket, the plastic casing slick with water. One of a dozen he had cycled through these past weeks. He dialed.

Jules picked up on the second ring. "Yeah?"

"It's time," Shadow said. His voice was steady, but his chest felt tight. "I'm going to end this."

Silence stretched. Just breath on the other end.

"You want in?" Shadow pressed. "Meet me. If not, stay out of the way."

A long pause. Then Jules's voice, low and sharp: "End it the right way. Or don't come back. And watch who you keep around."

The line clicked dead.

Shadow stared at the phone, then dropped it onto the wet pavement. He crushed it beneath his heel until it snapped, sparks faint under the rain.

He turned, stepped into the night, and disappeared into the dark.

* * *

Doc's Hideout – Pre-Dawn

Shadow slipped through the warped back door of the brownstone, the hinges whining just enough to make him pause. He froze, listening. The silence wasn't calm. It was forced, like someone had scrubbed the sound away to make room for violence.

Each step creaked beneath him, heavy with more than weight. This wasn't a safe house. It was a stage for betrayal, where promises turned into traps and protection disguised itself as endings.

He found the core of the house: the war room.

Doc stood at the center, lit by the orange glow of a steel barrel fire. Smoke curled into the rafters. The smell was thick with plastic and ink, the ashes of control. Everything Doc had used to own people was burning.

SIM cards snapped in the flames. Photos shriveled and blackened. One showed Vivi and Jules. Another, E and Ty. Both were already burned halfway through.

Shadow stepped into the light, gun raised.

"You should've stayed gone," Doc said without turning.

"You should've died years ago."

Doc chuckled, low and almost fond. "And give you the throne? Please. You were never built to rule. Just shine pretty on a shelf."

Shadow moved closer, anger sharp but controlled. "I was your insurance."

Doc turned slowly, the fire outlining the hard edges of his face. He looked older, but not weaker. "This city doesn't run on loyalty," Doc said. "It runs on leverage and dollar signs. You don't lead with truth. You lead with the right information at the right time."

Shadow understood exactly what Doc meant: here, power never came from loyalty or truth. It came from twisting the story and making people believe it.

"You ran it on fear. You burned every root you touched."

Doc nodded. "Because roots rot. You have to dig em' up to plant new ones. And I needed someone who could survive that. You survived, didn't you?"

"I did. But you forgot one thing."

Doc tilted his head. "What's that?"

Shadow fired. One shot. The bullet slammed into Doc's side, just below the ribs. Blood spread across his jacket fast, his hand clutching the wound. His grin stayed.

"Didn't I teach you to shoot for the head?" Doc rasped.

Shadow went to fired again. The lights cut out.

CRACK.

A shot. A flash from the left.

Shadow dropped behind an armchair, his breath loud in his ears. Boots scrambled above him. Wood splintered. Something heavy hit the ground.

A body.

He stayed still.

A voice broke the dark, low and tense. "Elijah!"

Dad.

Then again, desperate. "Move!"

Shadow lunged, reaching for the glint of steel across the floor. His fingers scraped the gun but missed.

Backup lights flickered on. The fire flared.

Tiny. Jules's old soldier. Loyal. Brutal. Dead. His body slumped against the wall, blood pooling from his chest.

Shadow's chest heaved. Doc was gone.

The back door hung open, curtains fluttering in the draft. The fire hissed louder.

Jules stepped inside, gun raised. His silhouette was older now, heavy with truths that couldn't be undone.

"He's gone," Shadow said.

Jules looked at the body, then at the flames eating the last of Doc's secrets. "He planned this. Every piece."

Shadow stared at the fire, the smoke curling like fingers around the past. "He wanted me to watch it all burn."

Outside, sirens wailed. Louder. Closer.

"Go," Jules said.

Shadow looked at him. Really looked. "You sure?"

"This isn't your fault. Not tonight."

No goodbyes. Only breath. Only memories. Shadow slipped into the hallway, his coat trailing fire-colored shadows.

Jules straightened. When boots thundered onto the porch, he walked out, dropped his gun, and sank to his knees with his hands behind his head. Red and blue lights washed over him as officers shouted. He didn't resist.

Before they pulled him up, Jules turned his head, searching the darkness. For a moment, it seemed their eyes met in an unspoken exchange.

Then they dragged him away, while the fire inside devoured the last of Doc's names.

* * *

Just Before Dawn

Shadow burst through the back door into the alley, breath ragged, skin slick with sweat. Cold slapped him full in the face, sharp as betrayal. Sirens screamed nearby. No longer background noise, they were bloodhounds in full pursuit.

He didn't think. Just ran.

Every muscle burned. His lungs were on fire. Water splashed from puddles; trash bags exploded at his heels. He vaulted a fence, scraped his palms on the landing, then sprinted across the length of a narrow lot.

His shoes caught on wet metal as he scaled a fire escape. Up. Over. The roof met him like a slap. He kept moving. The city blinked below, pink-gray light bleeding over the skyline. Dawn. Unforgiving.

But the image wouldn't leave him: his father on the porch, gun dropped, knees to the ground. Jules turning his head, searching the dark. Searching for him.

Shadow didn't look back. He's been running for so long his knees buckled. A dog barked. Tires screeched in the distance. The breath in his lungs was tight. He peeled off his jacket, flipped it inside out, gray to black. Slipped under a hanging sheet from a second-story window and vanished in a wash of laundry and shadow.

A cruiser rolled past the alley mouth. He didn't move. Footsteps. Gun raised. Eyes wide. Just his echo. He exhaled, heart threatening to split in two.

Shadow ducked through a loose chain-link gate and slipped into an old tunnel beneath the tracks.

He collapsed against the graffiti wall. Ribs screaming. The pain was real. Real meant alive.

His fingers brushed the hem of his jacket. A bump. He pulled it off. Tracker. Blinking.

Ty...

He dropped it. Crushed it underfoot. Ground it into the concrete until the light died. Then kicked it into the dark.

They were close. But one step behind. And that's all a shadow needs.

* * *

Morning – Fog / Lonely Silence

Shadow moved through the city. The sun had only just risen, but the light already felt like judgment. Fog clung to the streets like a shroud, turning every building into a gravestone. Even the birds stayed quiet, as if the morning itself wasn't allowed to begin.

Six hours had crawled by since Jules was taken away, each one heavy with sirens and the pressure of police drawing closer. Shadow had already switched hideouts twice, forced to move when patrols pressed too near. This new safehouse sat above a pawn shop with windows still boarded from the riots. The stairs groaned beneath his weight, the locks weak with rust. His hands trembled as he turned the key, stiff from cold and exhaustion.

Inside, the air hit harder. Peeling wallpaper, mold in the corners, and the sour scent of rot and old paint clung to the walls. It felt like a place that had been hiding secrets for too long.

He shut the door and wedged a chair under the knob before sliding down the wall to the floor. He didn't sit so much as collapse, folding in on himself like something broken and left behind.

His hands searched his pockets even though he already knew what he carried. Jade's voice broke through the haze in his mind: *If you survive, come find me.*

No address. No plan. Just belief. Just her faith that he could make it back.

He held onto those words until his vision blurred. Tears pressed at the edges, but he wouldn't let them fall. Crying would mean Elijah was still alive inside him. But Elijah hadn't made it out.

Jules was gone. Ty had betrayed him. Doc was still out there. But Shadow was alive.

That meant the story wasn't finished. Only the first book.

Outside, the fog pressed low against the rooftops. Inside, Shadow leaned back and closed his eyes.

Not to rest.

To decide.

Because Jade was still waiting. And no matter the danger, her life was the one he refused to let anyone take.

SHADOWS NEVER LEAVE

Three months had passed. Three months of running, hiding, asking the right questions, and following whispers through the city's cracks. Every lead brought him closer, but also left more bodies and burned bridges behind. By the time the bus hissed to a stop, Elijah's body carried every mile, every fight, every night he spent wondering if Jade was even still alive.

The sun sank behind the inland skyline, streaking gold through the smog as the bus pulled away in a cloud of exhaust. Elijah stood on the sidewalk, staring up at the chipped stucco of the apartment building. He had finally found her.

The stairs groaned under his weight. The hallway smelled like old wood and bleach. Second floor, end unit. A broken doorbell dangled by a single wire.

He lifted his hand to knock. Paused. He remembered her words: *If you survive, come find me.* He wasn't here for redemption or forgiveness. Those didn't exist in their world. He was here because this was the plan. Because after everything he had lost, Jade was the one-person worth finding.

Two knocks. Footsteps inside. A pause. A deadbolt slid. The door cracked open. Jade.

Her eyes widened for a heartbeat, then narrowed. She looked older, survival carved into her face. Braids pulled back, sleeves rolled, no makeup. She didn't look surprised. Just tired.

"You made it," she said.

He nodded. "Barely."

The door stayed half open. Her eyes scanned him: bruises, stitches near his jaw, the limp in his stance. His clothes hung looser. His face, harder.

"Still going by Shadow?"

He flinched. "Not anymore."

"Good," she said, soft but firm.

For a moment, silence pressed between them. All the memories, the close calls, the scars, spoken and unspoken, hung heavy like smoke.

She opened the door the rest of the way. "You hungry?"

He stepped inside. The apartment was small, clean, quiet. A steaming bowl of soup sat waiting on the counter. One light flickered overhead. On the muted TV, a news report played: grainy footage of Jules in handcuffs, headlines scrolling across the bottom. "Big Record Label Executive Arrested for Murder." The screen cut to a sketch of Elijah's face with a bold red banner: WANTED. Police commentary scrolled across the ticker, reporting that Doc Blackwell had disappeared and authorities were scrambling to track him down.

Elijah froze, his jaw tightening. He couldn't look away.

Jade noticed but said nothing. She moved past him, took the bowl from the counter, and set it in front of him. Then she sat across the table, her eyes locked on his.

"You know it's not over, right?" she asked.

"I know."

"They'll come harder. Smarter. With new names and old money."

He stirred the spoon but didn't eat. "Then we get new names too. Go farther away from here."

Her gaze stayed steady, sharp as glass. "So what do we do now?"

Elijah looked up. "Now we stand our ground."

She nodded once.

Outside, the wind picked up. The city never slept, but for that moment, it was quiet. Not safe. Just quiet. And in the silence, Elijah finally let himself breathe.

Some names are earned.
Others are inherited.
But in the dark, when the city forgets your face,
Only the truth can save you.

ABOUT THE AUTHOR

Dominic Dorsey is a writer, visionary, and legacy architect who creates work rooted in ownership, truth, and purpose. *Shadow Scholar: Lessons in the Dark* began as a joke on a livestream with friends. One line turned into a challenge, that challenge became a pitch, and that pitch became this novel.

Dominic writes for those who live between worlds, balancing image and identity, pressure and potential, privilege and pain. He is also the founder of UrbanFellowship Strategic Capital LLC, a company dedicated to creating stories that can be owned, passed down, and remembered.

ACKNOWLEDGEMENTS

This book was never a solo project, no matter whose name is on the cover.

Thank you to everyone who challenged me, supported me, and believed I'd follow through. What started as a joke on a livestream turned into a journey. What started as a spark turned into this.

To my people in the stream—you lit the match.

To my family—you kept the fire going.

To the ones who doubted me—you added fuel.

And to every late night, setback, and restart, this is what it looks like when you finish anyway.

Finally, thank you to Fred Aceves, my editor, for sharpening my words, guiding my vision, and helping me bring this story to life.

www.ingramcontent.com/pod-product-compliance
Lightning Source LLC
Chambersburg PA
CBHW030225120726
47903CB00005B/1367